AUDREY NIFFENEGGER

Her Fearful
Symmetry

VINTAGE BOOKS
London

Published by Vintage 2010

4 6 8 10 9 7 5 3

First published in Great Britain in 2009 by
Jonathan Cape

Vintage
Random House, 20 Vauxhall Bridge Road,
London SW1V 2SA

www.vintage-books.co.uk

Addresses for companies within The Random House Group
Limited can be found at: www.randomhouse.co.uk/offices.htm

The Random House Group Limited Reg. No. 954009

A CIP catalogue record for this book
is available from the British Library

ISBN 9780099524182

The Random House Group Limited supports The Forest
Stewardship Council (FSC), the leading international forest
certification organisation. All our titles that are printed on
Greenpeace approved FSC certified paper carry the FSC logo.
Our paper procurement policy can be found at
www.rbooks.co.uk/environment

Mixed Sources
Product group from well-managed
forests and other controlled sources
www.fsc.org Cert no. TT-COC-2139
© 1996 Forest Stewardship Council
FSC

Typeset in Vendetta Light by Palimpsest Book Production Limited,
Grangemouth, Stirlingshire
Printed and bound in Great Britain by
CPI Bookmarque, Croydon CR0 4TD

For Jean Pateman,
With Love.

She said, 'I know what it's like to be dead.
I know what it is to be sad.'
And she's making me feel like I've never been born.

The Beatles

PART ONE

☞═ THE END ═☜

Elspeth died while Robert was standing in front of a vending machine watching tea shoot into a small plastic cup. Later he would remember walking down the hospital corridor with the cup of horrible tea in his hand, alone under the fluorescent lights, retracing his steps to the room where Elspeth lay surrounded by machines. She had turned her head towards the door and her eyes were open; at first Robert thought she was conscious.

In the seconds before she died, Elspeth remembered a day last spring when she and Robert had walked along a muddy path by the Thames in Kew Gardens. There was a smell of rotted leaves; it had been raining. Robert said, 'We should have had kids,' and Elspeth replied, 'Don't be silly, sweet.' She said it out loud, in the hospital room, but Robert wasn't there to hear.

Elspeth turned her face towards the door. She wanted to call out, *Robert*, but her throat was suddenly full. She felt as though her soul were attempting to climb out by way of her oesophagus. She tried to cough, to let it out, but she only gurgled. *I'm drowning. Drowning in a bed . . .* She felt intense pressure, and then she was floating; the pain was gone and she was looking down from the ceiling at her small wrecked body.

Robert stood in the doorway. The tea was scalding his hand, and he set it down on the nightstand by the bed. Dawn had begun to change the shadows in the room from charcoal to an indeterminate grey; otherwise everything seemed as it had been. He shut the door.

Robert took off his round wire-rimmed glasses and his shoes. He climbed into the bed, careful not to disturb Elspeth, and folded himself around her. For weeks she had burned with fever, but now her temperature was almost normal. He felt his skin warm slightly where it touched hers. She had passed into the realm of inanimate objects and was losing her own heat. Robert pressed his face into the back of Elspeth's neck and breathed deeply.

Elspeth watched him from the ceiling. How familiar he was to her, and how strange he seemed. She saw, but could not feel, his long hands pressed into her waist – everything about him was elongated, his face all jaw and large upper lip; he had a slightly beakish nose and deep-set eyes; his brown hair spilled over her pillow. His skin was pallorous from being too long in the hospital light. He looked so desolate, thin and enormous, spooned around her tiny slack body; Elspeth thought of a photograph she had seen long ago in *National Geographic*, a mother clutching a child dead from starvation. Robert's white shirt was creased; there were holes in the big toes of his socks. All the regrets and guilts and longings of her life came over her. *No*, she thought. *I won't go.* But she was already gone, and in a moment she was elsewhere, scattered nothingness.

The nurse found them half an hour later. She stood quietly, taking in the sight of the tall youngish man curled around the slight, dead, middle-aged woman. Then she went to fetch the orderlies.

Outside, London was waking up. Robert lay with his eyes closed, listening to the traffic on the high street, footsteps in the corridor. He knew that soon he would have to open his eyes, let go of Elspeth's body, sit up, stand up, talk. Soon there would be the future, without Elspeth. He kept his eyes shut, breathed in her fading scent and waited.

The letters arrived every two weeks. They did not come to the house. Every second Thursday, Edwina Noblin Poole drove six miles to the Highland Park Post Office, two towns away from her home in Lake Forest. She had a PO box there, a small one. There was never more than one letter in it.

Usually she took the letter to Starbucks and read it while drinking a venti decaf soy latte. She sat in a corner with her back to the wall. Sometimes, if she was in a hurry, Edie read the letter in her car. After she read it she drove to the parking lot behind the hot-dog stand on 2nd Street, parked next to the dumpster and set the letter on fire. 'Why do you have a cigarette lighter in your glove compartment?' her husband, Jack, asked her. 'I'm bored with knitting. I've taken up arson,' Edie had replied. He'd let it drop.

Jack knew this much about the letters because he paid a detective to follow his wife. The detective had reported no meetings, phone calls or email; no suspicious activity at all, except the letters. The detective did not report that Edie had taken to staring at him as she burned the letters, then grinding the ashes into the pavement with her shoe. Once she'd given him the Nazi salute. He had begun to dread following her.

There was something about Edwina Poole that disturbed the detective; she was not like his other subjects. Jack had emphasised that he was not gathering evidence for a divorce. 'I just want to know what she does,' he said. 'Something is . . . different.' Edie usually ignored the detective. She said nothing to Jack. She put up with it, knowing that the overweight, shiny-faced man had no way of finding her out.

The last letter arrived at the beginning of December. Edie retrieved it from the post office and drove to the beach in Lake Forest. She parked in the spot farthest from the road. It was a windy, bitterly cold day. There was no snow on the sand. Lake Michigan was brown; little waves lapped the edges of the rocks. All the rocks had been carefully arranged to prevent erosion; the beach resembled a stage set. The parking lot was deserted except for Edie's Honda Accord. She kept the motor running. The detective hung back, then sighed and pulled into a spot at the opposite end of the parking lot.

Edie glanced at him. *Must I have an audience for this?* She sat looking at the lake for a while. *I could burn it without reading it.* She thought about what her life might have been like if she had stayed in London; she could have let Jack go back to America without her. An intense longing for her twin over-came her, and she took the envelope out of her purse, slid her finger under the flap and unfolded the letter.

> *Dearest e,*
> *I told you I would let you know – so here it is – goodbye.*
> *I try to imagine what it would feel like if it was you – but it's impossible to conjure the world without you, even though we've been apart so long.*
> *I didn't leave you anything. You got to live my life. That's*

enough. Instead I'm experimenting – I've left the whole lot
to the twins. I hope they'll enjoy it.
    Don't worry, it will be okay.
    Say goodbye to Jack for me.
    Love, despite everything,
        e

Edie sat with her head lowered, waiting for tears. None came, and she was grateful; she didn't want to cry in front of the detective. She checked the postmark. The letter had been mailed four days ago. She wondered who had posted it. A nurse, perhaps.

She put the letter into her purse. There was no need to burn it now. She would keep it for a little while. Maybe she would just keep it. She pulled out of the parking lot. As she passed the detective, she gave him the finger.

Driving the short distance from the beach to her house, Edie thought of her daughters. Disastrous scenarios flitted through Edie's mind. By the time she got home she was determined to stop her sister's estate from passing to Julia and Valentina.

Jack came home from work and found Edie curled up on their bed with the lights off.

'What's wrong?' he asked.

'Elspeth died,' she told him.

'How do you know?'

She handed him the letter. He read it and felt nothing but relief. *That's all,* he thought. *It was only Elspeth all along.* He climbed onto his side of the bed and Edie rearranged herself around him. Jack said, 'I'm sorry, baby,' and then they said nothing. In the weeks and months to come, Jack would regret this; Edie would not talk about her twin, would not answer questions, would not speculate about what Elspeth might have bequeathed to their daughters, would not say how she felt or let him even mention Elspeth. Jack wondered, later, if Edie would have talked to him that afternoon, if he had asked her. If he'd told her what he knew, would she have shut him out? It hung between them, afterwards.

But now they lay together on their bed. Edie put her head on Jack's chest and listened to his heart beating. *'Don't worry, it will be okay'* . . . *I don't think I can do this. I thought I would see you again. Why didn't I go to you? Why did you tell me not to come? How did we let this happen?* Jack put his arms around her. *Was it worth it?* Edie could not speak.

They heard the twins come in the front door. Edie disentangled herself, stood up. She had not been crying, but she went to the bathroom and washed her face anyway. 'Not a word,' she said to Jack as she combed her hair.

'Why not?'

'Because.'

'Okay.' Their eyes met in the dresser mirror. She went out, and he heard her say, 'How was school?' in a perfectly normal voice. Julia said, 'Useless.' Valentina said, 'You haven't started dinner?' and Edie replied, 'I thought we might go to Southgate for pizza.' Jack sat on the bed feeling heavy and tired. As usual, he wasn't sure what was what, but at least he knew what he was having for dinner.

Elspeth Noblin was dead and no one could do anything for her now except bury her. The funeral cortège passed through the gates of Highgate Cemetery quietly, the hearse followed by ten cars full of rare-book dealers and friends. It was a very short ride; St Michael's was just up the hill. Robert Fanshaw had walked down from Vautravers with his upstairs neighbours, Marijke and Martin Wells. They stood in the wide courtyard on the west side of the cemetery watching the hearse manoeuvring through the gates and up the narrow path towards the Noblin family's mausoleum.

Robert was exhausted and numb. Sound seemed to have fallen away, as though the audio track of a movie had malfunctioned. Martin and Marijke stood together, slightly apart from him. Martin was a slender, neatly made man with greying close-cropped hair and a pointed nose. Everything about him was nervous and quick, knobbly and slanted. He had Welsh blood and a low tolerance for cemeteries. His wife, Marijke, loomed over him. She had an asymmetrical haircut, dyed bright magenta, and matching lipstick; Marijke was big-boned, colourful, impatient. The lines in her face contrasted with her modish clothing. She watched her husband apprehensively.

Martin had closed his eyes. His lips were moving. A stranger might have thought that he was praying, but Robert and Marijke knew he was counting. Snow fell in fat flakes that vanished as soon as they hit the ground. Highgate Cemetery was dense with dripping trees and slushy gravel paths. Crows flew from graves to low branches, circled and landed on the roof of the Dissenters' chapel, which was now the cemetery's office.

Marijke fought the urge to light a cigarette. She had not been especially fond of Elspeth, but she missed her now. Elspeth would have said something caustic and funny, would have made a joke of it all. Marijke opened her mouth and exhaled and her breath hung for a moment like smoke in the air.

The hearse glided up the Cuttings Path and disappeared from sight. The Noblin mausoleum was just past Comfort's Corners, near the middle of the cemetery; the mourners would walk up the narrow, tree-root-riddled Colonnade Path and meet the hearse there. People parked their cars in front of the semicircular Colonnade, which divided the courtyard from the cemetery, extricated themselves and stood looking about, taking in the chapels (once famously described as 'Undertaker's Gothic'), the iron gates, the War Memorial, the statue of Fortune staring blank-eyed under the pewter sky. Marijke thought of all the funerals that had passed through the gates of Highgate. The Victorians' black carriages pulled by ostrich-plumed horses, with professional mourners and inexpressive mutes, had given way to this motley collection of autos, umbrellas and subdued friends. Marijke suddenly saw the cemetery as an old theatre: the same play was still running, but the costumes and hairstyles had been updated.

Robert touched Martin's shoulder, and Martin opened his

eyes with the expression of a man abruptly woken. They walked across the courtyard and through the opening in the centre of the Colonnade, up the mossy stairs into the cemetery. Marijke walked behind them. The rest of the mourners followed. The paths were slippery, steep and stony. Everyone watched their feet. No one spoke.

Nigel, the cemetery's manager, stood next to the hearse, looking very dapper and alert. He acknowledged Robert with a restrained smile, gave him a look that said, *It's different when it's one of our own, isn't it?* Robert's friend Sebastian Morrow stood with Nigel. Sebastian was the funeral director; Robert had watched him working before, but now Sebastian seemed to have acquired an extra dimension of sympathy and inner reserve. He appeared to be orchestrating the funeral without actually moving or speaking; he occasionally glanced at the relevant person or object and whatever needed doing was done. Sebastian wore a charcoal-grey suit and a forest-green tie. He was the London-born son of Nigerian parents; with his dark skin and dark clothes he was both extremely present and nearly invisible in the gloom of the overgrown cemetery.

The pall-bearers gathered around the hearse.

Everyone was waiting, but Robert walked up the main path to the Noblin family's mausoleum. It was limestone with only the surname carved above the oxidised copper door. The door featured a bas-relief of a pelican feeding her young with her own blood, a symbol of the Resurrection. Robert had occasionally included it on the tours he gave of the cemetery. The door stood open now. Thomas and Matthew, the burial team, stood waiting ten feet along the path, in front of a granite obelisk. He met their eyes; they nodded and walked over to him.

Robert hesitated before he looked inside the mausoleum. There were four coffins – Elspeth's parents and grandparents – and a modest quantity of dust which had accumulated in the corners of the small space. Two trestles had been placed next to the shelf where Elspeth's coffin would be. That was all. Robert fancied that cold emanated from the inside of the mausoleum, as though it were a fridge. He felt that some sort of exchange was about to take place: he would give Elspeth to the cemetery, and the cemetery would give him . . . what, he didn't know. Surely there must be something.

He walked with Thomas and Matthew back to the hearse. Elspeth's coffin was lead-lined, for above-ground burial, so it was incongruously heavy. Robert and the other pall-bearers shouldered it and then conveyed it into the tomb; there was a moment of awkwardness as they tried to lower it onto the trestles. The mausoleum was too small for all the pall-bearers, and the coffin seemed to have grown suddenly huge. They got it situated. The dark oak was glossy in the weak daylight. Everyone filed out except Robert, who stood hunched over slightly with his palms pressed against the top of the coffin, as though the varnished wood were Elspeth's skin, as though he might find a heartbeat in the box that housed her emaciated body. He thought of Elspeth's pale face, her blue eyes, which she would open wide in mock surprise and narrow to slits when she disliked something; her tiny breasts, the strange heat of her body during the fevers, the way her ribs thrust out over her belly in the last months of her illness, the scars from the port and the surgery. He was flooded with desire and revulsion. He remembered the fine texture of her hair, how she had cried when it fell out in handfuls, how he had run his hands over her bare scalp. He thought of the curve of Elspeth's thighs, and of the bloating and putrefaction that were already transforming her, cell by cell. She had been forty-four years old.

'Robert.' Jessica Bates stood next to him. She peered at him from under one of her elaborate hats, her stern face softened by pity. 'Come, now.' She placed her soft, elderly hands over his. His hands were sweating, and when he lifted them he saw that he'd left distinct prints on the otherwise perfect surface. He wanted to wipe the marks away, and then he wanted to leave them there, a last proof of his touch on this extension of Elspeth's body. He let Jessica lead him out of the tomb and stood with her and the other mourners for the burial service.

'The days of man are but as grass: for he flourisheth as a flower of the field. For as soon as the wind goeth over it, it is gone: and the place thereof shall know it no more.'

Martin stood on the periphery of the group. His eyes were closed again. His head was lowered, and he clenched his hands in the pockets of his overcoat. Marijke leaned against him. She had her arm through his; he seemed not to notice and began to rock back and forth. Marijke straightened herself and let him rock.

'Forasmuch as it hath pleased Almighty God of his great mercy to take unto himself the soul of our dear sister here departed, we therefore commit her body to its resting place; earth to earth, ashes to ashes, dust to dust; in sure and certain hope of the resurrection to

eternal life through Our Lord Jesus Christ; who shall change the body of our low estate that it may be like unto his glorious body, according to the mighty working, whereby he is able to subdue all things to himself.'

Robert let his eyes wander. The trees were bare – Christmas was three weeks away – but the cemetery was green. Highgate was full of holly bushes, sprouted from Victorian funeral wreaths. It was festive, if you could manage the mind-flip required to think about Christmas in a cemetery. As he tried to focus on the vicar's words he heard foxes calling to each other nearby.

Jessica Bates stood next to Robert. Her shoulders were straight and her chin was high, but Robert sensed her fatigue. She was Chairman of the Friends of Highgate Cemetery, the charity that took care of this place and ran the guided tours. Robert worked for her, but he thought she would have come to Elspeth's funeral anyway. They had liked each other. Elspeth had always brought an extra sandwich for Jessica when she came to have lunch with Robert.

He panicked: *How will I remember everything about Elspeth?* Now he was full of her smells, her voice, the hesitation on the telephone before she said his name, the way she moved when he made love to her, her delight in impossibly high-heeled shoes, her sensuous manner when handling old books and her lack of sentiment when she sold them. At this moment he knew everything he would ever know of Elspeth, and he urgently needed to stop time so that nothing could escape. But it was too late; he should have stopped when she did; now he was running past her, losing her. She was already fading.

Nigel closed the mausoleum door and locked it. Robert knew that the key would sit in a numbered compartment in a drawer in the office until it was needed again. There was an awkward pause; the service was over, but no one quite knew what to do next. Jessica squeezed Robert's shoulder and nodded to the vicar. Robert thanked him and handed him an envelope.

Everyone walked together down the path. Soon Robert found himself standing again in the courtyard. The snow had turned to rain. A flock of black umbrellas opened almost at once. People got into cars, began to proceed out of the cemetery. The staff said things, hands patted him, there were offers of tea, something stronger; he didn't quite know what he said to people, but they tactfully withdrew. The booksellers all went off to the Angel. He saw Jessica standing at the office window, watching him. Marijke and Martin had been standing apart; now they came to meet him. Marijke was leading Martin by the arm. His head was still bowed and he seemed to be intent on each sett in the courtyard as he walked across it. Robert was touched that he had managed to come at all. Marijke took Robert's arm, and the three of them walked out of the cemetery and up Swains Lane. When they reached the top of Highgate Hill they turned left, walked for a few minutes and turned left again. Marijke had to let go of Robert in order to hurry Martin along. They walked down a long narrow asphalt path. Robert opened the gate, and they were home. All three apartments in Vautravers were dark, and the day was giving way to evening so that the building seemed to Marijke even more heavy and oppressive than usual. They stood together in the entrance hall. Marijke gave Robert a hug. She didn't know what to say. They had already said all those things, and so she said nothing and Robert turned to let himself into his flat.

Martin's voice came out hoarse. He said, 'Sorry.' The word startled each of them. Robert hesitated and nodded. He waited to see if Martin would say anything else. The three of them stood together awkwardly until Robert nodded again and disappeared into his flat. Martin wondered if he had been right to speak. He and Marijke began to climb the stairs. They paused on the second landing as they passed Elspeth's door. There was a small typed card tacked to it that said NOBLIN. Marijke reached out and touched it as she passed. It reminded her of the name on the mausoleum. She thought that it would every time she went by it, now.

Robert took his shoes off and lay on his bed in his austere and nearly dark bedroom, still wearing his wet woollen coat. He stared at the ceiling and thought of Elspeth's flat above him. He imagined her kitchen, full of food she would not eat; her clothes, books, chairs which would not be worn or read or sat in; her desk stuffed with papers he needed to go through. There were many things he needed to do, but not now.

He was not ready for her absence. No one he loved had died, until Elspeth. Other people were absent, but no one was dead. *Elspeth?* Even her name seemed empty, as though it had detached itself from her and was floating untethered in his mind. *How am I supposed to live without you?* It was not a matter of the body; his body would carry on as usual. The problem was located in the word *how*: he would live, but without Elspeth the flavour, the manner, the method of living were lost to him. He would have to relearn solitude.

It was only four o'clock. The sun was setting; the bedroom became indistinct in shadow. He closed his eyes, waited for sleep. After some time he understood that he would not sleep; he got up and put on his shoes, went upstairs and opened Elspeth's door. He walked through her flat without turning on any lights. In her bedroom he took his shoes off again, removed his coat, thought for a moment and took off the rest of his clothing. He got into Elspeth's bed, the same side he had always slept on. He put his glasses in the same spot they had always occupied on the nightstand. He curled into his accustomed position, slowly relaxing as the chill left the sheets. Robert fell asleep waiting for Elspeth to come to bed.

Marijke Wells de Graaf stood in the doorway of the bedroom she had shared with Martin for the last twenty-three
years. She had three letters in her hand, and she was debating
with herself about where to leave one of them. Her suitcases
stood on the landing by the front stairs with her yellow trench
coat neatly folded over them. She had only to leave the letter
and she could go.

Martin was in the shower. He had been in there for about
twenty minutes; he would stay in the shower for another hour
or so, even after the hot water ran out. Marijke made a point
of not knowing what he was up to in there. She could hear
him talking to himself, a low, amiable mumble; it could almost
have been the radio. *This is Radio Insanity,* she thought, *coming
at you with all the latest and greatest OCD hits.*

She wanted to leave the letter in a place where he would
find it soon, but not too soon. And she wanted to leave it in
a spot that wasn't already problematic for Martin, so that he'd
be able to pick the letter up and open it. But she didn't want
to put it in a place which would be contaminated by the presence of the letter, which would then be forever associated with
the letter and therefore out of bounds to Martin in the future.

She'd been pondering this dilemma for weeks without
settling on a spot. She'd almost given up and resolved to
post the letter, but she didn't want Martin to worry when she

didn't come home from work. *I wish I could leave it hovering in midair,* she thought. And then she smiled and went to get her sewing kit.

Marijke stood in Martin's office next to his computer, trying to steady her hands enough to thread the needle in the pool of yellow light from his desk lamp. Their flat was very dark; Martin had papered over the windows and she could only tell that it was morning by the white light that showed through the Sellotape at the edges of the newspaper. Needle threaded, she whipped a few stitches around the edge of the envelope and then stood on Martin's chair to tape the end of the thread to the ceiling. Marijke was tall, but she had to stretch, and for a moment she had a sensation of vertigo, wobbling on the chair in the dark room. *It would be a bad joke if I fell and broke myself now.* She imagined herself on the floor with her head cracked open, the letter dangling above her. But a second later she recovered her balance and stepped off the chair. The letter seemed to levitate above the desk. *Perfect.* She gathered her sewing things and pushed in the chair.

Martin called her name. Marijke stood frozen. 'What?' she finally called out. She set the sewing supplies on Martin's desk. Then she walked into the bedroom and stood at the closed bathroom door. 'What?' She held her breath; she hid the remaining two letters behind her back.

'There's a letter for Theo on my desk; could you post it on your way out?'

'Okay.'

'Thanks.'

Marijke opened the door a crack. Steam filled the bath-room and moistened her face. She hesitated. 'Martin . . .'

'Hmm?'

Her mind went blank. '*Tot ziens*, Martin,' she finally said.

'*Tot ziens*, my love.' Martin's voice was cheerful. 'See you tonight.'

Tears welled in her eyes. She walked slowly out of the bedroom, edged her way between the piles of plastic-wrapped boxes in the hall, ducked into the office, picked up Martin's letter to Theo and continued through the front hall and out the door of their flat. Marijke stood with her hand on the doorknob. A random memory came to her: *We stood here together, my hand on the doorknob just like this. A younger hand; we were young. It was raining. We'd been grocery shopping.* Marijke closed her eyes and stood listening. The flat was large, and she couldn't hear Martin from here. She left the door ajar (it was never locked) and put on her coat, checked her watch. She hefted her suit-cases and carried them awkwardly down the stairs, glancing briefly at Elspeth's door as she went by. When she came to the ground floor she left one of her envelopes in Robert's mail basket.

Marijke did not turn to look at Vautravers as she let herself out of the gate. She walked up the path to the street, rolling her suitcases behind her. It was a cold damp January morning; it had rained in the night. Highgate Village had a feeling of changelessness about it this morning, as though no time at all had passed since she'd arrived there, a young married woman, in 1981. The red phone box still stood in Pond Square, though there was no pond in Pond Square now, nor had there been for as long as Marijke could remember, just gravel and benches with pensioners napping on them. The old man who owned the bookshop still scrutinised the tourists as they perused his obscure maps and brittle books. A yellow Labrador ran across the square, easily eluding a shrieking toddler. The little restaurants, the dry-cleaners, the estate agents, the chemist — all waited, as though a bomb had gone off somewhere, leaving only young mums pushing prams. As she posted Martin's letter to him, along with her own, Marijke thought of the hours she'd spent here with Theo. *Perhaps they'll arrive together*.

The driver was waiting for her at the minicab office. He slung her suitcases into the boot and they got into the car. 'Heathrow?' he asked. 'Yes, Terminal Four,' said Marijke. They headed down North Hill toward the Great North Road.

Somewhat later, as Marijke queued at the KLM desk, Martin got out of the shower. A spectator unfamiliar with Martin might have worried about his appearance: he was bright red, as though a superhuman housewife had parboiled him to extract impurities.

Martin felt good. He felt clean. His morning shower was a high point of his day. His worries receded; troubling things could be tackled in the shower; his mind was clear. The shower he took just before teatime was less satisfactory because it was shorter, crowded by intrusive thoughts and Marijke's imminent return from her job at the BBC. And the shower he took before going to bed was afflicted by anxieties about being in bed with Marijke, worries about whether he smelled funny, and would she want to have sex tonight or put him off until some other night? (there had been less and less sex lately) not to mention worries about his crossword puzzles, about emails written and emails unanswered, worries about Theo off at Oxford (who always supplied less detail about his daily life and girlfriends and thoughts than Martin would have liked; Marijke said, 'He's nineteen, it's a miracle he tells us anything,' but somehow that didn't help and Martin imagined all sorts of awful viruses and traffic accidents and illegal substances; recently Theo had acquired a motorcycle – many, many rituals had been added to Martin's daily load in order to keep Theo safe and sound).

Martin began to towel himself. He was an avid observer of his own body, noting every corn, vein and insect bite with deep concern – and yet he had hardly any idea what he actually looked like. Even Marijke and Theo existed only as bundles of feelings and words in Martin's memory. He wasn't good at faces.

Today everything proceeded smoothly. Many of Martin's washing and grooming rituals were organised around the idea of symmetry: a stroke of the razor on the left required an identical stroke on the right. There had been a bad period a few years ago when this had led to Martin shaving every trace of hair from his entire body. It took hours each morning, and Marijke had wept at the sight of him. He had eventually persuaded himself that extra counting could be substituted for all that shaving. So this morning he counted the razor strokes (thirty) required to actually shave his beard, and then deliberately put the razor down on the sink and counted to thirty thirty times. It took him twenty-eight minutes. Martin counted quietly, without hurrying. Hurrying always mucked things up. If he tried to rush he wound up having to start again. It was important to do it well, so that it felt complete.

Completeness: when done correctly, Martin derived a (fleeting) satisfaction from each series of motions, tasks, numbers, washing, thoughts, not-thoughts. But it would not do to be *too* satisfied. The point was not to please himself, but to stave off disaster.

There were the obsessions – these were like pinpricks, prods, taunts: *Did I leave the gas on? Is someone looking in the back-door window? Perhaps the milk was off. Better smell it again before I put it in the tea. Did I wash my hands after taking a piss? Better do it again, just to be sure. Did I leave the gas on? Did my trousers touch the floor when I put them on? Do it again, do it right. Do it again. Do it again. Again. Again.*

The compulsions were answers to the questions posed by the obsessions. *Check the gas. Wash my hands. Wash them very thoroughly, so there can be no mistake. Use stronger soap. Use bleach. The floor is dirty. Wash it. Walk around the dirty part without touching it. Use as few steps as possible. Spread towels over the floor to keep the contamination from spreading. Wash the towels. Again. Again. It feels wrong to enter the bedroom this way. Wrong how, exactly? Just wrong. Do it right foot first. And turn to the left with my body – there, that's it. That feels better. But what about Marijke? She has to do it this way too. She won't like it. Doesn't matter. She won't do it. She will. She has to. It feels too wrong if she doesn't. As though something dreadful will happen. What, exactly? Don't know. Can't think about it. Quick – multiples of 22: 44, 66, 88 . . . 1,122 . . .*

There were good days, bad days, very bad days. Today was shaping up to be a good day. Martin thought about his time at Balliol, when he had played tennis every Wednesday with a bloke from his Philosophy of Mathematics course. There were days when he knew, even before he unpacked his racquet, that every stroke would be sweet. Today had that feeling about it.

Martin opened the bathroom door and surveyed the bedroom. Marijke had laid out his clothes on the bed. His shoes sat on the floor, neatly aligned with the legs of his trousers. Every article of clothing was arranged in a precise pattern. No piece of clothing touched any other. He contemplated the hardwood floor of the bedroom. There were spots where the finish of the wood had been worn away, places where the floor was warped from moisture – but Martin disregarded all that. He was trying to discern whether the floor was safe to walk on in his bare feet. Today, he decided that it was. Martin strode to the bed and began to dress himself very slowly.

As each piece of clothing settled onto his body, Martin felt increasingly secure, enveloped in the clean, worn fabric. He was very hungry, but he took his time. Eventually, Martin slid his feet into his shoes. The shoes were problematic. The brown Oxfords were a sort of negotiation between his clean body and the always unnerving floor. He disliked touching them. But he did, and managed to tie the laces. Marijke had offered to get him trainers with Velcro straps, but Martin felt aesthetically repelled by the very idea.

Martin always dressed in sober, dark clothing; he exuded

formality. He did not go so far as to wear a tie around the flat, but he always looked as though he had just removed one, or was looking for a tie to put on before he rushed out the door. Since he had stopped leaving the flat, his ties stayed on the rack in his wardrobe.

Dressed, Martin walked cautiously through the hall and into the kitchen. His breakfast was laid out on the kitchen table. Weetabix in a bowl, a small jug of milk, two apricots. He pressed the button on the electric kettle, and in a few minutes the water boiled. Martin had few compulsions associated with food (they mainly involved chewing things a certain number of times). The kitchen was Marijke's domain, and she always made him take whatever was bothering him to another part of the flat. He tried never to turn on the stove, because he found it impossible to be sure that he'd turned it off again and would stand for hours with his hand on the knob, turning it back and forth. But he could make tea with the electric kettle, and he did so.

Marijke had left the newspapers next to his bowl of cereal. They were pristine, still neatly folded. Martin felt a little surge of gratitude – he liked to be the first to open the fresh newspapers, but he never got to them before she did. He unfurled the *Guardian* and went directly to the crossword.

Today was Thursday, and for Thursdays Martin always set a crossword with a scientific theme. This particular one concerned astronomy. Martin scanned it briefly to be sure that everything was correct. He was especially proud of the puzzle's form, which sprawled across the grid in the shape of a rather boxy and completely symmetrical spiral galaxy. He then turned to the solution for yesterday's puzzle, a strict Ximenean which had been set by his fellow compiler Albert Beamish. Beamish set under the name Lillibet; Martin had no idea why. He'd never met Beamish, though they spoke on the phone occasionally. Martin always imagined him as a hairy man in a ballet costume. Martin's own setting name was Bunbury.

Martin opened *The Times*, the *Daily Telegraph*, the *Daily Mail* and the *Independent* and began combing through them for interesting news items. The crossword he was working on at the moment was about the history of warfare in Mesopotamia. He wasn't sure if this was going to fly with his editor, but like any artist he felt the need to express his preoccupations through his work, and Iraq had been much on Martin's mind lately. Today the news was full of an especially bloody suicide bombing in a mosque. Martin sighed, got his scissors and began cutting out the articles.

After breakfast, he washed up (in a fairly normal fashion) and stacked the papers neatly (though they had become somewhat lace-like). He went into his office, bent over to turn on the desk lamp. As he straightened up something brushed his face.

Martin's first thought was that a bat had somehow got into the office. But then he saw the envelope, swinging gently on its thread, hanging from the ceiling. He stood and considered it. His name was written on it in Marijke's bold handwriting. *What have you done?* His mind went blank, and he stood in front of the dangling envelope with his head bowed and his arms crossed protectively over his chest. At last he reached out and took it, giving a little tug that detached the thread from the ceiling. He opened it slowly, unfolded the letter, groped for his reading glasses and put them on. *What has she done?*

                                                        6 January
Lieve Martin,

My darling husband, I am sorry. I cannot live this way any more. By the time you are reading this letter I will be on my way to Amsterdam. I have written to Theo to tell him.

I don't know if you can understand, but I will try to explain. I need to live my life without being always vigilant to calm your fears. I am tired, Martin. You have worn me out. I know that I will be lonely without you, but I will be more free. I will find myself a little apartment and open the windows and let the sun and the air come in. Everything will be painted white, and I will have flowers in all the rooms. I will not have to always enter the rooms with my right foot first, or smell bleach on my skin, on everything I touch. My things will be in their cupboards and drawers, not in Tupperware, not wrapped in cling film. My furniture will not wear out from being scrubbed too much. Maybe I will have a cat.

You are ill, Martin, but you refuse to see a doctor. I am not coming back to London. If you want to see me, you can come to Amsterdam. But first you would have to leave the flat, so I am afraid that we may never see each other again.

I tried to stay but I failed.

Be well, my love.

Marijke

Martin stood holding the letter. *The worst thing has happened.* He could not take it in. *She's gone.* She would not come back. *Marijke.* He bent slowly at his waist, hips, knees, until he was crouching on the floor in front of his desk, the harsh light shining on his back, his face inches from the letter. *My love. Oh my love . . .* All thought fled from him; there was only a great emptiness, the way the water draws back before a tsunami. *Marijke.*

Marijke sat on the train, watching the flat grey land along the track from Schiphol Airport as it blurred past her. It had been raining; the sky was low. *I'm almost home.* She checked her watch. By now Martin must have found her letter. She took her mobile phone out of her bag and opened it. No calls. She snapped it shut. The rain streaked sideways across the train's windows. *What have I done? I'm sorry, Martin.* But she knew she would not be sorry once she was home, and only Amsterdam could be home to her now.

Robert had given a special tour of the Western Cemetery to a group of antiquarians from Hamburg, and now he stood under the arch by Highgate Cemetery's main gate, waiting for his group to buy postcards and collect their belongings so he could shoo them out and lock up. In the winter there were no regular weekday tours. He liked the subdued, workaday quality the cemetery had on these quiet days.

The antiquarians straggled out of the former Anglican chapel that served as a makeshift gift shop. Robert shook the green plastic donation box at them, and they threw in their change. He always felt embarrassed at this little transaction, but the cemetery didn't pay VAT on donations, so everyone at Highgate begged as enthusiastically as they could manage. Robert smiled and waved the Germans out, then turned the old-fashioned key in the massive gate's lock.

He went into the office and put the key and the donation box on the desk. Felicity, the office manager, smiled and dumped out the contents. 'Not bad, for such a dreary Wednesday,' she said. She held out her hand. 'Walkie-talkie?'

Robert patted his mackintosh pocket and said, 'I'll bring it back.'

'Are you going out, then?' Felicity asked. 'It's starting to rain.'

'Just for a bit.'

'Molly's on the gate across the way. Could you give her these?'

'Okay.'

Robert took the pamphlets from Felicity and an umbrella from the stand by the stairs. He headed across Swains Lane. Molly, a lean elderly woman who wore green dungarees and an anorak, sat on a folding chair inside the Strathcona and Mount Royal memorial, which lurked in pink granite splendour just beside the Eastern Cemetery's gate. She peered out of the gloom patiently and took the pamphlets from Robert, tucking them into the little rack that sat beside her. The pamphlets featured Karl Marx on their covers; he and George Eliot were the star attractions among the dead on this side of the cemetery.

'D'you want to go in and warm up?' Robert asked her.

Molly's voice was slow, raspy, sleepy; she had a slight Australian accent. 'I'm all right – I've got the heater on. Have you had your visit?'

'No, I just got done with the tour.'

'Well go on, then.'

As he recrossed Swains Lane, Robert thought about the way Molly had said 'your visit' as though it were now part of the official daily schedule of the cemetery. Perhaps it was. He thought about the way the staff had made space for his grief as if it were a tangible thing. Out in the world people drew back from it, but at the cemetery everyone was accustomed to the presence of the bereaved, and so they were matter-of-fact about death in a way that Robert had never appreciated until now.

The drizzle turned to rain as Robert came to Elspeth's mausoleum. He put up his umbrella with a flourish and sat down on the steps with his back against the door. Robert leaned his head back and closed his eyes. Less than an hour ago he had walked right past this spot with his tour. He had been chatting to the group about wakes and the extreme measures the Victorians had taken for fear of being buried alive. He wished that the Noblin tomb was not on one of the main paths; it was impossible to give a tour without passing Elspeth, and he felt callous leading groups of gawking tourists past the small structure with her surname carved into it. It had never bothered him when it was only her family's grave – but he had never met her family. For the first time he properly understood why Jessica was so adamant about decorum in the cemetery. He had been inclined to tease her about that. For Jessica, Highgate was not about the tours, or the monuments, not about the supernatural or the atmosphere or the morbid peculiarities of the Victorians; for her, the cemetery was about the dead and their grave owners. Robert was working, rather slowly, on a history of Highgate Cemetery and Victorian funerary practices for his doctoral thesis. But Jessica, who never wasted anything and was supremely adept at putting people to work, had said, 'If you're going to do all that research, why don't you make yourself useful?' So he began to lead tours. He found that he liked the cemetery itself much better than anything he wrote about it.

Robert settled into himself. The stone step he sat on was cold, wet and shallow. His knees jutted up almost to shoulder height. 'Hello, love,' he said, but as always felt absurd speaking out loud to a mausoleum. Silently he continued: *Hello. I'm here. Where are you?* He pictured Elspeth sitting inside the mausoleum like a saint in her hermitage, looking out at him through the grate in the door with a little smile on her face. *Elspeth?*

She had always been a restless sleeper. When she was alive her sleep was punctuated by tossing and turning; she often stole all the blankets. When Elspeth slept alone she lay spreadeagled across the bed, staking her territory with limbs instead of a flag. When she slept with Robert he was often awoken by a stray elbow or knee, or by Elspeth's legs thrashing as though she were running in bed. 'One of these nights you're going to break my nose,' he'd said to her. She had acknowledged that she was a dangerous bed mate. 'I apologise in advance for any breakage,' she'd told him, and kissed the nose in question. 'You'll look good, though. It'll add a certain hooliganish glamour to you.'

Now there was only stillness. The door was a barrier he could have passed through; there was a key in Elspeth's desk, in addition to the one in the cemetery office. Elspeth's body sat in a box a few feet away from him. He chose not to imagine what three months had done to it.

Robert was struck once again by the finality of it all, summed up and presented to him as the silence in the little room behind him. *I have things to tell you. Are you listening?* He had never realised, while Elspeth was alive, the extent to which a thing had not completely happened until he told her about it.

Roche sent the letter to Julia and Valentina yesterday. Robert imagined the letter making its way from Roche's office in Hampstead to Lake Forest, Illinois, USA, being dropped through the letter box at 99 Pembridge Road, being picked up by one of the twins. It was a thick, creamy envelope with the return address of Roche, Elderidge, Potts & Lefley – Solicitors debossed in glossy black ink and the twins' names and address written in the spidery handwriting of Roche's ancient secretary, Constance. Robert imagined one of the twins holding the envelope, her curiosity. *I'm nervous about this, Elspeth. I would feel better if you'd ever met these girls. You don't have to live with them – they could be awful. Or what if they just sell the place to someone awful?* But he was intrigued by the twins, and he had a certain irrational faith in Elspeth's experiment. 'I can leave it all to you,' she'd said. 'Or I can leave it to the girls.'

'Let the girls have it,' he had replied. 'I have more than enough.'

'Hmm. I will, then. But what can I give you?'

They were sitting on her hospital bed. She had a fever; it was after the splenectomy. Elspeth's dinner sat untouched on the wheeled bedside table. He was massaging her feet, his hands slippery with the warm, fragrant oil. 'I don't know. Could you arrange to be reincarnated?'

'The twins are rumoured to be pretty close copies.' Elspeth smiled. 'I'll make them come and live in the flat if they want it. Shall I leave you the twins?'

Robert smiled back at her. 'That could backfire. That could be quite . . . painful.'

'You'll never know if you don't give it a whirl. But I want to give you something.'

'A lock of hair?'

'Oh, but it's bad hair now,' she said, fingering her downy silver fuzz. 'We should have saved a bit when I still had my real hair.' Elspeth's hair had been longish, wavy, the colour of winter butter.

Robert shook his head. 'It doesn't matter. I just wanted something of you.'

'Like the Victorians? It's a pity it isn't longer. You could make earrings or a brooch or something.' She laughed. 'You could clone me.'

He pretended to consider it. 'But I don't think they've worked all the bugs out of cloning. You might turn out morbidly obese, or flipper-limbed or whatnot. Plus I'd have to wait for you to grow up, by which time I'd be a pensioner and you'd want nothing to do with me.'

'The twins are a much better bet. They're fifty per cent me and fifty per cent Jack. I've seen photos, you really can't see him in them at all.'

'Where are you getting photos of the twins?'

Elspeth covered her mouth with her hand. 'Edie, actually. But don't tell anyone.' Robert said, 'Since when are you in touch with Edie? I thought you hated Edie.'

'Hated Edie?' Elspeth looked stricken. 'No. I was very angry with Edie, and I still am. But I never hated Edie; that would be like hating myself. She just . . . she did something quite stupid that bollixed up our lives. But she's still my twin.' Elspeth hesitated. 'I wrote to her about a year ago – when I first got diagnosed. I thought she ought to know.'

'You didn't tell me.'

'I know. It was private.'

Robert knew it was childish to feel hurt. He didn't say anything.

She said, 'Ah, come on. If your father got in touch would you tell me all about it?'

'I would, actually.'

Elspeth put her thumb in her mouth and bit gently. He had always found this highly sexual, a huge turn-on, but now it was somehow devoid of that power. She said, 'Yes, of course you would.'

'And what do you mean they are half you? They're Edie's kids.'

'They are. They are her kids. But Edie and I are identical twins, so her kids equal my kids, genetically.'

'But you've never even met them.'

'Does it matter so much? All I can say is, you haven't got a twin, so you can't know how it is.' Robert continued to sulk. 'Oh, don't. Don't be that way.' She tried to move towards him, but the tubes in her arms overruled her. Robert carefully set her feet on a towel, wiped his hands, got up and reseated himself on the arc of white sheet next to her waist. She took up almost no space at all. He placed one hand on her pillow, just beside her head, and leaned over her. Elspeth put her hand on his cheek. It was like being touched with sandpaper; her skin almost hurt him. He turned his head and kissed her palm. They had done all these things so many times before.

'Let me give you my diaries,' Elspeth said softly. 'Then you'll know all my secrets.'

He realised later that she had planned this all along. But

then he had only said, 'Tell me all your secrets now. Are they so very terrible?'

'Dreadful. But they're all very old secrets. Since I met you I've lived a chaste and blameless life.'

'Chaste?'

'Well, monogamous, anyway.'

'That'll do.' He kissed her, briefly. She was more feverish now. 'You ought to sleep.'

'Do my feet more?' She was like a child asking for her favourite bedtime story. He resumed his place at her feet and squeezed more oil onto his hands, warmed it by rubbing it between his palms.

Elspeth sighed and closed her eyes. 'Mmm,' she said after a while, arching her feet. 'That's bloody marvellous.' Then she had slept, and he'd sat there holding her slippery feet in his hands, thinking.

Robert opened his eyes. He wondered briefly if he had fallen asleep; the memory had been so vivid. *Where are you, Elspeth? Perhaps you're only living in my head now.* Robert stared at the graves across the path, which were dangerously tilted. One had trees growing on both sides; they had lifted the monument slightly off its base so that it levitated an inch or so in the air. As Robert watched, a fox trotted through the ivy that choked the graves behind the ones on the main path. The fox saw him, paused for a moment and disappeared into the undergrowth. Robert heard other foxes howling to each other, some close by, some off in the deeper parts of the cemetery. It was the mating season. The daylight was going; Robert was chilled and wet. He roused himself.

'Goodnight, Elspeth.' He felt silly saying it. He got up and began to walk back to the office, feeling much the way he had as a teenager when he realised that he was no longer able to pray. Wherever Elspeth might be, she wasn't here.

Julia and Valentina Poole liked to get up early. This was curious, because they were out of school, unemployed and rather indolent. There was no reason for the twins to be up with the dawn; they were early birds who weren't particularly interested in getting the worm.

On this particular Saturday in February the sun was not quite up. The twelve inches of snow that had fallen overnight looked bluish in the half-light; the huge trees that lined Pembridge Road bowed under the weight of it. Lake Forest was still asleep. The yellow-brick ranch house where the twins lived with their parents felt quiet and snug under the snow. All the usual traffic, bird and dog noises were stilled.

Julia turned up the heat while Valentina made hot chocolate from a mix. Julia went into the family room and clicked on the TV. When Valentina came into the room with the tray, Julia was standing in front of the TV flicking through the channels even though she knew what they wanted to watch. It was always the same, every Saturday. The twins loved the sameness, even as they felt incapable of enduring it for one more minute. Julia paused on CNN. President Bush was talking to Karl Rove in a conference room. 'Nuke them,' said Valentina. The twins gave the finger to the president and his aide in unison, and Julia changed the channels until she got to *This Old House*. She turned the sound up, careful not to blast it and risk waking their parents. Valentina and Julia settled onto the couch, wrapped around each other, with Julia's legs resting on Valentina's lap. Mookie, their aged tabby cat, sat next to Valentina. They pulled the plaid wool blanket over themselves, warmed their hands with their mugs of chocolate and stared at the TV, lost to everything else. On Saturday mornings they could watch four reruns of *This Old House* back to back.

'Soapstone kitchen counters,' said Julia.

'Mmm-hmm,' said Valentina, entranced.

The family room was dim; the only light came from the television and the front window. But if the light had been stronger the room would have been hard to look at, because everything in it was Kelly green, bright red plaid, or related to golf. The entire house was aggressively decorated. All the furnishings were either overstuffed, covered in chintz, made of brushed metal or frosted glass, or painted in colours with names that sounded like ice-cream flavours. Edie was an interior decorator; she liked to practise on their house, and Jack had given up trying to have any say in the matter. The twins were convinced that their mother had the most egregious taste in the entire world. This was probably not true; most Lake Forest homes were decorated in more expensive versions of the same. The twins liked the family room because it was their dad's, and therefore ironically hideous. Jack took a certain pleasure in acquiescing to the demands of his tribe as long as he was comfortable.

The twins themselves looked odd in this house. Actually, they looked odd everywhere they went.

They were twenty years old, on this winter Saturday. Julia was the older twin by six (to her, very significant) minutes. It was easy to imagine Julia elbowing Valentina out of the way in her determination to be first.

The twins were very pale and very thin, the kind of thinness that other girls envy and mothers worry over. Julia was five feet, one and a half inches tall. Valentina was one quarter of an inch shorter. Each twin had fine, floating, white-blonde hair, bobbed at their ear lobes, hanging in spiderweb curls around their faces, giving them the look of dandelions gone to seed. They had long necks, small breasts, flat stomachs. The vertebrae in their spines were visible, long straight columns of bumps under their skin. They were often mistaken for undernourished twelve-year-olds; they might have been cast as Victorian orphans in a made-for-TV movie. Their eyes were large, grey and so wide-set that they appeared almost wall-eyed. They had heart-shaped faces, delicate upturned noses, bow lips, straight teeth. Both twins bit their fingernails. Neither had any tattoos. Valentina thought of herself as awkward, and wished that she had Julia's splendid air of belonging. In truth, Valentina looked fragile, and this attracted people to her.

The thing that made the twins peculiar was hard to define. People were uneasy when they saw them together without knowing exactly why. The twins were not merely identical: they were mirror-image twins. The mirroring was not limited to their appearance, but involved every cell in their bodies. So the small mole on the right side of Julia's mouth was on the left side of Valentina's; Valentina was left-handed, Julia right-handed. Neither looked freakish by herself. The marvel was most evident in X-rays: while Julia was organised in the usual way, Valentina was internally reversed. Her heart was on her right side, with all its ventricles and chambers inverted. Valentina had heart defects which had required surgery when she was born. The surgeon had used a mirror to help him see her tiny heart in the way he was accustomed to seeing. Valentina had asthma; Julia rarely had so much as a cold. Valentina's fingerprints were almost the opposite of Julia's (even identical twins don't have exactly the same fingerprints). They were still essentially one creature, whole but containing contradictions.

The twins sat attentively, watching a gigantic house near the Atlantic Ocean being reshingled, sanded, painted. Dormers were restored, a chimney rebuilt. A new inglenook replaced one that had been torn out.

The twins were avid for things that belonged to the past. Their bedroom looked as though it had once been part of another house, as though it had strayed and been adopted by this ordinary ranch house out of charity. When the twins were thirteen they had stripped the blowsy floral wallpaper off their walls, sent all their stuffed animals and dolls to AMVETS and declared their room a museum. The current exhibit was an old birdcage stuffed with plastic crucifixes, which rested on a crocheted doily draped over a small table which had been completely covered with Hello Kitty stickers. Everything else in the room was white. It was a bedroom for Des Esseintes' sisters.

Outside, snow blowers began to roar. It was becoming a

clear, blindingly sunny morning. As the credits rolled on the fourth episode of *This Old House*, the twins sat up, stretched, turned off the TV. They stood at the window squinting in their paisley bathrobes, watching Serafin Garcia (who had been mowing their lawn and blowing their snow since they were babies) as he cleared the driveway. He saw them and waved. They waved back.

They heard their parents stirring, but knew that this did not mean they would be getting up any time soon. Edie and Jack both liked to sleep in on the weekends. The night before they had been at a party at the Onwentsia Club; the twins had heard them come in around three. ('Shouldn't it be the other way around?' Julia said to Valentina, not for the first time. 'Shouldn't it be us causing *them* anxiety?') The twins moved on to the next part of their usual Saturday morning: pancakes. They made enough so that when Edie and Jack eventually did emerge, they could microwave some pancakes if they felt like eating. Julia made the batter, and Valentina poured it onto the griddle and stood staring at the pale yellow circles as air bubbles formed and popped. She loved flipping the pancakes. She made five baby pancakes for herself and five for Julia. Julia made coffee. They ate in the kitchen, sitting at the island surrounded by African violets and a cookie jar that looked like a gnome.

After breakfast the twins washed the dishes. Then they put on jeans and hooded sweatshirts with BARAT printed on them. (This was the local college; the twins had attended it for a semester and then dropped out, claiming that it was a waste of their time and Jack's money. It was the third college they had attended. They had originally matriculated at Cornell; Julia had stopped attending classes in the spring semester, and when she was asked to leave Valentina came home with her. At the University of Illinois they'd lasted a year, but Julia refused to go back.) The mailperson trudged up the walk and shoved the mail through the slot. It landed on the floor of the foyer with a loud thud. The twins converged on it.

Julia grabbed the bundle and began to spew each piece of mail onto the dining-room table. 'Pottery Barn, Crate and Barrel, ComEd, Anthropologie, letter for Mom . . . letter for us?' The twins rarely received mail; all of their correspondence took place online. Valentina took the heavy envelope from Julia's hand. She stood weighing it, feeling the texture of the paper. Julia took it back from her. They glanced at each other. *It's from a law firm. It's from London.* The twins had never been to London. They'd never left America. London was where their mom was from, but Edie and Jack seldom spoke about that. Edie was an American now – she had gone native, or faux native; the Poole family lived in a suburb of Chicago that had pretended, from its inception, to be an English village. The twins had noticed that Edie's accent tended to reappear when she was mad, or trying to impress someone.

'Open it,' said Valentina. Julia's fingers fumbled with the stiff paper. She moved to the living-room window and Valentina followed her. Valentina stood behind Julia and put her chin on Julia's shoulder and her arms around Julia's waist. The twins looked like a two-headed girl. Julia raised the letter so Valentina could see it better.

Julia and Valentina Poole
99 Pembridge Road
Lake Forest, IL 60035 USA

Dear Julia and Valentina Poole,
I regret to inform you of the death of your aunt, Elspeth
Alice Noblin. Though she never met you, she was interested
in your welfare. Last September, knowing that her illness
would soon result in her death, she made a new will. I am
enclosing a copy of this document. You are her residuary
legatees; that is, she has bequeathed to you her entire estate,
with the exception of a few minor bequests to friends and
charities. You will receive this inheritance when you reach
the age of twenty-one.

The bequest is given to you with the following conditions:

1) Ms Noblin owned an apartment in London, in
Vautravers Mews, Highgate, N6. It borders Highgate
Cemetery in Highgate Village, a very lovely part of London
indeed. She bequeathed this apartment to you on the
condition that you both live in it for one year before you
may sell it.

2) The entire bequest is given on the condition that no
part of it shall be used to benefit Ms Noblin's sister,
Edwina, or Edwina's husband, Jack (your parents). Also,
Edwina and Jack Poole are forbidden to set foot in the flat
or inspect its contents.

Please let me know if you care to accept Ms Noblin's
estate on these terms. I am always available to answer any
questions you may have in regard to this matter.

Ms Noblin's executor is Robert Fanshaw. He will be your neighbour if you accept your aunt's bequest as he lives in the flat just below hers. Mr Fanshaw can also assist you in matters pertaining to the estate.

Regards,

Xavier Roche

Roche, Elderidge, Potts & Lefley LLP – Solicitors

54D Hampstead High Street

Hampstead, London, NW3 1QA

Julia and Valentina exchanged looks. Julia flipped to the next page. The handwriting was disturbingly similar to Edie's.

Dear Julia and Valentina,

Hello. I was hoping to meet you both some day, but now that won't happen. You might wonder why I am leaving all my flotsam and jetsam to you and not to your mother. The best reason I can give is that I feel rather hopeful about you. I wonder what you might make of it all. I thought it might be interesting, even fun.

Your mother and I have been estranged for the last twenty-one years. She can tell you about that if she wants to. You may think that the conditions of my will are a bit harsh; I'm afraid you will just have to decide for yourselves whether to accept on these terms. I am not trying to create discord in your family. I'm trying to protect my own history. A bad thing about dying is that I've started to feel as though I'm being erased. Another bad thing is that I won't get to find out what happens next.

I hope you will accept. It gives me great pleasure to think of the two of you living here. I don't know if this makes a difference, but the flat is large and full of amusing books, and London is an amazing place to live (though rather expensive, I'm afraid). Your mother tells me you have dropped out of college but that you are autodidacts; if so, you may enjoy living here very much.

I wish you happiness, whatever you may choose to do.

With love,

Elspeth Noblin

There were more sheets of paper, but Julia put the sheaf down and began pacing around the living room. Valentina perched on the back of an armchair and watched Julia orbiting the coffee table, the sofa, then winging off to circle the dining-room table a few times. *London*, thought Valentina. The thought was large and dark, the word was like a giant black dog. Julia stopped, turned and grinned at Valentina. 'It's like a fairy tale.'

'Or a horror movie,' said Valentina. 'We're, like, the ingénues.'

Julia nodded, resumed pacing. 'First, get rid of the parents. Then, lure the unsuspecting heroines to the spooky old mansion—'

'It's only a flat.'

'Whatever. Then—'

'Serial killers.'

'White slavery.'

'Or it's like, you know, Henry James.'

'I don't think people die of consumption any more.'

'They do in the Third World.'

'Yeah, well, the UK has socialised medicine.'

Valentina said, 'Mom and Dad won't like it.'

'No,' said Julia. She ran her fingers across the dining-room table and discovered a bunch of crumbs. She went into the kitchen, moistened a washcloth and wiped the table.

Valentina said, 'What happens if we don't accept?'

'I don't know. I'm sure it says in the letter somewhere.' Julia paused. 'You can't seriously be thinking about not accepting? This is totally what we've been waiting for.'

'What's that, sweetie?' Edie stood squinting at them from the archway between the living room and the hallway. Her hair was mussed and she had a generally crumpled aspect. Her cheeks were very pink, as though someone had pinched them.

Julia said, 'We got a letter.' Valentina scooped it off the side table and brought it to her mother. Edie looked at the return address and said, 'I can't possibly deal with this before I've had my coffee.' Valentina went to pour her a cup. Edie said, 'Julia, go wake up your dad.'

'Um . . .'

'Tell him I said so.'

Julia bounded down the hall. Valentina heard her shrieking *'Dad-deeeeeeee'* as she opened their parents' bedroom door. *Nice*, Valentina thought. *Why not just use an ice pick?* Edie went hunting for her reading glasses. By the time Jack lumbered into the dining room she had read the first few pages of the letter and was making her way through the will.

Jack Poole had once been handsome, in a corn-fed, college-athlete sort of way. His black hair now had a sumptuous grey streak. He wore it longer than the other guys at the bank. He was quite tall and towered over his petite wife and daughters. The years had coarsened his features and thickened his waistline. Jack wore suits so much of his waking life that on the weekends he liked to be slovenly. At the moment he was wearing an ancient maroon bathrobe and a splitting, enormous pair of sheepskin slippers.

'Fee, fi, fo, fum,' Jack said. This was an old joke, the rest of it lost in the mists of the twins' earliest childhood. It meant, *Get me some coffee or I will eat you.* Julia poured a cup for her father and set it before him. 'Okay,' he said. 'I'm up. Where's the fire?'

'It's Elspeth,' said Edie. 'She's not just leaving it to them, she's prying them away from us.'

'Say what?' Jack held out his hand and Edie put part of the letter into it. They sat next to each other, reading.

'Vindictive bitch,' Jack said, without much emotion or surprise. Julia and Valentina sat down at the table and watched their parents. *Who are these people? What happened? Why did Aunt Elspeth hate them? Why do they hate her?* The twins widened their eyes at each other. *We'll find out.* Jack finished reading and groped in his bathrobe pocket for his cigarettes and lighter. He put them on the table but did not light one; he glanced at Valentina, who frowned. Jack put his hand over the pack to reassure himself that it was there. Valentina took her inhaler from her sweatshirt pocket, set it on the table and smiled at her father.

Edie looked up at Valentina. 'If you don't accept, most of it goes to charity,' she said. The twins wondered how much of their conversation she had overheard. Edie was reading a codicil of the will. It instructed someone named Robert Fanshaw to remove all personal papers from the flat, including diaries, letters and photographs, and bequeathed these papers to him. Edie wondered who this Robert person was, that her sister had made him custodian of all their history. *But the main thing is she's arranged for the papers to not be in the flat when the twins arrive.* That was the thing Edie had most feared, the intersection of the twins and whatever Elspeth had left in the way of evidence.

Jack put the letter from Elspeth on the table. He sat back in his chair and looked at his wife. Edie held the will at arm's length and scowled at it, rereading. *You don't seem all that surprised, darling,* thought Jack. Julia and Valentina were watching Edie read. Julia looked rapt, Valentina anxious. Jack sighed. Although he had been trying to push his daughters out of the ranch house and into the real world, the world he had in mind was college, preferably an Ivy League college on a full scholarship. The twins' SAT scores were almost perfect, though their grades were wildly uneven and by now their transcripts would give any director of admissions pause. He imagined Julia and Valentina safely ensconced at Harvard or Yale, or even at Sarah Lawrence; heck, Bennington would be okay. Valentina glanced at him and smiled, raised her nearly invisible eyebrows just slightly. Jack thought about Elspeth as he had last seen her, weeping in line at the airport. *You don't remember her, girls. You have no idea what she was capable of.*

Jack had been relieved when Elspeth died. *I didn't realise you had any more tricks up your sleeve, Miss Noblin.* He had never failed to underestimate her. He stood up, scooped his cigarettes and lighter into his palm and headed for the den. He shut the door, leaned against it and lit up. *At least you're dead.* He inhaled smoke and let it stream through his nostrils slowly. *One Noblin sister is the most anyone should have to cope with in a lifetime.* He considered that he had ended up with the right sister, after all, and was thankful. He stood smoking, and thought about other ways things might have turned out. By the time Jack re-entered the dining room he felt steadier, almost cheerful. *Wonderful substance, nicotine.*

Edie was sitting very straight in her chair; the twins each leaned forward, elbows on the table, chins in hands, Valentina listing sideways as Julia said, 'But we never met her; why would she leave us anything? Why not you?'

Edie regarded them silently as Jack sat down in his chair. Julia said, 'How come you never took us to London?'

'I did,' Edie replied. 'We went to London when you were four months old. You met your grandmother, who died later that year, and you met Elspeth.'

'We did? You did?'

Edie got up and walked down the hall to her bedroom. She disappeared for a few minutes. Valentina said, 'Did you go too, Daddy?'

'No,' said Jack. 'I wasn't too popular over there then.'

'Oh.' *Why not?*

Edie came back holding two American passports. She handed one to Valentina and the other to Julia. They opened the passports, stared at themselves. *It's weird to see new baby pictures.* The stamps said HEATHROW AIRPORT, 27 APRIL 1984 and O'HARE INTERNATIONAL AIRPORT, JUNE 30, 1984. They traded and compared the photos. Without the names it was impossible to tell which twin was in each photo. *We look like potatoes with eyes,* Julia thought.

The twins laid the passports on the table and looked at Edie. Edie's heart beat fast. *You have no idea. Don't ask. It's none of your business. Just let me be. Let me be.* She stared back at them, poker-faced. 'Why didn't she leave it to you, Mom?' asked Valentina.

Edie glanced at Jack. 'I don't know,' she said. 'You'd have to ask her.'

Jack said, 'Your mother doesn't want to talk about it.' He gathered the papers that were strewn across the table into a stack, tapped the bottom of the stack against the table to align it and handed it to Julia. He stood up. 'What's for breakfast?'

'Pancakes,' said Valentina. They all stood, all tried to segue into the normal Saturday-morning routine. Edie poured herself more coffee and steadied the cup with two hands as she drank it. *She's frightened,* Valentina thought, and was frightened herself. Julia walked down the hall doing a little dance, holding the will over her head as though she were fording a rising river. She went into their bedroom and closed the door. Then she began jumping in place on the thick carpeting, her fists pounding the air over her head, shouting silently, *Yes! Yes! Yes!*

That night the twins lay in Julia's bed, facing each other. Valentina's bed was rumpled but unused. Their feet were touching. The twins smelled faintly of sea kelp and something sweet; they were trying out a new body lotion. They could hear the settling noises their house made in the night. Their bedroom was dimly illuminated by the blue Hanukkah lights they had strung around the wrought-iron headboards of their beds.

Julia opened her eyes and saw that Valentina was staring at her. 'Hey, Mouse.'

Valentina whispered, 'I'm afraid.'

'I know.'

'Aren't you?'

'No.'

Valentina closed her eyes. *Of course not.*

'It'll be great, Mouse. We'll have our own apartment, we won't have to work, at least for a while; we can do whatever we want. It's, like, total freedom, you know?'

'Total freedom to do what, exactly?'

Julia shifted onto her back. *Oh God, Mouse, don't be such a Mouse.* 'I'll be there. You'll be there. What else do we need?'

'I thought we were going back to college. You promised.'

'We'll go to college in London.'

'But that's a year from now.'

Julia didn't answer. Valentina stared into Julia's ear. In the semi-dark it was like a little mysterious tunnel that led into Julia's brain. *If I were tiny I would crawl in there and tell you what to do and you would think it was your own idea.*

Julia said, 'It's only for a year. If we don't like it we'll sell it and come back.'

Valentina was silent.

After a while Julia took her hand, interlaced their fingers. 'We've got to prepare. We don't want to be like those dumb Americans who go to Europe and only eat at McDonald's and speak English real loud instead of the local language.'

'But they speak English in England.'

'You know what I mean, Mouse. We need to study.'

'Okay.'

'Okay.' They shifted so that they lay side by side, shoulders touching, hands clasped. Valentina thought, *Maybe in London we can have a bigger bed.* Julia stared at the terrible Home Depot light fixture on the ceiling, mentally listing all the things they would need to find out about: exchange rates, vaccinations, soccer, the Royal Family . . .

Valentina lay in Julia's bed thinking about the inside of Julia's ear, how her own ear was the exact reverse, and if she pressed her ear against Julia's and trapped a sound, would it oscillate back and forth endlessly, confused and forlorn? *Would I hear it backwards? What if it was a London sound, like cars driving on the wrong side of the road; then maybe I would hear it forwards and it would be backwards for Julia. Maybe in London everything will be opposite from here . . . I'll do what I want; no one will be the boss of me . . .* Valentina listened to Julia breathing. She tried to imagine what she would do if it was just her, on her own. But she had never done anything on her own, so she struggled to formulate some kind of plan, and then gave up, exhausted.

Edie lay in bed waiting for Jack to fall asleep. Usually she tried to get to sleep first, because Jack snored, but tonight her mind was racing and she knew it was pointless to even try. Finally she turned onto her side and found Jack facing her with his eyes open.

'It'll be all right,' said Jack. 'They've been away before and it was all right.'

'This is different.'

'Because it's Elspeth?'

'Maybe,' she said. 'Or, just – it's so far away. I don't want them there.'

He put his arm around her waist and she burrowed into him. *I'm safe. I'm safe here.* Jack was her bomb shelter, her human shield. 'Remember when they were at Cornell?' he said. 'How great it was to have the house to ourselves?'

'Yeah . . .' It had been a revelation: married life without children was a blast. For a while, anyway.

'They're twenty years old, Edie. They should have been long gone. We should have sent them to separate schools,' said Jack.

She sighed. *You don't understand.* 'It's too late. Elspeth's taken it out of our hands.'

'Maybe she's done us a favour.'

Edie didn't reply. Jack said, 'When you were their age you were very eager to be on your own, as I recall.'

'That was different.'

He waited for her to continue. When she didn't, he said, very quietly, 'Why, Edie? Why was it different?' But she pressed her lips together and closed her eyes. He said, 'You could tell me.'

She opened her eyes and smiled. 'There's nothing to tell,

Jack.' She turned again, so she faced away from him. 'We should try to sleep.'

That was close, he thought. He wasn't sure if he was disappointed or relieved. 'Okay,' Jack said. They lay together for a long time, listening to each other's breathing, until Jack began to snore and Edie was alone with her thoughts.

The invention of the Internet had allowed Martin to abandon the outside world. Or rather, the Internet had enabled him to relegate that world to the role of support system for his world, the one that flourished inside his flat.

Martin had not expected Marijke to leave him. She had acquiesced in his rituals, had aided and abetted his increasingly stringent compulsions, for almost twenty-five years. He couldn't understand why she would leave now. 'You are like a bad pet,' she'd told him. 'You're like a human squirrel that never goes out, that just sits in the flat all day and all night, licking the same spot. I want to be able to open the windows. I want to walk into my own flat without having to put bags on my feet.' They'd had this conversation in the kitchen. The windows were taped shut and papered over, and both of them were wearing plastic bags over their socks. Martin was empty-handed; he had nothing he could use to counter Marijke's assertion. He *was* a human squirrel and he knew it. But who would take care of him if she left? 'You're a fifty-three-year-old PhD with a telephone and a computer. You'd be fine. Get Robert to take out the rubbish.' Two days later, Marijke was gone.

She left him with two weeks' worth of frozen meals and a list of websites and telephone numbers. Sainsbury's delivered groceries and cleaning products; Marks & Spencer sent pants and socks. Robert posted his letters and carried the rubbish down to the dustbin.

At the end of the day, it wasn't a bad way to live. There was no one to please but himself. He missed Marijke terribly, but he did not miss her reproving glares, her loud sighing, the way she rolled her eyes when he asked her to leave a room and come in again because she'd entered with the wrong foot first. Marijke wasn't there to frown when he ordered five thousand pairs of latex surgical gloves from a dodgy outfit on the Internet. While he was at it, he also bought a kit for measuring blood pressure, a gas mask and a desert-camouflage army-surplus jumpsuit which the site claimed could withstand chemical weapons.

There were bargains to be had. From a different site he ordered four fifty-litre drums of bleach. This brought Robert to his door.

'Martin, there's a bloke downstairs with an enormous amount of bleach. He says you ordered it, and it has to be signed for. Do you think it's safe to have that much bleach around the house? The containers have all sorts of scary pictographs of hands with smoke coming off them, and warnings galore. Are you sure this is a good idea?'

Martin thought it was a brilliant idea; he was always running out of bleach. To Robert he only said that he would be very careful, and to please put the bleach in the kitchen.

The more Martin delved into the cyber world, the more he realised that there was absolutely nothing he couldn't have brought to his door, for a fee. Pizza, cigarettes, beer, free-range eggs, the *Guardian*, postage stamps, light bulbs, milk: all this and more appeared when required. He ordered books by the dozen from Amazon, and soon the unopened boxes piled up in the hall. He missed browsing in Stanfords, the map shop on Long Acre, and was overjoyed when he discovered their website. Maps began to arrive, along with guidebooks to places Martin had never visited. Inspired, he ordered everything Stanfords offered on Amsterdam, and covered his bedroom walls with maps of that city. He traced what he imagined might be Marijke's routes. He guessed, correctly (though he did not know it), that she lived in the Jordaan district. He assigned her a routine and mentally accompanied her as she rode her bike along canals and shopped for all the odd vegetables she loved that he wouldn't eat. Fennel, Jerusalem artichokes, rocket. He didn't consider any of it to be food. Martin lived on tea, toast, eggs, chops, potatoes, beer, curry, rice and pizza. He had a weakness for pudding. But in his imagination Marijke lingered in Amsterdam's outdoor markets, filling the basket of her bike with freesias and Brussels sprouts. He remembered walks he and Marijke had taken together there decades before, marvellous spring evenings when they were besotted with each other and Amsterdam seemed hushed and the sounds of boats and seagulls bounced off the seventeenth-century canal houses as though they were recordings being played back from the past. Martin would stand in his bedroom with the tip of his index finger pressed to the map over the location of the radio station where Marijke now worked. He would close his eyes, repeat her name silently, moving his lips, one hundred times. He did this to prevent himself from calling her. Often it sufficed. Other times he had to call. She never answered. He imagined her flipping open her mobile, frowning at his number, flipping it closed.

Martin's desk was an island of normality in the wreck of his flat. He had succeeded in keeping his work space compulsion-free; if an obsession began to trouble him at his desk he would get up and take it to some other part of the flat to deal with it. Aside from cleaning rituals at the beginning and end of each work session, Martin had maintained his desk as a peaceful oasis. His computer had been for work only; email had been for corresponding with editors and proofreaders. In addition to setting his crossword puzzles, Martin also translated various obscure and ancient languages into various modern ones. He belonged to one online forum that existed to allow scholars worldwide to debate the merits of various texts and to amuse each other by ridiculing the work of translators who didn't belong to the forum.

But now the Internet began to interfere with his cherished desk-isle, and he found himself monitoring eBay auctions of aquarium filtering machines and checking Amazon every ten minutes or so to see how his crossword books were selling. They always had depressing numbers like 673,082 or 822,457. Once his latest had made it up to 9,326. It had given him a happy afternoon, until he logged on before going to bed and found it at 787,333.

Martin discovered that while he could find Young Girls Hot to Meet You!!!, Big Busted!?! S*xy Moms and a plethora of other opportunities to satisfy his lust and other people's avarice, he could not find Marijke on the Web. He Googled her repeatedly, but she was one of the rare, delicate creatures who managed to exist completely in the actual world. She had never authored a paper or won a prize; she had kept her phone number unlisted and didn't partake in any chat rooms or list-servs. He thought she must have email at work, but she wasn't listed in the radio station's directory. As far as the Internet was concerned, Marijke didn't exist.

As the days went by, Martin began to wonder if there had ever been a woman named Marijke who lived with him and kissed him and read him Dutch poems about the beginning of spring. Months disappeared, and Martin worked on his crosswords and translations, washed his hands until they bled, counted, checked, admonished himself for washing and counting and checking. He microwaved a monotonous array of frozen foods, ate at the kitchen table while reading. He did his laundry, and the clothes got thinner from too much bleach. He could hear the weather sometimes; rain and sleet, rare thunder, wind. He sometimes wondered what would happen if he stopped all the clocks. The cyber world ran outside of time, and Martin thought that he might cycle around the clock untethered. The idea made him depressed. Without Marijke he was only an email address.

Martin lay in their bed each night imagining Marijke in her bed. Over the years she had become a little plump, and he loved her roundness, he loved the warmth and heft and curve of her under the covers. She snored sometimes, softly, and Martin listened in the dark until he could almost hear her small snores drifting through her Amsterdam bedroom. He would say her name over and over until it devolved into meaningless sounds – *mah REI kuh, mah REI kuh* – it became an entry in a dictionary of loneliness. He thought of her alone in her bed. He never allowed himself to wonder if Marijke might have found someone else. He could not bear to even frame the question in his mind. Only when he had imagined her quite completely, the folds of her face against the pillow, the hump of her haunch under the blankets; only then could Martin let himself sleep. He often woke to find that he had been crying.

As each night passed he found it more difficult to evoke Marijke precisely. He panicked and pinned up dozens of photographs of her all over the flat. Somehow this only made things worse. His actual memories began to be replaced by the images; his wife, a whole human being, was turning into a collection of dyes on small white rectangles of paper. Even the photographs were not as intensely colourful as they had once been, he could see that. Washing them didn't help. Marijke was bleaching out of his memory. The harder he tried to keep her the faster she seemed to vanish.

Robert sat at his desk with the lights off, watching through the front windows as Vautravers' tangled front garden disappeared in the dusk. It was June, and the light seemed to hang there, as though the garden had fallen out of time and become an enormous image of itself. The moon rose, almost full. He got up and shook himself, gathered his night scope and a torch and walked through his flat to the back door. He slipped down the steps quietly; Martin worried about intruders. Robert avoided the gravel path through the back garden, instead squishing across the mossy earth to the green door in the garden wall. He unlocked it and passed through the wall into the cemetery.

He was standing on asphalt, the roof of the Terrace Catacombs. There were steps at both ends of the catacombs; tonight he took the western steps and headed towards the Dickens Path. He didn't use the torch. It was dark under the thick canopy of leaves, but he had done this route in the dark many times.

He liked Highgate Cemetery best at night. At night there were no visitors, no weeds to pull, no enquiries from journalists – there was only the cemetery itself, spread out in the moonlight like a soft grey hallucination, a stony wilderness of Victorian melancholy. Sometimes he wished he could stroll with Jessica along the dim paths, enjoying the evening noises, the animals that called out to each other in the distance and stilled as he passed. But he knew that Jessica was at home, asleep, and that she would certainly exile him from the cemetery if she knew about his night sojourns. He rationalised, telling himself that he was patrolling, protecting the cemetery from vandals and the self-described vampire-hunters who had plagued it in the 1970s and '80s.

Robert did sometimes meet other people in the cemetery at night. Last summer, for a short while, there had been a railing missing in the spiked iron fence that ran along the south-western edge of the cemetery. It was during this period that Robert began to see children in the cemetery in the evenings.

The first time, Robert was sitting in the midst of a cluster of graves from the 1920s. He had cleared a place for himself in the tall grass and was sitting very quietly, looking through his video camera with the night-vision scope on, hoping to videotape the family of foxes whose burrow was just twenty feet from where he sat. The sun had set behind the trees, and the sky was yellow above the silhouettes of the houses just beyond the fence. Robert heard a rustling sound and turned his camera in that direction. But instead of foxes, the viewfinder suddenly filled with the spectre of a child running towards him. Robert nearly dropped the camera. Another child appeared, chasing the first one; little girls in short dresses, running between the graves silently, breathing hard but running without calling out. They were almost upon him when a boy shouted, and they both turned and ran to the fence, squeezed through the gap, and were gone.

Robert reported the broken railing to the office the next morning. The children continued to play in the cemetery in the evenings, and Robert occasionally observed them, wondering who they were and where they lived, wondering what they meant by the strange games they silently played among the graves. After a few weeks a man came and put the fence right again. Robert walked along the street that evening and felt a bit sad as he passed the three children gathered there with their hands on the railings, peering into the cemetery, not speaking.

Robert's PhD thesis had begun as a work of history: he imagined the cemetery as a prism through which he could view Victorian society at its most sensationally, splendidly, irrationally excessive; in their conflation of hygienic reform and status-conscious innovation, the Victorians had created Highgate Cemetery as a theatre of mourning, a stage set of eternal repose. But as he did the research Robert was seduced by the personalities of the people buried in the cemetery, and his thesis began to veer into biography; he got sidetracked by anecdote, fell in love with the futility of elaborate preparations for an afterlife that seemed, at best, unlikely. He began to take the cemetery personally and lost all perspective.

He often sat with Michael Faraday, the famous scientist; Eliza Barrow, who had been a victim of the notorious serial murderer Frederick Seddon; he spent time brooding over the unmarked graves of foundlings. Robert had whiled away a whole night watching as falling snow covered Lion, the stone dog that kept watch over Thomas Sayers, the last of the bare-fisted prizefighters. Sometimes he borrowed a flower from

Radclyffe Hall, who always had an abundance of blooms, and relocated it to some remote and friendless tomb.

Robert loved to watch the seasons revolve in Highgate. The cemetery was never without some green; many of the plants and trees had symbolised eternal life to the Victorians, and so even in winter the haphazard geometry of the graves was softened by evergreens, cypress, holly. At night stone and snow reflected back moonlight, and Robert sometimes felt himself become weightless as he crunched along the paths through a thin coverlet of white. Occasionally he brought a ladder from Vautravers' garden shed and climbed up to the grass in the centre of the Circle of Lebanon. He would lean against the three-hundred-year-old Cedar of Lebanon, or lie on his back and watch the sky through its gnarled branches. There was seldom a visible star; they were all hidden by light pollution from London's electric grid. Robert watched aeroplanes blinking through the Cedar of Lebanon's leaves. At such times he felt a powerful sense of rightness: under his body, beneath the grass, the dead were quiet and peaceful in their little rooms; above him the stars and machines roamed the skies.

Tonight he stood by the Rossettis and thought about Elizabeth Siddal. He had rewritten the chapter devoted to her numerous times, more for the pleasure of thinking about Lizzie than because he had anything new to say about her. Robert fondled her life's trajectory in his mind: her humble beginnings as a milliner's girl; her discovery by the Pre-Raphaelite painters, who enlisted her as a model; her promotion to adored mistress of Dante Gabriel Rossetti.

Unexplained illnesses, her long-awaited marriage to Rossetti; a stillborn daughter. Her death by laudanum poisoning. A guilt-ridden Dante Gabriel, slipping a unique manuscript of his poems into his wife's casket. Seven years later, the exhumation of Lizzie at night, by bonfire light, to retrieve the poems. Robert relished all of it. He stood with his eyes closed, imagining the grave in 1869, not so hemmed in by other graves, the men digging, the flickering light of the fire.

After what seemed to him a long time, Robert followed the obscure path back through the graves and began to wander.

He was unable to believe in heaven. In his Anglican childhood he had imagined a wide, spacious emptiness, sunlit and cold, filled with invisible souls and dead pets. As Elspeth began dying he'd tried to revive this old belief, digging into his scepticism as though belief were simply an older sediment, accessible through strip-mining layers of sophistication and experience. He reread Spiritualist tracts, accounts of hundred-year-old seances, scientific experiments with mediums. His rationality rebelled. It was history; it was fascinating; it was untrue.

On these nights in the cemetery Robert stood in front of Elspeth's grave, or sat on its solitary step with his back against the uncomfortable grille-work. It did not bother him when he stood by the Rossetti grave and couldn't feel the presence of Lizzie or Christina, but he found it disturbing to visit Elspeth and find that she was not 'at home' to him. In the early days after her death he'd hovered around the tomb, waiting for a sign of any sort. 'I'll haunt you,' she'd said when they'd told her she was terminal. 'Do that,' he had replied, kissing her gaunt neck. But she was not haunting him, except in memory, where she dwindled and blazed at all the wrong moments.

Now Robert sat at Elspeth's doorstep and watched as dawn came over the trees. He could hear the birds stirring, singing, rioting and splashing across the street in Waterlow Park. Every now and then a car whooshed past along Swains Lane. When there was enough light for him to read the inscriptions on the graves across from Elspeth, Robert got up and made his way towards the back of the cemetery and the Terrace Catacombs. He could see St Michael's, but Vautravers was invisible beyond the wall. He walked up the steps at the side of the Terrace Catacombs and across the Catacombs roof to the green door. Fatigue clutched him. It was an effort to make it all the way into his flat before sleep overtook him. Outside, the cemetery assumed its daytime aspect; dawn gave way to day, the staff arrived, phones rang, the natural and the human worlds spun on their separate but conjoined axes. Robert was asleep in his clothes, his muddy trainers beside the bed. When he presented himself, noonish, at the cemetery's office, Jessica said, 'My dear boy, don't you look all in. Have some tea. Don't you ever sleep?'

London was baking under a cloudless July sky. Robert reclined on a decrepit wicker chaise longue in Jessica Bates' back garden, a gin and tonic sweating in his hand. He was watching Jessica's grandchildren preparing to play croquet. It was Sunday afternoon. He had a vague sense of being in the wrong place; usually he and Jessica would both have been at the cemetery. On a glorious Sunday like this there would be loads of tourists clustered at the gates, wielding cameras and protesting at the rules about proper attire and no water bottles. They would be whingeing about the £5 charge for the tour and pointlessly insisting on bringing in prams and children under eight. But for some reason today there had been extra guides, and he and Jessica had been sent off with orders from Edward to 'amuse yourselves, we'll be *fine* here, don't even *think* about us.' So now Jessica, who was eighty-four and incapable of leisure, was in her kitchen putting together lunch for twelve, and Robert (who had offered to help and been firmly escorted outside) lay idly watching as the children pounded the hoops and stake into the ground.

The grass was too long for croquet, but no one seemed to mind. 'I wanted to get some sheep to crop the grass, but Jessica overruled me,' said James Bates. Jessica's husband sat tucked into his lawn chair with a thin blanket; it made Robert hotter just to look at him. He was a tall man who had shrunk with age, and his gentle voice trembled a bit. He had large glasses that magnified his eyes, frail bones and a decisive manner. He had been a headmaster and now served as the cemetery's archivist.

James gazed at his grandchildren fondly. They were bickering over the rules and trying to choose teams. He longed to get out of his chair, to walk across the lawn and play with them. He sighed and looked down at the book of crosswords in his lap. 'This is quite ingenious,' he said, turning the page towards Robert. 'All the clues are mathematical equations, then you translate the answers into letters and fill it in.'

'Ugh. Is that one of Martin's?'

'Yes, he gave it to me for Christmas.'

'Sadistic devil.'

The children had arranged themselves around the first hoop and began to knock the coloured balls through it. The bigger children waited patiently for the smallest child to make her shot. 'Well played, Nell,' said the tallest boy. James pointed his pen at Robert. 'How are you getting on with Elspeth's estate?'

A small feud erupted between two cousins over a ball hit out of bounds. Robert's mind returned to Elspeth, who was never far from his thoughts. 'Roche is corresponding with the twins. Elspeth's sister was threatening to contest the will, but I think Roche has convinced her she'd lose. It must be something about America, this urge to litigate.'

'I still find it curious that Elspeth never mentioned having a twin.' James smiled. 'It's hard to imagine another one like her.'

'Yes . . .' Robert watched the children decorously tapping the balls across the lawn. 'Elspeth said she and Edie weren't very much alike in their personalities. She used to just hate being mistaken for her. Once we were in Marks & Spencer and this woman walked up to Elspeth and started chatting away, and it turned out that she was the mother of some boy Edie had gone out with. Elspeth was quite awful to her. The woman went off in a huff, and Elspeth had this rather puffed-up look about her, like one of those Brazilian frogs that get very large and spit at things that want to eat them.'

James laughed. 'She was very large for such a small woman.'

'I used to carry her around. I carried her across Hampstead Heath once – she'd broken a heel.'

'Such high heels she used to wear.'

Robert sighed and thought about Elspeth's dressing room, which doubled as an impromptu shoe museum. He had spent part of an afternoon there recently lying on the floor, petting her shoes and wanking off. He flushed. 'I don't know what to do with all her stuff.'

'Surely you needn't do anything; when the twins come they'll have to sort it out.'

'But they might throw things away,' said Robert.

'That's true; they might.' James eased himself into a different position in his chair. His back hurt. He wondered why Elspeth had left all her worldly possessions to these girls, who might come and heave everything she'd loved into a skip. 'Have you ever met them?'

'No. Actually, *Elspeth* never met them. She and Edie hadn't spoken to each other since Edie ran off with Elspeth's fiancé.' Robert frowned. 'It's a very odd will, really. The twins inherit most of the estate, but not until they're twenty-one, at the end of this year. And they only inherit the flat if their parents never set foot in the place.'

'That's a bit vengeful, don't you think? How did she expect you to enforce that?'

'She just threw that in because she couldn't stand the idea of Edie or Jack getting their hands on anything of hers. She knew it wasn't practical.'

James smiled. 'Such Elspethness. Why leave it to their daughters, then? Why not to you?'

'She left me the things that mattered to me.' Robert stared across the lawn, not seeing. 'She was rather secretive about the twins. I think she had a sort of soft spot for them *because* they were twins; she imagined herself as Auntie Elspeth, even though she never even sent them birthday cards. It's the extravagance of the thing that appealed to her, you know. It will completely alter their lives, and scoop them right out of their parents' laps and into Elspeth World. What they will do with it is anyone's guess.'

'Pity she won't be able to meet them.'

'Yes.' Robert felt disinclined to discuss the will any further. The croquet game was degenerating into a free-for-all. Some of the younger boys were using their mallets as swords, and the girls were throwing Nell's ball over her head as she leapt between them trying to rescue it. Only the two oldest boys were still doggedly hitting the balls through the hoops. At this moment Jessica happened to walk into the garden, noticed the mayhem, and stood with her arms akimbo, the very image of indignation. 'Ahem,' she said. 'What *are* you *doing*?' Jessica had a voice that rose and fell like a swooping kite. The children instantly stopped what they were doing and looked self-conscious, like cats that have fallen off something ungracefully and now sit licking themselves, pretending nothing has happened. Jessica walked carefully to where Robert and James sat. Two of her friends had broken their hips recently, so she had temporarily modified her habit of striding boldly wherever she went. She pulled up a chair and sat down next to James.

'How's the lunch?' he asked her.

'Oh, it'll be a while, the chicken's roasting.' Jessica blotted her forehead with her handkerchief. Robert realised that he was not going to be able to eat roast chicken in this heat. He pressed his glass full of almost-melted ice to his cheek. Jessica looked him over. 'You don't look well,' she told him.

'No sleep,' he replied.

'Mmm,' Jessica and James said together. They exchanged glances. 'Why's that?' Jessica asked.

Robert looked away. The children had reverted to their game. Most of them were clustered around the stake in the middle, though Nell was flailing at a ball that was stuck in a clump of irises. She whacked and the irises came flying out of the dirt. He looked at Jessica and James, who were watching him uneasily. 'Do you believe in ghosts?' Robert asked.

'Certainly not,' said Jessica. 'That's a lot of claptrap.' James smiled and looked down at Martin's crossword puzzle in his lap.

'Well, right, I know you don't believe in *ghosts*.' Highgate Cemetery had suffered from the attentions of paranormalists and satanists in the past. Jessica spent a great deal of time discouraging Japanese television programmes and enthusiasts of the supernatural from promoting Highgate as a sort of haunted-cemetery Disneyland. 'I just . . . I've been going into Elspeth's flat, and I have this feeling that she's . . . there.' Jessica's mouth turned down at the corners as though he'd made an off-colour joke. James looked up, curious. 'What sort of feeling do you mean?' he asked Robert.

Robert considered. 'It's rather intangible. But, for example, there's something very odd about the temperature in her flat. I'll be sitting at her desk, sorting papers, and I'll suddenly be very cold in one specific part of my body. My hand will be freezing cold and then it will go up my arm. Or the back of my neck . . .' Robert paused, staring at his drink. 'Things move, in her flat. Tiny, tiny movements: curtains, pencils. Movement at the edge of my peripheral vision. Things aren't where I put them when I come back. A book fell from the desk onto the floor . . .' He looked up and caught James shaking his head slightly at Jessica, who put her hand over her mouth. 'Yeah, okay. Never mind.'

Jessica said, 'Robert. We're listening.'

'I'm losing it.'

'Well, perhaps. But if it makes you feel better . . .'

'It doesn't.'

'Ah.' The three of them sat quietly.

James said, 'I saw a ghost once.'

Robert glanced at Jessica. She had a rather resigned

expression, her smile one-sided, her eyes half-closed. Robert said, 'You saw a ghost?'

'Yes.' James shifted in his chair, and Jessica leaned over and adjusted the pillow that supported his lower back. 'I was quite small, only a lad of six. So let me see, that would have been in 1917. I grew up just outside of Cambridge, and the house my family lived in at that time had once been an inn. It was built around 1750. It was very large and draughty and stood by itself at a crossroads. We didn't use the second floor, all of our bedrooms were on the first floor. Even the maid slept on the first floor.

'My father was a don at St John's, and we used to have a great many visitors come to stay with us. Ordinarily there were enough rooms to accommodate everyone, but on this occasion there must have been more visitors than usual, because my younger brother, Samuel, was put to sleep in one of the unused bedrooms on the top floor.' James smiled to himself. 'Sam was generally a pretty cool customer, as the Americans say, but he howled all night, until my mother went up and took him to sleep in her room.'

Robert said, 'I didn't know you had a brother.'

'Sam died in the war.'

'Oh.'

'So, the next night, I was to sleep in the second-floor room—'

'Wait. Did Sam tell you why he'd cried?'

James said, 'Sam was only four, and of course I teased him, so he wouldn't say. At least that's what I remember. So, I was put to bed upstairs. I remember lying there with the blanket pulled up to my chin, my mother kissing me good-night, and there I was in the dark, not knowing what terrible thing might be ready to slink out from the wardrobe and smother me . . .'

Jessica smiled. Robert thought it might be a smile for the morbidly fantastical imaginations of children.

'So what happened?'

'I fell asleep. But later that night I woke up. There was moonlight coming in through the window, and the shadows of tree branches fell onto the bed, waving gently in the breeze.'

'And then you saw the ghost?'

James laughed. 'Dear chap, the branches *were* the ghost. There weren't any trees within a hundred yards of that house. They'd all been cut down years before. I saw the ghost of a tree.'

Robert thought about it. 'That's rather elegant. I was expecting ghouls.'

'Well, that's just it, you see. I think perhaps if that sort of thing does happen – ghosts – it must be more beautiful, more surprising than all these old tales would have us believe.'

Robert happened to look at Jessica while James was speaking. She was gazing at her husband with an expression that combined patience, admiration, and something very private that seemed to Robert like the distillation of a life-time of marriage. He felt a sudden need to be alone. 'Do you have any ibuprofen?' he asked Jessica. 'I think the sun's given me a headache.'

'Of course, let me get it for you.'

'No, no,' he said, getting up. 'I'll just have a lie down before we eat.'

'There's some Anadin in the cabinet in the ground-floor loo.'

Jessica and James watched Robert walk stiffly across the terrace and into the house. 'I'm really worried about him,' Jessica said. 'He's lost the plot, a bit.'

James said, 'She's only been dead eight months. Give him some time.'

'Ye-es. I don't know. He seems to have stopped – that is, he's doing all the things one does, but there's no heart in him. I don't think he's even working on his thesis. He's just not getting over her.'

James met his wife's anxious eyes. He smiled. 'How long would it take you to get over me?'

She held out her bent hand, and he took it in his. She said, 'Dear James. I don't imagine I would ever get over you.'

'Well, Jessica,' said her husband, 'there's your answer.'

Inside the house, Robert stood in the dim ground-floor hallway with two tablets in his hand. He swallowed them without water and leaned his forehead against the cool plaster wall. It felt marvellous after the relentless sunlight. He could hear the children calling to each other, croquet abandoned for some other game. Now that he was alone he wanted to go back outside, to distract himself, talk of something else. He would go back in a few minutes. His throat felt constricted;

the pills had gone down the wrong way. He realised that he was leaving sweat on the wall, and wiped it with his forearm. Robert shut his eyes and thought of James, a small boy sitting up in bed, staring at the shadows of absent trees. *Why not*, he thought. *Why not?*

Elspeth Noblin had been dead for almost a year now, and she was still figuring out the rules.

At first she had simply drifted around her flat. She had little energy and spent a great deal of time staring at her former possessions. She would doze off and reawaken hours, perhaps days later – she couldn't tell, it didn't matter. She was shapeless, and spent whole afternoons rolling around on the floor from one patch of sunlight to another, letting it heat every particle of her as though she were air, so that she rose and fell, warmed and cooled.

She discovered that she could get into small spaces, and this led to her first experiment. Her desk had one drawer which she had never been able to open. It must have been stuck, because the key that unlocked all the others didn't work on the lower left-hand drawer. It was a shame; it would have been handy for keeping files. Now Elspeth drifted into it through the keyhole. It was empty. She was slightly disappointed. But there was something about being in the drawer that she liked. Being compressed into two cubic feet gave her a solidity that she quickly became addicted to. She didn't have separate body parts yet, but when she crowded into the drawer Elspeth felt sensations akin to touch: feelings that might be skin against hair, tongue against teeth. She began to stay in the drawer for long periods, to sleep, to think, to calm herself. *It's like going back to the womb*, she thought, happy to be contained.

One morning she saw her feet. They were hardly there, but Elspeth recognised them and rejoiced. Hands, legs, arms, breasts, hips and torso followed, and finally Elspeth could feel her head and neck. It was the body she had died in, thin and scarred by needle holes and the wound where the port had been, but she was so glad to see it that for a long time she didn't care. She gained opacity gradually – that is, she could see herself better and better; to Robert she was quite invisible.

He spent a lot of time in her flat, winding up her business, wandering around touching things, lying on her bed curled up with some piece of her clothing. She worried about him. He looked thin, ill, depressed. *I don't want to see this,* she thought. She vacillated between urgently trying to make him aware of her and leaving him alone. *He won't get over it if he knows you're here,* she told herself.

He's not getting over it anyway.

Sometimes she would touch him. It seemed to affect him like an icy draught; she could see the goosebumps rise on his skin as she ran her hands over him. He felt hot, to her. She could only feel warmth and coolness now. Rough and smooth, soft and hard: these were lost to her. She had no sense of taste or smell. Elspeth was haunted by music; songs she had loved, or hated, or barely even noticed now played in her mind. It was impossible to be rid of them. They were like a radio played at low volume in a neighbouring flat.

Elspeth liked to close her eyes and caress her own face.

She had substance under her own hands, even though the rest of the world slid through her as though she were walking in front of a film projected on a screen. She no longer went through any daily rituals of washing, dressing or applying make-up: calling a favourite jumper or dress to mind was enough to find herself wearing it. Her hair did not grow, much to Elspeth's disappointment. It had been hard to see it all fall out, handful by handful, and when it had begun to come in again it was someone else's hair, silver-grey in exchange for her blonde. It felt coarse when she ran her hands over it.

Elspeth was no longer reflected in mirrors. It drove her mad – she already felt marginal, and not being able to see her own face made her lonely. She sometimes stood in her front hall, looking intently into the various mirrors, but the most she caught was a dark, smudgy indication, as though someone had begun to draw on the air with charcoal and then rubbed it out, incompletely. She could hold out her arms and see her own hands quite visible before her. She could bend over and stare at her well-shod feet. But her face eluded her.

Being a ghost was mostly like that: it forced her to feed off the world. She no longer possessed anything. She had to take her pleasure in the doings of others, in their ability to move objects, consume food, breathe air.

Elspeth badly wanted to make noise. But Robert could not hear her, even when she stood inches away from him and yelled. Elspeth concluded that she had nothing to make a sound with – her ethereal vocal cords weren't up to the task. So she concentrated on moving things.

At first things were utterly unresponsive. Elspeth would

gather all her substance and fury and hurl herself at a sofa cushion or a book: nothing would happen. She tried to open doors, rattle teacups, stop clocks. The results were indiscernible. She decided to retrench, and began to attempt very small effects. One day she triumphed over a paper clip. By dint of patient tugging and pushing she managed to move it half an inch over the course of an hour. She knew then that she was not a negligible being: she could affect the world if she tried hard enough. So every day Elspeth practised. Eventually she could push the paper clip off the desk. She could flutter curtains and twitch the whiskers of the stuffed ermine who sat on her desk. She started to work on light switches. She could make a door sway a few inches, as though a breeze had come through the room. To her joy, she succeeded in turning the pages of a book. Reading had been Elspeth's great pleasure in life, and now she could indulge in it again, as long as the book was left lying open for her. She began to work on pulling books from their places on the bookshelves.

As insubstantial as objects were to Elspeth, or she to them, the walls of the flat were absolute barriers and she could not pass beyond them. She didn't mind this at first. She worried that if she went outside she would be dispersed by wind and weather. But eventually she became restless. If her territory had included Robert's flat she would have been content. She tried many times to sink through the floor, but only ended up in a sort of puddle, like the Wicked Witch of the West. Attempts to slide under the front door into the hallway were also unsuccessful. She could hear Robert down in his flat, taking a shower, talking to the TV, playing Arcade Fire on the stereo. The sounds filled her with self-pity and resentment.

Open windows and doors were inviting, but useless. Elspeth found herself dispersing, shapeless but still in the flat, as she tried to pass through them.

Elspeth wondered: *Why? What is all this for? I understand the rationale behind heaven and hell, reward and punishment, but if this is limbo, what is the point? What am I supposed to be learning from the spiritual equivalent of house arrest? Is every dead person consigned to haunt his or her former home? If so, where are all the other people who lived here before me? Is this an oversight on the part of the celestial authorities?*

She had always been lax when it came to religion. She had been C. of E. in the same way everyone else was: she supposed she believed in God, but it seemed rather uncool to make a fuss about Him. She had seldom been in church unless someone was dead or being wed; in retrospect she felt even more remiss because St Michael's was practically next door. *I wish I could remember my funeral*. It must have happened while she was rolling around the floor of the flat in an amorphous mist. Elspeth wondered if she should have been more assiduous about God. She wondered if she was going to be stuck in her flat for all eternity. She wondered if someone who was already dead could kill herself.

Edie and Valentina sat together in Edie's workroom, sewing. It was the Saturday before Christmas; Julia had gone downtown with Jack to help him shop. Valentina pinned the dress pattern to yards of violet silk, careful to lay out the pieces without wasting fabric. She was making two identical dresses, and she wasn't sure she'd bought enough silk.

'That's good,' Edie said. The room was warm in the afternoon sun, and she felt a little sleepy. She offered Valentina her best scissors and watched the steel work through the thin material. *That's such a great sound, the blades moving together that way.* Valentina handed Edie the pieces, and Edie began to transfer the seam lines from the pattern to the fabric. They passed the silk back and forth, working companionably out of long habit. Once the fabric was marked and unpinned and repinned without the pattern, Valentina sat at her sewing machine and carefully stitched the dress together while Edie began to pin and cut out the second dress.

'Look, Mom,' said Valentina. She stood and held the front of the dress against her chest. Static electricity wrapped the skirt around her with a crackle. There were no sleeves yet, and the seams were raw; Edie thought the dress was like a costume for a fairy in a Christmas pantomime. 'You look like Cinderella,' Edie said.

'Do I?' Valentina went to the mirror and smiled at her reflection. 'I like this colour.'

'It suits you.'

'Julia wanted me to make them in pink.'

Edie frowned. 'You'd look like twelve-year-old ballerinas. We could have made hers pink.'

Valentina caught her mother's eye, then looked away. 'It wasn't worth the hassle. She wanted whatever I was making for myself.'

'I wish you'd stand up to her more often, sweet.'

Valentina peeled the dress away from her and sat down at the machine. She began to make the sleeves. 'Did Elspeth boss you around? Or did you boss her?'

Edie hesitated. 'We didn't . . . It wasn't like that.' She laid the second dress flat on the table and began to roll the tracing wheel over the seam lines. 'We did everything together. We never liked to be alone. I still miss her.' Valentina sat still, waiting for her mother to continue. But Edie said, 'Send me photos of the flat, will you? I imagine it must be full of our parents' furniture; Elspeth loved all that heavy Victorian stuff.'

'Okay, sure.' Valentina turned in her chair and said, 'I wish we weren't going.'

'I know. But it's like your dad says: you can't stay home forever.'

'I wasn't going to.'

Edie smiled. 'That's good.'

'I wish I could stay in this room forever, and sew things.'

'That sounds like a fairy tale.'

Valentina laughed. 'I'm Rumpelstiltskin.'

'No, no,' said Edie. She put down the dress pieces and went to Valentina. Edie stood behind her and put her hands on her shoulders. She leaned over and kissed Valentina on her forehead. 'You're the princess.'

Valentina looked up and saw her mother smiling at her upside down. 'Am I?'

'Of course,' said Edie. 'Always.'

'So we're going to live happily ever after?'

'Absolutely.'

'Okay.' Valentina had an acute moment, an awareness of a memory being formed. *We're going to live happily ever after? Absolutely.* Edie went back to the other dress, and Valentina finished the first sleeve. By the time Jack and Julia got home, Valentina was wearing the violet dress and Edie was crouching in front of her with a mouthful of pins, hemming the skirt. It was all Valentina could do to hold still; she wanted to twirl and make the dress flare out like a carnival ride. *I'll wear it to the ball,* she thought, *when the prince invites me to dance.*

'Can I try it on?' said Julia.

'No,' said Edie through the pins, before Valentina could speak. 'This one is hers. Come back later.'

'Okay,' said Julia, and she turned and ran off to wrap the presents Jack had bought.

'See,' said Edie to Valentina. 'You just open your mouth and say "No".'

'Okay,' said Valentina. She twirled and the dress flared. Edie laughed.

Jack walked into his den and found the twins watching a movie. It was midnight and usually all three of them would have been in bed by now.

'That looks somewhat familiar,' said Jack. 'What are you watching?'

'*The Filth and the Fury*,' Julia said. 'It's a documentary about the Sex Pistols. You and Mom gave it to us for Christmas.'

'Oh.' The twins were sprawled together on the couch, so Jack lowered himself into the recliner. As soon as he was seated he felt exhausted. Jack had always enjoyed Christmas, but the days after Christmas seemed vacant and cheerless. The effect was compounded by the fact that the twins were leaving for London in a few days. *Where did the time go? Five days until their twenty-first birthdays. Then gone.*

'How's the packing going?' he asked.

'Okay,' said Valentina. She turned off the sound on the TV. 'We're going to be over the weight limit.'

'Somehow that's not surprising,' Jack said.

'We need to get converters, you know, to plug in our computers and stuff.' Julia looked at Jack. 'Can we go downtown with you tomorrow?'

'Sure. We'll have lunch at Heaven on Seven,' Jack said. 'Your mom will want to come with.' Edie had been shadowing the twins for weeks, hoarding them, memorising them.

'That's cool, we can go to Water Tower. We need new boots.'

Valentina watched Johnny Rotten singing silently. *He looks deranged. That's a great sweater.* She and Julia had studiously prepared for the trip to London, reading *Lonely Planet* and Charles Dickens, making packing lists and trying to find their new flat on Google Earth. They had speculated endlessly about Aunt Elspeth and the mysterious Mr Fanshaw, had been very pleasantly surprised by the amount of money in their new bank account at Lloyds. Now there was hardly anything left to do, which created an odd void, a feeling of restless dread. Valentina wanted to leave right this minute, or never.

Julia watched her father. 'Are you okay?'

'Yeah, I'm fine. Why?'

'I dunno, you seem kind of wiped.' *You've gained a huge amount of weight and you sigh a lot. What's wrong with you?*

'I'm okay. It's just the holidays.'

'Oh.'

Jack sat trying to imagine the house/his marriage/his life without the twins. He and Edie had been avoiding the subject for months, so now he thought about it obsessively, oscillating between fantasies of marital bliss, his actual memories of the last time the twins had left home and his worries about Edie.

For some time before Elspeth's death Edie had been distracted. Jack had hired the detective in hope of discovering the reason for her absent-mindedness, her vacant stare, her bright, false cheer whenever he asked her about it. But the detective could only observe Edie; he had no answers for Jack's questions. After Elspeth's death Edie's distraction had been replaced by a profound sadness. Jack could not comfort her. He could not seem to say the right thing, though he tried. Now he wondered how Edie would fare once the twins were gone.

Each time the twins left for college, things started out well. Jack and Edie revelled in their freedom: there would be late nights, loud sex, spur-of-the-moment amusements and slightly excessive drinking. But then a kind of bleakness always set in. Soon it would be upon them, their empty house. They would eat dinner together, just the two of them; the evening would stretch out before them in silence, to be filled with a DVD and perhaps a walk down to the beach or the club. Or they would retreat to opposite ends of the house, he to surf the Internet or read a Tom Clancy novel, Edie to work on her needlepoint while listening to an audio book. (She was currently listening to *Brideshead Revisited*, which Jack thought was pretty much guaranteed to produce a serious bout of depression.)

Tonight he didn't see much to look forward to after the twins were gone. He felt grateful to them for having stuck around as long as they had, grateful to Edie and Elspeth for having arranged things so that Julia and Valentina could grow up in this ugly, comfortable house, so he could be Dad, so the girls could sit here in his room watching Johnny Rotten spastically singing 'God Save the Queen' with the sound turned off; suddenly Jack was overwhelmed with a gratitude that felt like grief, and he struggled out of his chair, muttered goodnight and left the room, afraid that if he sat there one minute longer he would cry or blurt out something he'd regret. He walked into his bedroom, where Edie slept curled up, faintly blue in the clock-radio light. Jack undressed silently, got into bed without brushing his teeth and lay there in an abyss, unable to imagine any happiness for himself ever again.

Valentina turned off the TV. The twins rose and stretched. 'He seems really down,' said Valentina.

'They're both, like, suicidal,' replied Julia. 'I wonder what will happen when we're gone?'

'Maybe we shouldn't go.'

Julia looked impatient. 'We have to go somewhere, eventually. The sooner we're gone, the sooner they'll get over it.'

'I guess.'

'We'll call them every Sunday. They can come and visit.'

'I know.' Valentina took a breath. 'Maybe you should go to London and I'll stay here with them.'

Julia experienced a frisson of rejection. *You'd rather stay with Mom and Dad than be with me?* 'No!' She paused, trying to quell her irritation. Valentina watched, a little amused. 'Mouse, we both have to—'

'I know. Don't worry. I'm coming with you.' She pressed against Julia, put her arm around Julia's shoulders. Then they turned out the light and walked to their room, glancing at their parents' door as they passed.

Robert stood in Elspeth's office. The twins would arrive tomorrow. He had brought along an external hard drive and a few boxes from Sainsbury's; these stood empty and open next to Elspeth's enormous Victorian desk.

Elspeth sat on her desk and watched Robert. *Oh, you don't look happy, love.* She had no idea how much time had passed. Had she died months ago? Years? Something was happening; until now Robert had kept her flat unchanged. He'd thrown out most of the food and cancelled her credit cards. She no longer received mail. He had closed her business and written personal letters to her customers. It was becoming very dusty in the flat. Even the sunlight seemed dimmer than she remembered; the windows needed washing.

Robert went through the drawers of Elspeth's desk. He left the stationery and the invoices. He took some packets of photographs and a notebook she'd doodled in while she talked on the telephone. He went to the bookshelves and began carefully removing the ledgers she'd used as diaries, dusting them and placing them in the boxes. *Open one*, Elspeth said. *Open that one.* But of course Robert couldn't hear her.

He worked in silence. Elspeth felt slighted; sometimes he talked to her when he was in the flat. Photo albums, a shoebox full of letters, notebooks went into the boxes. She wanted to touch him but held back. Robert plugged the hard drive into her computer and transferred her files. Then he wiped the computer of everything except the system and applications. Elspeth stood behind him and watched. *How strange, to feel sad about the computer. I must really be dead now.* Robert unplugged the hard drive and put it in a box.

He began roaming through the flat, box in hand, Elspeth trailing behind him. *The bedroom,* she urged silently. When he got there he stood in the doorway for a few minutes. Elspeth flowed by him and sat on the bed. She looked at him: there was something about her sitting here and the way he stood there and the light, the way the light bathed the room in dusty warmth. *In a moment he'll come over here and kiss me.* Elspeth waited, forgetting. They had done this so many times.

Robert opened the door of her dressing room. He put the box down and opened a drawer. He put a few camisoles, a couple of bras and some of her fancier knickers into the box. He stood surveying her shoes. *He'll take the pink suede heels,* Elspeth thought, and he did. He adjusted the position of the other shoes so there was no gap. *Don't forget the letters.* He opened a drawer full of jumpers and smelled each one. The one he picked was a nondescript blue cashmere; she imagined it must not have been dry-cleaned since she'd worn it last. He opened another drawer and scooped their sex toys into the box. *You missed one,* Elspeth said, but he shut the drawer.

Robert reached up and retrieved a box from the top shelf. Elspeth smiled. She had counted on him to be thorough, and he was. He set it beside the box full of clothing.

Robert cleared out the bathroom. He threw most of her toiletries in the bin, but stood holding her diaphragm for a moment. *What a daft thing to get sentimental about*, she thought. Then that, too, went into the bin.

He shut the bathroom door and stood next to the bed, thinking. Then he lay down on the bed. Elspeth lay beside him, careful not to touch, hopeful. *What if I don't see you again?* He was taking the things she had given him; he was leaving the flat. *Don't be shy, sweet. It's just you and me.* She cheered when he undid his belt buckle and unzipped his fly. She imagined herself naked beside him, and she was.

Sometimes he imitated her technique, but today he was rougher, more utilitarian with himself. Elspeth watched Robert's face. She sat up and leaned over him; his eyes were closed. She touched his hair. She put her face close to his, let his breath warm her. *So warm, so solid.* She would have given anything to be alive with him then, to touch him. Elspeth knew that her touch was cold to him; whenever she'd tried to touch him he would shiver and shrink. So she knelt beside him, watching.

She had often marvelled at the play of expression in Robert's face during sex. Desire, concentration, pain, endurance, hilarity, desperation, release: she sometimes felt as though she were watching a pageant of the extremes of Robert's soul. Today it was determination, a kind of grim plea; it seemed to take a long time, and Elspeth began to be anxious. *Enjoy it, at least. For both of us.* She watched his hands on his cock, watched the way his toes curled, the sideways jerk of his head as he came. His body went slack. Robert opened his eyes and stared through Elspeth at the ceiling. *I'm here, Robert.*

A tear rolled halfway across his cheek. *Don't, sweet. Don't cry.*

Elspeth had never seen Robert cry, not even in hospital, not even when she'd died. *Oh, hell. I don't want you to be so miserable.* She reached down and touched the tear. Robert turned his head, startled.

I'm here I'm here I'm here. She looked around for something she could move, and began to sway the curtains, slightly. But Robert was sitting up, wiping his hands, fastening his trousers, not watching. She tried to shake the box of sex toys and knickers, but it was too heavy for her. She stood in the middle of the room, exhausted. Robert went into the bathroom and washed, came out holding the bin bag full of her things. He put it down and began straightening the bedclothes. Elspeth sat on the bed while he did this, and when he leaned over she put her hands against his chest, reaching through his shirt, touching his skin lightly. He recoiled.

'Elspeth?' He was whispering, urgent.

Robert. She ran her hands over his skin, slowly: back, hips, legs, cock, stomach, hands, arms. He stood with his head turned and lowered, his eyes closed. She imagined what he might feel – perhaps it was like ice cubes moving over his body? She pushed her hands into him and he gasped. *You're so warm,* she thought, and knew what he must feel; her immaterial coldness must be the opposite of his lovely hot liquid body. She took her hands away. She could still feel his warmth in her hands. She looked at them, expecting them to glow a bit. Robert had crossed his arms over his chest and stood hunched over, shivering. *Oh sweet, I'm sorry.*

'Elspeth,' he whispered. 'If that's you – do something – do something only you'd know – an Elspeth thing . . .'

She put the tip of her finger between his eyebrows and slowly stroked it down his nose, his lips, his chin. She did it again.

'Yes,' he said. 'My God.' He sat down on the bed again, elbows on knees, head in hands, and stared at the floor. Elspeth sat next to him, ecstatic. *Finally!* She was virtually drunk with relief. *You know I'm here!*

Robert groaned. Elspeth looked at him: his eyes were screwed up tight and he was rhythmically hitting his forehead with both fists. 'I've completely – lost – my bloody – mind. *Shit.*' He got up, grabbed the boxes and the bin liner, and walked quickly back to her office. Elspeth followed, disbelieving. *Wait – Robert – don't –*

He hefted each box, strode down the hall and across the landing and carted it all down the stairs to his flat. She stood at her open front door, listening to his footsteps moving through his flat and then back up the stairs. She let him walk right through her each time he came up, and trailed after him, catching stray mutterings as he stalked along.

'Jessica said I was losing the plot, and right she was! "You're going to make yourself ill," she said, and damned if I haven't . . . What have I been playing at, she's not coming back . . . Oh God, Elspeth.'

The door shut. Elspeth was alone, again. *Tears*, she thought, as though she were summoning a jumper. She put her hand to her face and felt tears. *Gosh, I'm crying.* She paused to marvel at her new accomplishment. Then she turned to face her silent flat.

PART TWO

Julia and Valentina Poole walked off the plane and into
Heathrow Airport. Their white, patent-leather shoes hit the
carpeting in perfect step, with movie-musical precision. They
wore white knee socks, white pleated skirts that ended four
inches above their knees, and plain white T-shirts under white
woollen coats. Each twin wore a long white scarf and wheeled
a suitcase behind her. Julia's suitcase was pink and yellow terry
cloth, and had a Japanese cartoon-monkey face that leered at
the people walking behind her. Valentina's blue-and-green suitcase's cartoon face was a mouse. The mouse looked both
regretful and shy.

Outside the airport windows the morning sky was blue.
The twins made their way through the endless corridors, stood
to the right on people-movers, followed exhausted passen-
gers down ramps and stairs. They stood in the queue for the
Immigration officials, holding hands, yawning. When their
turn came, the twins handed over their virginal passports.

'How long will you be staying?' asked the tired woman
in the uniform.

'Forever,' said Julia. 'We've inherited a flat. We've come to
live in it.' She smiled at Valentina, who smiled back. The
woman scrutinised their residency visas, stamped their passports and waved them into the UK.

Forever, Valentina thought. *I will live forever with Julia in our apartment in London, which we have never seen, surrounded by people we haven't met, forever.* She squeezed Julia's hand. Julia winked at her.

The black cab was draughty and cold. Valentina and Julia dozed in the back seat, their feet crowded by piles of luggage, still clutching each other's hands. London streets flashed by or stood still; other drivers whooshed along, following incomprehensible traffic laws. Julia and Valentina had learned to drive, but as the taxi wove through congested serpentine streets, Julia realised that driving in London was going to be impossible, even for her, and certainly for the Mouse. The Mouse didn't like to get lost, didn't like to be in strange places. Plus they didn't own a car. Julia resigned herself to taxis and public transportation. She watched a red double-decker bus swaying along beside them. Everyone inside looked tired and bored. *How can you be bored? You live in London! You're breathing the same air as the Queen and Vivienne Westwood!*

The taxi passed a tube station. People swarmed out of it. Julia looked at her watch, which read 4.15. She reset it to 10.15. They turned onto Highgate Road, and Julia thought they must be getting close. She looked at Valentina, who was sitting up now and staring out the window. The taxi began to climb a steep hill. SWAINS LANE. 'Is that like Lover's Lane?' Valentina asked. 'More like swine, miss,' said the driver. 'They used to drive the pigs along here.' Valentina blushed. Julia took out her lipstick and applied it without a mirror, offered it to Valentina, who did the same. They looked at each other. Julia reached out and wiped a tiny bit of errant pink lipstick from the corner of Valentina's mouth. Over the radio came a long string of code-like names and numbers: *Tamworth one, Burton Albion one; Barnet nil, Woking nil; Exeter City nil, Hereford United one; Aldershot two, Dagenham and Redbridge one* . . . 'Football scores, miss,' said the driver when Julia asked.

They reached the top of the hill and drove along a narrow street with a park on one side, brick houses on the other. A large church stood in the middle of the block, and the cab pulled up halfway between it and the blank-faced stucco building just after it. 'Here it is. Vautravers Mews.' The driver took Julia's money. She was shocked when she realised they'd just spent almost $120 on a cab ride. She tipped ten per cent. 'Thank *you*,' said the driver. Valentina opened the taxi door and cold wet wind rushed at her.

'I don't see it,' she called to Julia. The church was on the left, and the stucco building was number 72. Between them was a narrow asphalt path that descended precipitously into gloom. It was overshadowed by a huge brick wall that bounded the church's property. But Valentina couldn't see any house that might be theirs.

'It'll be along here,' said the taxi driver. 'Shall I help you with those?' He picked up an impossible number of suitcases and walked down the path. Julia and Valentina followed, wheeling their terry cloth suitcases. The little path led them behind the stucco house, and then they saw a high stone wall with spikes set on top. Rampant birch trees spilled over it. Valentina smelled damp earth, and it made her homesick. Julia was opening a heavy wooden gate with a large key. The gate swung silently, and Julia disappeared behind the wall. The driver had placed the suitcases in a neat row; Valentina stood on the asphalt near them, reluctant to go in. The driver looked at her curiously. He was a thinnish, oldish man with watery blue eyes. He wore a bright green cardigan and brown plaid trousers. 'Are you all right, miss?' he asked.

'Yes. I'm fine,' said Valentina, although she actually felt somewhat nauseated.

'Come on, Mouse!' Julia yelled. Her voice sounded muffled and remote.

'You're Americans?' said the driver.

'Our aunt left us her apartment in her will,' Valentina said. Then she felt foolish. Why should he care?

'Ah,' said the driver. This seemed to satisfy his curiosity about them. Valentina felt a surge of gratitude. He wasn't going to ask about them being twins. Maybe he felt that would be too personal. Or maybe he hadn't noticed. She loved it when people failed to notice.

'Mouse!'

The driver gave her a little smile. 'Go on, then.' Valentina smiled back, and dragged her suitcase through the gate.

Julia was standing at the front door with her hand on the doorknob. She waited for Valentina to make her way over the squishy moss that covered the stones in the footpath. Valentina looked at the great dark bulk of Vautravers, at the black windows and elaborate ironwork, and shivered. It wasn't quite raining, but it wasn't exactly not raining either. She heard the driver squelching along the path behind her. Julia opened the door.

They stepped into the front hall. In contrast to the outside of the building, it was warm, neat and virtually empty. The walls were painted a pinkish grey, a colour that reminded Valentina of brains. To the right was a closed oak door with a tiny hand-lettered card that read FANSHAW. In front of them a small table held three empty baskets; an umbrella leaned against the table. To their left was a staircase, which curved and rose above their heads. Valentina thought there ought to be a little bottle labelled DRINK ME, but there wasn't.

'You can just leave those here,' said Julia to the driver. Valentina said, 'Thank you.' The driver replied, 'Good luck, then,' and was gone. Valentina felt a little bereft. 'Come on,' said Julia. She bounded up the stairs as though she'd been released from gravity. Valentina followed more sedately.

On the next landing a faded Oriental carpet appeared. The stairs continued, but the twins stopped. The card on the door was pale green, and NOBLIN was typed on it, apparently with an actual typewriter. Julia inserted the key into the keyhole. She had to wiggle it back and forth a few times before she got the lock open. She looked back at Valentina. Valentina took Julia's hand, and together they walked into their new home.

The front hall was full of umbrellas and mirrors. The twins were reflected eighteen times in as many mirrors, and their reflections were reflected, and on and on. They were startled by this; both stood perfectly still and were each unsure which reflection belonged to which girl. Then Julia turned her head: half of the reflections also turned; the effect was diminished. 'Spooky,' said Julia, to mar the silence. Valentina said, 'Uh-huh.' She put a hand out in front of her like a blind person and moved through the passageway from the hall into a large dark room.

Elspeth was dozing in her drawer. Voices woke her.

As Julia stepped into the front room behind Valentina, she had a sensation of being underwater, as though the room were at the bottom of a pond. All the things in the room were bulky shadows; Valentina was a slim shadow moving in the gloom. Julia heard a noise (which was Valentina tripping over a pile of books), and then light entered the room as Valentina drew the curtains on the tall wide windows. The light was cold and grey and sort of particulate. The room was very dusty.

'Look, Julia – an owl!' It hung suspended from the high ceiling, in place of an absent light fixture that had left a small hole with wires coming out of it. The owl's wings were spread and its talons were open to grasp some small prey. Julia reached up and carefully touched one of the feet, which set the owl spinning, slowly. 'It's an owlicopter,' she said, and Valentina laughed.

Elspeth stood in the doorway, watching the twins. *Oh, I missed you. I wanted to see you again, and now you're here.* She hugged herself, eager and apprehensive.

As Edie had predicted, all of the furniture was heavy, ornate and old. The sofas were pale pink velvet, beast-footed, many-buttoned. There was a baby grand piano (the twins were distinctly unmusical) and a vast Persian rug which was chrysanthemum-patterned, soft to the touch, and had at one time been deep red, now faded in most places to dull pink. Everything in the room seemed to have been drained of colour. Julia wondered if the colour had all collected somewhere else; perhaps it was in some closet, and when they opened that door it would all flood back into the objects it had deserted.

She thought of Sleeping Beauty, and the palace, still for a hundred years, full of motionless courtiers. Edie and Jack preferred new things. Julia ran her finger across the piano, leaving a trail of shining black amid the dull dust. Valentina sneezed. Both girls looked at the doorway as though expecting to be caught intruding on the silence of the flat.

Elspeth stepped forward, about to speak, then realised they couldn't see her.

There were books everywhere: entire walls of bookcases, piles of books on tables, on the floor. Valentina knelt to collect the pile she had tripped over, a little island of bestiaries and herbals. 'Look, Julia, a manticore.' The twins wandered back into the hall. Elspeth followed them.

They crossed a rather bare dining room, which contained only a formal table and chairs and a large sideboard; a little tufted ottoman stood orphaned in a corner. Bleak daylight seeped in through huge French windows that led to a diminutive balcony. The twins could see the church rising over a wall of ivy.

Next, a room that was meant to be a parlour but had been used by Elspeth as an office. There was an enormous, ornate desk with a clunky fifties office chair. On the desk sat a scruffy computer, heaps of papers, more books, a credit-card-processing machine, a delicate white-and-gold teacup with long-evaporated tea at the bottom and apricot lipstick staining the rim. Bookcases lined the walls, stuffed with reference books and a complete *OED*. An anomalous shelf was bare and dust-free. The room was bursting with flattened packing boxes, bubble wrap, file cabinets and a small stuffed ermine, which

peered at them from its perch atop a set of library-card catalogue drawers. The room seemed to have been neatened
without actually becoming neat. Valentina sat down at the
desk and pulled out the centre drawer. It contained invoice
pads, Smints, paper clips, rubber bands and business cards:

ELSPETH NOBLIN

RARE AND USED BOOKS

BOUGHT AND SOLD

enoblin@bookish.uk.com

Valentina said, 'Do you think all these books were for her,
or to sell? I wonder if she had a shop?'

'I think this was the shop,' said Julia. 'None of these
receipts has an address on it. I bet she worked from here.
Besides, the will didn't mention anything besides this place.'

'I wish Mom knew more. It's so lame that they didn't talk
to each other.' Valentina got up and examined the ermine. It
stared back at her, insouciant. 'What do you suppose his name
was?' Valentina asked. She thought, *It's sad that we don't know.*

Margaret, Elspeth thought. *Her name was Margaret.*

'He looks like George Bush.' Julia headed back through
the dining room as she spoke, and Valentina followed her.

A swinging door at the far end of the room led to the
kitchen. It was old-fashioned, and the appliances were, by the
twins' American standards, dollhouse-sized. Everything was
compact, serviceable, white. The only thing that seemed new
was the dishwasher. Valentina opened a cupboard and found
a washing machine inside. There was a contraption that sprung

into a complicated configuration of clothes line and metal. 'Guess that's the dryer,' said Julia, refolding it. The electrical outlets were shaped differently here. All the kitchen implements were subtly weird, foreign. The twins exchanged uneasy looks. Valentina turned on the tap, and water spurted out with a grunt. She hesitated, then ran her hands under the rust-coloured stream. It took a while to get warm.

Elspeth watched the twins puzzling over her very ordinary belongings. She listened to their American accents. *They're strangers; I didn't expect that.*

Behind the kitchen was a small bedroom. It was full to the brim with boxes and dusty furniture. There was a tiny, plain bathroom attached to it. The twins realised that it must have been intended for a servant. Here was the back door and the fire escape, here an almost-empty pantry. 'Mmm,' said Julia. 'Rice.'

Back to the hall ('We should collect two hundred dollars every time we go through here,' said Valentina) and into the bedrooms. There were two, connected by a splendid white marble-tiled bathroom. Each bedroom had a fireplace, elaborate built-in bookshelves, windows with window seats.

The other bedroom, which had obviously been Elspeth's, overlooked the back garden, and Highgate Cemetery.

'Look, Julia.' Valentina stood at the window, marvelling.

Vautravers' back garden was small and austere. Though the front yard was a deranged tangle of bushes, trees and clumpy grass, this little back garden was almost Japanese in its arrangement of gravelled sloping walks, a stone bench and modest plants.

'I can't believe it's so green in January,' said Julia. Back home in Lake Forest the snow lay ten inches thick on the ground.

There was a green wooden door in the brick wall that separated the garden from the cemetery.

'I wonder if anyone goes in,' said Valentina. The ivy around the door was tidily clipped back.

'I will,' said Julia. 'We'll go on picnics.'

'Mmm.'

Beyond the wall, Highgate Cemetery spread before them, vast and chaotic. Because they were on a hill, they might have seen quite far down into the cemetery, but the density of the trees prevented this; the branches were bare, but they formed a latticework that confused the eye. They could see the top of a large mausoleum, and a number of smaller graves. As they watched, a group of people strolled towards them along a path and then stopped, evidently discussing one of the graves. Then the group continued towards them and disappeared behind the wall. Hundreds of crows rose into the air as one. Even through the closed window they could hear the rush of wings. The sun abruptly came out again and the cemetery changed from deep shade and grey to dappled yellow and pale green. The gravestones turned white and seemed to be edged with silver; they hovered, tooth-like amid the ivy.

Valentina said, 'It's a fairyland.' She had been nervous about the cemetery. She had imagined smells and vandalism and creepiness. Instead it was verdant, full of mossy stone and the soft tapping noises of the trees. The group of people wandered away from them, strolling down the path on the opposite side from which they'd come. Julia said, 'They must be tourists, with a guide.'

'We should do that. Go on the tour.'

'Okay.' Julia turned and considered Elspeth's bedroom. There was a huge nest-like bed, with numerous pillows, a chenille bedspread and an elaborate painted wooden head-board. 'I vote we sleep in here.'

Valentina surveyed the room. It *was* nicer than the other bedroom; larger, cosier, brighter. 'Are you sure we want the room that overlooks the cemetery? It seems weird, you know; like, if this was a movie, there would be all these zombies or something creeping out of there at night and climbing up the ivy and grabbing us by our hair and turning us into zombies. Plus it was Aunt Elspeth's bedroom. What if she died in here? I mean, it seems like we're sort of asking for it, you know?'

Julia felt impatience rise up in her throat. She wanted to say, *Don't be an idiot, Valentina*, but that was not the way to soothe the Mouse when she was being irrational. 'Hey, Mouse,' she cooed. 'You know she died in the hospital, not here. That's what the lawyer told Mom, remember?'

'Ye-ssss,' Valentina replied.

Julia sat down on the bed and patted the coverlet, inviting. Valentina walked over and sat next to Julia. They both lay back on the soft bed, their thin white legs dangling over the edge. Julia sighed. Her eyelids wanted to close for just a second, just a moment more, just one more minute . . .

'This must be jet lag,' Valentina said, but Julia didn't hear her. In a minute Valentina too was asleep.

Elspeth walked over to the bed. *Here you are, all grown up.*

How strange this is, you here. I wish you had come before . . . I didn't realise, it would have been so simple. Too late, like everything else. Now Elspeth leaned over the twins and touched them very lightly. Her reading glasses hung around her neck, and they brushed against Valentina's shoulder as Elspeth bent over her. She saw how the little mole by Julia's right ear repeated itself by Valentina's left ear. She put her head on their chests and listened to their hearts. Valentina's had a disturbing swoosh, a whisper instead of a beat. Elspeth sat on the bed next to Julia and petted Julia's hair: it barely moved, as though a miniature breeze had come in through the closed windows.

Like, but unlike. Elspeth saw in Julia and Valentina the strangeness, the oneness that had always so discomfited people in herself and Edie. She thought of things that Edie had written to her about the twins. *Do you mind Julia bossing you all the time, Valentina? Have either of you got any friends? Lovers? Aren't you a bit old to be dressing alike?* Elspeth laughed. *I sound like a nagging mother.* She felt exhilarated. *They're here!* She wished she could welcome the twins somehow, sing a little song, do an elaborate pantomime demonstrating how glad she was that they'd arrived to alleviate the boredom of the afterlife. Instead she gave each twin a delicate kiss on the forehead and settled cat-like on the pillows to watch over their sleep.

Almost an hour later, Valentina stirred. She had a little dream as she woke. She was a child, and Edie's voice came floating into her ears, telling her to get up, it was snowing and they would have to leave early for school.

'Mom?'

Valentina sat up hurriedly and found herself in a strange

room. It took her a moment to think where she was. Julia was still asleep. Valentina wanted to call their mother, but their cell phones didn't work internationally. She found a telephone by the bed, but when she raised the receiver it was disconnected. *No one can call us, and we can't call anyone.* Valentina started to feel lonely, in the enjoyable manner of those who are seldom alone. *If I left now, before Julia wakes up, no one could find me. I could just vanish.* She slid off the bed carefully. Julia didn't stir. There was a dressing room connected to Aunt Elspeth's bedroom, a kind of walk-in closet with a built-in dresser and a full-length mirror. Valentina glanced at herself in the mirror: as always, she looked more like Julia than herself. She opened a drawer in the dresser, found a vibrator, and shut the drawer again, embarrassed. Elspeth stood in the doorway, slightly apprehensive. She watched as Valentina tried on a pair of red platform heels. They were just a bit long, maybe a half-size. They would fit Julia better. Valentina took a grey Persian-lamb coat off its hanger and put it on. Elspeth thought, *She's a mouse in sheep's clothing.* Valentina rehung the coat and went back into the bedroom. Elspeth let her walk through her. Valentina shivered and rubbed her upper arms briskly with her hands.

Julia woke and turned her face towards Valentina. 'Mouse,' she said thickly.

'I'm here.' Valentina climbed back onto the bed. 'Are you cold?' She pulled the bedspread over the two of them and twined her fingers into Julia's hair.

Julia said, 'No.' She closed her eyes. 'I had such a bizarre dream.'

Valentina waited but she did not continue.

Eventually Julia said, 'So?'

'. . . Yes.' They smiled at each other, their faces pumpkin-coloured in the filtered light under the chenille.

Elspeth stood watching them, fused together into a single form under the coverlet. She had not seriously worried that they might refuse her, but she was still giddy with pleasure now that she understood that they would stay. *Think of all the things that will happen to you – to us! Adventures, meals . . . Books will be taken off shelves and opened. There will be music and perhaps parties.* Elspeth twirled around the bedroom a few times. She swapped the red wool jumper and brown corduroy trousers she'd been wearing for a bottle-green strapless gown she had once worn to a summer ball up at Oxford. She hummed to herself, twirling out through the bedroom door, into the hall where she danced up the walls and across the ceiling *à la* Fred Astaire. *I've always wanted to do that. Hee hee.*

'Did you hear something?' asked Valentina.

'Huh? No,' replied Julia.

'It sounded like mice.'

'Zombies.' They giggled. Julia got off the bed and stretched. 'Let's bring up the luggage,' she said. Elspeth followed them to the door and made little skipping steps as she watched the twins dragging their belongings into her flat, ecstatic with novelty as they hung their clothes next to hers, stuck bottles of shampoo in the shower and plugged their laptops in to charge. After some discussion, they set up Valentina's sewing machine in the guest bedroom, where it was to gather dust for months. Elspeth watched them with delight. *You're beautiful,* she thought, and was surprised to be so surprised. *You're mine.* She felt something like love for these girls, these strangers.

'Well, here we are,' said Julia, after they had emptied their suitcases and fussed over the placement of every sweater and hairbrush.

'Yep,' agreed Valentina. 'I guess.'

The following morning Julia and Valentina went to see Mr Xavier Roche, their solicitor. Actually, he was Elspeth's solicitor; the twins had inherited him along with the rest of Elspeth's things. For many months now Mr Roche had been sending them papers to be signed, as well as instructions and keys and dry, admonitory emails.

Their cab deposited them in front of a faux-Tudor Hampstead office block. The firm of Roche, Elderidge, Potts & Lefley was above a travel agency. The twins climbed the narrow stairs and found themselves in a small anteroom which contained a door, a bare desk, a swivel chair, two uncomfortable armchairs, a small table and a copy of *The Times*. The twins sat in the armchairs for ten minutes, feeling anxious, but nothing happened. Finally Julia got up and opened the door. She beckoned to Valentina.

In the next room was another desk, but this one was occupied by a neat, elderly secretary and an enormous beige computer. The office was done in a style that Elspeth had always referred to as 'Early Thatcher'. To the twins it seemed oddly modest; it was their introduction to the British proclivity for making certain things important and shabby, expensive and self-deprecating all at once. The secretary ushered them into another office decorated in the same style but with more books, and said, 'Please sit down. Mr Roche will be with you directly.'

Mr Roche, when he arrived, was startling, even Dickensian, but not in the way the twins had imagined. He was an old man. He had been quite small to begin with and had shrunk with age; he walked using a stick, slowly, so that the twins had plenty of time to consider his comb-over, his prodigious eyebrows and his well-made but loose-fitting suit as he crossed the carpet and took each of their hands in turn, gently. 'The Misses Poole,' he said, in a grave voice. 'It is a great pleasure to meet you both.' He had dark eyes and a prominent nose. Julia thought, *He looks like Mom's gnome cookie jar.* Elspeth had sometimes called him Mr Imp, though never in his hearing.

'Let's sit here at the table, shall we?' he said, moving incrementally. Valentina pulled out a chair for him and then the twins stood and waited while he eased himself into it. 'It's so much nicer and more informal than the desk, don't you think? Constance will bring us some tea. Oh, thank you, my dear. Now then, tell me all about your adventures. What have you done since you've arrived?'

'Slept, mostly,' said Julia. 'We're pretty jet-lagged.'

'And has Robert Fanshaw been to see you?'

'Um, no. But we just got here yesterday,' Julia said.

'Ah, well, I expect he'll come by today, then. He's very eager to meet you.' Mr Roche smiled and looked at each of them in turn. 'You are astonishingly like your mother's side of the family. If I didn't know better I'd think I was sitting with Edie and Elspeth, twenty years ago.' He poured them each some tea.

Valentina asked, 'You knew them then?' Mr Roche was so ancient that she would have believed it if he claimed acquaintance with Queen Victoria.

He smiled. 'Dear child, my father was your great-grandfather's solicitor. I dandled your grandfather on my knee when he was tiny, and when your mother and aunt were small they used to sit on that carpet and play with blocks whilst I talked to their parents, just as the three of us are talking now.' The twins smiled back at him. 'It's a pity that Elspeth is no longer here to greet you. But I can tell you that she was excited about your coming to live here, and she has provided for you quite handsomely. I hope the terms of the will are clear?'

'We have to live in the flat for a year before we can sell it,' said Julia.

'Mom and Dad can't visit us,' said Valentina.

'No, no,' said Mr Roche. 'I certainly *hope* your parents will come and visit you; that isn't what Elspeth meant. She only stipulated that they aren't to be *in* the flat.'

'But why not?' said Valentina.

'Ah.' Mr Roche looked regretful. He spread his gnarled hands, tilted his head. 'Elspeth often kept her own counsel. Have you asked your mother? No, I imagine she wouldn't want to discuss it.' Mr Roche watched the twins as he spoke. It seemed to Julia that he was expecting some kind of reaction from them. 'People can be odd about their wills. All sorts of strange things get put into wills, often with unintended effects.'

He waited for them to say something. The twins shifted in their chairs, embarrassed by his scrutiny. Finally Julia said, 'Oh?' But Mr Roche only lowered his eyes and reached for a folder.

'Now then,' he said, 'let me show you how your money is invested.' The twins found the next half-hour confusing but thrilling. They had made money babysitting, and had spent one summer as counsellors at a Girl Scout camp in Wisconsin, but they had never imagined possessing the sums Mr Roche spread before them.

'How much is there all together?' Julia asked.

'Two and a half million pounds or so, if we include the value of the flat.'

Julia glanced at Valentina. 'We can live on that pretty much forever,' she said. Valentina frowned.

Mr Roche shook his head very slightly. 'Not in London. You'll be surprised at what things cost.'

Valentina said, 'Can we work here?'

'You don't have the proper visas, but we can certainly apply. What sort of work do you do?'

Valentina said, 'We aren't sure yet. But we're planning to go back to school.'

'Actually, we're done with school,' said Julia.

Mr Roche looked from one to the other and said, 'Ah.'

'We were curious,' said Julia. 'Why did Aunt Elspeth leave everything to us? I mean, we're really grateful and all, but we don't understand why she never came to see us but she left us her stuff.'

Mr Roche was silent for a moment. 'Elspeth was not a very . . . nurturing sort of woman, but she did have a strong family feeling.' He added, 'I'm afraid I really couldn't say why, but here we are.'

Couldn't say, or wouldn't say? the twins wondered.

'Can I answer any other questions?'

Valentina said, 'We don't exactly understand how the

heating works in the apartment. It was kind of cold in there last night.'

'Robert can help you with that; he's a very practical chap,' Mr Roche said. 'Do say hello to him for me, and ask him to give me a ring – there are one or two things we ought to go over.' He bid them goodbye. Julia turned back as they were leaving and found him standing with both hands on his stick, watching them with a bemused expression.

When they got back to Vautravers the building was quiet and cheerless. In the front hall Julia said, 'Maybe we should just knock on his door.'

'Who?'

'This Robert Fanshaw guy. We could ask about the heat.'

Valentina shrugged. Julia knocked; she could hear the sound of a television playing faintly in the flat. Julia waited and then knocked again, louder, but no one came to the door. 'Oh well,' she said, and they went upstairs.

Martin put the phone down on the bed. The bed was an island. Around the bed was a sea of contamination. Martin had been crouching on the bed for four hours. Luckily there were survival tools there in bed with him: the telephone, some bread and cheese, his worn copy of Pliny. Martin wanted very much to leave the bed. He needed to pee, and he was hoping to get some work done today. His computer sat waiting for him in the office. But somehow Martin sensed, he *knew,* that there had been a hideous accident in the night. The bedroom floor was covered with filth. Germs, shit, vomit: someone had got into the flat and smeared this horrible slime over the floor. *Why?* Martin wondered. *Why does this always happen? Is this possible? No, it's not real. But what can I do about it?*

As if he had asked the question out loud, an answer came to him: *Count backwards from a thousand, in Roman numerals. Touch the headboard while you do it.* Of course! Martin began to comply, but faltered at DCCXXIII and had to start again. As he counted, he wondered, with a separate part of his brain, why this was necessary. He lost track again, started again.

The telephone rang. Martin ignored it and tried to focus on counting. It rang three more times, then the answering machine picked up. *Hello, this is Martin and Marijke Wells. We're not here now. Please leave a message.* Beep. A pause. 'Martin? Come on, pick up, I know you're there. You're always there.'

Robert's voice. 'Martin.' A click. Martin realised that he had lost track of his counting again. He threw the telephone across the bedroom. It smashed against the wall and began to buzz. Martin was horrified. Now he would have to replace the phone. It was on the floor, contaminated. The light in the bedroom was afternoon light, slanted. He had failed to escape from the bed. Once again, he had allowed his madness to rule him.

But an idea came to him. Yes: he would simply move the bed. The bed was large, wooden, antique. Martin clambered to the footboard and began to rock the bed, to propel the bed towards the bathroom. The bed moved in inches, its small wooden wheels scraping the floorboards. But it did move. Martin was sweating, concentrating, almost joyous. He rode the bed across the bedroom, inch by inch, and finally, stepping onto the bath mat, he was free.

A few minutes later, just as he had finished peeing and was beginning to wash his hands, Martin heard Robert moving through the flat and calling his name. He waited until Robert was in the bedroom before he said, 'In here.' He heard a sound which he thought was probably Robert moving the bed back to its usual location.

Robert stood outside the door. 'Are you all right in there?'

'I'm fine. I think I've broken the phone. Could you unplug it?'

Robert walked away and came back with the telephone in his hands. 'It's fine, Martin.'

'No, it's . . . it was on the floor.'

'So it's contaminated?'

'Yes. Could you take it away? I'll order a new one.'

'Martin, couldn't I just decontaminate it for you? This is the third phone in what? A month? I was just listening to a report on Radio 4 about how British landfills are chock-full with old computers and mobiles. It seems a shame to toss a perfectly functional phone.'

Martin didn't answer. He began to wash his hands. It always took a long time for the water to get hot enough. He was using carbolic soap. It stung.

Robert said, 'Are you coming out any time soon?'

'I think it might be a while.'

'Can I do anything?'

'Just take the phone away.'

'All right.'

Martin waited. Robert stood on the other side of the door for a minute, then left. Martin heard the front door slam. *I'm sorry.* The phrase began to repeat in his head, until he replaced it with another, more secret refrain. The water was satisfyingly hot now. It was going to be a long afternoon.

Robert went back to his own flat and called Marijke at work. She had told him not to do this unless there was an emergency, but she never answered her mobile and she wasn't returning calls. She worked at VPRO, one of the quirkier Dutch radio stations. Robert had never been to the Netherlands. When he imagined Holland he thought of Vermeer paintings and *The American Friend*.

Strange Dutch ringing sounds: a voice, not Marijke's. Robert asked for Marijke and the voice went to get her. Robert stood in his front room with his phone pressed to his ear, listening to the noises of the radio station. He could hear muffled voices: *'Nee, ik denk van niet . . .' 'Vertel hem dat het onmogelijk is, hij wil altijd het onderste uit de kan hebben . . .'* Robert imagined the receiver sitting on Marijke's desk like a marooned insect. He imagined Marijke walking towards it, her plain, gently creased face, her tired green eyes, her mouth red with too-bright lipstick and tense at the corners, seldom quite smiling. Robert pictured her in an orange jumper she used to wear for days at a time every winter. Marijke's fingers were never still, always holding a cigarette or a pen, picking at imaginary lint on someone's collar, fiddling with her limp hair. She drove Robert crazy with her fidgeting.

Now she picked up the receiver.

'Hallo?' Marijke had a sultry voice. Robert always told Martin she could have made a fortune in phone sex. In her old job at the BBC she had read the afternoon traffic reports; sometimes men appeared in the lobby of Broadcasting House asking for her. At VPRO she was a very popular programme host on a show that mostly featured stories about human-rights catastrophes, global warming and terribly sad things that happened to animals.

'Marijke. It's Robert.'

He felt her discomfort come at him through the telephone ether. After a pause, she said, 'Robert, hello. How are you?'

'I'm fine. Your husband is not fine.'

'What do you want me to do? I am here, he's there.'

'I want you to come home and take him in hand.'

'No, Robert, I won't do that.' Marijke covered the phone with her hand and said something to someone, then returned to him. 'I'm absolutely not coming back. And he can't even walk downstairs to get the mail, so I don't imagine we'll be seeing each other soon.'

'At least ring him.'

'Why?

'Persuade him to take his medicine. Cheer him up. Hell, I don't know. Don't you have any interest in helping him sort himself out?'

'No. I've done that. It's not a joke, Robert. He's hopeless.'

Robert stared out the window at Vautravers' chaotic front garden, which sloped up away from the house so that it was like watching an empty raked stage. As Marijke declared her complete lack of interest in Martin's future, the twins opened the front door of Vautravers and walked up the footpath to the gate. They were dressed in matching baby-blue coats and hats and carried lavender muffs. One twin was swinging her muff on its wrist-strap; the other twin pointed at something in a tree, and both girls burst out laughing.

'Robert? Are you there?'

One twin walked slightly in front of the other; to Robert they appeared to be two-headed, four-legged, two-armed. They let themselves out of the gate. Robert closed his eyes, and an afterimage formed on the backs of his eyelids, a silhouette-girl shimmering against darkness. He was enchanted. They were like an early Elspeth, a previous version that had been withheld from him until now. *They're so young. And so strange. My God, they look like they're about twelve.*

'Robert?' His eyes flew open; the twins had gone.

'Sorry, Marijke. What were you saying?'

'I have to go. I'm on deadline.'

'Er – right, then. Sorry to have bothered you.'

'Robert, is something wrong?'

He thought about it for a moment before he answered. 'I just saw something rather marvellous.'

'Oh,' said Marijke. 'What was it? Where are you?' For the first time she sounded interested in the conversation.

'Elspeth's twins have arrived. They just walked through the front garden. They're a bit . . . surprising.'

'I didn't know Elspeth had children.'

'They belong to Edie and Jack.'

'The famous Edie.' Marijke sighed. 'I never quite believed in Edie; I always suspected Elspeth might have invented her.'

Robert smiled. 'I was never sure about Jack, myself. The legendary fiancé who eloped with the demon twin to America. It seems they were real after all.'

Marijke covered the phone with her hand. When she spoke again it was to say, 'I really do have to go, Robert.' She paused. 'Do they look like Elspeth?'

'If you come home you can see for yourself.'

She laughed. 'I'll call him, but I'm not coming to London. It never quite was my home, you know, Robert.' Marijke had lived in London for twenty-six years. For twenty-five years she had lived with Martin. Robert couldn't imagine how she had done it. He pictured her with other Dutch people, tall sturdy people who spoke five languages and ate herring they bought from little carts on the streets. In London Marijke had always seemed worried and deprived. Robert wondered if her return to her own city had restored what she had craved.

'He's waiting for you, Marijke.' Silence, static over the phone. Robert relented. 'They do look rather like Elspeth. They're more blonde, though. They aren't as fierce as Elspeth, either, I don't think. They look like kittens.'

'Kittens? How incongruous. Well, kittens will be good for the place. You gloomy men could use some kittens. I must go, Robert. But thanks for calling.'

'Bye, then, Marijke.'

'Bye.'

Marijke stood in her cubicle with her hand on the receiver. It was a little after three o'clock, and she could spare a few minutes, despite what she'd said to Robert. She should do it now. Martin had caller ID, so she would only call him on her mobile. She felt a pang of guilt. When she'd left, a year ago, she had called every few weeks. Now she had allowed two months to go by without calling. She held the phone to her ear, counting the rings. Martin always answered on the seventh ring; yes, here he was.

'Hello?' He sounded interrupted; she wondered what he had been doing when the phone rang, but she knew better than to ask.

'*Hallo*, Martin.'

'Marijke . . .'

She stood with the phone pressed hard against her ear. She had always loved to hear him say her name. Now it made her sad. Marijke leaned over with the mobile still pressed against her ear and then crouched down next to her desk, so that when she looked up she saw only the walls of her cubicle and the acoustical tiles of the ceiling. 'Marijke, how are you?'

He did not sound any different than the last time she'd spoken to him.

'I'm fine. I got promoted. I have an assistant now.'

'Stellar, that's excellent.' There was a pause. 'Male or female?'

She laughed. 'Female. Her name is Ans.'

'Hmm, okay, well, that's great. I don't want you being swept off your feet by some young Adonis with' – here Martin lowered his voice – 'fab-u-lous e-nun-cia-tion.'

'Don't worry, you, there's nobody here but us radio geeks. The young ones are too busy chatting each other up to be bothered with the likes of me.' Marijke felt oddly pleased that Martin imagined she was beset by suitors. She could hear him lighting a cigarette, and then the soft exhalation of smoke.

'I quit smoking,' she told him.

'Surely not. What will you do with your hands? Your poor hands will go crazy without a ciggy to occupy them.' Martin's tone was caressing, but Marijke could hear the effort to be casual. 'When did you give up?'

'Six days, twelve hours, and' – she looked at her watch – 'thirteen minutes ago.'

'Well, marvellous. I'm jealous.' At the word *jealous* there was a mutual pause.

Marijke combed her brain for a new topic. 'What are you working on? The Assyrians?' Martin occasionally worked for the British Museum, and the last time they'd talked he had mentioned some Aramaic inscriptions that he was translating.

'Mmm, I finished those. They've got me onto a little trove of poems, an Augustan lady named Marcella is supposed to have written them. If they were real they would be rather exciting; there are hardly any surviving works by women from that period. But they aren't quite right. I think that Charles has been hoodwinked, alas.'

'How do you know they are not right? Surely Charles had them vetted?'

'As objects, they seem fine. But the language is wrong in all sorts of small ways. It's sort of how it would be if you decided to forge some new Shakespearean sonnets; even though your modern English is lovely and charming, you would make odd little mistakes with the archaic turns of phrase, the grace notes that would have come naturally to a writer of that time. I think the writer is a twentieth-century Frenchman with an excellent command of nineteenth-century Latin.'

'But aren't they copies of copies? Perhaps the mistakes were introduced . . .'

'Ah, well, they were found at the library at Herculaneum, you see, so they were supposed to be the genuine article. I must call Charles today. He'll be hopping . . .'

Marijke's boss appeared in the entrance of her cubicle, looked around confusedly and discovered her sitting on the floor. Marijke looked up at Bernard from her crouch and mouthed, *Martin*. Bernard rolled his eyes and continued to loom over her, his sparse grey hairs standing up as though he were a cartoon character who had been electrocuted. He pointed to his watch. She stood up and said, 'I've got to go, Martin. I'm on deadline.'

Martin experienced a jolt — talking to Marijke was so

comforting, so normal and right, that he had almost forgotten; it had been so much like the conversations they used to have every day, he had forgotten that it would soon be over. And when would she call again? He panicked.

'Marijke . . .'

She waited. She wished Bernard would stop looking at her. She made a little rotating motion with her free hand: *Yes, I know. I'll be off in a moment.* Bernard wiggled his enormous eyebrows at her warningly and went back into his office.

'Call again soon, Marijke.'

'Yes.' She wanted to. She knew she wouldn't. '*Groetjes*, my love.'

'*Doeg! Ik hou van je . . .*' They both paused. She hung up first.

Martin stood in his office, holding his mobile. A crowd of emotions filled him. *She called. She said 'my love'. I should have asked her more questions, I talked too much about my work. She said she would call soon. How soon? But she didn't say she would call until I asked her to call. But she called today, so she will call again. When will she call? I should write down questions to ask her. She gave up smoking – that's amazing. Maybe I should too. We could do it together, next time she calls I could tell her. But when will she call?* Martin shook another cigarette from the pack and lit it. *She called me. A minute ago, we were talking.* He pressed the mobile to his cheek. It was warm. He felt affection for the little phone; it had brought Marijke's voice to him. Carrying the phone in one hand and the cigarette in the other, Martin walked to the kitchen. When he got there he walked back to his office again. *She called me. She promised to call again. She called. When will she call again? Maybe I should give up smoking . . .*

Marijke flipped her phone shut and put it in her pocket. She finished the piece for Bernard, emailed it to him. She heard the *ping* from his computer that said the piece had crossed the twelve feet between their desks. Someone said, 'You're on air in fifteen minutes.' She nodded and made her way towards the studio, but detoured into the loo, where she leaned against the wall and cried. *He doesn't change.* She wished she hadn't called. On the phone it was too easy to remember Martin as he had once been. Marijke washed her face and ran to the studio, where her engineer gave her an annoyed look. Months would go by before she called Martin again.

Robert had been imagining the arrival of the twins for a year.
He had whole conversations with them in his mind: he told
them about London, the cemetery, Elspeth; he chatted to them
about restaurants, his thesis, all sorts of things. As he
went about his days in the long year of their imminent arrival,
Robert noted points of interest – *There's Dick Whittington's cat.
They'll want to know about that . . . I'll take them to Postman's Park,
to the Hunterian Museum, to the John Soane. We'll ride the London Eye
at sunset.* He and Elspeth had done all these things together.
*We'll go round Dennis Severs' house at Christmas. And the Foundling
Museum.* Robert became, in his imagination, the tour guide of
the twins' London lives, their indispensable sherpa, their native
speaker. They would naturally come to him with their little
dilemmas and queries; avuncular, he would advise them and
aid them in their London initiation. Robert had looked forward
to the twins. He had enveloped them with so many witticisms,
expectations and hopes that now, when Julia and Valentina had
finally actually arrived, Robert was quite frightened of them.

He had thought that he would simply walk upstairs, knock
on their door and introduce himself. But the sound of their
footsteps and laughter paralysed him. He watched them come
and go, traipsing through the front garden in matching frocks,
carrying bags of groceries, flowers, an ugly lamp. *Why do they
need a lamp? Elspeth has plenty of lamps.*

They knocked on his door once or twice a day. Each time, Robert stood motionless, interrupted at his desk, or during his dinner; he could hear them speaking softly to each other in the hall. *Just open the door*, he told himself. *Don't be such a wanker.*

He hesitated before their twinness; they seemed sublime and inviolable together. Each morning he watched them navigating the slippery path to the gate. They appeared so self-sufficient, and conversely so reliant on each other, that he felt rejected without having ever exchanged a word with either of them.

One bright chilly morning Robert stood at his front window, coffee in hand, wearing his coat and hat, waiting. Eventually he heard the twins galumphing down the stairs. He watched them cross the yard and let themselves out of the gate.

Then he followed them.

They led him across Pond Square, through Highgate Village and along Jackson's Lane to Highgate tube station. He hung back, let them disappear, then panicked that a train might come and whisk them off. He ran down the escalator. The station was nearly deserted; it was half eleven. He found them again on the southbound platform, positioned himself just close enough to get into the same carriage. They sat near the middle doors. He sat across from them, fifteen feet away. One twin studied a pocket tube map. The other leaned back in her seat and studied the adverts. 'Look,' she said to her sister, 'we could fly to Transylvania for a pound each.' Robert was startled to hear her soft American accent, so different from Elspeth's confident Oxbridge voice.

He avoided looking at them. He thought of a cat his mum had, Squeak; every time they took it to the vet's surgery, that cat tucked its head under Robert's arm and hid. She seemed to think that if she couldn't see the vet, the vet couldn't see her. Robert did not look at the twins, so they would not see him.

They got off at Embankment and changed for the District line. Eventually they emerged from Sloane Square station and wandered haltingly into Belgravia, stopping often to consult their *A–Z*. Robert never came to this part of London, so he, too, became quickly lost. He hung back, keeping his eye on them and feeling pervy and gormless, not to mention highly noticeable. Smart young Sloanes of both sexes marched past him, toting inscrutable shopping bags, mobiles clamped to their ears. Little fogs of breath emanated from their mouths as they rushed by, chatting to themselves like actors rehearsing. The twins seemed tentative and childish by comparison.

They wandered into a side street and became suddenly excited, skipping along and craning their necks at the shop numbers. 'Here!' said one. They went into a tiny hat shop, Philip Treacy, and spent an hour trying on hats. Robert watched them from across the street. The twins took turns with the hats, turning in front of what must have been a mirror. The shop girl smiled at them and offered an enormous lime-green spiral. A twin put it on her head and all three of them looked quite pleased.

Robert wished that he smoked, as it would have provided an excuse to stand about in the street looking pointless. *Maybe I should go and have a pint. They look as though they'll be at this all afternoon.* The twins were exclaiming over a plastic orange disc that reminded Robert of the dinner-plate-like halos in medieval paintings. *I need a disguise. Maybe a beard. Or a hazmat suit.* The twins came out of the shop without any bags.

Robert trailed them all over Knightsbridge, watching them window-shop, eat crêpes, gawk at other shoppers. Mid-afternoon, they vanished into the underground. Robert let them go and took himself to the British Library.

He put his things in a locker and went upstairs to the Humanities 1 reading room. The room was crowded and he found a seat between a beaky woman surrounded by books about Christopher Wren and a hirsute young man who seemed to be researching Jacobite housekeeping practices. Robert did not order any books; he didn't even check on the books he had previously ordered. He put both palms flat on the desk top and closed his eyes. *I feel odd.* He wondered if he was coming down with the flu. Robert was aware of a split within himself – he was filled with contradictory emotions, which included shame, exhilaration, accomplishment, confusion, disgust with himself and a strong desire to follow the twins again tomorrow. He opened his eyes and tried to pull himself together. *You can't spy on them like this. They'll notice sooner or later.* Robert imagined Elspeth chiding him: 'Don't be gutless, sweet. Just open the door the next time they knock.' Then he thought she would have laughed at him. Elspeth never understood shyness. *Don't laugh at me, Elspeth,* Robert said to her in his mind. *Don't.*

The call light at his desk lit up. Robert realised that he must be sitting in someone else's seat. He glanced around, then got up and left the reading room. He took the tube home. As he walked down the path to Vautravers he saw lights in the windows of the middle flat, and his heart contracted in joy. Then he remembered it was only the twins. *Today was a one-off. Tomorrow I'll knock on their door and introduce myself properly.*

The next morning he followed them to Baker Street and paid twenty quid to wander around Madame Tussauds at a discreet distance from the twins as they made fun of wax versions of Justin Timberlake and the Royal Family. The day after that they all went to the Tower and then took in a puppet show on the Embankment. Robert began to despair. *Don't you ever do anything interesting?* Days passed in a blur of Neal's Yard, Harrods, Buckingham Palace, Portobello Road, Westminster Abbey and Leicester Square. Robert sensed the twins' determination: they seemed to be circling London's most public spheres, looking for a rabbit hole into the real city underneath. They were trying to construct a personal London for themselves out of the *Rough Guide* and *Time Out*.

Robert had been born in Islington. He had never lived anywhere but London. His geography of London was a tangle of emotional associations. Street names evoked girlfriends, school mates, boring afternoons playing truant and doing nothing in particular; rare outings with his father to obscure restaurants and the zoo, raves in east-London warehouses. He began to pretend that the twins were taking him on school outings, that they were all three attending an exotic public school with odd uniforms and a curriculum of tourism. He stopped thinking about what he was doing, or worrying very much about being caught. Their obliviousness frightened him.

They lacked the urban camouflage skills young women ought to have. People stared at them all the time, and they seemed to be aware of this without making very much of it, as though being the objects of constant attention was natural to them.

They led and he followed. He went to the cemetery intermittently. When Jessica asked, he told her he was working at home on his thesis. She looked at him curiously; later he noticed the messages piled up on his answering machine and understood that she thought he was avoiding her.

Then the twins stayed in several days running. One twin did little errands by herself. Robert worried. *I should go up and check on them.* By now he felt that he knew them well, but he had never spoken to them. He missed them. He berated himself for becoming immersed in their lives. Still, he hesitated to begin. He found himself spending whole days sitting quietly in his flat, listening, waiting, worrying.

⋙ SICK DAY ⋘

Valentina didn't feel well that morning, so Julia went to the Tesco Express to buy chicken soup, Ritz crackers and Coke, which the twins considered to be the proper cuisine for invalids. As soon as Julia left, Valentina dragged herself out of bed, threw up in the toilet, went back to bed and lay on her side, knees pulled to her chest, burning with fever. She stared at the rug, tracing the gold-and-blue shapes with her eyes. She began to fall asleep.

Someone leaned over and looked at her closely. The person did not touch her; she merely had the feeling that someone was there, that this person was concerned about her. Valentina opened her eyes. She thought she saw something dark, indistinct. It moved towards the foot of the bed. Valentina heard Julia come in the front door, and she woke up completely. There was nothing at the foot of the bed.

In a little while, Julia came into the room with a tray. Valentina sat up. Julia put the tray down and gave her a glass of Coke. Valentina rattled the ice cubes against the glass, touched it to her cheek. She took a tiny sip of Coke, then a bigger sip. 'There was something weird in the room,' she said.

'What do you mean?' asked Julia.

Valentina tried to describe it. 'It was like a smudge in the air. It was worried about me.'

'That's nice of it,' Julia said. 'I'm worried about you too. Want some soup?'

'I think so. Can I just have the soup part and not all the noodles and stuff?'

'Whatever.' Julia went back to the kitchen. Valentina looked around the bedroom. It was just its regular morning bedroom-self. The day was sunny, and the furniture seemed warm and innocent. *I must have dreamed it. How bizarre, though.*

Julia came in and gave her the soup in a mug. She put her hand on Valentina's forehead exactly the way Edie did. 'You're burning up, Mouse.' Valentina drank some soup. Julia sat at the foot of the bed. 'We should find you a doctor.'

'It's just the flu.'

'Mouse . . . you know you can't not have a doctor. Mom would freak. What if you have an asthma attack?'

'Yeah . . . Can we call Mom?' They had called home yesterday, but there was no rule that said they couldn't call twice in one week.

'It's 4 a.m. at home,' Julia said. 'Later we can.'

'Okay.' Valentina held out the mug. Julia put it on the tray. 'I think I want to sleep.'

''kay.' Julia drew the curtains, took the tray and left.

Valentina curled up again, content. She closed her eyes. Someone sat next to her and smoothed her hair. She fell asleep smiling.

Valentina didn't like the underground. It was dark and fast and dirty; it was crowded. She didn't like being pressed against people, feeling someone's breath on her neck, hanging onto a pole and being pitched against sweaty men. Most of all, Valentina did not like being underground. Somehow, the fact that the whole thing was *called* the underground made it worse. She took the bus whenever she could.

She tried not to let Julia know that the tube frightened her, but somehow Julia guessed. Now, every time they went out, Julia would spread out the tube map on the dining-room table and plot out elaborate routes that necessitated at least three changes. Valentina never said anything. She trudged along beside Julia, rode endless escalators into bottomless underground stations. Tonight they were going to the Royal Albert Hall to see a circus. They began at Archway. At Warren Street the twins had to change from the Northern line to the Victoria line, and found themselves moving with a number of other people down a long white-tiled corridor. Valentina held Julia's hand. She mentally checked the zipper of her purse, thinking of pickpockets. Valentina wondered if everyone could tell they were Americans. The crowd moved like syrup.

Valentina noticed a man walking in front of them.

He was quite tall and had ear-length, brown wavy hair. He wore a white button-down shirt tucked into brown corduroy trousers and carried a thick paperback book. He wore wingtip shoes without socks. The man walked with the long, loose-jointed stride of a Labrador retriever or a tree sloth. He was soft-bodied and pallid. Valentina wondered what he was reading. The twins followed him onto an elevator. He walked ahead of them through tunnels and then they stood behind him on the escalator, one of the long ones that made Valentina feel as though the world had tilted, as though she were subject to some new, weird gravity. Finally they found the platform for the Victoria line.

Valentina tried to catch a glimpse of the book's title. It ended in *sis*. Kafka? Too thick. He wore small gold wire-rimmed glasses and had a kind face, a face with lots of jaw and a long narrow nose, which he proceeded to stick into his book. His eyes were brown and hooded, heavily lashed. The train was coming. It was packed, and the doors opened and shut without anyone getting off or on. The man glanced up and resumed reading.

Julia was talking about an accident she had seen that morning, in which a pedestrian, an older woman, had been hit by a moped. Valentina tried not to listen. Julia knew she was afraid of crossing the streets. Valentina always stubbornly waited for the green man, even when there were no cars in sight, even when Julia skipped across the street and stood waving at her from the other side. 'Stop it,' she said to Julia. 'If you don't shut up I'm going to stay home forever, and you'll have to carry all the groceries yourself.' Julia looked surprised, and to Valentina's relief, she was silent.

The next train was in one minute. This one was less

crowded, and the twins pushed their way into it. Julia delved her way towards the middle of the carriage, but Valentina stood clinging to the pole near the door. As the train pitched forward, Valentina looked up and saw that the man she had been watching was standing pressed against her. He caught her eye, and she looked away. He smelled like grass, as though he had been mowing a lawn, and sweat, and something Valentina couldn't place. Paper? Dirt? It was a good smell, whatever it was, and she inhaled it as though it had vitamins in it. Someone's shopping bag was chafing her leg. Valentina glanced up again. The man was still watching her. She blushed, but held his eyes. He said, 'You don't like the tube much, do you?'

'No,' said Valentina.

'Nor I,' he said. His voice was pleasant and low. 'It's too intimate.'

Valentina nodded. She was watching the man's mouth as he spoke. His mouth was wide, the upper lip a bit rabbit-like, showing his slightly protuberant teeth, teeth that could have used orthodontia. She thought of the years she and Julia had spent at Dr Weissman's, having their teeth straightened. She wondered what their teeth would have looked like if they'd just been left alone.

'Are you Julia, or Valentina?' he asked.

'Valentina,' she replied, and was instantly appalled at her own boldness. But how did he know their names? The train slid into a station, throwing her off balance. The man caught her by the elbow, held her up until the train stopped. *This is Victoria*, said the disembodied female voice of the underground.

'Mouse! This is our stop, Mouse, we have to change here.'

Julia's voice rose above the wall of people between them as the doors opened. Valentina twisted her head to look at the man.

'I have to get off,' she told him. There was something reassuring about the way he regarded her, as though they were travelling together and had been riding this train for hours.

'Where are you going?' he asked her. Julia was pushing her way towards them. Valentina stepped off the train.

'The circus,' she said as Julia landed next to her. He smiled; the doors closed; the train moved forward. Valentina stood for a moment, watching. The man raised his hand, hesitated, waved.

'Who was that?' Julia asked. She took Valentina's hand, and they began walking with the crowd to catch the District line.

'I don't know,' Valentina replied.

'He was cute,' said Julia. Valentina nodded. *He knew our names, Julia. We don't know anyone here. How did he know our names?*

Robert watched Valentina and Julia as they slid away. He got off at the next stop, Pimlico, walked to the Tate Gallery, and sat on its steep front steps staring at the Thames, deeply agitated. *What are you so afraid of?* he asked himself, but he could not answer.

It was very late at night, past 2 a.m., and the twins were asleep.
It had been a chilly evening. The twins still hadn't figured out
the heating system – tonight it didn't seem to want to come
on, even though it was colder than it had been. They were used
to their overheated American home; all through the evening
they had each placed their hands on the radiators, wondering
why they were lukewarm. Now they slept with several quilts
covering them. They had found a hot-water bottle in a drawer,
so they had that tucked under their feet. Valentina lay on her
side in a foetal ball. Her thumb was not actually in her mouth;
it hovered nearby, as though she had been sucking on it and
it had become bored and wandered away. Julia spooned around
Valentina, her body pressed into Valentina's and her arm resting
along Valentina's thigh. This was a habitual sleeping position
for the twins; it echoed the way they had slept *in utero*. Their
faces were set in different expressions: Valentina slept lightly,
her brow furrowed and her eyes squinched up. Julia twitched
with a dream. Her eyes raced back and forth under her shell-
thin eyelids. In her dream, Julia was on a beach, back home in
Lake Forest. There were children on the beach. They shrieked
with pleasure; they were knocked over by little waves. Julia felt
the wet of the lake on her skin and twisted in her sleep. In her
dream it began to rain. The children raced back to their parents,
who packed up the toys and sunblock lotion. The rain was

coming down in sheets. Julia tried to remember, *Where is the car?* – she was running now—

Water splashed Julia's face. She put her hand to her cheek, still dreaming. Valentina woke up, sat up and looked at Julia. A thin trickle of water began to pour from the ceiling and onto the quilts, just where Julia's breasts were.

'Ugh, Julia, wake up!'

Julia woke with a snort. It took her a minute to understand the situation. Valentina had already run to the kitchen and returned with a gigantic soup pot by the time Julia crawled out of bed. Valentina stuck the pot under the leak, and the water rattled in it. The bed was soaked. The ceiling plaster above the bed was slick and crumbly. The twins stood watching as the water collected in the pot. Small pieces of plaster bobbed in the water like cottage-cheese curds.

Valentina sat down in the armchair next to the bed. 'What do you think?' she asked. She was wearing boxer shorts and a spaghetti-strap T-shirt, and she had goosebumps all over her arms and her thighs. 'It's not raining.' She tilted her head back, stared at the ceiling. 'Maybe someone was going to take a bath and left the water running?'

'But why doesn't it leak over here, then?' Julia walked into the bathroom and flipped on the light. She scrutinised the ceiling. 'It's totally dry,' she told Valentina.

They looked at each other as more water trickled into the pot. 'Huh,' said Julia. 'I don't know.' She put on her bathrobe, an old pink silk thing she had found at Oxfam. 'I'd better go upstairs and see.'

'I'll come too.'

'No, stay down here in case the pot overflows' – which was a good idea because the water was indeed threatening to reach the top of the pot.

Julia marched out of the apartment and up the stairs. Julia had never gone upstairs before. There were piles of newspapers, mostly the *Guardian* and the *Telegraph*, stacked on the landing. The door stood ajar. Julia knocked. No one responded.

'Hello?' she called. All she could hear was a noise that sounded like something being sanded, a rhythmic, abrasive noise. Someone, a man, was speaking in a low voice.

Julia stood in front of the door nervously. She didn't know anything about the neighbours. She wished she had brought Valentina with her. What if these people were satanists, or child-abusers, or people who cut up inquisitive young women with chainsaws? Did they have chainsaws in Britain, or was that only an American serial-killer thing? Julia stood with her hand on the doorknob, hesitating. She imagined water filling their whole flat, all of Aunt Elspeth's furniture floating around, Valentina swimming from room to room trying to save stuff from the deluge. She opened the door and walked in, calling 'Hello?' as she went.

The flat was very dim, and Julia immediately ran into a pile of boxes that filled the hall. She had a sense of many objects oppressively close together. Somewhere there was a light, across the hall, in another room, but here there was only a dim reflection. The wooden floor felt sticky and gritty under her bare feet. There were pathways within the hall; on each side of the pathways were stacks of boxes. The boxes reached the ceiling, towered ten feet from the floor. Julia wondered if the boxes had ever fallen down and crushed anyone. Maybe there were people buried under the piles of stuff? She navigated by touching the boxes with her hands, like a blind woman. She could smell cooked meat and fried onions. The sweet smell of tobacco. The sharp, complicated smell of bleach-based cleaner. Rotting fruit; lemons? Soap. Julia tried to sort out the smells. They made her nose itch. *Please, God, don't let me sneeze*, she thought, and she sneezed.

The muttering and the sanding stopped abruptly. Julia stood still. The noises resumed after what seemed to Julia to be an eternity. Her heart pounded, and she turned to see if she had left the front door open, but it had vanished. *Breadcrumbs*, Julia thought. *String. I'll never find my way out of here.*

The boxes disappeared under her fingertips, and she stretched her hand out and felt a closed door. This would be the front bedroom, if this were their flat. The noise was louder now. Julia crept down the hall. Finally she stood in the doorway of the back bedroom, and she looked in.

The man had his back to her. He crouched, knees bent, only his feet and the scrubbing brush touching the floor as he washed it. Julia was reminded of a man imitating an anteater. He wore jeans and nothing else. The overhead light was intense, much too bright for the small room, and the bed was huge. There was a lot of clothing and books and junk scattered around. There were maps and photographs pinned to the walls. The man was reciting something in a foreign language as he scrubbed. He had a beautiful voice, and Julia knew that whatever he was saying, it was sad and violent. She wondered if he were a religious fanatic.

The floor was dark with water. The man reached into the pail and brought the scrubbing brush out full of suds and more water. Julia watched him. After a while, she realised that he was simply scrubbing one section over and over again. The rest of the floor remained dry.

Julia began to feel desperate. She wanted to say something, but she didn't know how to begin. Then she told herself that she was behaving like the Mouse, and that gave her the impetus to speak.

'Excuse me,' Julia said softly. The man had his hand in the pail, and he was so startled that he jerked it over, and water spilled across the floor. 'Oh!' Julia said. 'Oh, I'm sorry, I'm so sorry! Here, let me . . .' She dashed across the spreading water, into the bathroom, and came darting back with towels. The man crouched on the floor, watching her, with an expression of incredulity, almost stupefaction. Julia worked at containing the flood, using the towels as fabric dams, like sandbags. She dashed back into the bathroom, bringing another armful of towels, babbling apologies. Martin was so struck by Julia's energy and by her non-stop stream of contrition that he simply stared at her. Her pink robe had come undone, and her hair was messed up. She had the general appearance of a small girl who had been riding a waltzer in her nightclothes. She was showing a lot of leg, and Martin thought that it was charming of this girl to barge into his flat wearing an old dressing gown and knickers, and although he didn't understand what she was doing here, he felt relieved to see her. The overwhelming anxiety he had been feeling was gone. Martin dried his hands on his trousers. Julia finished drying the floor, wadded up all the towels and heaved them into the bathtub. She returned to the bedroom feeling pleased with herself, and saw Martin crouching with his arms folded across his chest, looking up at her.

'Um, hello,' said Martin. He extended his hand, and Julia grasped it and pulled. She noticed as she let go of his hand that it was bleeding; a thin glaze of blood covered her palm. Martin had expected her to shake his hand, so he was surprised to find himself standing. Julia, in turn, was surprised at how agile Martin was. She found herself staring up at a slender, middle-aged man whose horn-rimmed glasses were askew. He seemed rather knobbly to her; his knees and elbows and knuckles were prominent. He was not at all hairy. Julia noticed that his chest was a little concave. She blushed and looked up. He had short salt-and-pepper hair. He seemed kind.

'I'm Martin Wells,' he said.

'I'm Julia Poole,' Julia replied. 'I live downstairs.'

'Oh, of course. And . . . you were lonely?'

'No, see, the water . . . Our bed's right under here, and there was a lot of water coming through the ceiling, and it, like, woke us up.'

Martin blushed. 'I'm terribly sorry. I'll call someone to fix it, he'll put it right for you.'

Julia looked away, at the pail and the scrubbing brush, at the wet floor. She looked back at Martin, puzzled. 'What are you doing?' she asked.

'Cleaning,' he replied. 'I'm washing the floor.'

'Your hands are bleeding,' Julia told him.

Martin looked at his hands. The palms were criss-crossed

with open cracks from long hours in water. His hands were shiny and bright red. He looked back at Julia. She was looking at the bedroom, at the stacks of boxes that lined the walls.

'What's in the boxes?' she asked.

'Things,' he replied.

Julia abandoned tact. 'You live like this?'

'Yes.'

'You're one of those people who wash all the time. Like Howard Hughes.'

Martin didn't know what to say, so he simply said, 'Yes.'

'Cool.'

'Um, no, it isn't, at all.' Martin went into the bathroom, opened the medicine cabinet and took out a tube of lotion, which he began to rub onto his hands. 'It's an illness.' He straightened his spectacles with a lotiony finger. Julia felt that she had made a faux pas.

'I'm sorry.'

'That's all right.'

There was an awkward pause during which neither looked at the other.

Julia began to feel nervous. *I was right before – he's mentally ill.* She said, 'I should go back downstairs. Valentina is probably wondering.'

Martin nodded. 'I'm sorry about your ceiling. I'll ring up someone first thing tomorrow. I would come down myself—'

'Yes?'

'But I never leave my flat.'

Julia was disappointed, even though she had been intent on getting away from him just moments before. 'Not at all?'

'It's part of . . . my illness.' Martin smiled. 'Don't look like that. You are quite welcome to come and visit *me*.' He guided Julia through the maze of boxes. When they arrived at his front door he let her open it and step into the landing. 'I hope you will come again. For tea? Tomorrow, perhaps?'

Julia stood on the well-lit landing and peered at Martin, who hung back from the door in his dark hall. 'Okay,' she said. 'Sure.'

'And your sister is welcome, as well.'

Julia felt a tiny pang of possessiveness. If he met Valentina he would probably like her better. Everyone did. 'Um, I'll see if she's available.'

Martin smiled. 'Until tomorrow, then. Four o' clock?'

'Okay. It was nice to meet you,' Julia said, and fled downstairs.

Valentina had just emptied the soup pot when Julia returned. The ceiling was still dripping and the bedding was a sodden mess. The twins stood together and surveyed the damage. 'So what happened?' Valentina asked.

Julia told her, but she had trouble describing Martin. Valentina looked horrified when Julia said they'd been invited to tea. 'But he sounds awful,' said Valentina. 'He never leaves his apartment?'

'I dunno. He was super polite. I mean, yeah, he's obviously crazy, but in a nice eccentric English way, you know?' The twins began to strip the quilts off the bed. They carried them into the bathroom and tried to wring the water out of them. 'I think maybe these are ruined.'

'No, it's only plaster. It should rinse out. Maybe we could

soak them?' Valentina put the stopper in the plughole and began to run warm water into the tub.

'Anyway, I said I'd come and have tea and you can come if you want. I think you should at least meet him. He's our neighbour.'

Valentina shrugged. They finished stripping the bed and left the soup pot sitting on the mattress to collect the drips. They put themselves to bed in the spare bedroom (which was rather clammy) and each went to sleep worrying about home repair and tea.

The twins found virginity burdensome, each in her own way.

Julia had experimented some. In high school she had let boys kiss and/or fondle her in cars, in the bedrooms of friends' parents at parties when those parents were out of town, once in a ladies' room at Navy Pier, and several times on the doorstep of Jack and Edie's unimpressive ranch house, which she always wished was a gigantic Victorian with a porch – so she could sit with the boy in a porch swing and eat ice cream and they could lick it off each other's lips while Valentina spied on them from the darkened living room. But there was no porch, and the kisses were as lacklustre as the house.

Julia remembered fending off boys on the beach, behind the shelter in West Park after ice skating, in a music-practice room at the high school. She remembered each boy's reaction, the various shadings of confusion and anger. 'Well, why d'ya come in here, then?' the boy in the practice room had asked her, and she had no answer.

What did she want? What was it she imagined these boys could do to her? And why did she always stop them before they could do it?

Valentina was more sought after, and not as proficient at saying no. During the twins' teen years it was Valentina who was singled out by the quiet boys, and by the boys who thought of themselves as nascent rock stars. While Julia chose boys who weren't interested in her and then chased them, Valentina dreamily ignored them all and won hearts. She was always surprised when the boy who sat behind her in Algebra declared his love as she unchained her bike; when the editor of the school paper asked her to the prom.

'You should let them come to you,' Valentina said, when Julia complained about the discrepancy. But Julia was impatient, and cared about being passed over. These things are fatal to romance, especially if a more indifferent version of yourself is nearby.

Sex was interesting to Valentina, but the individual boys she might have had sex with were not. When she focused her attention on a boy, that boy always seemed to her unfinished, dull, absurd. She was used to the profound intimacy of her life with Julia, and she did not know that a cloud of hope and wild illusion is required to begin a relationship. Valentina was like the veteran of a long marriage who has forgotten how to flirt. The boys who followed her through the hallways of Lake Forest High School at a safe distance lost their ardour when it was met with polite bewilderment.

And so the twins had remained virgins. Julia and Valentina watched all of their high school and college friends disappear one by one into the adult world of sex, until they were the only people they knew who lingered in the world of the uninitiated. 'What was it like?' they asked each friend. The answers were vague. Sex was a private joke: you had to be there.

The twins worried about virginity individually, and they worried about it together. But the most basic problem was one they never talked about: sex was something they couldn't do together. Someone would have to go first, and then the other would be left behind. And they would each have to pick different guys, and these guys, these potential boyfriends, would want to spend time alone with one or the other; they would want to be the important person in Julia or Valentina's life. Each boyfriend would be a crowbar, and soon there would be a gap; there would be hours in the day when Julia wouldn't even know where Valentina was, or what she was doing, and Valentina would turn to tell Julia something and instead there would be the boyfriend, waiting to hear what she was about to say, although only Julia would have understood it.

It was a delicate thing, their private world. It required absolute fidelity, and so they remained virgins, and waited.

Julia presented herself at Martin's door at exactly four o' clock the next afternoon; Valentina had had an attack of shyness and refused to come. A man had arrived that morning and had begun to repair their bedroom ceiling, so Julia felt she ought to keep her promise.

Julia wore jeans and a white blouse. When Martin answered the door she was startled to see that he wore a suit and tie. He was also wearing latex surgical gloves, which made him look like a TV butler.

'Do come in,' he said. He led her through the flat to the kitchen, which was surprisingly cosy, though the windows were covered in newspaper and tape. 'We always eat in here,' Martin said. 'The dining room has been taken over by boxes.' He said this as though he had no idea how it had come to pass.

'You have a family?' It had not occurred to Julia that anyone might be married to this crazy person.

'Yes, I have a wife and a son. My wife is in Amsterdam and my son is up at Oxford.'

'Oh. Is she on vacation?'

'I suppose you could put it that way. I'm not really sure when she's coming back, so I've been making shift for myself. Things are a little improvisational here at the moment.' Martin had set out three places at the kitchen table. Julia sat down at the one that faced the back door, *in case I need to escape.*

'Valentina couldn't come. She isn't feeling too well,' Julia said; it was sort of true.

'That's unfortunate. Another time,' said Martin. He felt pleased with himself; he had contrived, at short notice, a very passable afternoon tea. There were fish-paste sandwiches, as well as cucumber and cress; there was a Victoria sponge cake. He had set out Marijke's mother's china, and there was a little jug of milk and a bowl of sugar cubes. He thought it looked quite as nice as what Marijke would have done. 'What kind of tea would you like?' he asked.

'Earl Grey?'

He pressed the button on the electric kettle and plopped a tea bag into the teapot. 'This isn't how it's supposed to be done, but one gets lazy.'

'How are you supposed to do it?'

'Oh, you warm the pot, you use loose tea . . . but I can't taste the difference, and I drink a lot of tea, so the ritual has devolved somewhat.'

'Our mom uses tea bags,' Julia assured him.

'Then that must be correct,' said Martin gravely. The water boiled (he had actually boiled it a few times before Julia arrived, just to make sure the kettle was working) and Martin made tea. Soon they were both seated, drinking tea and eating sandwiches. Well-being pervaded Martin. He had not realised how much he'd missed sharing a meal with another human. Julia looked up and saw him beaming at her. *He might be insane, but he's very cheerful.*

'So, um, how long have you lived here?' she asked him.

'Twenty-some years. We lived in Amsterdam when we were first married, and then we lived in St John's Wood. We bought this flat just before Theo was born.'

'Have you always . . . stayed in?'

Martin shook his head. 'That's a recent development. I used to work at the British Museum, translating ancient and classical languages. But now I work from home.'

Julia smiled. 'So they bring the Rosetta Stone and all that here to you?' The twins had been to the British Museum the previous week. Julia thought of Valentina bending over Lindow Man, nearly in tears.

'No, no. I don't often need the actual objects. They take photographs and make drawings – I use those. It's all become so much easier now everything is digital. I suppose some day they'll just wave the objects over the computer and it will sing the translation in Gregorian chant. But in the meantime they still need someone like me to work it out.' Martin paused, then said, rather shyly, 'Do you like crossword puzzles?'

'We aren't very good at them. Mom does the New York Times ones. She tried to teach us, but we can only do Mondays.'

'Your Aunt Elspeth was a whiz at them. I used to set special cryptics for her birthday.'

Julia wanted to ask about Elspeth, but she understood that Martin was actually inviting her to ask him about his puzzles, so to be polite she said, 'You make crosswords?'

'I do. I set them for the Guardian.' Martin said this as

though he were confessing to a secret identity as a superhero.

Julia arranged her face into what she hoped was an expression of appropriate awe. 'Wow. We never thought of anybody making them. They just kind of appear in the paper, you know?'

'It is an underappreciated art form.' *Ask her about herself, you're monopolising the conversation.* 'What do you do?'

'We don't know yet. We haven't decided.'

Martin sipped his tea and looked at Julia quizzically. 'Do you often refer to yourself in the first person plural?'

Julia frowned. 'No – I mean me and Valentina. We haven't found anything we both want to do as a profession.'

'Do you both have to do the same thing?'

'Yes!' Julia paused and reminded herself that she was talking to a stranger, not the Mouse. 'I mean, we want something we can do together. So maybe we could do two slightly different jobs that fit together somehow.'

'What sorts of things do you each like to do?'

'Well, Valentina likes clothes. She likes to take clothes and make new things out of them, you know, like she might take your suit and slit open the back and make a corset or a bustle or that kind of thing. She's, like, a slave to Alexander McQueen.' Julia glanced at the place setting meant for Valentina and wondered what her twin was doing; Martin pictured himself wearing a bustle and smiled.

'And you?'

'Um. I don't know. I like to find out about things. I guess.' Julia looked at her plate as she said this. The rim of the plate was painted with blue morning glories. *Why do I feel like I'm at the edge of a hole?*

Martin said, 'More tea?' Julia nodded. He poured. 'You're quite young, aren't you? My son doesn't know what he wants to do yet either. He's studying maths, but he doesn't have the passion for it. I imagine he'll end up in finance and spend all his time planning exotic holidays. Everything he enjoys is somewhat dangerous.'

'Like what?'

'Oh – motorcycling. I think he goes mountain climbing, but no one will confirm or deny that. It's just as well I don't know.'

'You worry about him?'

Martin laughed. He hadn't felt so light-hearted in months. 'Dear child, I worry about *everything*. But yes, I worry about Theo in particular. That's just the nature of parents. The moment Theo was conceived, I started to worry about him. I don't think it's done him a whit of good, but I can't help it.'

Julia thought of Martin washing the floor. *You're like a dog licking the same spot over and over.* 'So you wash things?'

Martin leaned back in his chair and folded his arms across his chest. 'That's very perceptive. Yes, that's right.' He looked at Julia and she looked back at him. They each experienced a little jolt of recognition. She thought, *He's insane and I understand him. But maybe he isn't completely crazy. Like a sort of lucid craziness, like a dream.* Martin said, 'You like to find out about things. What sort of things?'

Julia tried to put it into words. 'Just — everything. I'm curious about things that people aren't supposed to see — so, for example, I liked going to the British Museum, but I would like it better if I could go into all the offices and storage rooms, I want to look in all the drawers and — discover stuff. And I want to know about people. I mean, I know it's probably kind of rude, but I want to know why you have all these boxes and what's in them and why all your windows are papered over and how long it's been that way and how do you feel when you wash things and why don't you do something about it?' Julia looked at Martin and thought, *Now he's going to ask me to leave.* They sat in uncomfortable silence for what seemed a long time. Then Martin smiled.

'You're very — American, aren't you?'

'Is that a euphemism for "very rude"? Yes, I am very rude. Sorry.'

'No, no, don't apologise. That's *my* job. More tea?'

'No thank you. If you give me too much caffeine I totally lose all restraint. Maybe that already happened,' Julia said.

Martin poured himself another cup of tea. 'Do you actually want to know all those things?' he said. 'Because if I answer all your questions I might lose my air of mystery, and you won't come and visit me again.'

'I would visit you.' *You're the oddest person I've ever met, you couldn't get rid of me if you tried.*

Martin opened his mouth, hesitated, then said, 'Do you smoke?'

'Yes,' Julia replied. Martin brightened. He left the table and came back with a pack of cigarettes and a lighter. He shook a cigarette out of the pack and offered it to Julia. She took it and put it to her lips, let him light it for her and immediately had a severe coughing fit. Martin jumped up and fetched her a glass of water. When she could speak she said, 'What the hell was that?'

'Gauloises. They're unfiltered – I'm sorry. I wasn't trying to kill you.'

She handed him the lit cigarette. 'Here, I'll just inhale your second-hand smoke.'

Martin took a deep drag and let the smoke trickle from his mouth. Julia thought she had never seen such an expression of raw pleasure on anyone's face. She understood then how he had managed to woo and marry a girl: *He just looked at her like that.* Julia wished someone would look at her that way. Then she felt confused.

Martin said, 'Curiosity killed the cat.' He took another drag on his cigarette.

'I know. But I just feel like my head's going to explode if I don't find out . . . whatever it is.'

'You would make a good scholar.'

Julia was fascinated to see that smoke came out of his mouth in little gusts as he spoke. *I thought Dad was a hardcore smoker, but this guy is definitely in another league.* 'I can't sit still that long. I want to find out *now,* and then find out the next thing.'

'A journalist, then.'

Julia looked dubious. 'Maybe. But what about Valentina?'

She noticed that Martin had removed his surgical gloves in order to smoke the cigarette. They lay crumpled beside his cup and saucer.

'Don't you think that each of you might be happier pursuing your own interests?'

'But we're *together* – we've always done things together.'

'Hmm.'

Julia had the uncomfortable feeling that someone had snuck upstairs before she'd arrived and told Martin the Mouse's point of view on things. 'What?' she said, resentfully.

'It's a pity you won't meet Elspeth. She had some interesting things to say about being a twin.'

Julia was all attention. 'Like what?'

Martin asked, 'Would you like some cake?' Julia shook her head. 'I think I will have a small piece,' he said. He delicately cut a sliver of cake and laid it on a plate, then ignored it as he continued to smoke. 'Elspeth thought that there was a limit to how far the twin relationship should go, in terms of each person giving up their own individuality. She felt that she and your mother had exceeded that boundary.'

'How?'

Martin shook his head. 'She didn't tell me. You ought to ask Robert; if she told anyone it would have been him.'

'Robert Fanshaw? We haven't met him yet.'

'Hmm. I'd have thought he'd've been round to introduce himself first thing. How odd.'

'We've knocked on his door, but he's never home. Maybe he's out of town,' Julia said.

'I just saw him this morning. He arranged for your ceiling to be repaired.' Martin smiled. 'He ticked me off properly for annoying you.' Martin stubbed out his cigarette and then carefully put on his gloves.

'Huh. I wonder how come . . . I mean, what's he like?'

Martin ate a bite of cake and Julia waited while he chewed and swallowed. 'Well, he was very devoted to Elspeth. I think perhaps her death has unhinged him a bit. But he's a good fellow, he's very patient with all my mishaps.'

'Do you have a lot of – Um, should we expect the ceiling to cave in all the time?'

Martin looked embarrassed. 'That's only happened once before. I'll try very hard not to do that again.'

'Do you have a choice about it?'

'There's a little bit of leeway. Usually.'

Julia felt dizzy from all the cigarette smoke. 'Can I use your washroom?'

Martin said, 'Of course.' He pointed towards the servant's room. 'There's one in there.' Julia rose unsteadily and made her way through the box-filled room into the tiny bathroom. There were more boxes stacked in the bathtub. *It must be like living in a self-storage unit.* She used the toilet and splashed water on her face and felt better. When she got back to the kitchen she said, 'So what's in the boxes? I mean, it looks like you just moved in.'

Martin regarded her tolerantly. 'All right, Miss Pandora Poole. As a special treat you may open a box.'

'Any box?'

'Maybe. I can't always remember what's in them, so it doesn't much matter which box.'

They both stood up. *It's like Easter. Or Christmas.* 'Any hints?'

'No,' he said. 'Most of them aren't too exciting.' They moved into the dining room. Julia stood staring at the towering piles of boxes. Martin said, 'Perhaps you could pick one from the top? So we don't have to shift them all?'

Julia pointed at a box and Martin carefully took it off the pile and handed it to her. It was embalmed in tape, so he went and got a Stanley knife. She put the box on the floor and sliced into it, kneeling beside it. When she opened the box Martin stood back as though it might explode.

It was full of plastic. At first Julia thought plastic was the only thing in the box, but as she delved into it she realised that there were a number of items, each wrapped in plastic and taped. She looked up at Martin. He stood in the doorway, nervously tugging at his gloved fingers. 'Should I stop?' she asked.

'No. Unwrap something.'

She groped in the box and pulled out a small plastic package. She unwrapped it slowly. It was an earring, a single pearl in an elaborate silver setting. She offered it up to Martin. He leaned forward to look. 'Ah,' he said. 'That's Marijke's. She'll want that back.' He did not take it from Julia.

She said, 'Do you think the other earring is in here?' He nodded. She went through the box until she found a similar package. When she had both earrings Julia stood up.

She went to Martin and held out her hand. He cupped his gloved hands together and she put the earrings into them. Then she put all the plastic back in the box, and placed it back on the pile. She didn't want to know what else was in there. They went back to the kitchen and stood awkwardly next to their chairs. Martin put the earrings carefully into Valentina's teacup. He said, 'Sometimes a thing is . . . too much . . . and it has to be isolated and put away.' Martin shrugged. 'So what's in the boxes is . . . emotion. In the form of objects.' He looked at Julia. 'Is that what you wanted to know?'

'Yes.' It seemed like a completely sensible system. 'Thank you.'

'Any other questions?'

She stared at her shoes. 'I'm sorry. I didn't mean . . . it was nice of you . . .' She stopped because she was about to cry.

'Hey, hey, it's all right, child.' Martin put his thumb under her chin and lifted her face. 'No harm done.' She blinked at him. 'Don't look so tragic.'

'I felt like I really was Pandora for a minute there.'

'No, not at all. But I'm going to send you home now, I think.'

'Can I come again?' It seemed urgent to Julia, to know.

'Yes,' said Martin. 'That would be delightful. You know, you're very like your aunt. Please do visit again. Any time,' he added.

'Okay,' said Julia. 'I will. Thank you.' They navigated the aisles between the boxes until they stood at Martin's front door. He watched as Julia disappeared, foreshortened, down the stairs. She stopped and waved just before vanishing. He heard her door open and close, heard her calling 'Mouse!' and an answering call. 'Goodness,' Martin said to himself, and turned and shut his door.

It was a dreary Saturday evening in mid-February. Rain was lashing the windows; Elspeth wondered if perhaps that would wash any of the grime off them. Julia and Valentina were eating their dinner in front of the TV. *They're going to get some kind of vitamin deficiency*, Elspeth thought. *They never seem to eat anything green.* Tonight it was tinned chicken soup, peanut butter on toast and semi-skimmed milk. The twins watched copious amounts of television (Julia joked that they had to learn the language somehow), but tonight they seemed to be making a point of sitting down to watch a particular programme. It turned out to be *Doctor Who*.

Elspeth hovered above them, lying on her stomach, chin resting on folded arms. *Isn't there anything else on TV?* She was a snob about science fiction and hadn't seen an episode of *Doctor Who* since the early eighties. *Eh, I suppose it's better than nothing.* She watched Julia and Valentina watching the television. They ate their soup slowly from mugs and looked keen. Elspeth happened to glance at the screen in time to see the Doctor walk out of the Tardis and into a defunct spaceship.

That's David Tennant! Elspeth zoomed over to the television and sat herself a foot away from it. The Doctor and his companions had discovered an eighteenth-century French fireplace on the spaceship. A fire burned in the hearth. *I want a fire*, Elspeth thought. She had been experimenting with warming herself over the flames of the stove on the rare occasions that the twins cooked anything. The Doctor had crouched down by the fire and was conversing with a little girl in Paris in 1727 who seemed to be on the other side of the fireplace. *Is it sad to fancy David Tennant when you're dead? This is a very strange programme.* The little girl turned out to be the future Madame de Pompadour. Clockwork androids from the spaceship were trying to steal her brain.

'Cyber-steampunk, or steam-cyberpunk?' asked Julia. Elspeth had no idea what she meant. Valentina said, 'Look at her hair. Do you think we could do that?'

'It's a wig,' said Julia. The Doctor was reading Madame de Pompadour's mind. He put his hands on her head, palms enclosing her face, fingers delicately splayed around her ears. *Such long fingers*, Elspeth marvelled. She placed her small hand on top of David Tennant's. The screen was deliciously warm. Elspeth sunk her hand into it, just an inch or so.

'God, that's weird,' said Valentina. There was a dark silhouette of a woman's hand superimposed over the Doctor's. He let go of Madame de Pompadour's face, but the black hand remained where it was. Elspeth took her hand away; the screen hand stayed black. 'How did you do that?' said the Doctor. Elspeth thought he was speaking to her, then realised that Madame de Pompadour was answering him. *I must have burned out the screen. What if I could do that with my face?* She tucked her entire self into the TV and found herself looking out through the screen. It was wonderful inside the television, quite warm and pleasantly confining. Elspeth had only been in there for a second or two when the twins saw the screen go black. The TV died.

'Drat,' said Julia. 'It looks like a newish set too.' She got up and started fiddling with the buttons, to no avail.

'Maybe it's under warranty,' said Valentina. 'I wonder where she got it?'

John Lewis, Elspeth remembered. *But I think the warranty must have expired by now.* She passed out of the television and stood before it, hoping it would revive. *That was rather exciting – they saw me! Well, they saw my hand.* She waited for the screen to flicker back to life, but it remained stubbornly dark. *Think about this. I short-circuited an electrical thing. Am I electrical? What am I made of, anyway?* She stared down at her hands, which, to her, looked like . . . hands. Elspeth floated over to a floor lamp which stood in a corner of the room. It was turned off. She reached through the fixture and touched her fingers to the base of the light bulb. It began to glow, faintly. *Ah, that's bloody brilliant.* She looked to see if the twins were noticing, but they weren't.

'Maybe that guy upstairs would let us watch his TV,' said Valentina. Her reluctance to meet Martin was evenly matched by her desire to see the rest of the episode.

'I'm not sure he has one,' said Julia. 'It was kind of hard to tell with all the stuff he's got piled up.' They stood looking at each other in silence, irresolute.

'Maybe there's a Scrabble set around here somewhere.' Valentina got up, and Julia followed her out of the room. Elspeth stood holding the light bulb, feeling a distinct sense of anticlimax. *It's in the wardrobe in the guest bedroom,* she thought.

She let the light bulb go, and the glow vanished. She could hear the twins ransacking her office. *I've got to get more serious about this. I wish I'd read more ghost stories, I'm sure I could have found some tips in Le Fanu and that lot. Maybe there's something on Wikipedia. I wonder if I can turn on the computer? No, I'd probably just wreck it.* Elspeth climbed back into the defunct television, which was still warm. *What's wrong with me? I feel positively fuck-witted, I think death has knocked fifty points off my IQ. I used to be able to reason. Now I just waft around making random experiments regarding the nature of existence. And wallowing in self-pity.*

When the last of the heat was gone from the TV, Elspeth left it and wandered into the guest room. The wardrobe stood slightly open. The Scrabble set was on the top shelf, under the Monopoly box and an old cribbage board. Elspeth got onto the shelf and behind the games. She began pushing. It was useless; the boxes were too heavy for her. *Sod it.*

She went to her office to see what the twins were doing. They were sitting together on the floor, huddled over an old issue of *The Face*. Elspeth felt irritated. *Idiot girls. You're sitting in a flat that's chock-full of fabulous printed matter and what are you reading about? Morrissey.*

'Don't,' said Valentina.

'Don't what?' replied Julia.

'Don't be mad at me. It's not my fault about the TV.'

'I'm not mad at you.' Julia put the magazine down and looked at Valentina. 'I'm kinda bored, but not mad.'

'Huh. I just felt this – like you were really annoyed with me.'

'Well, I'm not.'

'Okay.'

They went back to their reading. Elspeth crouched on the floor a few feet away and stared at them. Valentina raised her head and surveyed the room, perplexed. Seeing nothing, she looked down again. Julia turned the page.

All right then, Elspeth thought. *We're getting somewhere, you and I.*

Valentina said, 'It's so cold in here. Let's just go to bed.' Julia put the magazine away and flipped the light switch. Elspeth sat by herself in the dark, listening to the twins brushing their teeth. When the flat was quiet she went to her desk and touched her fingers to the light bulb in the desk lamp. It glowed.

⤞⚌ SQUIRRELS ⚌⤝

For days Martin had been hearing noises in the eaves. Something was scampering, clawing, scratching in the space between his ceiling and the roof. Martin called Robert. Robert called the pest-control man, whose name was Kevin.

Kevin duly arrived first thing Monday morning. He was an enormous man, at least twenty stone, both tall and wide. He didn't say anything as Martin and Robert led him through the darkened rooms with their piles of boxes. Martin wondered how such an immense human was going to manage to get through the small trapdoor in the dressing-room ceiling that provided access to the eaves.

Kevin pulled down the ladder, took out a torch and squeezed himself through the hole with a soft grunt. Robert and Martin heard his boots treading from joist to joist. Martin felt a bit queasy, staring up at the hole. Something might come running out of it. Perhaps whatever it was had fleas; perhaps Kevin would bring the fleas down with him on his boots. He seemed to be up there a long time. Martin became very uneasy. Robert said, 'You don't have to stand here. Why don't you go and have a fag at your desk. I'll wait for him.' Martin shook his head. The faint boot treads seemed to be moving around the outer perimeter of the building. 'Have you ever been up there?' Robert asked.

'When we first lived here Marijke went up. And we had

some problems with the roof, but that was before you came. It's just boards and insulation.' Martin wondered if he could persuade Kevin to remove his boots before he stepped off the ladder. Not likely.

The boot treads approached; Kevin appeared in the opening, lowered himself onto the ladder. Martin stared at his boots. Robert said, 'See anything?'

'There's nowt up there,' said Kevin. 'You've got very empty eaves.'

'Hmm,' said Robert. 'They must be on the roof, not in the roof.'

'That'll be it, perhaps.'

Robert saw him out and came back upstairs. Martin was scrubbing the dressing-room floor.

'Well?' said Robert.

'That's a deep subject,' Martin replied.

'My grandfather used to say that.'

Martin said, 'Why haven't you introduced yourself to Elspeth's girls? They've been here for six weeks.'

Robert leaned against the doorjamb and thought about it. 'I don't know. I've been rather busy. I had their ceiling fixed, though.' He watched Martin scrubbing and said, 'You might use a bit less water when you do that, or you'll be bringing down their dressing-room ceiling as well and all Elspeth's shoes will be ruined.'

'They're charming. Or, one of them is. I haven't met the other one. She was quite Elspeth-like.'

'In what way?'

'That devastating forthrightness. Elspeth could wield it

better, of course – Julia seems a bit out of control. But really, she's a lovely girl. Nothing to be afraid of.'

Robert made a little snorting sound that Martin correctly translated as *Kindly back off*. 'These noises you've been hearing. Are you sure they're animal noises? I noticed the big oak has grown over the roof. Perhaps we need to call a tree surgeon and get things trimmed up. It couldn't hurt.'

'All right.' Martin was convinced that the eaves were infested with something, but he knew better than to insist on it now that the pest-control man had checked things out and found nothing. Martin knew that there were two realities: the actual one and the felt one. In the past he had tried to explain, but Robert didn't understand and invariably started talking about medication in a serious, almost patronising manner. Martin stopped scrubbing and stared at the floor, then closed his eyes and consulted his feeling about the floor. The urge to clean it was satisfied. He stood up and gathered his bucket and brush.

'How's your book coming along?' he asked Robert.

'Fine. I'm off to the Royal Society of Medicine today. I'm helping Dr Jelliffe with his pamphlet on all the medical practitioners buried in Highgate.'

'Oh, what fun,' Martin said wistfully. Of all the things he missed about the world, researching in actual libraries ranked near the top. Robert opened his mouth to say something, changed his mind. Martin said, 'Say hello to the doctor, then. And for heaven's sake go and introduce yourself to those twins.'

Robert smiled and gave Martin an enigmatic look. 'Okay.

I'll get right on it.' He left Martin's flat and went down the stairs. On the first-floor landing he stood facing the door, staring at the little card with Elspeth's name on it. He raised his hand to knock, then didn't, and continued walking down the stairs and into his flat.

It was a grey, cold day. Rain was imminent. Julia and Valentina were walking up Primrose Hill. They were bundled up against the cold, and the effort of walking uphill made their cheeks pink. Julia had bought a book called *Super-Mini British Slang Dictionary* in an Oxfam shop. She occasionally referred to it as they walked.

'*Bubble and squeak*,' Julia said.

Valentina pondered. 'It's something to eat. Is it steak and kidney pie?'

'No, steak and kidney pie is steak and kidney pie.'

'Well, it's like a stew.'

'Cabbage and potatoes chopped up and fried together,' said Julia. 'Okay, here's a good one: *codswallop*.'

'Nonsense.'

'Very good, A-plus for our Mouse. Now you do some for me.' Julia handed Valentina the book. The twins reached the top of the hill. London spread out before them. The twins were unaware of it, but Winston Churchill had often stood on the spot they happened to be standing on, thinking over strategy during World War II. The twins were disappointed with the view. Chicago was dramatic; if you went to the top of the John Hancock Center you felt a little bit of vertigo and saw a city full of huge buildings beside a gigantic body of water. Standing on Primrose Hill, the twins saw Regent's Park, which was drab in February, and tiny buildings in the distance all around.

'It's bloody cold up here,' said Julia, jumping up and down and hugging herself.

Valentina frowned. 'Don't say "bloody". It's swearing.'

'Okay. It's jolly cold up here. It's blooming cold. Gorblimey, it's cold up here.' Julia began to do a sort of dance. It involved running in circles, skipping and hopping in place every now and then while throwing her body sideways. Valentina stood with her arms crossed, watching Julia carom around. Now and then Julia bumped into her. 'C'mon, Mouse,' Julia said, grabbing Valentina's mittened hands. They two-stepped around in a circle for a few minutes until Valentina was out of breath. She stood leaning over with her hands on her knees, wheezing.

'You okay?' Julia asked. Valentina shook her head and her hat fell off. Julia replaced it. After a few more minutes Valentina's breathing returned to normal. Julia felt as though she could jog up and down the hill ten times without getting as winded as Valentina had been after a couple minutes of dancing. 'You okay now?'

'Yeah.' They began to walk down the hill. The wind dropped almost instantly. Valentina felt her lungs unclench. 'We should figure out how to get a doctor.'

'Yeah.' They walked in silence for a while, following the same train of thought: *We promised Mom we'd find a doctor right away and not wait until Valentina has some kind of emergency. But we've only been here six weeks, so really this is still 'right away'. Besides, there's a hospital just down Highgate Hill, so if anything does go wrong we could go to the emergency room. But we're still not insured, so we'd end up having to tell Mom and Dad. But how do we figure out the National Health Service? Maybe that lawyer who did Aunt Elspeth's will could explain it.*

'We should call Mr Roche,' they said in unison, and laughed.

Julia said, 'Jinx.'

Valentina said, 'I'm better now.' Then she had the feeling she often had lately, of being watched. Sometimes it went away; she hadn't felt it up on the hill. She turned and looked around, but they were alone on the street except for a young woman pushing a pram with a sleeping baby in it. The houses shut them out with blank narrow faces, windows curtained. The twins walked down some steps to the path along the Regent's Canal; the canal was placid, with wide paths on each bank. The houses loomed over them in strange perspective, as though the twins were walking underneath a transparent street. Cold fat raindrops fell sporadically. Valentina kept looking over her shoulder. There was a teenage boy on a bike; he rode past them without a glance. Someone was keeping pace with them on the street above. Valentina could hear footsteps crunching alongside them as they walked.

Julia noticed Valentina's unease. 'What is it?'

'You know.'

Julia was about to say the same thing she'd been saying for days, which was: *That's crazy, Mouse.* But suddenly she became aware of the footsteps too. She looked up. There was nothing to see but the wall and the railing and the houses. She stopped walking and so did Valentina. The footsteps continued, *one, two, three, four,* then stopped. The water had exaggerated the footsteps; now their absence was enlarged by the canal lapping at its cement banks. Julia and Valentina stood facing each other, heads tilted to catch the sound. They waited and the footsteps waited. The twins turned and walked back the way they'd come. The footsteps walked on, away from them, hesitated, and then continued, growing faint as they moved away.

The twins came to the steps. They ascended to the street. In the distance was a man in a long overcoat, walking away from them hurriedly. Valentina frowned. Julia said, 'Do you want to go home?'

Yes, but not in the way you mean. 'No,' said Valentina. She had the feeling more intensely inside the flat. 'Let's go to the V&A and look at Queen Caroline's clothes.'

'Okay,' said Julia. They stopped while Julia consulted the *A–Z.* Valentina stood watching, but whatever it was had gone.

Elspeth felt that she was on the verge of a breakthrough. She had been giving serious thought to haunting. *There's a balance between the aesthetics and the practical side of it. I've been muddling around trying to do the things living people do, messing with objects and such. But I can do things they can't do: I can fly and pass through walls and blow out TVs. I'm not exactly matter so I must be energy.* Elspeth wished she'd paid more attention to physics. Most of her knowledge of the hard sciences came from quiz shows and crossword puzzles. *If I'm energy, then what?* She didn't understand why Valentina seemed to be able to sense her while Julia couldn't. But Elspeth redoubled her efforts: she followed Valentina around the flat, turning lights on and off. Valentina complained to Julia about the old wiring and worried that the building was going to burn down. When the twins were out Elspeth gave herself exercises to do: cast a shadow, make a Tesco's receipt float a few inches off the dining-room table. (She couldn't manage either task.) She imagined grand tableaux: *I'll pull all the books off the shelves, break all the windows, play the 'Maple Leaf Rag' on the piano.* But she was too weak to sound even one note. She walked over the piano keys, stomping as hard as she could in her yellow Doc Martens. The keys depressed a few millimetres; she thought she heard the strings whisper, but really there was nothing at all. She was more successful with doors; if the hinges were well oiled she could close a door by leaning against it and pushing with all her might.

So she kept practising. *If I'd worked out this hard when I was alive I could have lifted a Mini Cooper.* The results were gradual, but definite. The most effective thing Elspeth did was simply to stare at Valentina.

Valentina didn't like it. She seemed to pick up on Elspeth's emotional states. But even when Elspeth tried to project bright-ness and smiles, Valentina was uneasy. She would look around, get up and move, abandoning her book, taking her cup of tea to some other room. Sometimes Elspeth followed her and sometimes she let her escape. Elspeth tried staring at Julia, just to be fair, but Julia was impervious.

One morning Elspeth came upon them at breakfast in the dining room. As she entered the room Valentina was speaking. '. . . I don't know, it's like, a ghost, just, you know, a presence. Like someone's there.' Valentina looked around the room, which was bright with morning sun. 'It's here now. It wasn't a minute ago.'

Julia obediently cocked her head and sat still, trying to feel the ghost. Then she shook her head and said, 'Nope.'

Do something, Elspeth thought. She was excited because Valentina had actually used the word *ghost*. Elspeth walked behind Julia's chair and bent over her, wrapped her arms around Julia's shoulders and placed her hands over Julia's heart. Julia let out a little shriek and exclaimed, 'Yowza!' Elspeth let go of her and Julia huddled in her chair, shivering.

'What?' said Valentina, alarmed.

'It just got super cold in here. Didn't you feel it?'

Valentina shook her head and said, 'It's the ghost.' Elspeth ran her fingers up Valentina's arm. She was afraid to embrace Valentina the way she had just done to Julia; she wasn't sure Valentina's heart would stand it. Valentina rubbed her arm and said, 'It is kind of draughty in here.' Both of them sat concentrating, waiting. *Now, it's now or never.* Elspeth scanned the room for anything delicate enough for her to move. She managed a slight quivering of Valentina's spoon against her teacup. The twins sat watching it, looking at each other, then back to the spoon. Elspeth illuminated the light bulbs in the wall sconces. The room was bright and the twins didn't see her do it, so she went back to rattling the spoon.

'Well?' said Valentina.

Julia said, 'I don't know. What do you think?' *Humour her.*

'Something's going on.'

'Ghosts?'

Valentina shrugged. Elspeth felt a surge of delight: *We're on the verge.* Valentina said, 'It's happy.'

'How do you know?' Julia asked.

'Because I suddenly felt happy, except I'm not happy. It was like it came from outside me.'

'At least it's not a mean ghost. You know, like in *Poltergeist*, where they put the house on top of the cemetery,' Julia said. She looked at Valentina doubtfully.

'You think it's something from the cemetery?' Valentina imagined a vaporous slimy dead thing climbing over the cemetery wall, up the side of the house and into their flat. 'Ugh.' She stood up, ready to flee.

'This is getting weird,' Julia said. 'Let's go out.' Julia could see that the Mouse was freaking; it would be better to get moving, to go outside.

Valentina said, 'We're going out, ghost. Please don't follow us, I hate it when you do that.'

What are you talking about? I never leave the flat. Elspeth watched the twins as they dressed and then followed them to the front door. Valentina said, 'Bye, ghost,' in a voice tinged with hostility, and let the door slam in Elspeth's face. She tried not to take it personally.

The following night it snowed. Valentina and Julia walked carefully down the icy path that led from South Grove to Vautravers. There was only half an inch of snow, but they were wearing smooth-soled leather shoes, and the path descended at an angle that made walking without traction an adventure. They were discussing whether clearing the path was their problem or their neighbours'. St Michael's wall threw the path into shadow. Above them the night sky was bright; the full moon and the snow had turned Highgate Village into a glittering fairyland. Julia was smoking a cigarette. Its orange tip floated a few inches from her shadowed face, bobbing along as they walked, then arcing down as Julia took it from her lips and blew the invisible smoke above her head.

Valentina was annoyed; Julia would smell like smoke in bed, and her breath would reek in the morning. But she didn't say anything. Valentina figured if she kept quiet about it, Julia wouldn't start smoking all the time just to bug her. Just then Julia inhaled too deeply and had to stop and cough for a minute. Valentina stood staring past Julia's hacking frame and it was then that she saw a small white thing scurrying through the ivy, straight up the church's wall. It was about the size of a squirrel, and Valentina wondered if they had white squirrels here in London. Then she thought of the ghost, and her throat contracted. The thing darted towards the top of the wall and then seemed to hang there, as though it knew it was being watched. Julia stopped coughing and straightened up.

'Look,' Valentina whispered, pointing. The white thing heaved itself onto the top of the wall, and as it stood up silhouetted the twins saw that it was a cat, a little cat: a kitten. It stretched itself and sat down on the wall. It looked down at them, scorning their inferior position. The wall was fifteen feet high, so the kitten appeared both small and incongruous.

'Whoa,' said Julia. 'Can cats *do* that? It's like a monkey.'

Valentina thought about a white tiger they had seen once in a circus. It had placed its paw on the shoulder of its keeper so gently, as though it meant to dance with him. The tiger had walked on a tightrope ten feet off the ground.

'It's the Death-Defying Kitten,' Valentina said. 'Do you think it lives in the cemetery?'

'It's the Little Kitten of Death,' said Julia. 'Hi, Little Kitten of Death!' She made what were meant to be cat-calling noises – *sk-sk-sk* – but the kitten shrugged itself and disappeared over the wall. They could hear it thrashing through the ivy on the other side.

When they got home, Valentina put an old chipped teacup full of milk and a saucer of tuna fish out on the dining-room balcony. Julia noticed it the next morning at breakfast.

'What's that for?'

'The Little Kitten of Death. I want it to come up to us.'

Julia rolled her eyes. 'More likely you'll just get raccoons. Or those foxes.'

'I don't think they climb like that.'

'Raccoons climb anywhere they please,' Julia said, munching her buttered toast.

The tuna and milk sat there all day, attracting a few curious birds. Valentina snuck into the dining room a few times to see if anything had visited, but the cup and saucer sat untouched until dinner.

'That's gonna attract ants if you leave it there long enough,' said Julia.

'It's winter. All the ants are hibernating,' said Valentina. Later she dumped the milk down the sink, washed the cup and refilled it with fresh milk; likewise the tuna. She put the cup and saucer back in their positions on the balcony and went to bed.

The following morning Valentina opened the French windows to the balcony and inspected the cup and saucer. She was pleased to see that something had been at them: the tuna was gone and the milk was only about half as full as it had been the night before. She removed the dishes before Julia came in. That night she filled them and put them on the balcony, turned out the lights and sat on the floor of the dining room, waiting.

She could hear Julia moving around the flat. At first she was just moving: undressing for bed, washing her face, brushing her teeth. Then she began moving through the apartment in search of Valentina. 'Mouse?' Julia's footsteps went down the hall and into the front of the flat. 'Mouse?' Valentina sat silent, as though they were playing hide-and-seek. Julia was walking along the hall, she was outside the dining room. *Warmer, warmer.* 'Mouse? Where are you?' She opened the door and saw Valentina sitting in the pool of moonlight beside the French windows. *Hot.* 'What are you doing?'

'*Ssh.* I'm waiting for the kitten,' Valentina whispered.

'*Ohh.* Can I wait too?' Valentina wondered how it was possible for Julia's whispering to be louder than her normal speaking voice.

'Okay,' Valentina replied, 'but you have to be totally silent.' The twins sat side by side on the floor. Neither of them had a watch. Time passed.

Julia stretched out on the floor and fell asleep. It was cold in the room, and colder on the floor. Julia was wearing sweatpants and a long-sleeved Wilco T-shirt she had stolen from Luke Brenner, a boy she'd had a crush on in high school. Valentina thought about getting some pillows and blankets for Julia, who looked uncomfortable. Valentina was fully dressed, but her hands and feet and nose were cold. She considered making herself a cup of tea. She got up and left the room.

When Valentina came back with the tea, the pillows and the blankets, Julia was awake. She put her finger to her lips as Valentina came in. There was a rustling noise, as though something was swimming through dry leaves. Valentina sank to the floor, cushioned in pillows. She set the tea down silently.

Julia looked over at her twin, whose eyes shone in the half-shadow. Valentina hadn't washed her hair that day, and it hung lank and darkish. Valentina breathed deeply, focused on the cup and saucer. Julia smiled and looked at the cup and saucer too. She loved it when Valentina wanted something badly.

The noises came closer, then stopped. The twins were still. Everything paused, and then the white kitten launched itself from the wall onto the balcony.

It was small and thin. The twins could see its ribs. The kitten had immense, bat-like ears. Its fur was matted and short. But somehow it was not pathetic; it came off as determined. There was nothing especially preternatural about it. It was businesslike, and immediately ran to the saucer to gulp down the tuna fish. The twins could see its sides working as it fed. Valentina thought of the jellyfish she had once seen washed up on a Florida beach. The kitten was so thin she felt as though she could see all its internal organs. It was a female kitten. Valentina was entranced.

The kitten finished eating and sat cleaning herself. She looked at them briefly (or in their direction; Valentina wasn't sure the kitten could see them, since the moon had moved and they now sat in shadow). Then she hopped off the balcony and rustled away.

Julia held out her palm, and Valentina high-fived her. 'That was really cool, Mouse. Are you going to keep feeding her?'

Valentina smiled. 'I'm going to adopt her. Before you know it she'll be wearing a collar and sitting on my lap.'

'But don't you think she's a little . . . feral? What if she's not litter-box trained?'

Valentina shot Julia a look. 'She's a kitten. She'll learn.'

The scene was repeated on subsequent nights. Valentina went to Sainsbury's and bought tins of cat food and a litter box. Each night she sat and waited for the Little Kitten of Death to arrive. Usually she sat well back from the French windows and simply watched. After five nights of this she left the windows slightly open, and tried to entice the kitten inside, but this only frightened it, and Valentina had to start again. The kitten was truly wild, and would not be coaxed.

'I thought she'd be sitting on your lap by now,' Julia teased.

'You try,' retorted Valentina.

Julia gave it some thought, and that night she showed up in the dining room with a spool of thread from Elspeth's sewing box. She waited for the kitten to finish her meal, then rolled the spool out onto the balcony. The kitten eyed it suspiciously. Julia tugged a bit on the thread. The kitten put out a tentative paw. Soon the kitten was chasing the spool across the balcony, madly pouncing and hopping, waiting for the next tug on the thread. But as soon as Julia pulled the spool into the room, the kitten looked up, saw Julia and darted off the balcony into the ivy.

'Nice try,' Valentina said. She was secretly pleased that the kitten had not come in for Julia either, though by now Valentina wanted the kitten so badly that it almost wouldn't have mattered.

In the end, it was neither Valentina nor Julia who lured the Little Kitten of Death indoors. One Tuesday night in late

February, Valentina prepared the kitten's food and was nego-
tiating the dining-room door with the tray in her hands when
she heard something skittering, ivy rustling. The French
windows were ajar, and cold air flowed into the room. Out
on the balcony the kitten frisked and pounced. The spool of
thread jerked and rolled, controlled by an imperceptible hand:
now just outside the white kitten's grasp, now flicking across
the balcony, checked by the kitten's spread paw. Valentina
stood still. The spool of thread spun into the space between
one of the doors and the sill. It rocked there, enticingly. The
kitten hesitated. It gathered itself, and pounced. Its
momentum sent it scooting forward into the room. The door
shut behind it.

Valentina and the kitten stared at each other, equally
shocked. They recovered at the same moment. Valentina put
the tray on the floor. The kitten began to run back and forth,
scrambling on the parquet floor for an escape. Valentina shut
the dining-room door and put her back against it.

'Who's there?' she said. She meant it to sound normal,
but her voice came out squeaky. 'Who is it?' The spool of
thread sat immobile on the floor. Everything in the room was
still, except the kitten, who flattened herself under the skirts
of the ottoman and hid. Valentina stood listening, or rather,
feeling the room with her body, trying to discern whether there
was anything there. But she was shaking, and she couldn't
feel anything besides the cold air and the kitten's fright. Then
something pushed on the other side of the door she was
leaning against. Valentina went weak.

'Mouse?' It was only Julia. Valentina let out her breath

and opened the door a crack. 'Come in quick,' she said. Julia did, slipping through six inches of open door and pushing it closed. 'Did you catch her?' Julia asked, her face alight.

'No,' said Valentina. 'The ghost caught her.' She expected Julia to be scornful, but Julia looked at Valentina and saw that she was shaking. Julia flipped the light switch and the dining room filled with the weak light of the chandelier.

'C'mere,' said Julia. She pulled out one of the spindly chairs that clustered around the dining-room table and Valentina sat down on it. Julia glanced around the room. 'So if the ghost caught her, where is she?'

'She's under that ottoman.'

Julia got down on her hands and knees in front of the ottoman and carefully lifted the fringe. She saw a small animal with glowing green eyes that bared its teeth and hissed at her. 'She's all yours,' said Julia.

Valentina smiled. 'Here, put the tuna close to the ottoman. Maybe she'll come out to eat.'

Julia did this. 'Hey,' she said, 'how did the ghost do it?' She had decided to put aside her disbelief in the ghost for the moment. Julia liked the idea of a ghost that made itself useful.

'The ghost did it just the same way you did, only the kitten couldn't see the ghost, so she just pounced right into the room and then the ghost shut the door.'

'So maybe that means the ghost watches us?' Julia was getting creeped out in spite of herself. 'Because otherwise how would the ghost even know you *wanted* the kitten? Did you leave the spool of thread here, or was it in the sewing box?'

'No, it was here.'

'Hmm.' Julia was pacing back and forth with her hands clasped behind her back. Valentina thought of a Sherlock Holmes movie they had seen over and over on Channel Nine when they were kids. Holmes was always pacing. Valentina half-expected Julia to say, *It's elementary, my dear Watson*, but Julia only sat down on the floor and stared at the ottoman, frowning. 'Do you think the ghost is still here?'

Valentina looked around. There weren't very many places a ghost could be in here; the dining-room was somewhat bare. 'I guess,' she said. 'But the ghost is mostly a *feeling*, at least before tonight. It's not like I've ever *seen* it. And I don't *feel* it right now.'

Elspeth stood on top of the dining-room table. She was wearing a blue chiffon cocktail dress and spiked heels with fishnet stockings. Elspeth delighted in the fact that she could walk on the smooth wood of the table without marring it. She was also tremendously pleased that she had caught the kitten, and that Valentina had seen her do it. *That's it, then. I've done it! They've got to believe in me now.*

The Little Kitten of Death sat under the ottoman, enraged. She knew that there was tuna quite close by, but she did not want to give anyone the satisfaction of seeing her eat it. After a while, Julia grew bored with watching the ottoman and went to bed. Valentina put a litter box in the dining room, hoping that the kitten wouldn't pee all over everything. She turned out the lights and also went to bed. Elspeth sat on the table, waiting.

'*Sk-sk-sk*,' she said, knowing the kitten couldn't hear her.

After half an hour of complete silence, the kitten crept out and looked around, circling the room, hunting for a way out. Elspeth hopped off the table and sat on the ottoman. She waited for the kitten to calm down, stroked it as it gulped down the tuna. It didn't notice.

Jessica stood in front of the Eastern Cemetery's gates on a brisk Sunday in early March, watching the visitors assembled before the main gate on the Western side. They were an unpromising lot: an American couple wearing intimidating trainers and impressive cameras; a quiet, middle-aged man with a receding hairline and binoculars; three young Japanese men in baggy denim trousers and baseball caps; a woman with a rather aerodynamic-looking pram, and a stout man with an enormous backpack, who paced back and forth with bouncy energy.

A black van sped along Swains Lane. The gilt, circus-poster-style lettering on its side said only TEMERITY.

Indeed, thought Jessica. She checked her watch. It was quarter to three. She glanced behind her at Kate, a round, pleasant, American volunteer who was chatting with some grave owners about the renovations to the Eastern Cemetery's wall. When Jessica returned her gaze to the group at the gate she saw that they had been joined by two girls dressed from head to toe in white. The girls stood by themselves, holding hands. They wore white hooded sweatshirts with fur trim, white miniskirts, leggings and boots. Their white knitted caps were almost the same colour as their hair. The girls had their backs to Jessica, but she knew without seeing their faces that they must be twins. *How darling they are.* She wondered if they realised how muddy the cemetery paths were, and whether they were younger than sixteen.

Julia and Valentina stood in front of the gates, shifting from foot to foot and shivering. Julia wondered where everyone was; all was quiet inside the gates. She could see a wide court-yard beyond the gatehouse and a colonnade which extended in a half-circle around it. She heard someone using a walkie-talkie, but there were no people in sight. Across the road was the other half of the cemetery, where Karl Marx was buried. It looked more open, more like a regular American cemetery. The guidebook said that the Western Cemetery was more interesting, but could only be visited on the tour. Anyway, it was the Western side that the twins' windows overlooked.

Jessica crossed Swains' Lane, strode through the little crowd and unlocked the massive gates. She was dressed entirely in shades of violet and mauve, and wore a hat that Valentina instantly coveted, a large-brimmed felt affair with a sweeping black feather tucked in the band. Valentina and Julia's first impression was of royalty, a duchess, perhaps, who had come to the cemetery for the afternoon to cut a ribbon or visit a loved one and had stayed on to help out. This notion was not immediately dispelled when she spoke. 'Do come in now, my dears. Has everyone read the notices? Right, please leave *all* luggage *in* the office. I'm *terribly* sorry, but no children under the age of eight are allowed in the Western Cemetery. Photographs may be taken for Personal Use Only. *This* way, please, kindly *perch* yourselves in front of the War Memorial on the far side of the courtyard there. We'll be *right* with you.' The twins obediently sat on a bench and waited.

Robert walked out of the office with the ticket box, distracted by a crossword clue James had just read to him. He joined Jessica and they crossed the courtyard together. He saw the twins and his stomach clenched. The sensation reminded him of stage fright; then he realised it was guilt.

'Don't charge them,' he said to Jessica.

'Why ever not?'

'They're grave owners.'

'Surely n—oh,' she said, looking more carefully. 'I see.' They continued walking. 'Will you be all right, then? Shall I ask Kate to give the tour?'

'Don't be silly. I've got to meet them eventually.'

The twins watched them arrive. Julia elbowed Valentina. 'Isn't that the guy you met on the tube?' she whispered. Valentina nodded. She watched Robert tearing tickets, Jessica accepting £5 from each person. The twins were at the end of the row of benches. When she had taken the money from the American couple Jessica closed her money box and winked at them. Julia held out £10, but Jessica shook her head and smiled. The American woman gave them an annoyed look. Julia squeezed Valentina's hand.

'Welcome to Highgate Cemetery,' Jessica said. 'Robert will be your guide. He is one of our most Learned Guides, an historian of the Victorian era, and is writing a book about this cemetery. *All* of our work is done on a voluntary basis, and every year we must raise over three hundred and fifty thousand pounds *just* to keep the cemetery open.' Jessica flirted with them as she spoke, and exhibited the green box. 'As you leave, a volunteer will be stationed at the gate with this green box, and *any* help you can give will be Much Appreciated.' Robert watched the tourists fidget. Jessica wished them a Pleasant Tour and went back to the office. She felt a flutter of excitement. *Why?* She stood at the office window and watched Robert gather his group in front of the Colonnade. He stood two steps up and spoke to them, looking down, gesturing. From where they stood, the tourists could not see anything but greenery and the steps. *Those girls look extraordinarily like Elspeth. How amazing life is. I hope he'll be all right. He looked a bit pale.*

Robert tried to clear his mind. He felt as though he were watching himself, as though he had separated into two Roberts, one of whom was calmly giving a tour, the other mute with nerves, trying to think what he might say to the twins. *Bloody hell, you'd think you were seventeen. You don't have to talk to them. They'll talk to you. Wait.*

'At the beginning of the nineteenth century,' Robert began, 'London's graveyards were shockingly overcrowded. Burial in churchyards had been the custom for hundreds of years. People were flocking to the city: there was an industrial revolution going on, and the factories needed workers. There was no space left to bury anyone, yet people died anyway. In 1800, London's population was approximately one million. By the middle of the century it was well over two million. The churchyards couldn't keep up with the relentless pace of death.

'The churchyards were also a health hazard. They contaminated the ground water and caused epidemics of typhoid and cholera. Since there was no space for more graves, corpses had to be disinterred so that the newly dead could be buried. If you've read your Dickens, you know what I'm talking about: elbows poking out of the ground, grave robbers stealing the dead to sell them to the medical schools. It was an absolute shambles.

'In 1832, Parliament passed a bill allowing the establishment of private, commercial cemeteries. In the next nine years, seven cemeteries were opened, situated in a ring around what was then the edge of the city. These became known as the Magnificent Seven: Kensal Green, West Norwood, Highgate, Nunhead, Brompton, Abney Park and Tower Hamlets. Highgate was opened in 1839, and it quickly became the most desirable burial ground in London. Let's go up the steps, and you'll see why.'

The twins were at the back of the group, so all they saw was other people's legs as they ascended. When they got to the top, Robert was standing with the group ranged in a circle around him. They saw a dense clamour of large, tilting graves, crowded and encroached on by trees and greenery. Valentina had a powerful feeling of recognition. *I've been here before! – but not really; maybe I dreamed it?* A crow flew close over their heads and swooped across the courtyard, landing on the apex of the chapels' roof. Valentina wondered what that would be like, to fly brazenly through the cemetery; she wondered what the crow thought about the whole thing. *It's so strange, to put people in the ground and put stones on top of them.* She felt a surge of wonder that people should all agree to be put in the ground together.

Robert said, 'We're standing on top of the Colonnade.

If you'll look towards the chapels – there, where you came in: there were two chapels, Anglican and Dissenters', joined together in one building, quite unique. We are in the Western Cemetery, the original part. There are seventeen acres, and two of those are set aside for Dissenters – that is, Baptists, Presbyterians, Sandemanians and other Protestant sects. Highgate was so popular that by 1854 they needed to expand, and so the London Cemetery Company bought the twenty acres across Swains Lane to create the Eastern Cemetery. This led to a problem. Once the service had been conducted in the Anglican chapel, how were they to get the coffin over to the Eastern side without taking it off consecrated ground? They couldn't consecrate Swains Lane, so instead they used typical Victorian ingenuity and dug a tunnel under the road. At the end of the service, the coffin would be lowered by a pneu-matic lift down into the tunnel. The pall-bearers would meet it and take it across, where it would ascend on the Eastern side in a touching allusion to the Resurrection.'

Julia thought, *He looks really pleased with himself, like he invented the whole thing.* She felt kind of crabby, cold and damp. She glanced at Valentina, who was staring at the guide with rapt attention. Robert ran his eyes over the group. Most of them had their cameras ready, itching to take photos, to move on. He saw Valentina staring at him and turned to the grave they were standing next to.

'This grave belongs to James William Selby, who was, in his day, a famous coachman. He was fond of driving fast and in all weathers. The whip and horn signify his profes-sion, the inverted horseshoes tell us that his luck has run out.

In 1888 Selby accepted a wager to drive from London to Brighton in less than eight hours. He made it in seven hours and fifty minutes, using seven teams of horses. He won a thousand pounds, but died five months later. We speculate that his winnings might have been used to buy him this very handsome memorial. Mind the path — it's fairly bad today.'

Robert turned and began walking uphill. He could hear the tourists scrambling after him. The main path was rocky, muddy and full of tree roots and holes. He could hear cameras clicking like digital insects as they walked. His stomach was churning. *I wonder if I could park them all at Comfort's Corners and just go and quietly puke in the shrubbery?* He soldiered on. He showed them the Gothic-style grave with the empty stone chair, signifying that the occupant was gone, never to return. He led them to the tomb of Sir Loftus Otway, an enormous family mausoleum which had once featured large panels of glass: 'You could look down into the tomb and see the coffins. This wasn't for our voyeuristic pleasure, mind you — many Victorians hated the thought of being buried six feet under, and quite a number of the burials in this cemetery are above ground . . .' He told them about the Friends of Highgate Cemetery, how they had saved Highgate. 'Before the First World War the staff included twenty-eight gardeners. Everything was tidy, spacious and serene. But all the able-bodied men went to fight, and things were never quite the same. The vegetation began to take over, they ran out of space to make new graves, the money stopped coming in . . . and in 1975 the Western side was padlocked and essentially abandoned to satanists, nutters, vandals, Johnny Rotten—'

'Who's he?' one of the young Japanese men wanted to know.

'Lead singer of the Sex Pistols, used to live nearby, in Finchley Park. Right, so you may have noticed that the neighbourhood surrounding this cemetery is a bit posh, and the neighbours got alarmed about the grave-desecrating and the wrong element hanging round. A group of local people got together and bought Highgate Cemetery for fifty quid. Then they went about trying to put it right again. And they invented what they call "Managed Neglect", which means just what it sounds like: they didn't try to make it all tidy and imitate what the Victorians had done. They work things in such a way that you see what time and nature have made of the place, but they don't let it go so far that it gets dangerous. It's a museum, in a sense, but it's also a working Christian burial ground.' Robert glanced at his watch. He needed to get them moving; Jessica had spoken to him only yesterday about Getting the Tour Back in a Timely Manner. 'This way.'

He led them at a faster pace to Comfort's Corners, then began to tell the story of Elizabeth Siddal Rossetti. As always, Robert had to fight the urge to tell the group everything he knew; they would be here for days, gradually collapsing with fatigue and hunger while he went on and on. *They mainly want to see the place. Don't bore them with too much detail.* He walked them to one of his favourites, a ledger-style tomb with a bas-relief of a weeper, a woman sitting up at night with the coffin. 'Before modern medical technology, people had a difficult time determining when someone was really dead. You might think that death would be pretty blatant, but there were a number of famous cases in which a dead body sat up and went on living, and many Victorians got the jim-jams just thinking about the possibility of being buried alive.

'Being a practical people, they attempted to find solutions to the problem. The Victorians invented a system of bells with strings attached that went through the ground and into the coffin, so if you woke up underground you could pull on your bell till someone came to dig you up. There's no record of anyone being saved by one of these devices. People made all sorts of odd stipulations in their wills, such as asking to be decapitated as insurance against an undesired revival.'

'What about vampires?'

'What *about* vampires?'

'I heard there was a vampire here in the cemetery.'

'No. There were a bunch of attention-seeking idiots who claimed to have seen a vampire. Though some people do say that Bram Stoker was inspired to write *Dracula* by an exhumation here at Highgate.'

Valentina and Julia hung back at the edge of the group. They were having decidedly different experiences. Julia wanted to leave the group and go exploring. She detested lectures and professors and Robert was making her itch. *You're just bloviating. Get on with it.* Valentina was not following Robert's commentary very closely because she was occupied with an

idea that had been nudging at her since Jessica had introduced him: *You're Elspeth's Robert Fanshaw. That's how you knew
us.* She was disquieted by the thought that he must have seen
them before without them knowing. *I should tell Julia.* Valentina
glanced at Julia. *No, better wait. She's in a mood.*

Robert turned and led them further uphill, stopping at
the entrance to the Egyptian Avenue. He waited for the
American couple to catch up; they tended to fall behind as
they tried to photograph everything. *You'll never make it, folks,
there's 52,000 graves in here.* One of the Japanese men said,
'Wow.' He drew it out so that it sounded like *whoooohow.*
Robert loved the drama of the Egyptian Avenue; it looked like
a stage set for *Aida.*

'Highgate Cemetery, in addition to being a Christian burial
ground, was a business venture. In order to make it the most
desirable address for the eminent Victorian dead, it needed
what every posh neighbourhood needs: amenities. In the late
1830s, when Highgate opened, all things Egyptian were quite
popular, and so here we have the Egyptian Avenue. The
entrance is based on a tomb at Luxor. It was originally coloured,
and the Avenue itself was not so dark and gloomy. It was open
to the sky, and there were none of these trees that lean over
it now . . .'

'The mausoleums in the Avenue can hold eight to ten
people. There are shelves inside for the coffins. Note the
inverted torches – the keyholes are upside down as well. The
holes on the bottom of the doors let the gases escape.'

'Gases?' asked the quiet man with the binoculars.

'As the bodies decomposed, they gave off gases. They used

202 · AUDREY NIFFENEGGER

to put candles in there with them to burn it off. Must have
been rather spooky at night.' They went through the Egyptian
Avenue and stood at the other end, the twins hugging themselves for warmth even in the strong sunlight. Robert looked
at them and was hit by a memory of Elspeth standing in
almost the same spot, her face tilted to catch the sun. *Oh, you
. . . He* faltered. Everyone waited for him to continue. *Don't
look at them. Don't think about her.* Robert stared at the ground
for a moment and then pulled himself together.

'We are standing in the Circle of Lebanon. This was the
most coveted address in the cemetery. It gets its name from
the enormous Cedar of Lebanon tree you see up there above
the mausoleums. The tree is approximately three hundred
years old now, but even when Highgate Cemetery was founded
it would have been impressive. The land was originally part
of the estate of the Bishop of London, and when they came
to make the Circle they cut down around the tree; it stands
on what was originally ground level. Imagine trying to shift
all that earth with 1830s equipment. The inner circle was made
first, and it proved so popular that the outer circle was begun
twenty years later. You can see the changing tastes in archi-
tecture, from Egyptian to Gothic.'

Robert led them through the Circle. *This is not getting easier.*
He glanced at his watch and resolved to skip a few graves.

'This is the mausoleum of Mabel Veronica Batten and
her lover, Radclyffe Hall . . . Here we have a columbarium.
The name comes from the Latin *columba*, meaning "dove",
and originally meant compartments for doves to live in . . .
Follow me up these stairs, please . . . Right. This is the grave

of George Wombwell, a famous menagerist. He got his start by buying two boa constrictors from a sailor . . .' Robert skipped over Mrs Henry Wood, the Carter family's faux-Egyptian tomb and Adam Worth and led the visitors around the top of the Circle to admire the view of St Michael's. He then herded them to stand between the Terrace Catacombs and the enormous Beer family tomb. The twins realised that they were looking at the huge mausoleum they could see from their bedroom window. They backed up, trying to see over the Catacombs, but although they could see Martin's flat, their own wasn't visible.

'Julius Beer was a German Jew who arrived in London with no money and made his fortune on the Stock Exchange . . .' Valentina was thinking about the fact that she had never exactly thought about death. The cemetery at home in Lake Forest was tidy and spacious. Jack's parents were buried there in a modest plot with matching pink granite markers. The twins had never met any of their grandparents. *We don't know anyone who died. It's hard to imagine not being here, or Julia not here* . . . She felt a spasm of loneliness, or homesickness — she wasn't sure which. Valentina watched Robert. He was ignoring her; he seemed to be deliberately focusing on the man with the binoculars. *He knew Elspeth. He was her lover. He could tell us about her.*

'. . . Julius Beer was unable to secure a position in Victorian society, because in addition to being a foreigner and Jewish, he had made his money rather than inheriting it. So he erected this rather large mausoleum where no one could possibly miss it. The Beer mausoleum blocks the view if you happen to be promenading on the roof of the Terrace Catacombs, as Victorian ladies liked to do of a Sunday afternoon.' Valentina thought of the green door in their back garden. She imagined herself and Julia wearing crinolines, strolling atop the hundreds of rotting bodies lying in the dark nasty Terrace Catacombs. *Those Victorians sure knew how to have fun.*

Robert led them along paths, past the Dissenters' section; he showed them Thomas Sayers' grave, where Lion the stone dog kept patient vigil; skipped Sir Rowland Hill, inventor of the Uniform Penny Post. He passed the Noblin family mausoleum without comment. Fifty yards on, Robert turned to say something to the group and saw that he had lost Julia and Valentina. They were standing in front of the Noblins, arm in arm, conferring. Robert parked the group in front of Thomas Charles Druce and jogged back to the twins.

'Hello,' he managed.

They went still, like rabbits looked at too directly. Valentina said, 'You're Robert Fanshaw, aren't you?' Julia thought, *What?*

Robert's stomach lurched. 'Yes. That's right.' A look passed between Valentina and Robert that Julia could not interpret. 'We'll talk after the tour, shall we?' he said, and walked with them back to the front of the group. He fumbled through Thomas Charles Druce's exhumation, skipped murder victim Eliza Barrow and also Charles Cruft of dog-show fame. He somewhat regained his form while talking about Elizabeth Jackson and Stephan Geary, then fairly hustled the group down the Cuttings Path. Jessica was waiting for them at the gate with the green box. Robert said to her, 'I'm just going to take the twins back and show them their family grave.' He half-hoped Jessica would refuse him, but she only smiled and waved him along.

'Don't be long,' Jessica said. 'You know we're short-handed today.' As Robert walked towards Valentina and Julia he saw them framed together before the arch over the Colonnade stairs, two white statues radiant against the gloom. It seemed to him inevitable that he should meet them here.

'Come on, then,' he said. They followed him, alert and curious. He felt their eyes on him as he led them up the stairs and along the paths. The twins grew uneasy; on the tour Robert Fanshaw had seemed garrulous, eager to please; now he led them through the cemetery without comment. The sounds of the cemetery itself filled the silence: the squish of their boots on the path, the whisper and roar of the wind in the trees. Birds, traffic. Robert's overcoat flapped behind him and Valentina recalled the retreating figure she had seen that day by the canal. She began to be frightened. *No one knows we're here.* Then she remembered the duchess at the gate and felt reassured. They came to the Noblin mausoleum.

'So,' Robert said, feeling like an absurd parody of a Highgate tour guide, 'this is your family's grave. It belongs to you, and you can come and visit whenever you like, whenever the cemetery is open. We'll make you a grave owners' pass. There's a key in Elspeth's desk.'

'A key to what?' Julia asked.

'This door. You also have a key to the door between our back garden and the cemetery, though we're asked by the cemetery staff not to use it.'

'Do you go in?'

'No.' His heart was pounding.

Valentina said, 'We've been wondering about you. We wondered — why we didn't see you. We thought maybe you were out of town or something—'

'Martin said you weren't,' interrupted Julia.

'So we were confused, because Mr Roche said you would help us . . .' Valentina looked up at Robert, but he was looking at his feet and it seemed like a long time before he replied.

'I'm sorry,' he said.

He was unable to look at the twins, and they pitied him, although neither was at all sure why. Julia was amazed to see this man who had been so voluble, so eager to tell them more than anyone could possibly want to know about the cemetery, now standing inarticulate and frightened. His hair hung over his face; his posture was abject. Valentina thought, *He's just very shy — he's afraid of us.* Because Valentina was shy herself — because she had spent her life with an extrovert who never tired of mocking her timidity — since she had never met a person who seemed normal and was abruptly revealed to be acutely inhibited; because there was a profound intimacy in observing Robert's fear; because she was emboldened by Julia's presence: Valentina stepped closer to Robert and put her hand on his arm. Robert looked at her over the rims of his glasses.

'It's okay,' she said. He felt, without being able to express it to himself, that something lost had been restored to him.

'Thank you,' he replied. He said it quietly but with such intensity that Valentina fell in love with him, though she had no name for the feeling and nothing to compare it to. They might have stood that way for a long while, but Julia said, 'Um, maybe we should go back,' and Robert said, 'Yes, I told Jessica we wouldn't be long.' Valentina felt as though the world had paused. Now it continued; they walked together side by side down the Colonnade Path.

Julia asked Robert about his thesis, and his answer carried them back to the cemetery's gate. As they passed the office door Jessica popped out; Robert guessed that she had been watching for them. She took the twins' hands in hers and said, 'Elspeth was *very* dear to us all. We're *delighted* to finally meet you both. I do hope you'll come and visit often.'

'We will,' said Julia. She liked the idea of getting behind the scenes, of finding out what went on in the cemetery when the tourists left. Valentina met Jessica's eyes and smiled. Robert was standing slightly behind Jessica, watching them. 'Bye,' Valentina said as she and Julia slipped through the gate. Valentina's face showed Robert something that filled him with apprehension – her face mirrored his own feelings. He understood and he didn't want to know.

'Goodbye, my dears,' said Jessica. She turned the key in the lock and watched as the twins walked up Swains Lane. *Why so worried?* she asked herself. *They're darling.* Robert had disappeared into the office. She found him counting out the change into little plastic bags.

'Are you all right?' she asked him.

'I'm fine,' he said, without looking at her. She was about to question him further when the walkie-talkie squawked out Kate's request: more tickets for the Eastern gate. Jessica grabbed a book of tickets and left Robert to his mood. The rest of that Sunday was a blur of guides and visitors, counting receipts and closing; by the time she thought about Robert again they were standing by the Western gates, locking up.

Phil and some of the younger guides were headed up the hill to have a pint at the Gatehouse. 'D'you want to come along?' Phil asked Robert.

'No,' Robert said. He wanted a drink, but he didn't want to talk to anyone. He wanted to think about the afternoon, to relive it, to make it come out differently, to arrive at some other conclusion. 'No, I think I'm coming down with something.' He turned and walked off, startling the rest of them with his abrupt departure.

'What's eating him?' Kate asked Jessica.

Jessica shook her head. 'With our Robert one never quite knows,' she replied. 'It's probably just Elspeth.' Everyone agreed that yes, it was probably Elspeth. They went up the hill to the Gatehouse and gossiped about Robert for a while, then lost interest and turned to the more urgent pleasures of trading stories about odd things that had happened that day on their tours and trying to outdo each other in their knowledge of obscure cemetery anecdotes. Kate drove Jessica home, and they agreed that something was definitely amiss with Robert and that Elspeth was at the bottom of it. Having settled that, they turned their attention to Monday's funerals.

Robert went home and gathered a glass, a bottle of whisky and the key to the green door, then let himself into the cemetery. He didn't venture forth but sat down with his back to the wall and poured himself some whisky. He sat there staring absently at the top of Julius Beer's mausoleum and drinking until evening fell. Then he returned unsteadily to his flat and went to bed.

Days went by and nothing much happened. Julia and Valentina tried to civilise the Kitten, cajoling her with food and little balls of aluminium foil, sitting in the dining room chatting to her while she regarded them sceptically from underneath a chair. Elspeth played with her when the twins were out or asleep, glad to have someone to engage with, even if that someone was an angry white kitten. Gradually the Kitten became less outraged and was allowed into other parts of the flat. She occasionally let herself be petted. To Elspeth's dismay she shredded the spine of a Hogarth Press *To the Lighthouse* and the back of the sofa. Valentina was delighted with the Kitten's progress and looked forward to what she described to Julia as 'total kitten happiness' in the near future.

The twins saw nothing of Robert, though they sometimes heard him showering or watching TV. He was hunkered down in his flat, slogging through a chapter about Highgate Cemetery as nature reserve. Every afternoon he went to the cemetery and took notes while Jessica and Molly tried to teach him about the flora and fauna. They chivvied him into going on nature walks and pointed out demure wild flowers that wouldn't bloom for months, taught him their Latin names, tut-tutted over invasive species, reminisced about long-ago cemetery landscaping triumphs and exclaimed over rare spiders. Robert wallowed in his own ignorance and tried to keep up with the two of them as they briskly dragged him into distant recesses of the cemetery. Molly and Jessica beamed at him whenever he managed to ask an intelligent question. It kept his mind off the twins, and he slept better for being thoroughly exhausted.

Julia visited Martin, but he politely asked her to come back in a few days as he was behind with his work. The moment she left he went back to cleaning the bathroom-floor tiles with straight bleach and a toothbrush. Marijke's birthday was coming up and Martin was worrying over whether he would be able to call her, and how he might send her a present. These problems had absorbed him for days, but he didn't find himself any nearer to solving them. More cleaning might do the trick.

Elspeth had relented in her haunting of the twins, at least for the time being, and steered clear of them. There was no point in forcing them to acknowledge her existence if they disliked her, and they had made it obvious that they were sceptical (Julia) or hostile (Valentina). Elspeth kept to herself, practised her peculiar pursuits and waited. So Valentina found herself suddenly free. Robert had ceased to shadow the twins, and Valentina no longer had the feeling of being watched on the street; she began to relax and enjoy their outings again.

The twins very seldom bought anything when they went shopping. They had a flat full of Elspeth's belongings, which they treated as though it were a combination archaeological dig/magic hat; whatever they required seemed already to be somewhere at hand. They made their life out of Elspeth's, as if they were hunter-gatherers living on top of ruined Troy.

Today they were in Harvey Nichols. The shop girls had

them pegged as non-customers, so service was slow, but the twins strutted about in Prada and Stella McCartney all afternoon with perfect contentment. In the dressing room Valentina turned things inside out, meditated on garment construction and fabrics. Julia watched her, happy in Valentina's happiness. A plan (not even a plan; a need, really) had been forming in Valentina's mind for some time, and later when they sat upstairs in the café drinking tea she said to Julia, 'I want to go to Central Saint Martins College and take some classes.'

'Classes? Why?'

'I want to be a fashion designer.' Valentina tried to smile confidently, as though she were presenting Julia with a delightful gift. 'Alexander McQueen went there.'

'Um. What am I supposed to do while you're doing that?'

'I don't know.' Valentina paused. She thought, *I don't care. Do whatever you want.* She wasn't sure whether she needed Julia's consent to take money out of their account. She would ask Mr Roche. Valentina didn't want to argue about it, so she said, 'You could be my manager?'

Julia pouted. 'That sounds kind of boring.'

'Well, don't, then.'

They sat in silence, staring off in opposite directions. The café had high ceilings, numerous small tables full of mums and prams, a safe ordinary clatter of silverware and dishes, laughing female conversation all around them. Valentina felt as though she had finally thrown down the gauntlet; she imagined a heavily fortified glove lying between them among the tea things. *I always back down, but not this time.* She said, 'We have to work someday. And you promised we'd go back to school when we got here.' Julia glared at her but didn't reply.

The waiter brought the bill. Julia paid. Valentina said, 'Let's look up the University of the Arts on the Web when we get home. Maybe there's something you would like.'

Julia shrugged. They walked through the shop without speaking and out onto Knightsbridge. Valentina thought the tube ought to be just to the left, but Julia turned right and began walking very quickly. They passed Hyde Park Corner tube station. Valentina said, 'There's the tube,' but Julia ignored her. They crossed into Mayfair and began to zigzag, making random turns, Julia leading, Valentina trotting after her. Valentina knew they would continue walking until Julia decided to speak to her again; meanwhile they would get thoroughly lost.

It was rush hour and the streets were crowded. The evening was clear and cold. Valentina saw familiar shops, squares, street names, but she had no internal map of London, no way to organise her surroundings; that was Julia's job, Valentina had not bothered to pay attention. Valentina began to be frightened. She wondered if she should just walk off and find a tube station; they were in central London; there ought to be stations all around. *I should leave her and go home.* Valentina had never tried that, abandoning Julia in the middle of a fight. She experienced a qualm at the thought of taking the tube by herself – she had never done it without Julia. Then she saw the familiar red, white and blue sign: OXFORD CIRCUS.

The twins crossed Regent Street and were immediately caught in a crush of people trying to enter the tube station.

There were currents within the crowd, and for a few minutes they found themselves walking against the stream. Julia was struck by how calm everyone was, as though they all did this every day at 6.30 p.m.; perhaps they did. Valentina was behind her, and Julia could hear her breathing hard. She reached her hand back and Valentina took it. 'It's okay, Mouse,' she said. They found the current of people moving in the direction they wanted to go. Now they were not pushed and jostled so much.

Valentina felt as though she were drowning. She could not draw a breath; she was pressed by people on all sides. All thought of going into the tube station vanished. She wanted only to get out of the crowd. Elbows and backpacks jabbed her. She heard the buses and cars going by a few feet away. People muttered their annoyance to themselves and each other, but to Valentina all the noise seemed muted.

There was a surge in the direction of the tube entrance. Julia was pushed forward, Valentina backwards. Julia felt Valentina's hand pull out of her grip. 'Mouse!' Valentina lost her footing and fell sideways into the oncoming people. A man said, 'Whoops! She's down! Stand back, please!' in a jocular tone, but no one could move. It was like being in a mosh pit. Hands groped for Valentina; she was put back on her feet. 'All right, then, luv?' someone asked. She shook her head; she could not answer. She heard Julia calling her name but couldn't see her. Valentina tried to catch her breath. Her throat closed; she tried to suck in air very slowly. She was walking, the crowd pushed her forward.

Julia stood outside the crowd, panicking. 'Valentina!' No answer. She dived into the crush again but could only see the people next to her. *Ohmigod.* She saw a flash of bright hair and lunged towards it. 'Watch it there.' Valentina saw Julia and put her hand to her throat. *I can't breathe.* Julia grabbed her, began to elbow and push at the people in front of them. 'She's having an asthma attack, let us out!' The crowd tried to part. No one could see what was happening. At last the twins spilled out onto the Oxford Street pavement.

Valentina leaned against a brightly lit shop window full of cheap shoes, gasping. Julia ransacked Valentina's purse. 'Where's your inhaler?' Valentina shook her head. *I don't know.* A concerned knot of bystanders watched. 'Here, use mine.' A teenaged boy, long hair occluding his face, skateboard in one hand, proffered an inhaler with the other. Valentina took it, sucked at it. Her throat opened slightly. She nodded at the boy, who stood with his free hand slightly extended, as though he might need to catch her. Julia watched Valentina breathe, tried to make her breathe by breathing deeply herself, willed Valentina to breathe. Valentina took a few more puffs on the inhaler, stood with her hand pressed against her sternum, breathing. 'Thanks,' she said eventually, handing it back to the boy.

'Sure, any time.'

The little crowd that had been watching dispersed. Valentina wanted to hide. She wanted to get out of the cold. Julia said, 'I'm going to get us a cab,' and strode off. It seemed like hours before Valentina heard her calling, 'Mouse! Over here!' and she could climb gratefully into the warmth of the black cab. Valentina plopped down on the seat and began scooping the contents of her handbag onto her lap until she found her inhaler. She sat with the inhaler clutched in her hand, weapon-like. Despair blossomed in her. *This is crazy. I can't spend my whole life as a Mouse.* Valentina glanced over at Julia, who was staring impassively out of the window at slow-moving traffic. *You think I need you. You think I can't leave you.* Valentina looked out at the unfamiliar buildings. London was endless, relentless. *If I had died in that crowd . . . ?* She imagined Julia calling their parents.

Julia looked at her. 'You okay?'

'Yeah.'

'We should get you a doctor.'

'Yeah.'

They rode back to Vautravers in silence. 'You want to look at that website?' Julia asked as they let themselves into the flat.

'No,' said Valentina. 'Never mind.'

Valentina and Julia were puzzled by an empty shelf in Elspeth's office. Since the office was jam-crammed with every conceivable kind of book, knick-knack, writing implement and other things useful and useless, space was in short supply – therefore the existence of a pristine, thoroughly empty shelf was a conundrum. It must have held something once. But what? And who had removed it? The shelf was twelve inches deep and eighteen inches wide. It was the third shelf from the bottom in the bookcase next to Elspeth's desk. Unlike the rest of the office, it had been somewhat recently dusted. There was also a locked drawer in the desk, for which they could find no key.

The former contents of the shelf were now sitting in Robert's flat, along with all the other things he'd removed from Elspeth's, in boxes on the floor next to his bed. He had not touched anything in the boxes except Elspeth's jumper and shoes, which he had placed in their own drawer in his desk. Now and then he would open the drawer and pet them, then close it and go back to his work.

He had placed the boxes on the side of his bed away from the door, so it was possible for him not to look at them for days. He considered putting the boxes in the spare bedroom, but that seemed unfriendly. Eventually he would have to explore the contents. Before Elspeth died he had thought he wanted to read her diaries. He thought he wanted to know everything, be privy to all her secrets. Yet for quite a long time he put off touching the diaries or bringing them into his flat. Now they were here, and still he did not open them. He had his memories, and he did not want them altered or disproved. As a historian he knew that any trove of documents has incendiary potential. So the boxes sat like unexploded ordnance on the floor of his bedroom and Robert did his best to ignore them.

⊷ BIRTHDAY GREETINGS ⊶

It was 12 March, a grey, lowering Saturday; Marijke's fifty-fourth birthday. Martin woke up at six and lay in bed, his mind flitting from happy anticipation (she would expect him to call and must surely answer the phone) to anxious consideration of his birthday tribute to her (a dauntingly complex cryptic crossword in which the first and last letters of each clue made multiple anagrams of her full name and the solution was an anagram of a line from John Donne's 'A Valediction: Forbidding Mourning'). He had given the crossword and her present to Robert, who had promised to send it express. Martin had decided to wait until two to call. It would be three o' clock in Amsterdam; she would have had her lunch and would be in a relaxed, Saturday-afternoon mood. He got out of bed and began to make his way through his morning routine, feeling like an only child waiting for his parents to wake on Christmas morning.

Marijke woke up confused, late in the morning, in weak sunlight that came through the shutters and onto her pillow. *It's my birthday. Lang zal ze leven, hieperderpiep, hoera.* She had no plan for the day, beyond coffee and cake with some friends that evening. She knew Martin would call, and hoped that Theo would – sometimes Theo forgot; he seemed to deliberately cultivate a protective layer of obliviousness. She always called Theo to remind him of Martin's birthday;

perhaps Martin did the same for her? She had dreamt about Martin, a very *aangename* dream of their old *gezellig* flat in St John's Wood. She had been washing dishes and he had come up behind her and kissed the nape of her neck. *Memory or dream?* She imagined his hands on her shoulders, his lips brushing her neck. *Mmm.* Marijke had been policing her erotic imagination since she'd left Martin. Usually she was quick to boot him out of her mind when he tried to sneak in, but this morning, for a birthday treat, she let the dream-memory unfurl.

The package arrived around noon. Marijke put it on her kitchen table and spent some minutes hunting for a Stanley knife as the package was almost completely covered with tape and beseechments to HANDLE WITH CARE. *It looks like it's from an insane person. But he's my insane person, my very own.* She ferreted through the plastic packing and pulled out a fat envelope and a pink box. The pink box contained a pair of cerulean-blue leather gloves. Marijke slipped them on. They fitted perfectly; they were soft as breath. She ran her gloved fingers over the invisible hairs on her arm. The gloves disguised her knobbly knuckles and age spots. She felt as though she'd been given new hands.

The envelope contained a letter and a crossword, with the solution in another, smaller envelope. Marijke opened the smaller envelope straight away; she had no talent for crosswords, and Martin knew this. She could never have begun to solve the masterpieces he made for her each year, and they both understood these birthday crosswords for what they were: a demonstration of devotion, the equivalent of the intricate, eye-popping jumpers Marijke knitted for Martin on his birth-days. Inside the envelope were two stanzas of the Donne poem:

> If they be two, they are two so
>> As stiff twin compasses are two,
> Thy soule the fixt foot, makes no show
>> To move, but doth, if th'other doe.
>
> And though it in the centre sit,
>> Yet when the other far doth rome,
> It leans, and hearkens after it,
>> And growes erect, as that comes home.

Marijke smiled. She opened the letter and a tiny package fell into her blue-gloved hand. She had to take the gloves off to open it. At first she thought it was empty – she shook the package and nothing came out. She probed with a finger, and found two bits of metal and pearl clinging inside. They spilled onto her palm. *Oh, oh! My earrings.* Marijke carried them to the window. She imagined Martin hunting among the boxes for days, excavating layers of plastic-embalmed possessions, just to find her earrings. *Lieve Martin.* She closed her hand around the earrings, closed her eyes and let herself miss him. *All this distance . . .*

She raised her head, looked at her one-room flat. It had been the hayloft of a livery stable in the seventeenth century. It had pitched ceilings, heavy beams, whitewashed walls. Her futon occupied one corner, her clothes hung in another

corner behind a curtain. She had a table with two chairs, a
tiny kitchen, a window that overlooked the little crooked
street, a vase of freesias on the windowsill. She had a
comfortable chair and a lamp. For more than a year now this
room had been her haven, fortress, retreat, her triumphant,
undiscoverable gambit in her marital game of hide-and-seek.
Standing there, clasping the earrings in her hand, Marijke
saw her snug room as a lonely place. *Apartment. A place to be
apart.* She shook her head to change her thoughts and opened
Martin's letter.

> *Lieve Marijke,*
> *Happy birthday, Mistress of my heart. I wish I could see you*
> *today; I wish I could embrace you. But since that isn't*
> *possible, I send you surrogate hands to slip over your own*
> *hands, to lurk in your pockets as you walk through your city,*
> *to warm you, to remind you of blue skies (it's grey here too).*
> *Your loving husband,*
> *Martin*

Perfect, Marijke thought. She arranged the gloves, the
earrings, the crossword and the letter on her table like a still
life. *It's almost too bad he's going to call and ruin it.*

Martin stood in his office with the phone in his hand,
watching the clock on the computer count up to two o' clock.
He was wearing a suit and tie. He was holding his breath.
When the clock hit 14:00:00 he exhaled and pressed 1 on
his speed dial.

'*Hallo*, Martin.'

'Marijke. Happy birthday.'

'Thank you. Thank you.'

'Has Theo called yet?'

Marijke laughed. 'I don't think he's even awake yet, hmm? How are you? What's new?'

'I'm fine. Everything's fine.' Martin lit a cigarette. He glanced at the list of questions on his desk. 'And you? Still no smoking?'

'Yes, no smoking. It feels amazing, you should try it. I can smell things. I had forgotten what things smell like, water, freesias. There are so many beautiful smells. Those gloves you sent, they smell like the first day of winter.'

'You like them?'

'Oh, it was all perfect. I can't believe you found my earrings.'

'The Americans have a new word for that: *regifting*. It seemed a bit miserly to send you your own earrings on your birthday, but having found them . . .' Martin thought of Julia putting the earrings into his hands. Marijke thought of the occasion upon which Martin had originally given her the earrings, which was Theo's birth.

'No, I was so happy . . . And the letter, and the cross-word . . .'

'Have you worked it out yet?' he teased her.

'*Ja*, I sat down and did it straight away, twenty minutes.' They both laughed.

There was a contented pause. 'What are you going to do for your birthday?' he said finally.

'Mmm, coffee and cake with Emma and Lise. I've told you about them.'

'Oh, right. And dinner?'

'No – I'll eat at home.'

'By yourself?' Martin was inspired. 'That's no good. Listen – let me take you out for dinner.'

Marijke frowned. 'Martin—'

'No, listen, here's how we'll do it. Pick a restaurant, somewhere nice. Make a reservation, wear something beautiful, bring your mobile. We'll talk on the phone, you have a lovely dinner, it will be almost as though we're together.'

'Martin, those kinds of restaurants don't allow mobiles. And I would feel conspicuous eating by myself that way.'

'I'll eat too. We'll eat together. Just in different cities.'

'Oh, Martin . . .' She weakened. 'What language?'

'Whatever you like. *Nederlands? Français?*'

'No, no. Something unusual, for privacy . . .'

'*Pāli?*'

'It would be a very short dinner, then.'

Martin laughed. 'Think about it and let me know. What time shall we dine?'

'Half eight your time?'

'Okay, I'll be here.' He thought perhaps he shouldn't have reminded her of that. 'Don't forget to charge up your mobile.'

'I know.'

'*Tot ziens.*'

'*Tot straks.*'

Martin put the phone in its cradle. He had been standing

in the same spot for the duration of the conversation, leaning over the phone on the desk. Now he straightened and turned, smiling – and his hand flew to his heart. 'Oh!'

Julia stood in the doorway, a dark form against the dim light. 'Sorry, I didn't mean to scare you.'

He lowered his face and closed his eyes, almost as though he were going to hide his head under a wing; he waited for his heart to slow. 'That's all right. Have you been there long?' He looked at her. She stepped into the room, and became only herself.

'No. Not very long. Was that your wife?'

'Yes.'

'Did she like the gloves?'

Martin nodded. 'Come into the kitchen, I'll make tea. Yes, she liked the gloves very much. Thank you for choosing them.' He followed her through the aisle of boxes that led across the dining room and into the kitchen.

'Um, Valentina actually picked them. She's the one with clothes-sense.' Julia sat down at the table and watched Martin getting out tea things. *He put on a tie to talk on the phone with his wife.* For some reason this made Julia a little depressed.

'You're like an old married couple, you and Valentina. You have everything divvied up, all the talents and the chores.' Martin glanced at her as he ran water into the electric kettle. There was something different about her. *What's wrong? She seems wrong.* 'Did someone hit you?' There was a bruise rising over Julia's cheekbone.

She put her fingers on the bruise. 'Do you have any ice?'

Martin went to the freezer and shifted things around until he found an ancient bag of frozen peas. 'Here.' Julia clamped the bag to her cheek. Martin went back to his tea-making. Neither of them said a word until he had finished pouring out.

'Choccie biccie?' he offered.

'Yeah, thanks.'

'Would you care to talk about it?'

'No.' Julia stared at her teacup, her expression hidden behind the peas. 'She didn't mean it.'

'Nevertheless.'

'How long have you and your wife been married?' she asked.

'Twenty-five years.'

'How long has she been gone?'

'One year, two months, six days.'

'Is she coming back?'

'No. She isn't.'

Julia leaned her elbow on the table, leaned her face into the peas so that she was regarding him at an angle. 'So . . . ?'

'One sec.' Martin walked to his office and gathered his cigarettes and lighter. By the time he returned to the kitchen he had worked out his answer. 'I'm going to Amsterdam.' He lit a cigarette and smiled, imagining Marijke's surprise.

Julia said, 'Great. When?'

'Oh, erm, soon. When I'm able to leave the house. Maybe in a week or two.'

'Oh.' She looked disappointed. 'So, like, never?'

'Never say never.'

'You know, I've been doing some research. They have drugs for OCD. And there's behavioural therapy.'

'I know, Julia,' he said gently.

'But—'

'Part of the condition is refusing treatment for the condition.'

'Oh.' She took the peas in both hands and tried to break up the big clumps. Martin thought the bruise had become darker, though the swelling had perhaps lessened. The peas made a crunching sound that Martin found distressing. 'It's not your problem, my dear. I'll get to Amsterdam eventually.'

Julia gave him a small smile. 'Yeah. Okay.' She sipped her tea, then put the peas against her cheek.

'Are you going to be all right?'

'What? Oh, sure, it's just a little sore.'

'Does that happen often?'

'Not since we were little. We used to hit and bite and spit and pull hair and everything, but we kind of grew out of it.'

Martin said, 'Will you be safe when you go back to your flat?'

Julia laughed. 'Of course. Valentina's my twin, she's not some huge monster. She's actually pretty timid, usually.'

'Mmm. Timid people can surprise you.'

'Well, she did.'

Martin smoked and thought about Marijke. *What will she wear?* He imagined her getting out of the cab, walking into a restaurant, flowers, white tablecloths. Julia thought about Valentina, who had locked herself in the dressing room. Julia had stood by the door, listening to Valentina sob, waiting. *Maybe I should go back.* She stood up.

'I'm going to see how she is.'

'Why don't you take these?' Martin handed her the packet of chocolate digestives. 'A peace offering.'

'Thanks. May I borrow the peas? We don't have any ice cubes.'

'Of course.' He stood up, smiling, and led the way through the boxes. *Peas, peace, piece, please, pleas . . . Say something.* 'Somehow I always thought Americans were obsessed with ice, all those iced drinks and such. You don't have a herd of little glaciers in your freezer?'

'No, they evaporated . . . You know, we're half-English. Maybe we're not totally average Americans, you know?'

'I'm sure you're not average at all,' Martin said. Julia smiled and went downstairs. *Peas, peace, pleas . . .* He looked at his watch. *Three hours and twenty-eight minutes to kill before dinner. Just enough time for a shower.*

Marijke sat at a long table in the Restaurant Sluizer, clutching her mobile under the tablecloth. She had explained her predicament to the head waiter, and he had kindly escorted her to a room that was usually reserved for private parties. He lit several candles and quickly cleared away a few of the surplus table settings, leaving her in solitary possession of a room that could have seated twenty. She skimmed the menu, even though she always ordered the same thing here.

Her phone rang just as the waiter brought her a glass of wine. 'Martin?'

'Hello, Marijke. Where are you?'

'Sluizer. In a private room.'

'What are you wearing?' he asked.

She glanced down; she was wearing slacks and a grey turtleneck. 'That red dress with the low back, open-toed heels, my earrings.' She actually was wearing the earrings. 'What are you having for dinner?'

'Mmm, I thought I'd go with the Seekh kabob of mutton starter, and then roast saddle of Oisin red deer with pickling spices for the mains. And a nice Merlot.'

'That sounds meaty. Where are you pretending to be?'

'The Cinnamon Club.'

'Isn't that the Indian restaurant that's in a library?'

'Yes.'

'I've never been there.'

'Neither have I, I'm experimenting.' Martin was ripping open boxes of frozen food as he spoke, his mobile clamped between head and shoulder. Chicken tikka masala and saag aloo. The Cinnamon Club didn't do take away. 'Are you having your usual sea bream?'

'Yes, indeed.' The waiter arrived and took her order. Marijke handed him her menu and stared at her own reflection in the restaurant window. In the soft light of the reflected candles she looked almost young. She smiled at herself.

'Did Theo call?' asked Martin.

'He did, yes. Just as I was going out, so we didn't talk long.'

'How is he?'

'He's fine. He may come and visit over the break. And he has a new girlfriend, I think,' said Marijke.

'Ah, that's news. Did he tell you much of anything?'

'Her name is Amrita. She's a foreign student, from Bangladesh. Her family has a tea-towel factory, or something like that. According to Theo, she's a looker *and* a genius. And she can cook, he says.'

'He sounds smitten. What sort of genius is she?' Martin pressed the buttons on the microwave and the food began to rotate.

'Maths. He explained but I'm afraid I didn't comprehend. You'll have to ask him yourself.'

Martin felt a sudden lightness, a temporary lifting of worry. 'That's excellent. They'll be able to talk about their work.' He and Marijke had met in a Russian class; they had always enjoyed being able to share the intricacies of translation, of one language melting into another. 'I was afraid he'd end up with a kindergarten teacher, one of those terribly cheerful women.'

'Mmm, don't marry him off yet.'

'Yeah, I know.' He poured himself more wine. 'That's the thing about living vicariously; it's so much faster than actual living. In a few minutes we'll be worrying about names for the children.'

She laughed. 'I have them all picked out. Jason, Alex and Daniel for the boys, and Rachel, Marion and Louise for the girls.'

'Six children?'

'Why not? *We* don't have to raise them.' Her food arrived. Martin removed his from the microwave. It looked rather colourless, and Martin wished himself at the Cinnamon Club in reality, not just imagination. Then he thought, *That's silly. I wish we were eating together, anywhere.*

'How's yours?' he asked her.

'Delightful. As always.'

When the table had been cleared and she was sipping her brandy, Marijke said, '*Diz-me coisas porcas.*' ('Talk dirty to me.')

'In Portuguese? Kind mistress, that's going to require a dictionary or two.' He went to his office, grabbed their Portuguese–English dictionary, went to their bedroom. He took off his shoes and climbed into bed. Martin thought for a moment, riffling through the dictionary's pages for inspiration. 'Okay, here we go. *Estamos a sair do restaurante. Estamos num táxi a descer a Vijzelstraat. Somos dois estranhos que partilham um táxi. Sentados tão afastados um do outro quanto possível, cada um olhando pela sua janela. Vai ser uma longa viagem. Olho de relance para ti. Reparo nas tuas belas pernas, collants de seda e saltos altos. O vestido subiu-te até às coxas, terá sido quando entraste no táxi, ou talvez o tenhas puxado para cima deliberadamente? Hmm, é difícil dizer . . .*' ('We're leaving the restaurant. We're in a taxi, driving down Vijzelstraat. We're strangers, sharing a cab. We're sitting as far apart as possible, each looking out of a window. It's going to be a long ride. I glance over at you. I notice your beautiful legs, silk stockings and high heels. Your dress has ridden up your thighs, maybe when you got into the taxi, or perhaps you deliberately pulled up your dress? Hmm, it's hard to tell . . .')

Marijke sat by herself at the long table, brandy in hand, mobile at her ear, her mind in the past and in a taxi meandering through the streets of Amsterdam. *I want you. I want us, the way we were before.*

'Marijke? Are you crying?'

'No. No, go on . . .' *Talk as long as you can, until the batteries run down, until dawn, until I see you again, my love.*

The next day was strangely mild, the kind of day that induces people to say, 'Global warming,' and smile ruefully. Robert woke up early to the sound of church bells and thought, *Today is the perfect day to picnic in Postman's Park.*

He gathered his courage, went upstairs and invited the twins. By noon he had assembled sandwiches, bottled water, apples and a bottle of Pinot Blanc into an ancient picnic basket borrowed from Jessica and James. He decided they should take the bus, partially to accommodate Valentina's tube phobia and partly because he thought the twins ought to get to know the bus system. By the time they arrived at the unassuming gates of the park all three of them were hungry, and the twins were quite lost.

Robert carried the picnic basket into the park and set it on a bench. '*Voilà*,' he said. 'Postman's Park.' He had not told them what to expect; they had imagined something like St James's or Regent's Park, and so they stood and looked about, perplexed. The park occupied a narrow space between a church and some nondescript buildings. It was neat, shady and devoid of people. There was a diminutive fountain, eight wooden benches, a scattering of trees and ferns, a low, shed-like structure at one end and some old tablet-style gravestones leaning against the buildings.

'It's a cemetery?' asked Julia.

'It was an old churchyard, yes.'

Valentina looked quizzical but said nothing. The park was sort of drab and she couldn't see why Robert had been so intent on bringing them here.

'Why is it called Postman's Park? I don't see any postmen. Or postpersons,' said Julia.

'The old Post Office was nearby. The postmen used to eat their lunch here.'

Valentina wandered over to a sign on the church wall. GUILD AND WARD CHURCH OF ST BOTOLPH-WITHOUT-ALDERSGATE. She looked at Robert, who smiled and shrugged. She took a few steps towards the shed at the back of the park.

'Warmer,' he said. Julia was there and Valentina hurried to join her. The shed building was covered in beautiful white tiles, which were lettered with blue inscriptions:

Elizabeth Boxall, aged 17 of Bethnal Green who died of injuries received in trying to Save a Child from a runaway horse, June 20, 1888.

Frederick Alfred Croft, Inspector. Aged 31 Saved a Lunatic Woman from suicide at Woolwich Arsenal Station. But was Himself run over by the Train. Jan. 11. 1878

The twins wandered back and forth, reading the plaques. There seemed to be hundreds of them.

*David Selves, aged 12 of Woolwich supported his drowning
playfellow and sank with him clasped in his arms
September 12, 1886*

'You're kind of sick, you know that?' Julia told Robert. He
looked slightly hurt.

'They're memorials to ordinary people who sacrificed
themselves for others. I think they're beautiful.' He turned to
Valentina, who nodded.

'They're nice,' she said. She wondered why Julia was being
so mean. Usually this was exactly the sort of thing they both
found interesting. There was something very strange about
the plaques; the stories were extremely abbreviated, hinting
at mayhem, but they were decorated with flowers and leaves,
crowns, anchors. The ornamentation belied the words:
drowned, burned, crushed, collapsed.

*Sarah Smith, Pantomime Artiste at Prince's Theatre died of
terrible injuries received when attempting in her
inflammable dress to extinguish the flames which had
enveloped her companion. January 24, 1863*

All these ordinary catastrophes crowded in on Valentina.
She went back to sit on the bench. Just to be sure, she got
out her inhaler and took two puffs. Julia and Robert watched
her.

'She has asthma?' Robert asked.

'Yeah. But I think at the moment she's trying to fend off
a panic attack.' Julia frowned. 'Why did you bring us here?'

'This was one of Elspeth's favourite spots. If she was around to give you the grand tour she would have brought you here herself.' They began walking towards Valentina. 'Shall we have lunch?' Robert unpacked the sandwiches and distributed food and drink to the twins. They sat in a row on the bench and ate quietly.

'Are you okay?' Robert asked Valentina.

She glanced at Julia and said, 'I'm fine. Thanks for bringing lunch, this is good.' *Say something nice, Julia.*

'Yeah, really good. What are we eating?'

'Prawn-mayonnaise sandwiches.'

The twins inspected the insides of their sandwiches. 'It tastes like shrimp,' said Julia.

'You would call it a shrimp-salad sandwich. Though I've never understood where the salad idea comes into it.'

Julia smiled. 'We've been trying to teach ourselves British. Logic does not apply.'

Valentina said, 'Have you ever been to America?'

'Yes,' Robert replied. 'Elspeth and I went to New York a few years ago. And the Grand Canyon.'

The twins were puzzled. 'Why didn't you come to see us?' Julia asked.

'We talked about that. But in the end she decided not to. There were some things she never told me. Perhaps if she'd known she was going to die . . .' Robert shrugged. 'She was reticent about her past.'

The twins looked at each other and silently agreed that Valentina would ask for the favour. 'But you have her papers, right? So you know everything now, right?' Valentina put down her sandwich and tried to seem casual.

'I do have her papers. I haven't read them.'

'What? How could you not read them?' Julia could not suppress her indignation.

Hush, Julia. I'll do it. 'Aren't you curious?'

'I'm afraid,' Robert said.

'Oh.' Valentina glanced at Julia, who looked about ready to run home and read Elspeth's papers whether Robert liked it or not. 'Well, we were wondering, um, if you would mind . . . If we could read them? I mean, we're living in her place with all her stuff, and we don't know her, and, you know, we're interested. In her.'

Robert was shaking his head before Valentina finished speaking. 'I'm sorry. I know she was your relation, and ordinarily I would gladly hand over the lot. But Elspeth told me you weren't to have them. I'm sorry.'

'But she's *dead*,' Julia said.

They sat in silence. Valentina was sitting next to Robert, and without Julia seeing she reached down and took his hand. Robert laced his fingers with hers. Valentina said, 'It's okay. Pretend we didn't say anything about it. We're sorry.' Julia rolled her eyes. Her bruise was smaller today, she had covered it with make-up, but Valentina felt bad just looking at her. She wondered if Robert had noticed.

'It's not my decision,' he said. 'And not knowing what's in there, I can't tell you why it would be better if you don't read her papers. But Elspeth did care about you, and I don't think she would have been so adamant about this if it wasn't important.'

'All right, all right,' said Julia. 'Never mind.'

Clouds had appeared in the narrow sky above the park and scattered drops of rain began to fall. Robert said, 'Perhaps we'd better pack up.' The picnic had been a failure, not at all the urban idyll he had imagined that morning. They filed out of the park, each dejected in various degrees. But on the bus Valentina sat next to Robert and Julia sat in front of them, and he offered her his hand. Valentina placed her hand in his and they rode in surprised and contented silence back to Highgate.

Martin dreamt he was on the underground. It was a Circle-line train, the sort of carriage where all the seats face the aisle. At first he was the only passenger, but soon people began to get on, and he found himself staring at his knees to avoid looking at the crotch of the man crowded against him. He wasn't sure what station he was supposed to get off at; since it was the Circle line they would all come round again and again, so he stayed where he was, trying to remember where he was going.

Martin heard peculiar noises coming from the seats directly across from him – crunching, ripping, chewing sounds, which increased in volume as the train went on. Martin began to be anxious – the sounds worked on his nerves like grinding teeth. Something rolled up against his foot. He looked down. It was a walnut.

The train stopped at Monument and quite a few people got off. Now he could see across the aisle. Two young women sat together. They wore scuffed white trainers and medical scrubs, and each had a shopping bag resting on her lap. Both women had protruding eyes and pronounced overbites. They wore wary expressions, as though prepared to defend their bags against thieves. Both women delved in the bags with shovel-like hands, scooping out walnuts and ripping them open with their huge teeth.

'Wotchalookin' at?' said one to Martin. He could hear walnuts rolling all over the floor. No one else seemed to notice. Martin shook his head, unable to speak. To his horror, the women got up and seated themselves on either side of him. The one who had spoken before leaned over and put her mouth to his ear.

'We're squirrels in human form,' she whispered. 'And so are you.'

'We've got to get you to a doctor,' said Julia. Valentina nodded and wheezed.

But this was easier said than done. The twins were blissfully unaware of the intricacies of the NHS. Robert tried not to sound exasperated as he filled them in.

'You can't just show up and expect them to attend to your problem,' he told Valentina when the twins accosted him outside his door. He stood holding a sheaf of letters and waved them about for emphasis as he talked. 'You have to find out which GPs are accepting new patients and ring them to make an appointment to register. And then you fill out a pile of forms and give them your history. And *then*, and only then, are you allowed to make an appointment.' Valentina started to say something and coughed instead.

Julia shook her finger at Robert as though he had personally invented the National Health Service. 'No way,' she said. 'The Mouse needs a doctor right now.'

'Go over to Whittington Hospital, then, to A & E.' And that was what they ended up doing. Robert came with them.

Whittington Hospital was a sprawling thing located just down Highgate Hill, on the other side of Waterlow Park. They walked there. The spring wind was damp and stiff, and by the time they arrived Valentina was breathing in deep, stomach-clenching gasps.

After some questions and some waiting, Valentina was whisked away by a young Pakistani nurse. Julia and Robert could hear the nurse making low-pitched sounds of reassurance as she hustled Valentina through the double doors that separated the waiting room from the A & E department proper. They settled down to do the forms with the middle-aged, basset-jowled white man who sat at the intake desk.

'Allergies?'

'Tetracycline, mould, soy,' said Julia.

'Existing conditions?'

'Well,' said Julia, 'she has situs inversus.' The intake man, who had seemed utterly bored with them, now looked up at Julia and raised his eyebrows inquisitively. 'We are mirror twins, and she's mostly reversed inside. Her heart's over here,' Julia laid her hand on her chest, just to the right of her sternum, 'and her liver and kidneys and whatnot are all backwards of mine.' The man considered this, and then began typing rapidly.

'I didn't know that,' said Robert.

'Well, now you do,' said Julia irritably. 'It's not like it matters or anything, unless you're Valentina's doctor.'

'I meant the bit about you being mirror-image twins. I thought you were identical twins. That is, wouldn't mirror twins be more . . . opposite?'

Julia shrugged. 'We're pretty symmetrical, so it doesn't show that much in our faces. You can notice it better if you look at the way our hair parts, or our moles, or if you saw a pair of X-rays, then you could really see it, because she's so opposite. She has an asymmetric non-flail mitral-valve prolapse,' she added, to the intake man.

'What does that mean?' asked Robert.

'There's a valve that isn't formed right,' replied Julia. 'That's why I'm so worried about her breathing like that. It might put a strain on her heart, and then we'd be in big trouble.'

'I can't believe you've been in London for almost three months without getting her a doctor!' Robert was feeling extremely anxious, suddenly, and he spoke sharply.

She retorted, 'We were going to do it and we've just been putting it off 'cause we weren't sure how to find one. It's not like we haven't been thinking about it.' Julia knew that this was an inadequate reason, and it made her cross. She finished the paperwork and they went back to their seats in the waiting room.

The diagnosis was bronchitis. They took a cab up the hill, Valentina huddling in Julia's arms, coughing. In the front hall, back at Vautravers, the twins began to walk upstairs, and Robert tried to follow them. 'No,' said Julia. 'We're all right. Thanks.' She turned away brusquely.

Robert said, 'But she needs—'

'*I* take care of her. That's *my* job.' Julia watched Valentina slowly ascending the stairs, pausing on each step.

'I could get the prescription,' Robert offered.

Julia considered. It would be helpful; Boots was a bus ride away. 'Okay. Here.' She handed over the prescription as though she were doing Robert a favour, not the reverse. He went out the front door, a man on a mission. *I take care of her.*

Not you, Julia thought. She followed Valentina into their flat. She filled the hot-water bottle before she took off her coat, and went to the bedroom, where Valentina was slowly undressing.

'Where's Robert?' Valentina asked, as though she hadn't heard their conversation.

'He went to Boots,' Julia said.

Valentina got into bed without comment. Julia gave her the hot-water bottle, set up the vaporizer, fetched the book Valentina had been reading, made tea; she did all these things purposefully and quite happily, humming to herself as she accomplished all the little comforting tasks. She came into the bedroom with the tea to find the Kitten curled up near Valentina's head and Valentina herself asleep. The Kitten stretched out a paw and placed it protectively on Valentina's shoulder, eyeing Julia with suspicion. *You too?* Julia thought. *We all want to be her only one.* She set the tea tray on the bedside table. It occurred to Julia to wonder, *If I got sick, would everyone rush to my bedside?* The thought made her irritable. She never got sick; what was the point of wondering that? Valentina's breath rattled in her throat. Julia settled herself in the window seat with her own cup of tea, causing Elspeth, who had been there all along, to get up and stand next to the bed, biting her thumb, worrying. It was an anxious day for everyone: humans, cats and ghosts.

Edie sat at her dining-room table drinking coffee with the telephone at her elbow; she was not actually looking at the phone, just having it near because it was going to ring in a few minutes. Jack wandered over, carrying the Sunday *Times*. He began to separate it into his and hers piles. Edie put her hand out and he placed the business section in it. She flipped it open and ran her finger down the stock tables, making little *tsk*ing sounds as she did so. The phone rang. Edie took a sip of her coffee as though she were in no hurry and let it ring three times. Jack went down the hall to pick up in their bedroom.

'Mom?'

'Hi, Julia,' said Edie.

'Valentina?' said Jack.

'Hi, Dad,' said Valentina. She tried to make her voice sound normal but the effort sent her into a coughing fit.

'Oh my God,' said Edie. 'That doesn't sound good.'

'It's just bronchitis,' said Julia. 'We went to the doctor.'

'I'm better today,' Valentina said. She put her phone down and went into the bathroom to cough. Julia watched her standing bent over, elbows on the sink, hand over her mouth to suppress the sound of the coughing.

'Did they give you antibiotics? Are you taking that mucus-reducing stuff Dr Brooks gave you?' Edie and Julia embarked on a leisurely and detailed discussion of everything they could and should do for Valentina's bronchitis. Eventually Valentina came back to the phone.

'We met Robert Fanshaw,' she said, mostly in order to change the subject.

'Finally,' said Jack. 'Where's he been all this time?'

'He's helping us get signed up for the NHS,' Julia said.

'Oh,' said Edie. 'Huh. What's he like?'

'Mopey,' said Julia. 'Kind of freaky and weird. If he was our age he'd probably be a Goth, you know, all pierced and tattooed.'

'No,' said Valentina. 'He's nice. He's kind of shy, and you can tell he misses Elspeth. He has little glasses like John Lennon.' She wanted to say more, but had to put the phone down and cough.

'Valentina has a crush on him,' Julia informed them. Valentina drew her finger across her throat. *Don't, Julia.*

'Surely he's a bit old for her. He must be our age?' Jack said.

'I think he's younger. Mid-thirties, maybe?'

Valentina came back to the phone. 'I *don't* have a crush on him. But he's *nice*.' Edie thought, *Uh-oh*, but she knew better than to say anything. The conversation turned to the weather, movies, politics. After they all hung up Valentina said crossly, 'Now they're going to obsess. Why did you say that?'

'It will distract them from you being sick,' Julia replied.

'It's not true, though.'

Julia just laughed.

Edie and Jack hung up simultaneously and met in the hallway. 'Don't look so worried,' Jack said. 'She says it's nothing.'

Edie snorted. 'That's exactly when you should get very worried.'

He put his arm around her. 'She did sound awful.'

'Maybe we should go there. We wouldn't actually go to the flat, but just be in London. We could rent a flat nearby . . .' Edie nestled into him. She loved how big Jack was, how small she felt next to him. It was very comforting.

He stroked her head. 'How would you have felt if your mom followed you across the ocean and moved in across the street from us?'

'That was different.'

'They're managing. Let them be.'

Edie shook her head, but smiled at him. *That's it, just smile and be my Edie, that's enough for me.* He kissed the top of her head. 'It'll be all right.'

Robert and Jessica were having their afternoon tea in the upstairs office at Highgate Cemetery. Jessica fixed Robert with a Purposeful Look, and he steeled himself for one of her Talks. He expected the Talk to be about Not Letting The Tourists Slow Down The Tour By Taking Endless Videos, or even possibly Please Remember Not To Go About With Your Hands Thrust Into Your Pockets As It Looks Undignified, but she surprised him.

'Don't you think,' asked Jessica, 'that she is a bit too young for you?'

'A bit?'

'Ridiculously young for you?'

'Maybe,' Robert said. 'How young is too young?'

'Not so much in years, because I have known many people at twenty-one to be quite mature – but both of them seem so *very* young. They remind me of my girls at sixteen.'

'That has a certain appeal, Jessica.'

She waved her hand at him. 'You understand me. It seems strange that after Elspeth, who was such a dear girl, so level-headed and *not* a flibbertigibbet . . . Valentina seems an odd match for you.'

'Some people thought I was too young for Elspeth.'

'Did I say that?'

'I believe you did, actually. Here in this very office, as I recall.'

'Surely not.'

'I'm nine years younger than Elspeth. I'm catching her up, though.'

'Yes . . .'

'You're younger than James.'

'James is ninety-four. I'm eighty-five this July.'

'I wonder why it's more socially acceptable for the man to be older?'

'I believe the men arranged it that way.'

'Ah. I don't think you've ever mentioned how you and James met?'

Jessica hesitated before she answered. Robert thought, *It must be something rather risqué. She looks as though I've asked for her bra size.* 'We met during the war. I was James' assistant at Bletchley Park.'

'No kidding? I'd no idea. You were code breakers?'

'Actually, what we did was more . . . administrative.' Jessica pursed her mouth, as though she had said more than she thought strictly necessary.

'I thought you read Law.'

'One may do many things in a long life. I also played a great deal of tennis and brought up three children. There's time for all sorts of adventures.'

'And you saved the cemetery.'

'Not single-handedly, as you well know. Molly and Catherine, Edward . . . we had help from a great many dear people. Though of course there's never enough help for all the little things that need doing. That reminds me, would you take these with you up the hill on your way home and just drop them in Anthony and Lacey's letter boxes? It will save the stamps.'

'Of course.'

Jessica sighed. 'I must say, I do feel just a tiny bit fatigued thinking of all the letters I have to write.' She put her teacup on the desk and held out both hands to him. 'Come on, help the old thing out of her chair.'

Robert spent the afternoon sitting in the Strathcona mausoleum by the Eastern Cemetery gates, selling tickets and watching the landscaping team trimming trees. It was a slow day, and he had time to wonder if Jessica was right. Perhaps Valentina was too young for him. Perhaps he should let her be and go back to mourning Elspeth. Not that he had stopped; the thought of Elspeth was a sharp ache. But Robert had to admit that he didn't think of her quite as often as before, and that the arrival of the twins had coincided with this slackening of Elspeth's presence in his every waking thought. He felt ashamed, as though he were a sentinel who had abandoned a guard tower to the enemy.

But Elspeth wouldn't want me to spend the rest of my life mourning her. Would she? It was not exactly something they had discussed, but he felt wrong whether he devoted himself to her memory or allowed Valentina to waft into reveries that would have once featured Elspeth. He lived in a state of aroused guilt. It was very confusing, but somewhat pleasurable.

Early one morning Robert found Valentina sitting in the back garden with a Thermos of tea. He was letting himself in through the green door and had no idea she was there until she said, 'Good morning.'

'Good lord,' he said, after he'd stepped backwards and nearly broken his ankle on a gravestone. 'I mean, good morning.'

Valentina was sitting on the low stone bench and wearing a quilted dressing gown. Her feet were bare. 'Oh – I'm sorry!'

'Aren't you cold?' It was going to be a warm day, but the dawn was chilly.

'Yes, I am now. My tea's gotten cold.'

'Come in, why don't you?'

She glanced up at the first-floor windows. 'Julia's still asleep.'

Valentina picked her way across the damp moss and Robert held his door open for her. When she went in under his arm he felt as though he'd caught a bird.

'Do you want a jumper, or anything warm?'

'No, but maybe some more tea?' Robert put the kettle on. He went to change his muddy clothes. When he emerged

Valentina was standing at his desk. 'Who are all these women?'

The wall above Robert's desk was covered with postcards, magazine clippings, images printed off the Internet and copied from books, all of women. They radiated in a boxy sunburst pattern from the centre of the wall; there were clusters of them, as though they charted solar systems in a galaxy of women. 'Oh. Well, that's Eleanor Marx, Karl's daughter. That's Mrs Henry Wood. This is Catherine Dickens . . .'

'They're all buried at Highgate?'

'Yes, exactly.'

'No men?'

'The men are over here.' He had another galaxy tacked to the adjacent wall. 'I'd rather stare at the women when I'm blocked; the men are collectively somewhat dour.'

Valentina turned on the desk lamp, to see better. The kettle whistled and Robert bounded out of the room. He returned with Valentina's tea and she said, 'We saw that painting at the Tate.' She pointed to a postcard in the centre of the wall. 'Who is she?'

'That's Millais' *Ophelia*. The model is Elizabeth Siddal.' Robert felt his face flush just as Valentina turned to him. She said, 'You have lots of pictures of her.'

'She was Dante Gabriel Rossetti's muse. He painted her over and over. She was the It girl of the Pre-Raphaelites. I'm a little obsessed with her.'

'Why?'

'Why, indeed? She doesn't seem to have been especially attractive as a person; she was rather needy and sickly. Perhaps because she was beautiful and died young.' Robert smiled. 'Don't look so worried, it's a very mild obsession.'

'You seem to have a thing for dead girls,' Valentina said.

She was joking, but Robert replied defensively. 'Not because they're dead. Though unattainability is always attractive.'

'Oh.' *What does he mean by that?*

Robert cleared a space in the piles of paper and sat down on his desk. He offered her the swivel chair and she spun around 360 degrees with her bare feet stuck out in front of her, holding the mug of tea carefully level. She looked so childish that Robert found it painful to watch her. *I think dead girls are the least of my problems at the moment.*

Valentina said, 'You don't have very much furniture.'

'No. This place is far too big for me. And too expensive, really.'

'How come you live here, then?'

'It's all Elspeth's fault.'

Valentina grinned at him and spun around again. 'Same here.' She stretched out one bare foot and stopped her revolution, then spun slowly in the other direction. 'Did you move here because she was here?'

'We met in the front garden, actually. I was poking around because there was a To Let sign and I'd been looking for a flat that bordered the cemetery, because I wanted one of those little doors, you know, in the garden wall . . . So there I was, writing down the estate agent's number, when Elspeth hops out of the front door and says she's got the key and would I like to see the flat? Of course, I say *Yes, please*, because I did want to see it. And she showed me round. And it's immediately obvious that it's far too large, but there's nothing like an attractive woman in an empty flat . . .' Robert was lost in his story and temporarily oblivious to Valentina. 'So I ended up moving in. Though I must say, I was so thick-headed that it took me years to work out that she'd picked me up and not vice versa. I was very young.'

'When was that?'

Robert calculated. 'Almost thirteen years ago.'

'Oh.' *We were eight years old then.* Valentina had a sudden thought. 'Why didn't you live together? I mean, these apartments are huge, it seems funny to have two giant flats for two single people. And it's not like you have a lot of stuff.'

'No. I don't, do I?' Robert stared at Valentina's knees. 'Elspeth wasn't keen. She'd lived with someone once and hated it. I think she felt differently towards the end, when I was taking care of her all the time, I think she realised that it could have worked, us living together. I'm fairly self-sufficient and so was she. She liked to be alone, knowing I was nearby if she wanted me.'

'Our mom is like that.'

'Is she?'

'I think Dad is always kind of confused, you know, sometimes Mom seems like she's just visiting, she's super detached, and then she'll be, like, really fun and sort of more present, you know?' Valentina peered up at him. 'Was Elspeth like that?'

Robert paused to sort out her syntax. 'Yes,' he said. 'Sometimes she was far away, even when she was right there.'

He was thinking of a certain way Elspeth had, after they'd made love, of seeming to forget him even as he lay sweat-sticky collapsed over her.

'Yeah, totally. Did Elspeth like to boss everyone? Our mom is always in charge of everything all the time.'

'Hmm. I suppose she did, but then, I enjoy being bossed. I come from a family of aunts, I spent my childhood being ordered about by women.' He smiled at her. 'I get the impression that Julia bosses you.'

'I don't like it.' Valentina made a face. 'I don't want to boss anyone and I don't want to be bossed.'

'That seems reasonable.'

'What time is it?' Valentina asked. She sat up and put her mug on the desk, suddenly anxious.

Robert glanced at his watch. 'Half seven,' he told her.

'Seven thirty? I've got to go.' She stood up.

'Wait,' he said. 'What's wrong?' He slid off the desk and stood facing her.

'Julia will freak if she wakes up and can't find me.'

Robert hesitated. *She'll come back. Let her go.* He felt acutely alone even before Valentina turned to leave. He followed her to his back door. She put her hand on the doorknob. Awkwardness overcame them.

'Would you like to have dinner with me sometime?' he asked her.

'Yes.'

'This Saturday?'

'Okay.' She continued to stand there, waiting. It occurred to Robert that he might kiss her, so he did. The kiss surprised him because it had been so long since he'd kissed anyone but Elspeth. It surprised Valentina because she had hardly ever kissed anyone that way – to her, kissing had always been more theoretical than physical. Afterwards she stood with her eyes closed, lips parted, face tilted. Robert thought, *She's going to break my heart and I'm going to let her.* Valentina let herself out and padded up the steps. He heard their door latch. Robert stood there trying to sort out what had just happened, failed and gave in to giddy confusion. He made himself a drink and went to bed.

The following Saturday evening Robert presented himself at the twins' front door wearing a suit. Valentina slipped out and said, 'Let's go.' He had a glimpse of Julia in the hall mirrors, standing forlorn in dim light. He started to wave to her but Valentina was hurrying down the stairs so he followed. He glanced up just as Julia poked her head into the hallway. She scowled at him and closed the door.

He had ordered a minicab. 'Andrew Edmunds, in Soho,' he told the driver. They sped through Highgate Village, Kentish Town. Robert looked more attentively at Valentina and saw that she was wearing Elspeth's clothes, a black velvet dress and a white cashmere wrap which awoke memories of other evenings, years ago. Even the shoes had been Elspeth's. *What does she mean by that?* Then he realised that Valentina might not have brought evening clothes with her from America. He thought rather irritably that Elspeth had left the twins more than enough money to buy new clothes. Valentina seemed older in Elspeth's clothes, as though she had taken on bits of

Elspeth. She was staring out of the window. 'I never know where I am.'

Robert glanced past her and said, 'Camden Town.'

Valentina sighed. 'It all looks alike. And there's so much of it.'

'Don't you like London?'

She shook her head. 'I *want* to like it. It isn't home, though.'

It hadn't occurred to Robert that she wouldn't stay once the year was up; now he felt an urgency, a need to convince her of London's desirability. 'I can't imagine living anywhere else. But then, I grew up here. I think if I left I'd feel a bit cut off. All my memories are here.'

'Well, exactly. That's how I feel about Chicago.'

He smiled at her earnestness. 'Aren't you terribly young to be so nostalgic? I'm a fusty old historian, I've a right to be calcified. But you ought to be out having adventures.'

'How old are you?' she asked.

'I'll be thirty-seven the week after next,' he told her. He noticed that she did not contradict his description of himself as old.

Valentina smiled. 'We should have a party for you.'

At first Robert thought she meant *we* to mean the two of them, himself and her; then he realised she meant herself and Julia. He imagined Julia's likely reaction and said, 'I think we're having tea and cake at the cemetery; why don't you come by and meet everyone?'

'Okay.' She smiled. 'I've never been to a birthday party at a cemetery.'

'Oh, it isn't a party, just ourselves having a slightly more elaborate tea than usual. There won't be presents or anything of that sort.'

They began to exchange birthday stories: 'We went to the circus for the first time . . .' 'I ended up in hospital having my stomach pumped . . .' 'Julia was so mad . . .' 'My father showed up that morning and I had never met him before—'

'What?'

Robert paused, unsure whether he had meant to tell her this story so early in their acquaintance. He kept forgetting they barely knew one another. 'Erm, well. My parents weren't actually married to each other. In fact my father had another family, in Birmingham. They were his proper family – they still are – and they don't know about my mum and me. I didn't meet him until my fifth birthday. He showed up in a Lamborghini and took us out on a day trip to Brighton. It was the first time I ever saw the sea.'

'That's so weird. How come he waited all that time to see you?'

'He's a very self-absorbed man, and he doesn't like children. It's funny, too, because I have five half-siblings. My mother says he came to meet me because she finally asked him for money. After that he would come round occasionally, bring us impractical presents . . . He's quite entertaining, and completely undependable. When I was younger I used to worry that he was going to take me away from my mum and I'd never see her again.'

Valentina looked at Robert. *Is he joking?* If he was, she

couldn't detect it. The cab pulled up in front of the restaurant. Valentina had expected it to be large, well upholstered and quiet, but found herself in a tiny crowded room full of age-blackened wood and low ceilings. She had a rare sensation of being too big. *This is the real London, where the Londoners eat.* A welter of emotions hit her: triumph at finally being a non-tourist; satisfaction because she was here and Julia wasn't; inadequacy to the task of conversing with Robert. *What do you say to someone when he says he thought his dad was going to kidnap him? What would Julia say?* Once they were seated at a small table squeezed between an exuberant party of City people and a literary agent wooing an editor, Valentina said, 'Why would he do that?'

Robert looked at her over the menu and said, 'Sorry?'

'Um, your dad? You said . . . ?'

'Oh, right. I know now that he never would've, but he was always joking about it, saying how great it was, just him and me, and how he was going to take me up north . . . To me he was like a goblin. I was quite frightened of him until I was in my teens.'

Valentina looked at him wide-eyed, then took refuge in her menu, at a loss for a reply. *He seems so calm about it. I guess no matter what your family is like, you're not surprised.* She had the feeling, now very familiar to her, of being absurdly young and Midwestern.

I've gone too far, Robert realised. He said, 'Would you like a glass of wine? What are you having to eat?' They began to chat haltingly, righting the conversation with shared affection for Monty Python, anecdotes about the cemetery, the antics of Valentina's kitten, appreciation of the fennel soup. By the end of the meal they were easy with each other again, or at least less uneasy than they had thus far managed to be.

It was a long evening, alone in the flat. Julia considered going upstairs to see Martin, but she was angry at being left on her own and determined to have the most miserable evening possible. She was gratified that the TV was still broken.

Julia heated some tomato soup and sat in the dining room, eating while reading an old copy of *Lucky Jim* she'd found in Elspeth's office. Elspeth sat across from her and watched her. *Don't spill soup on that, it's a signed first.* Elspeth realised that she should have left more detailed instructions for the twins. Without meaning to be destructive, they were maddeningly casual with her things: they read rare editions of *Tristram Shandy* and *Villette* in the bath; they tucked Daniel Defoe pamphlets into their handbags to read on the tube. Elspeth yearned to snatch the book away from Julia. *But why do I mind? It's a book, she's reading it, I ought to be fine with that. I shouldn't be bothered that Valentina is wearing my clothes and having dinner with Robert – but I am, I am very bothered indeed.* Julia finished her soup, shut the book, cleared the dishes and washed up. She played with the Kitten until the Kitten got bored and disappeared into the dressing room to nap. Then Julia lay on the sofa in the front room and stared at the ceiling until she couldn't stand it and had to turn on her computer. She managed to kill a couple hours writing emails to a few long-neglected high-school

friends. Elspeth retreated to her drawer to sulk. At ten o' clock
Julia took a bath. At ten thirty she began to think that Valentina
really ought to be home any minute now. By midnight she
had called Valentina's phone three times and was beginning
to panic. Elspeth watched Julia pacing and had a premoni-
tion of . . . what? *Trouble. Danger.* It was too much, the past
repeating itself with unnerving variations. Elspeth imagined
all the places Robert might have taken Valentina, favourite
bars, cherished walks . . . *Come home, come here where I can keep
an eye on you.* Julia went to bed but lay awake, fuming. Elspeth
sat in the window seat. They waited.

'Would you like to walk along the South Bank?' Robert asked
Valentina. He had paid the bill, they were gathering themselves
to leave the restaurant. Valentina hesitated. She considered
the shoes she was wearing. They were pointy and spiky and
half a size too large. 'Sure,' she said.

They took a cab to Westminster Bridge. The streets were
strangely empty. Their footsteps sounded sharp on the pavement; they could hear laughter across the river. Valentina had
never been in Westminster at night. *It's so much nicer without
the crowds.* Robert led her across the bridge and down some
steps. They stood side by side at the railing looking over the
Thames at the Houses of Parliament. There was a low orange
moon slung just above Big Ben. Robert put his arm around
her. She stiffened. They stood that way for a few minutes, each
wondering what the other was thinking. Eventually he said,
'Shall we walk? You must be getting cold.'

'Yeah, a little,' she said. They went back up the steps. It

was a relief to Valentina to be walking. She was unsure of the protocol; she thought he would kiss her, but would he expect more than that? Did he imagine she would go home with him? Did he understand how impossible that would be? *What time is it?* Julia would be upset if she wasn't home soon. *She's upset anyway, but she'll totally freak out* . . . Valentina tried to read Robert's watch without him seeing. Then she remembered where she was and turned to see Big Ben. It was almost midnight. They walked past Waterloo Bridge, Blackfriars Bridge. Her feet were on fire. He was talking to her about an exhibit he'd seen at Tate Modern. She looked at each bench they passed with longing. They were near London Bridge when she said, 'Can we sit down?'

'Oh,' he said, realising. 'I'm awfully sorry – I forgot about your shoes.'

Valentina sank onto a bench and slipped her feet out of the shoes. She wriggled her toes and rotated her ankles. Robert stooped and picked up the shoes. He sat beside her, a hand in each shoe. The shoes were warm and a little damp. 'Your poor feet,' he said.

'They aren't my shoes,' she said.

'I know.' He put Elspeth's shoes on the bench. 'Here,' he said, holding out his hands. 'Give me your feet.'

She looked dubious but complied. He eased her around so she was leaning back on her elbows with her feet in his lap.

'Could you take off your stockings?'

'Don't look,' she said.

He began to massage her feet. At first she watched him,

but soon she let her head hang back and all he could see was her long neck and her little pointed chin. He gave himself over to her feet, feeling that he had achieved a new level of debauchery, giving a foot massage to a young girl in public. *I wonder if they arrest people for this?* He stopped thinking. The world shrank to their bench, her feet, his hands.

Valentina raised her head. She was dizzy and deeply relaxed. Robert leaned down and kissed her feet. 'There you are,' he said.

'Oh my God,' she said. 'I don't think I can walk.'

'I'll carry you,' he said, and he did.

It was almost 2 a.m. when Julia and Elspeth heard footsteps on the stairs. Julia jumped out of bed, unsure if she should go to meet Valentina or wait for her. Elspeth flew to the hall and saw the door open slowly; she saw that Robert was carrying Valentina; she saw him deposit her gently onto her bare feet; she saw Valentina teeter slightly, a shoe in each hand, and Elspeth knew as though she had seen it exactly what had passed between them. Valentina stood peering into the dark flat. She turned to Robert and gave him a small wave. He bowed slightly to her with a smile, handed her her stockings and went downstairs. Valentina stepped into the flat and closed the door. She made no sound as she walked into the bedroom.

Elspeth stayed in the hall. She had no appetite for the fight the twins were about to have. *Been there, done that.* She wanted to leave the flat, to be alone, to sort herself out. She wanted to find Robert and plead with him. *But what would*

I ask of him? What would I say? Elspeth wanted a stiff drink, a good long cry in the bath. She wanted to walk until she was exhausted enough to sleep. Instead she went into her office and looked out at the front garden in the moonlight. *Let me go*, she asked of whatever it was that held her here. *I want to die now, please; really die and be gone.* She waited, but there was no response. *Please, God, or whoever you are, please let me go.* She looked out at the garden, up at the sky. Nothing happened. She understood then that no one was listening. Anything that happened to her now would be her own doing.

Valentina crept into the bedroom, still holding the shoes and stockings. Julia sat on the bed in her pyjamas, feet dangling. She turned as Valentina came in. 'Do you know what time it is?'

'No.'

'It's nearly 2 a.m.'

'Oh.'

Julia hopped off the bed. Valentina thought, *I can use the shoes to defend myself if she tries to hit me.* They stood facing each other, each reluctant to say the next words that would provoke the argument. Julia thought, *We should just go to bed*; but she couldn't resist saying, 'Is that all you have to say? "Oh"?' She mimicked Valentina's attempt at innocence. *Oh, oh, oh.*

Valentina shrugged. 'It's not like I have a curfew. And you aren't my mom. And even if you were my mom, I'm twenty-one years old.' *So whatcha gonna do about it, huh, Julia?*

'It's common courtesy to let me know when you're coming

home, otherwise I worry.' *I'm more than Mom. You can't just go off on your own.*

'That's not my problem. You knew where I was and who I was with.' *You don't own me.*

'You went out for dinner. Dinner doesn't last until 2 a.m.!' *What were you doing for seven hours?*

'I went out on a date and none of this is any of your business!' *Let go of me!*

'It is! What do you mean?' *We don't have secrets from each other ever.*

'Don't you think it's time we started having our own lives?' *Oh, God, just let go, Julia.*

'We do! We have our own lives together—' *Valentina!*

'That's not what I mean!' Valentina threw the shoes across the room. They bounced harmlessly on the carpet. 'You know what I mean – I want my own life. I want privacy! I'm sick of being half a person.' She burst into tears. Julia stepped towards her and Valentina shrieked, 'Don't touch me! Don't—' and ran out of the room.

Julia stood with her arms at her sides, her eyes closed. *Tomorrow she'll be normal. It will be like this didn't happen.* She got back into bed and lay there trying to hear Valentina somewhere in the flat. Eventually she fell asleep and dreamt she was upstairs, in Martin's flat, wandering by herself through the endless paths between the piles of boxes.

Valentina put herself to bed in the spare bedroom. The sheets were clammy and she felt oddly sophisticated sleeping in her underwear. *I can't remember ever sleeping by myself.* She was too excited to actually sleep. The fight with Julia occupied her mind; the evening with Robert seemed weeks ago, a dim and pleasant interlude in the real battle. She saw herself as rational and victorious: *I won*, she thought. *I said exactly what I wanted to say, she was wrong, she knew I was right. From now on things will be different.*

In the morning the twins met shyly in the kitchen. They made scrambled eggs and toast, and had their breakfast together in the cold light of the dining room without saying very much. Things between them went back to normal, but things were different.

'You look terrible,' Julia said to Martin a few days later. 'I'm going to buy you some vitamins.'

'Now you sound like Marijke.'

'Is that good or bad?' They were in Martin's office. It was late afternoon; Valentina was at the cemetery with Robert, so Julia had come upstairs like a stray creature, complaining loudly that she had been deserted and hoping that Martin would watch TV with her. But Martin was working, so she hovered around him, bored but expectant.

Martin smiled and swivelled to look at her. In the dim light of the computer screen he seemed otherworldly; Julia thought him beautiful, though she knew it was the beauty of damage. His face was bluish and his hands were an extra-ordinary blood-orange colour in the warm desk-lamp light. 'It's nice. It's good to have someone worry about me, just a bit. I wouldn't want you to worry too much, though.'

An idea was forming in Julia's mind. 'I won't. But would you take vitamins if I got you some?'

Martin turned back to the screen. He was building the grid for a crossword. He clicked and three squares went black. 'Maybe. I'm not very good at remembering to take pills.'

'I could remind you. It could be my job.'

'I suppose it's easier than actually eating fruit and veg.'

Julia said, 'Okay, I'll go to Boots tomorrow.' She hesitated. 'Are you going to work all night?'

'Yes, I should have started this yesterday, but I got side-tracked. It's due the day after tomorrow.' Martin made a note on his handwritten sketch of the crossword. 'If you want to watch TV, go ahead.'

'No, I don't feel like watching by myself. I'll go downstairs to read.'

'Well, sorry to be such poor company, but I really do have to finish this or my editor will be at my door with a truncheon.'

'S'okay.' By the time Julia was back in her own flat her plan was complete.

'You can't do that,' Valentina said when Julia told her. 'You can't just give him medicine and not tell him.'

'Why not? He says refusing treatment is part of the disease. So I'm going to sneak it into him. He'll be glad when it works and he can go outside.'

'What about side effects? What if he's allergic? And how are you going to get your hands on medicine for obsessive compulsive disorder, anyway?'

'We'll just go to the doctor and pretend to have OCD. I've been reading about it, it's not hard to fake. I was thinking I would tell the doctor I'm super afraid of snakes. And maybe pluck out all my eyebrows.'

'Whadaya mean we? I'm not going with you.' Valentina held onto the arms of her chair as though she thought Julia might pull her out of it.

Julia shrugged. 'Okay, fine. I'll go by myself.'

It was much more complicated than she had anticipated, but Julia did eventually manage to get a prescription for Anafranil. She decanted the capsules into a vitamin bottle and presented herself in Martin's office one evening after dinner.

'Look, I remembered,' she said, shaking the bottle so the pills rattled.

He was bent over some photographs, lost in another language. 'Sorry, what? Oh, hello, Julia. What's that? That's very kind, thank you. Here, I'll put them next to the computer so I remember to take them.'

'No,' said Julia. 'I'll keep them and make sure you take them. That's our deal, right?'

'Was it?' he said. She went to the kitchen to get a glass of water. When she handed him one capsule and the glass, Martin let the pill rest in his palm and glanced at it. He looked up at her inquisitively but didn't say anything.

'Aren't you going to take it?' she asked nervously. ANAFRANIL 25 MG was printed right on the capsule; she was counting on Martin's near-sightedness to conceal that.

'Hmm? Oh, yes.' He put the pill in his mouth and gulped it down with water. 'There you are, Nurse.'

Julia laughed. 'You look better already.' She rattled the vitamin bottle flirtatiously and went downstairs. Valentina was sitting on the floor of Elspeth's office peering into her laptop.

'You're going to kill him,' Valentina said.

'No, I'm not. What are you talking about?'

'Look at this.' Valentina swivelled her computer towards Julia, who sat on the floor next to her. 'Look at the side effects.'

Julia read. *Blurred vision, constipation, nausea, vomiting, allergies, heart palpitations* . . . It was a long list. She looked at Valentina. 'I'm up there a lot. I see him more than a doctor would. I just have to monitor him, that's all.'

'What if he has a heart attack?'

'That's probably not going to happen.'

'What if he gets seizures? He's not going to tell you if he's suddenly impotent or constipated.'

'I just gave him a little dose.'

Valentina logged off and shut down the computer. She stood up. 'You're an idiot,' she told Julia. 'You can't just decide things for people. And you look weird without eyebrows.'

'You haven't even met him,' Julia said, but Valentina had already left the room. Julia heard her walking through the flat, out the front door and down the stairs. 'Fine,' Julia said. 'Be like that. You'll see.'

Robert's birthday dawned clear and balmy. He had gone to sleep at a reasonable hour the night before, so he bounded out of bed feeling oddly joyous and expectant. '*Dadadadadada – blahblahblahblah BIRTHDAY . . .*' He sang in the shower and ate a soft-boiled egg and toast. He spent a luxurious morning rewriting the chapter of his thesis devoted to Stephen Geary, Highgate Cemetery's architect. He presented himself at the cemetery before noon and pottered in the archives with James until it was time to give the two o'clock tour. All the familiar memorials seemed to salute him: *Eventually you'll be dead, too, but not today.* When he returned from the tour he found the ground-floor office empty except for Nigel, the cemetery's manager, and a young couple who were discussing the funeral arrangements for their baby. Robert hastily withdrew and went upstairs.

Valentina was perched on one of the office chairs, effacing herself. Jessica was on the phone; Felicity was making tea and talking softly to George, the stone carver, about a memorial he was designing; James called down to Jessica from the archives; Edward was photocopying and Phil was unboxing a cake. Thomas and Matthew came in, rather shyly, and the office seemed suddenly overfull as the burial team seldom came indoors and both of them were very tall.

'Look,' said Phil. 'I had them do the Egyptian Avenue in icing.'

'Wow,' said Robert. 'That's really . . . unappetising.'

'Yeah,' Phil said. 'Grey icing is not enticing.'

Felicity laughed when she saw the cake. Then everyone shushed, remembering the bereaved parents in Nigel's office below. 'That's brilliant,' she said in a whisper. She started placing little pink candles on the cake. Jessica put the phone down and said, 'Behave yourselves,' to no one in particular. She winked at Valentina and went downstairs.

The only people Valentina had met before besides Robert were Jessica and Felicity. When Robert came in he'd smiled at her and Valentina felt a jolt of confidence. She watched with surprise as Robert bantered with Phil and parried jokes about his advancing mortality with Thomas and Matthew. *It's like being a zoologist, watching the rare animal in its natural habitat.* Robert didn't seem at all shy here. He summoned Valentina from her chair in the corner and began to introduce her around, one hand touching her back lightly. Valentina was excited to be seen by Robert's friends as part of a couple, even as she was conscious of how much this would have irritated her if it was Julia claiming her instead of Robert.

James came down from the archives and gingerly settled at Jessica's desk. Jessica walked into the office followed by Nigel. 'Oh,' he said. 'What's the occasion, then?'

'We're having a twentieth of April party, Nigel,' Felicity said. 'Didn't you bring your costume?'

'It's Robert's birthday,' James told him.

'Of course it is,' said Nigel regretfully. 'I'm afraid my mind's somewhere else.'

'Is it all arranged?' James asked.

'Yes,' he replied. 'The funeral is on Monday at eleven.' A pall came over the office; no one liked babies' funerals. Robert thought, *It always rains when we bury the babies*. Then he thought that couldn't be true, really. *But I'll bring an umbrella just in case.*

'Oh dear,' Nigel said, noticing the cake. 'What happened there?'

'Hey, now,' said Phil, 'don't disrespect the cake.' He took a picture of it with his phone – 'for the archives.'

Felicity lit the candles. Everyone clustered round Robert, who stood looking self-consciously pleased as they sang 'Happy Birthday' to him. Valentina sang and felt as though she'd known all these people for years: Phil with his leather trench coat and tattoos; George with his shirtsleeves rolled up and his baritone voice, a pencil sketch of a gravestone loosely held in his graphite-smudged hands; Edward, who reminded Valentina of a leading man in an old black-and-white movie, dignified in his suit and tie, singing with his hands clasped in front of him, as though he were in church; Thomas and Matthew in their high boots and braces, smiling as they sang; Nigel sad-faced, as though the singing was a very solemn task which might have unpleasant consequences; Felicity kind and clear-voiced; Jessica and James singing breathily like overblown flutes – all singing together, *Happy birthday, happy birthday to you*. At the end of the song Robert closed his eyes and wished *just to be happy again* and blew out all the candles but one. There was a murmur of not-quite concern in the group, then he took another breath and finished off the last candle. Applause, laughter. Robert cut the cake and gave Valentina the first piece. She held the paper plate in one hand and the plastic fork in the other, and watched him hand out slices. Felicity poured tea into the cemetery's motley collection of mugs and china cups. Robert ate a bite of cake; the grey icing tasted just like any other colour. He glanced at Valentina and found her staring at him, solemn and silent in the midst of the conviviality. Suddenly Valentina smiled and he felt light-hearted: the past seemed to dissipate and it was all about the future now. Robert walked over to Valentina and they stood side by side, eating cake, happily quiet together amid the humming birthday party. *It's going to be all right*, he thought.

Jessica watched them. *She looks so much like Elspeth*, she thought. *It's quite unnerving.* She thought of the couple she had just met, the young parents. They had leaned into each other as they went out through the cemetery's gate as though confronting a strong wind imperceptible to anyone else. Robert and Valentina were not touching at all, but Jessica was reminded of that leaning together. *He seems happy enough.* She sighed and sipped her tea. *Perhaps it will be all right.*

Elspeth was working with dust. She couldn't think why she had not understood before the communicative powers of dust. It was light and she could move it easily; it was the ideal medium for messages.

When the twins first arrived in the flat, Julia had idly run her finger across the dust on the piano, leaving a shiny trail. It had been bothering Elspeth, and she had begun to laboriously put the dust back, to erase Julia's thoughtless defacement, when she realised that she had stumbled across what amounted to a *tabula rasa*. Dust was a megaphone that could amplify her distress call. She was so excited that she immediately went to her drawer to think over the possibilities.

What to say, now that she finally had the chance? *'Help, I'm dead.'* No, they can't do anything about that. It's better not to seem too pathetic. But I don't want to frighten them. I want them to know it's me, not a trick. She thought of Robert. She could write to him; he would know she was here.

The next morning was Sunday. It was raining and the front room was suffused with an even, feeble light. Elspeth floated above the piano. If she had been visible to anyone, she would have appeared as only a face and a right hand.

The twins were in the dining room, lingering over coffee and the remains of toast and jam. Elspeth could hear their amiable, desultory conversation, the mid-morning debate over what manner of amusements to pursue today. She shut them out and concentrated on the dull dusty expanse before her.

Elspeth placed a tentative fingertip on the piano. She recalled reading somewhere that household dust was largely comprised of shed human skin cells. *So perhaps I'm writing with bits of my former body.* The dust gave way, soft particles yielding as she traced a shiny path. She exulted in the ease of it; she took care with her writing, so that Robert must know it as hers. She spent almost an hour writing a few lines. The twins had gone out by the time she was finished. Elspeth hummed and hovered over her work, admiring the flourish of her signature, the exactness of her punctuation. With great effort she switched on the floor lamp she had once used to illuminate sheet music. *They can't miss that,* she crowed, and took a celebratory flight around the flat, shooting through doors and skimming ceilings. She managed to drop a lump of sugar on the Kitten's head as it slept on a chair partially tucked under the dining-room table. *What a glorious morning!*

Robert spent the day, which happened to be May Day, at the entrance to the Eastern Cemetery pointing a great many people, most of them Chinese, towards Karl Marx's grave. That evening he sat at his desk, exhausted. He stared at his computer and tried to work out what it was exactly that irritated him so about Chapter III. There was something wrong with the tone of the thing: it was a rollicking, almost jolly chapter about cholera and typhoid. It wouldn't do. He couldn't fathom why epidemics had once seemed so delightful.

He was highlighting all the essential bits in red when he heard someone banging on his door.

Both twins stood in the front hall looking solemn. 'Come upstairs,' said Valentina.

'What's wrong?'

'We have to show you something.'

Julia followed Valentina and Robert upstairs. She was conscious of feeling hopeful.

The flat was blazing with light. The twins escorted Robert to the piano and stepped back. He saw Elspeth's handwriting:

GREETINGS, VALENTINA AND JULIA

I AM HERE.

LOVE, ELSPETH

and:

ROBERT 22 JUNE 1992 E

Robert stood there, blank-minded. He put his hand out to touch the writing but Valentina caught his wrist. 'What does it mean? The date?' asked Julia.

'It's something . . . only she and I would know.'

Valentina said, 'She turned on that lamp.'

'What happened that day?' said Julia.

Valentina said, 'The writing looks just like Mom's.'

'What happened—'

'It's private, okay? It's between Elspeth and me.' Robert spoke sharply. The twins looked at each other and sat down on the sofa, hands folded. Robert read and reread the message. He thought about that first day: he stood in the front garden, taking down the estate agent's number off the To Let sign.

Elspeth was looking down at him through her front windows. She was waving and he'd waved back; she disappeared and came almost immediately – she must have run down the stairs. She was wearing a white sundress; she had her hair pulled back with a clip. She wore those cheap rubber sandals – *What were those called?* They flapped at the bottoms of her feet as she went ahead of him up the steps, into the flat. It was completely empty, that day, his flat. She took him through it but they talked about other things. What had they said to each other? He could not recall. He remembered only following her, the way the sundress revealed the wings of her back, the delicate vertebral knobs that vanished into the trough of her spine, the zipper of the dress, the tight waist and the full skirt. She had a slight tan that summer. Later they had gone upstairs, to her flat, and they had drunk shandy in this room and later still they had gone to her bedroom and he had unzipped that dress and it had fallen off her like a shell. She was warm under his hands. Later he rented the flat, but that afternoon he forgot why he was there, forgot everything but her bare feet, the way her hair kept escaping from the clip, her face without make-up, the way her hands moved. *I'm going to fall apart, Elspeth. I can't . . . I don't know what to feel.*

He stared at the writing. Valentina thought, *He doesn't feel that for me.* Julia waited. She wondered if Elspeth was in the room with them. The Kitten jumped up on the sofa and perched herself on one of its arms. She folded her paws under her chest and watched them, obviously indifferent to any spirits that might be present.

Finally Robert said, 'Elspeth?'

Each of them in turn felt their whole bodies go deep, fleeting cold. Robert said, 'Will you write something for us?' The twins got up and the three of them stood at the piano, watching the surface.

It was like a slow stop-action cartoon. The dust seemed to displace itself; the letters emerged through invisible agency: YES.

Elspeth saw that Robert was struggling to reconcile past with present, that he was excited and disturbed. Valentina watched him and Julia watched Valentina. *That's how it is*, Elspeth thought. *Hard on all of us.* She began to wander around the room, pushing at things. Doors swayed, drapes fluttered. Robert looked up from his contemplation of the piano as she turned a table lamp off and on a few times.

'Come here, sweet,' he said, and she flew to his side, suddenly happy. He felt her as a proximity, a cold presence. *How did I not understand, before? She was here, and I left her alone.* Robert thought of all his visits to her grave, thought of himself sitting for hours on the steps of the Noblin mausoleum chatting away pointlessly, remembered his evening by the river with Valentina and felt foolish and a little nauseated. *But I didn't really believe she was there. Did I?* He stood shaking his head. He stopped when he realised he was doing it. 'Tell us what it's like . . . How is it? . . . How are you?' Robert wanted to say things he could not say with the twins present. Elspeth positioned herself over the piano and began to consider the question. *How am I? Well, dead. Um, try to be positive about that. Hmm . . .* She made a little spiral in the dust while she thought about it. Robert remembered her pages and pages of spirals doodled whilst talking on the telephone. *You're here, really here.*

Valentina and Julia watched the shiny spiral appear, bystanders. *We're, like, the sheep at Jesus' birth,* Julia thought. Valentina wondered if Elspeth watched them all the time. *What does she know about us? Does she like us?* It all seemed very uncomfortable. Valentina tried to remember if either of them had ever said anything unkind about Elspeth. When the twins were tiny they had scared each other with the idea of God watching them every minute of every day. *You could never be good enough* . . . She watched Robert's face. He had forgotten her. He was waiting for Elspeth to write again.

Letters began to appear: LONELY. TRAPPED IN FLAT. HAPPY TO SEE V & J. MISS YOU.

Julia said, 'Is there anything you want?'

READ BOOKS. PLAY GAMES. PAY ATTENTION.

'Pay attention to you?'

YES. TALK TO ME, PLAY WITH ME. Elspeth wrote as quickly as she could. Her writing was uncontrolled and large, and she could see that the surface of the piano was not going to allow unlimited conversation. Just then the Kitten leapt on the piano keys with a musical crash and up onto the middle of the piano lid, obliterating Elspeth's writing as efficiently as a duster. 'Ugh,' said Valentina, scooping her up, 'bad girl.' She threw the Kitten onto the sofa. The Kitten, thus rejected, went under the piano to sulk.

Now half the dust was gone from the piano. Elspeth wrote along the edge of the music stand: R – SEANCES – OUIJA?

'Right, the Victorians used Ouija boards. And automatic

writing, spirits would possess the medium and speak through them. I mean, that's what the mediums pretended they were doing. But they were frauds, Elspeth.'

MAYBE.

'Right, okay. Do you want to try?'

OUIJA?

'I'll have to make the board.' He turned to the twins. 'Do you have a large sheet of paper? We need a notebook, a biro and a drinking glass to be the planchette.' Julia went to the kitchen and returned with a juice glass and a pen. Valentina brought the notebook and a few sheets of white paper from the computer printer. She taped them together.

Robert wrote the letters of the alphabet in three rows. He wrote the words YES and NO in the upper corners of the paper. He put the paper on the coffee table and the glass upside down in the centre of the paper.

Elspeth thought, *That glass is too heavy.* She managed to rattle it as though it were having its own private earthquake, but she could not make it glide even an inch.

Robert said, 'We need something that hardly weighs anything. Perhaps a bottle cap?' Julia ran back to the kitchen and returned with the round blue plastic safety strip she had peeled off the milk bottle that morning. 'Yes, brilliant,' Robert said. He placed it where the glass had been and it began to skitter around the paper *like it's glad to be out of the garbage can, it's like a happy water bug,* Julia thought. It was easy to imagine Elspeth here in the room when she wrote on the piano; when she moved the plastic strip it seemed as though the thing itself had become a creature, moving under its own volition.

Julia and Valentina sat down on the floor next to the coffee table. Robert sat on the sofa and leaned over the board. The plastic thing stopped expectantly, as though listening. The Kitten came over and began marching her hind legs and preparing to pounce. *Get that animal out of here*, Elspeth thought. As though Elspeth had spoken out loud, Valentina got up and put the Kitten in the dining room and shut the door.

When she had settled again Valentina asked, 'What do you mean you're trapped in the flat? Have you been here all the time?' She didn't say, *Are you watching us all the time?* even though she wanted to.

The plastic thing spelled slowly. No one touched it; it moved with intention along short straight paths. YES ALWAYS HERE CANT LEAVE Robert wrote down the letters in the note-book as the plastic circle paused over them. He thought that he should have included punctuation on the board.

Julia asked, 'What about heaven? Or, you know, all that stuff they tell you in church?'

NO EVIDENCE PRO OR CON JUST HERE WAITING

'Ugh,' said Julia. 'Forever? Does anything change?'

I GET STRONGER

'Does this happen to everyone who dies?'

DONT KNOW ONLY ME HERE Elspeth wanted to ask questions, not just answer them. HOWS EDIE she spelled before Julia could ask anything else.

The twins exchanged glances. 'She's fine,' said Valentina. 'She was sad that you said she couldn't visit us here,' said Julia.

The plastic circle spun around the paper aimlessly. Finally Elspeth spelled, DONT TELL EDIE

'Don't tell her what?' asked Robert.

DONT TELL IM GHOST DONT TELL ANYONE

'Nobody would believe us,' Valentina told her. 'You know Mom, she would think we were totally lying. And she would think it was, you know, mean.'

YES MEAN DO YOU SPEAK FRENCH

'Yes,' said Julia.

LATIN

'Uh, no.'

VENI HUC CRAS R UT TECUM EX SOLO COLLOQUAR

Robert smiled. Julia said, 'No fair having secrets.' Valentina thought, *They have years of secrets already.* She wanted to throw up. Robert reached over and stroked her hair. She looked at him doubtfully. Julia and Elspeth each felt a twinge of jealousy, and each felt strange about that for her own reasons.

Elspeth spelled out TIRED

'Okay,' said Robert.

GOODNIGHT

'Goodnight, sweet.'

'Goodnight, Aunt Elspeth.'

Robert and the twins stood up. There was an awkwardness; they had nothing to say to each other in front of Elspeth. They each would have liked to go somewhere else and burst into exclamations over the strangeness, how peculiar and how exciting and disturbing, and what about it? 'Well, goodnight, then,' Robert said, and went downstairs to his own flat. 'Goodnight,' said the twins, as they watched him leave. He shut his door and stood looking at his ceiling, completely gobsmacked. Then he started laughing and couldn't stop.

The twins heard him. They sat at the little coffee table, flicking the planchette back and forth, not speaking. Elspeth lay on the floor in the hall for a while, listening to Robert laughing, worrying about him. When he quietened down she went back to the front room. She touched each twin on the crown of her head. *Goodnight, goodnight.* Elspeth curled up in her drawer in an ecstasy of satisfaction.

The next morning was still damp and drab. Robert lay in bed listening to the twins walking around their flat. He was afraid they might stay in, the weather was so unpromising. He could hear their kitten galloping through rooms at random. *How can a creature that sounds like the cavalry look like an oversized lab rat?* Robert hauled himself out of bed. He made coffee and showered. By the time he had dressed and drunk his coffee the twins were at his door.

'Do you want to go to the Cabinet War Rooms with us?' Valentina asked.

'Erm – I do, but I had better do some work. I've got horribly behind on my thesis. Jessica's insinuating that I've given it up.'

'Oh, come anyway.' Julia spent a few minutes trying to persuade him, perfectly aware that she sounded insincere. Valentina looked beseeching. Robert gently urged them on their way, and they finally left without him. Robert watched through his front window as they angled their immense tartan golfing umbrella through the gate.

He waited until he thought they must be safely on the tube. Then he gathered pencil and paper and retrieved Elspeth's key from a little drawer in his desk. He went upstairs and let himself into the flat.

He stood in the hall and wondered how best to proceed. He decided that the dining-room table would be most comfortable and sat down with the Ouija board, plastic circle and his pad of paper before him.

'Elspeth?' He spoke softly. *Perhaps she's sleeping. Do dead people sleep?* 'Elspeth, I thought we might try automatic writing because it seems like a lot of work for you to push a planchette around a Ouija board. Do you want to try?'

He sat for what seemed to him a very long time, hand poised over the paper in silence, waiting.

He fell into a reverie that featured the many soft-boiled eggs he had eaten whilst sitting in this very chair at this very table. The first morning he had breakfasted with Elspeth she had asked, 'How d'you like your eggs?' and he'd replied, 'Soft-boiled.' He showed her how to cook them; Elspeth ate her eggs scrambled. And every breakfast thereafter she had presented him with a perfectly soft-boiled egg in a little blue egg cup. He wondered where the egg cup was. Robert was thinking about getting up to look for it when his hand went cold and jerked sideways. He looked around, saw nothing. He picked up the pencil and repositioned himself.

This time he let the tip of the pencil touch the paper. The cold came gradually into his hand. The pencil began to move over the paper.

Circles, loops, spiky lines that looked like seismographs filled the page. Robert sometimes felt his fingers gripping the pencil without his willing them to do it. Sometimes it seemed to be the pencil itself that moved with unseen volition. He leaned over the paper, watching. The meaningless lines became smaller, tighter. Robert remembered his infant school days, practising the alphabet with a thick pencil on coarse paper. His fingers ached from the cold.

WHAT ARE YOU THINKING ABOUT?

He let go of the pencil and it dropped on the table, inert.

'Soft-boiled eggs,' said Robert quietly.

The pencil spun around a few times, as though it was amused, or perhaps upset at being abandoned. Robert picked it up with his left hand, to give his right hand a chance to warm.

LOL I MISS YOU.

'Likewise. Understatement. I just . . . this is bollocks, Elspeth. I didn't understand. I've been having all these dreams about you, where you're alive and I've been ignoring you – there was one a week ago where I was looking for you in Sainsbury's and you had turned into a lettuce and I had no idea . . . and now it turns out that that is essentially the case . . . I mean, not that you are a lettuce, but that you are here and I didn't realise.'

NOT YOUR FAULT.

'I keep thinking I've let you down.'

I DIED. NOT YOUR FAULT.

'In my head I know that . . .'

The twins sat on the kitchen floor listening, ears pressed to the dining-room door. Julia glanced at the trail of muddy water they'd tracked across the linoleum. *I hope he won't come in here, 'cause there's nowhere to hide.* Valentina wished they had really gone to the museum. She didn't want to listen to whatever Robert had to say to Elspeth. She looked at Julia, who was sprawled in an uncomfortable posture so as to get her ear in the best possible spot. Julia was rapt; she loved spying on people.

Elspeth sat on the table, watching Robert's face as he spoke to her. It was as though he'd gone blind; he'd no idea where she was, so he sat gazing upward as he talked.

'. . . so I can't seem to get on, things are a bit meaningless. And now here you are, but not exactly.' Robert paused, waiting to see if Elspeth would reply. When she didn't, he said, 'Maybe I could come to you. If I died . . .'

NO.

'Why not?'

WHAT IF YOU ENDED UP STUCK IN YOUR FLAT?

'Ah.'

I COULDN'T BEAR IT IF YOU DIED.

Robert nodded. 'Let's talk about something else.'

They both became aware of the breathing at the same moment. Elspeth wrote, KEEP TALKING, and Robert began to tell her about something Jessica had said to him the day before, an anecdote about her law-school days. Elspeth went to the kitchen door and stuck her head through it. At first she didn't see anything. Then she looked down and saw the twins. Elspeth laughed and flew back to Robert. SPIES, she wrote. COME BACK ANOTHER DAY.

HOW WILL I KNOW WHEN TO COME? Robert wrote back.

I'M ALWAYS HERE, Elspeth replied.

'I've got to go, sweet. It's almost noon, I told Jessica I'd help with the newsletter.'

I LOVE YOU.

He opened his mouth to say it, then wrote it instead. I LOVE YOU TOO. ALWAYS.

Elspeth ran her finger over the writing. She wished she could have the paper, then thought, *No, it's just a thing.* Robert gathered up the notebook and put the chair back where it had been. He stood in the front hall, not wanting to leave her. A wave of cold passed through him. It made him feel nauseous. He waited for the feeling to pass, and left.

Elspeth went back to the kitchen expecting to find the twins. There were only thin trails of mud on the floor. Elspeth went to the back-door window and was able to see Valentina and Julia creeping down the fire escape, soundlessly. When they got to the bottom they ran across the moss and disappeared into the side garden. *They're cleverer than they look.* She wasn't sure if that was a problem; she was aware of mixed emotions – pride and wariness, nostalgia and exasperation. *I wish I could stow them away somewhere while I frolic with Robert.* She sighed. *What a bad mother I would have been.*

What is more basic than the need to be known? It is the entirety of intimacy, the elixir of love, this knowing. Robert gave himself over to it. He and Elspeth spent hours each day – whenever the twins were out of the flat – engrossed in each other, reliving with paper and pencil fragments of days that had once seemed ordinary but were now precious and in need of lapidary acts of shared memory.

'Do you remember the day you broke your toe?'

IN GREEN PARK.

'I'd never seen you cry.'

IT HURT. YOU WOULD'VE, TOO.

'I imagine so.'

THAT NICE TAXI DRIVER.

'Yes. And we ate all that ice cream, later.'

AND GOT DRUNK. THE HANGOVER WAS WORSE THAN THE TOE.

'Lord, I'd forgotten that.'

And:

'What do you miss most?'

TOUCHING. BODIES. DRINKING, THAT HEAT IN THE THROAT.
SUBSTANCE — HAVING TO ACTUALLY LIFT MY HAND OR LEG, TURN
MY HEAD. SMELLS. I CAN'T REMEMBER HOW YOU SMELL.

'I kept some of your clothes, but the scent has faded.'

TELL ME HOW YOU SMELL.

'Oh. Let's see . . .'

DIFFERENT PARTS SMELL DIFFERENT.

'Yes . . . my hands smell like pencils, and lotiony, it's that
cucumber one you used to buy me . . . I had pepperoni for
lunch . . . Hmm. I don't know if it's possible to know one's
own smell. Sort of like not being able to ever see one's own
face, don't you think?'

I CAN'T SEE MYSELF IN MIRRORS.

'Oh. That seems — lonely.'

YES.

'I wish I could see you.'

I'M ON YOUR LEFT, LEANING OVER YOU.

'Mmm. No. Perhaps you're in some other part of the
spectrum. Ultraviolet? Infrared?'

YOU NEED GHOST SPECS.

'Brilliant! We could patent them, people could walk down the street and see all the ghosts riding the bus, haunting Sainsbury's—'

YOU COULD WEAR THEM IN THE CEMETERY. LOADS OF GHOSTS THERE?

'I wonder. I mean, you aren't in the cemetery, which is where I rather expected to find you.'

TWINS ARE COMING.

'Oh dear. Till tomorrow, then.'

And:

WHAT ARE WE GOING TO DO? YOU CAN'T LIVE THIS WAY.

'What do you mean? I'm happy. That is, I'm happy, considering.'

VALENTINA IS IN LOVE WITH YOU.

Robert put down the pencil. He got up and walked around the perimeter of the dining room, his arms wrapped around his torso as though for warmth. Finally he sat down again. 'What do you want me to do?'

I DON'T KNOW.

He stood up again. 'I don't know what to say, Elspeth.' He gathered up the notebook and pencils and went downstairs. Elspeth thought, *Say you love me.* Two days went by before Robert reappeared in the dining room, notebook in hand. 'I've been thinking,' he said, and sat with his hand poised over the paper, waiting for Elspeth to turn up. She was already there but she made no sign to him. She sat on one of the straight-backed chairs across the table from him, arms folded, eyes slitted.

Finally Robert said, 'Elspeth, I've been trying to sort things out. About Valentina. And I'm just very . . . confused.'

Silence. Robert could hear his nervous system whining in his head. It was a soft dark rainy day and the dining room was very gloomy.

'Okay, then. I'll just sit here and talk to myself.' He paused. Elspeth waited. 'Elspeth, what did you think was going to happen? You died almost a year and a half ago. I spent a year just . . . mourning you, and wishing I could die, thinking quite seriously in fact of killing myself, and just when things seemed to be lifting somewhat, the twins arrived. And if you think back, you had hinted or, actually, you'd said it more than once, that you were sending the twins here as a sort of sub-stitute for yourself. And just as I began to regard them, or rather Valentina, in that light, you reappear – well, not appear, but you reveal yourself to be here, and while that's absolutely wonderful it does seem as if we are rather stuck.'

Elspeth had a feeling about Robert then that she had never had when she was alive. *He's going to leave me*, she thought. *He doesn't love me any more.* It was something about the tone of his voice.

'Elspeth, if I could come and get you – if I knew where to go and how – or even if I could join you, I would do it.'

She went and stood next to him, afraid to hear what he would say next and afraid to interrupt him.

'But we're both betwixt and between, aren't we? I'm caught here in my body, and you're caught . . . here, without any body at all; no body, no voice . . . I go downstairs and look at all these pages of writing, and I think I'm losing my mind.'

She caught his hand and made a jerky line with the pencil. When she got it under control she wrote: YOU WANT ME TO HAVE A BODY?

'It's what I'm used to,' he said. 'I'm sorry.'

Elspeth let herself rise, until she was looking down at Robert from the ceiling; she was somewhat entangled in the chandelier. She began to run her hands through the little crystals and Robert looked up. *It's as though I'm a cloud, and he's expecting rain.*

'If you want me to give up Valentina I'll do it.'

Is that what I want? she wondered. *Why does he make me decide?* She put her fingers to the base of one of the delicate flame-shaped light bulbs in the chandelier. It surged with light and exploded. Robert averted his face, put up his hands to shield his eyes. He sat that way for what seemed to Elspeth a long time. Then he said quietly, 'Why did you do that?' He picked up the pencil, put his hand over the paper gingerly, avoiding the shards of light-bulb glass.

SORRY SORRY SORRY. BY MISTAKE — I WAS THINKING.

'Are you angry with me?'

HURT & CONFUSED, NOT ANGRY.

'Wait here, Elspeth. I'm going to clean up the glass. It will give us both time to think.' He went to the kitchen and found the dustpan and brush. After he had swept up all the slivers and replaced the bulb he sat down again and stared at the paper. *He looks so depressed*, Elspeth thought. *It's not good for him to sit in the dark scribbling with the dead lady. If this were a fairy tale the princess would come and save him. The least I can do is let him go.*

IT'S ALL RIGHT, she wrote. IF VALENTINA MAKES YOU HAPPY, GO AHEAD.

'Elspeth—'

DON'T FORGET ME.

'Elspeth, listen . . .'

But she had left the room, and she did not come back to talk with him that day or for many days to come.

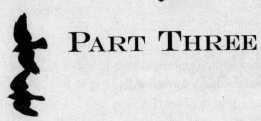

PART THREE

It was very early morning and Valentina woke before Julia, as she often did. She gently disengaged herself from Julia's arms and sat up in bed. The curtains were not quite closed; the light was pale and diffused. Something moved. Valentina wasn't properly awake and she saw it without really seeing. She thought it was the Kitten, but the Kitten was sleeping beside her on the bed. Valentina looked harder, and as she did the thing unfolded itself from where it had been sitting by the window and Valentina realised that she was seeing Elspeth.

It was like seeing from a long distance; Elspeth was faint and not sharply defined. *She looks just like Mom*, Valentina thought, but there was something about the way the ghost looked back at her that was unfamiliar and alien. Elspeth moved her mouth as though she were speaking and began to walk towards the bed. Until that moment Valentina had not been afraid but suddenly she was. The fear woke her up completely: Elspeth vanished. Valentina felt a cold touch on her cheek, then nothing. She slid off the bed and ran out of the flat, down the front stairs, then stood panting next to the mail baskets in her pyjamas.

Robert had only been asleep for an hour or so, and it took him some time to become aware of the knocking at his door. His first thought was that the house must be on fire. He came to the door in his underwear and poked his head out, squinting.

Valentina said, 'Can I come in?'

'Ah. Minute.' He walked to his bedroom and put on trousers and yesterday's shirt, then went back to the door and opened it wide. He said, 'Good morning,' and then, observing her more carefully, 'What's wrong?'

'I saw Elspeth,' she replied, and began to cry.

Robert put his arms around Valentina and said, 'Hush,' to the top of her head. After she had recovered somewhat, he said, 'I've been trying to see her for weeks. How did she look?'

'Like Mom.'

'Then why are you crying?'

'I've never seen a ghost before. I mean, you know, she's *dead*.'

'Yes. I know.' He led her into the kitchen. She sat at the table, and he began to make tea. Valentina blew her nose on a paper towel. Robert said, 'Did you have the impression that she was trying to appear to you? Or what happened, exactly?'

Valentina shook her head. 'I think when I first saw her she was sitting in the window seat looking out. It wasn't like she was especially trying to make me see her. When she noticed I was looking at her she came over to me and then I got scared and she disappeared.' Valentina paused. 'Actually, what I think it was, I don't think I was totally awake.'

'Oh,' Robert said. 'So you dreamt her?'

'No – I don't think so. But maybe it's like . . . you know how when you try to remember something, and you can't think of it, and then later when you're not trying to think about it any more it just pops into your head?'

'Yes?'

'Maybe I saw her because I forgot I couldn't see her.'

Robert laughed. 'I'll have to try that. Of course, she's not speaking to me lately, so I don't imagine she'll appear. How did she seem? Was she angry with you?'

'Angry? No, she was trying to tell me something, but it wasn't like she was mad or anything.'

The kettle boiled and Robert poured water into the teapot. He said, 'Don't you and Julia talk to her?'

'Sometimes. But she doesn't want to answer the questions we want to ask.'

Robert smiled and put the tea things on the table. 'Perhaps if you let Elspeth do the asking you'll eventually find out whatever it is you want to know.' He sat down across from Valentina.

'Maybe. I wish you'd just tell us.'

'Tell you what?'

'Whatever it is — we're not exactly sure, but there's some big secret about Elspeth and Mom. I mean, they were *twins*, and then they never spoke to each other again. What was that about?'

'I'm sure I couldn't say.'

'Couldn't, or wouldn't?' Valentina said irritably.

'Couldn't. I have no idea why Elspeth and Edie parted ways. It happened long before I met Elspeth, and she hardly ever mentioned your mother.' He poured out the tea.

Valentina watched steam rise from her mug.

Robert said, 'Why do you need to know? Your mother

doesn't want to tell you, and Elspeth took great care not to leave anything behind that might cause anxiety. Of course, that's assuming that there actually is a secret.'

'Mom is afraid we'll find out.'

'Isn't that a good reason to *leave it be*?' He said this more vehemently than he meant to; Valentina looked startled. 'Listen,' Robert said more quietly, 'sometimes when you finally find out, you realise that you were much better off not knowing.'

Valentina frowned. 'How would you know? And besides, you're a historian. You spend all your time finding out stuff about other people.'

'Valentina, it's one thing to research the Victorians, it's completely different when you unearth your own family skeletons.'

She didn't reply.

'Here. I'll give you a cautionary tale.' Robert drank some of his tea, and experienced a qualm. *Do I really want to tell her this?* But she was looking at him expectantly. He said, 'When I was fifteen, my mother suddenly came into a great deal of money. "Who gave you the money, Mum?" I asked her. "Oh, my Great Aunt Pru died and left it to me," she said. Now, I come from a family with a prodigious quantity of aunts, but I had never heard of this one; my mother's family could trace itself back to the Crusades but they didn't any of them have a bean. But that was her story, and she stuck to it.

'Then, about two weeks later, I was watching television and they were interviewing a new cabinet minister – and it was my father. He had a different name, but there he was. "Mum,"

I said, "come and look at this." We both sat there watching him do this interview, looking terribly smarmy and respectable.'

Valentina knew what was coming. 'So, the money came from your father?'

'Yes. He had finally got to a point in his career where she could ruin him quite spectacularly if she went to the tabloids. "Cabinet Minister's Double Life" would have been the headline, I suppose. So he paid up and I never saw him again. Except on TV, of course.'

Valentina understood something she had been afraid to ask. 'So that's why you don't have a job?'

'Yeee-ss,' Robert said. 'Though eventually, when I'm done with my dissertation, I'd like to teach, I think.' He sighed. 'I would rather have gone on being poor and seeing my father now and then.'

'I thought you didn't like him.'

'Well, he didn't care much for children, and I had just got to the age where we might have developed an actual understanding – but it was all a sham, anyway.'

'Oh.' Valentina thought she ought to say something. 'I'm sorry.'

Robert smiled at her. 'You're sounding more English by the day. No need to be sorry.' They heard Julia's footsteps in the kitchen above them. 'Should you go upstairs?'

'In a while.'

'Would you like some breakfast, then?'

'Sure.'

Robert collected eggs, bacon, butter and various other items from the fridge. 'How do you like your eggs?'

'Fried?'

While the bacon and eggs cooked he set out plates and cutlery, jam and juice; he made toast. Valentina watched him, comforted by his efficiency and delighted by the novelty of having a man serve her breakfast while he pretended not to notice that she was wearing pyjamas.

Robert slid the food onto their plates and sat down. They began to eat. Upstairs, Julia stomped across the kitchen. 'Somebody's not happy,' Robert said.

'I don't care.'

'Ah, well,' he said.

'I wish I could just leave,' Valentina said.

But you just got here. Robert said, 'Why don't you, then?'

Valentina sensed that he was – what? *Offended?* She said hastily, 'I don't mean you – I mean Julia. She thinks she owns me. She's, like, a total dictator about it.'

Robert hesitated, then said, 'At the end of the year, you can sell the flat and do what you like.'

Valentina shook her head. 'Julia won't sell it. Julia won't do anything that would let me be independent. I'm stuck.'

'You could go to Xavier Roche and ask him to divide the estate. There's enough money in the trusts that Julia could keep the flat and you could take your share in cash,' Robert said.

Valentina brightened. 'I could do that?'

'It's provided for in the will. Didn't you read it?'

'We did,' Valentina said vaguely, 'but I wasn't paying attention to the small print.'

'Elspeth said she regrets having stipulated that you both live here for a year. She's rather worried about you.'

'When did she say that?' Valentina asked.

'Last week.'

'Too late.'

'Yes,' Robert said. 'I think that watching you and Julia come unglued is too much like whatever happened to her and Edie.'

Valentina finished her eggs and wiped her mouth. 'I wish she'd tell us.'

Robert said, 'I think she would – I think it's your mother who doesn't want you to know.'

'What would you do if you were me?'

Robert smiled and ran his eyes over her pyjamas. 'All sorts of things,' he said. 'Shall I list them?'

'No – you know what I mean.' She blushed.

He sighed. 'I would make friends with Elspeth.'

'Oh.' She thought about this. 'I'm frightened of her.'

'That's because you only know her as cold blasts of air and such. She was wonderful when she was alive.'

'Why is Elspeth not speaking to you?'

'Sorry?'

'You said she wasn't—'

'Oh, so I did.' He got up to clear away the dishes. 'It's just a misunderstanding. It will pass.'

'Was she . . . was she more like Julia, or me?'

Robert shook his head. 'She was herself. She was plucky, like Julia, but also restrained, like you. She was very clever and she liked to have her own way. But she usually worked it so that I enjoyed whatever it was she'd manoeuvred me into doing.'

'It freaks me out that she watches us and we don't know she's there.'

'Perhaps you could use that as an excuse to treat each other more kindly?'

'What did she tell you?' asked Valentina.

He looked surprised. 'I can use my own eyes.'

She coloured deeply but did not reply. Robert said, 'From what I've been able to glean, Elspeth and Edie had an agreement that Elspeth wouldn't have anything to do with you and Julia. Elspeth seems to feel that she kept up her end of the bargain.' He returned the juice and butter to the fridge. 'But now I think she would like to get to know you a bit. Since you're here.' He began to run water into the sink. 'If it's any comfort, she probably spends less time hovering round than you imagine. She liked to be off on her own. If you put out a few books where she can get at them, or leave the TV on for her, I'm sure she'd let you be.'

'The TV's broken,' Valentina reminded him.

'Let's cope with that, then, shall we?' Robert was standing at the sink with his back to Valentina. He stared out of the window and thought of Elspeth. *You must be bored silly. No one to talk to, nothing to read.* He tried to imagine how Elspeth had felt when Valentina ran away from her in a panic. He turned to Valentina and said, 'Do you mind if I go up later and try to talk to her?'

Valentina shrugged. 'Sure, no problem. But why even ask? You're in our flat all the time, talking to her.'

'I hadn't realised I was so obvious.'

'We can use our own eyes.' She smiled.

'Touché.'

Valentina stood up and padded over to Robert. 'Thank you for breakfast.' He had his hands in the soapy water and she darted a kiss at his face just as he turned to her.

'Ouch,' he said. 'Let's do that properly.' Each kiss was a little lesson. Robert enjoyed them, though he was beginning to wonder if they would ever lead to a more advanced curriculum. His hands were wet but he slid them under her pyjama top and ran his palms over her breasts.

She whispered, 'That's nice.'

'It could be much nicer,' he offered.

'Mmm. Not . . . yet.' She stepped back, looking confused. Robert smiled.

'I have to go upstairs,' Valentina said.

'Okay.'

'I'm going to talk to Elspeth.'

'That's good,' he told her.

'And I'll be nice to Julia.'

'Also good.'

'See you later.'

'Yes.'

When Valentina returned to their flat she found Julia at the dining-room table, fully dressed and reading the newspaper over a cup of coffee with a lit cigarette in her hand.

'Hi,' Valentina said.

'Hi,' Julia replied without looking up.

'I wish you wouldn't smoke in the flat.'

'I wish you wouldn't run downstairs and screw Robert

when I'm sleeping, but that doesn't stop you, does it?' Julia kept her eyes on the newspaper.

'I haven't – we haven't – and that's none of your business anyway.'

Julia looked at Valentina. 'Whatever. Your pyjamas are all wet.' She put the cigarette to her lips, blew the smoke in Valentina's direction. Valentina went to take a shower. By the time she was dressed Julia had left the flat.

Valentina collected a stack of paper and some pens and pencils. She spread the Ouija board Robert had made onto the coffee table, and placed the plastic planchette carefully in the middle of it. 'Elspeth?' she called. 'Are you here?'

The planchette began to move. GOOD MORNING, it said. As Valentina watched, she saw Elspeth materialise, hovering over the board, pushing the little planchette with great concentration. Elspeth looked up at her and smiled.

Valentina smiled back. 'Tell me a story,' she said.

WHAT SORT OF STORY

'Tell me about you and Mom, when you were little . . .'

Elspeth tilted her head to the side and thought for a moment. She placed her finger inside the planchette and twirled it a few times. Then she knelt by the table and slowly began to spell: ONCE UPON A TIME THERE WERE TWO SISTERS NAMED EDIE AND ELSPETH . . .

Martin had a toothache. It had been coming on for days. Now it had arrived in his mouth, like a train, and he was unable to think of anything else. He stood in front of the bathroom mirror and tried to see the painful tooth by leaning his head back, opening his mouth and straining his eyes downward, but this merely caused him to fall over backwards and crack his shin on the bathtub. He gave up and took some codeine that Marijke had left over from her slipped disc. Then he went back to bed.

Later in the morning his phone rang. Since the phone was in bed with him, quite near his head, Martin felt as though it were his tooth that was ringing; the pain was excruciating. It was Marijke.

'Hallo, sailor, what of the sea?' She sounded quite cheerful.

'Still salty,' he said. 'How are you?' He sat up and fumbled for his glasses.

'What's wrong?' Marijke said. 'You sound asleep.'

'Oh . . . I've got toothache.' He felt a little ashamed of himself; he wanted her to feel sorry for him.

'Oh, *no*.' Marijke was sitting in her flat, having a leisurely Saturday morning in her comfortable chair with a detective novel on her lap and a bowl of crisps to hand. She had decided to call Martin in a mood of magnanimity. Now his toothache groped through the phone and demanded that she attend to it. 'Have you done anything for it? Which tooth?'

'One of the upper molars. On the right side. It feels like someone's kicking my face.'

Neither of them said anything, because there was no obvious remedy. Even if Martin could have gone to the dentist, he had no dentist to go to: Dr Prescott had left the NHS to practise privately; in the process he had dropped Martin from his patient list. Anyway, it didn't matter, because Dr Prescott didn't do home visits. Finally Marijke said, 'Maybe you should call Robert?'

'Why?'

'Maybe he could . . . no, never mind.'

Martin pressed his hand against his cheek. The tooth was throbbing more relentlessly. 'He's a clever chap, but I don't think he knows much about dentistry.' Martin climbed out of the bed and walked into the bathroom. Something was different – but he couldn't think what it was, not with his tooth pulsing whilst he was talking to Marijke and trying to find the bottle of codeine capsules – *Ah, there.* He swallowed two and wandered back to bed. As he got into bed he realised that he had just walked on the floor in his bare feet without giving it a thought. *Hmm.* The anxiety wasn't there; no compulsion urged itself upon him. He turned his attention back to Marijke.

'So what are you going to do?' she asked him.

'Sleep?'

'Shall I call Robert, then?'

'All right – tell him to come up with a pair of pliers.'

'Ugh,' she said. 'Go back to sleep.'

*   *   *

Later Martin was sitting at his kitchen table in a codeine fog, trying to eat lukewarm porridge. He heard Robert stumbling through the dark flat, calling his name. 'Here. The kitchen,' Martin said, with effort.

'Hey,' Robert said softly when he arrived in the kitchen. 'Marijke says you've fallen afoul of the tooth fairy.'

'Mmm,' Martin said.

'Listen – if I found a dentist – could you leave the flat?' Martin shook his head very slowly.

'You're *quite* sure?'

'I'm sorry . . .'

'Never mind. I'm going to make some calls. I'll be back soon, I hope.'

Time passed and Robert did not reappear. Martin put his head on the table and dozed. When he woke again Julia was sitting at the table reading yesterday's *Telegraph*. She had washed the dishes.

'Robert sent me,' she told him.

'Time is it?' Martin asked.

'Four-ish,' said Julia. 'Can I do anything? Tea?'

'Yes, please,' said Martin. Julia had brought the bag of frozen peas. Martin gratefully held it against his face. She got up and began to make tea.

Julia said, 'Robert's here.' Martin sat up and ran his hands over his hair so that it stood straight up and made him look surprised.

'Martin,' Robert said, 'I've brought Sebastian.'

Robert's friend Sebastian Morrow, the funeral director, stood in the kitchen doorway. Martin had always found Sebastian to be rather aloof; now he looked uncertain and reluctant, though resplendent in a beautiful deep-blue suit; his shoes gleamed and he held an ominous leather satchel.

'But I need a dentist,' said Martin, 'not an undertaker. Yet.'

Robert said, 'Before he became an undertaker Sebastian did the undergraduate course in dentistry at Barts.'

Julia rose from her seat and stood near the back door with her arms folded across her chest. *Only Robert would bring an undertaker to pull a tooth.*

Martin said, 'Why didn't you carry on with dentistry?'

Sebastian said, 'Dead people don't bite.' He lifted the satchel and asked, 'May I?'

'Please,' said Martin.

Robert spread a clean towel on the table, and Sebastian laid out his instruments: a syringe for the novocaine, a bottle of alcohol, wads of cotton and gauze. Robert took a cup and a bowl from the cupboard, and Sebastian put on an immaculate white coverall. He washed his hands and pulled on latex gloves.

As long as he'd been waiting for Robert to come, Martin had devoutly wished for an end to his agony. But now, watching Sebastian prepare, Martin began to feel unendurably anxious. 'Wait!' he said, grasping Sebastian's wrist. 'I have to . . . do something first.'

'Martin,' said Robert, 'we can't wait hours for you to—'

'Here, Martin,' said Julia, suddenly at his side, 'I'll do it for you, okay? You stay here and just tell me what to do, yeah?'

She leaned over and put her ear next to Martin's mouth, expectantly.

Martin hesitated. *Is it all right if she does it instead of me?* He tried to consult the inner feeling that arbitrated these things. It was mute. At last he whispered to Julia, and she nodded. 'Out loud?' Julia asked.

'No, but stand where I can see you.'

Sebastian said, 'Let's try to make you comfortable.' He and Robert rearranged Martin so he was leaning back in his chair with his head supported by telephone directories and towels on the table. Julia stood over him with a torch, shining it down at his face. She began to count, moving her lips silently. Martin fixed his eyes on Julia's lips and prayed.

'Open, please,' said Sebastian. 'Oh dear.'

Martin held Julia's hand tightly while he waited for the novocaine to work; her other hand shook and the torchlight wavered across his face. Martin had a blessed sensation of pain being lifted away from him. 'Steady, please,' Sebastian said. 'I've almost got it.' The next few minutes were rather bloody. Martin closed his eyes. There was a dull crack, and then some probing. 'That's it, then,' Sebastian said, sounding surprised. Martin smelled clove oil and alcohol. Sebastian packed cotton into the empty gum space. 'Bite down, please, gently.' Martin opened his eyes.

'All done,' said Sebastian, beaming. Martin sat up. The tooth lay in the bowl, brownish-grey and bloody-rooted and very much smaller than he'd imagined it. Julia was still counting and Martin put up his hand to tell her she could stop. 'Eight hundred and twenty-two,' she said.

'Is that all?' Martin tried to ask her, but his face was numb and she didn't understand him. The pain was gone, leaving a vacancy where there would be different pain when the anaesthetic wore off. 'You're a genius,' he mumbled to Sebastian.

'Not at all,' Sebastian said, but he looked relieved. 'Anyone can extract a tooth. I'm glad it came out in one piece though – it looks awfully fragile.'

'If we'd had proper facilities, could it have been saved?' Robert asked.

'No . . . but we would have known that before taking it out, instead of afterwards.' Sebastian began to wash up. Julia helped him. He packed his satchel and shook hands with Martin, who tried to pay him for his services. 'Certainly not, glad to help. You mustn't smoke for a couple of days, and keep ice on it, please. I have to run now – I was in the middle of something when Robert rang me.'

Robert saw Sebastian out. When he returned Martin said, 'What was he doing when you called him?' Martin imagined Sebastian leaning over an inert form on a steel table, wielding those shiny instruments . . .

'He was having tea at the Wolseley with a very lovely woman. She's been waiting in my flat while Sebastian worked on your tooth. That's one of the reasons it took me so long to bring him. That, and we had a hard time acquiring the novocaine. Which reminds me, we need to somehow get you antibiotics.'

Martin put his fingers to his cheek. 'Thank you. Thank you, both. All three of you.' He looked up at Robert.

'Must send him a bottle of whisky. And one for you too.'
Martin smiled lopsidedly at Julia. 'You too?'

She smiled back. 'No, thanks. It tastes like medicine.'

Martin said, 'That reminds me, Nurse; I should take my
vitamins.'

Julia looked embarrassed. 'It's not time yet.'

'I know, but I'm tired and I'm going to bed early. So be a
darling . . .'

'Okay,' Julia said. She went off to get the pills.

Robert said, 'What was that about?'

'Oh,' said Martin, 'she's been feeding me Anafranil. She's
pretending it's vitamins, and I'm pretending I believe her.'

Robert laughed. 'In my next life I'm coming back as a
pretty girl. That's so typical – you wouldn't do it for Marijke,
you wouldn't even listen to me banging on about it, but for
Julia you're a model patient.' Robert filled the electric kettle
and flicked the switch. 'Can you eat something?'

'I suppose I ought to.' Martin watched Robert setting out
the tea things. 'Really, though, I *am* taking it for Marijke.'

'Are you? Have you told her?'

'Not yet. I thought I might surprise her one of these days.'
Martin touched his cheek again; he could feel it swelling. He
stood up slowly and retrieved the bag of peas from the freezer.
Robert took the bag from him and wrapped it in a tea towel.
Martin held it against his cheek, thinking of Marijke. He
wanted to call her and tell her everything was all right, but he
didn't want Robert listening. Martin frowned and said, 'Did
Sebastian say I'm not to smoke?'

Julia came into the kitchen and looked at Robert. *Are you*

still here? Robert said, 'You can't smoke or use a drinking straw because the extraction has to scab over and sucking might dislodge the scab.'

Martin said, 'Oh,' so dismally that Robert and Julia both laughed. Robert said, 'What's Valentina up to?' and Julia mimed a hand writing on invisible paper. 'Really?' said Robert. 'Do you think she'd mind if I popped in?'

'I don't know,' said Julia. 'I don't think she wanted *me* around. But go ahead. I'll make the tea.'

Robert said to Martin, 'Just call if you need anything.'

Martin said, 'I'm fine now. Thank you again; that was . . . miraculous.'

'It was, wasn't it?' Robert said, and went off feeling pleased with himself.

Julia made tea and then poked around in the cabinets and refrigerator for possible dinner ingredients. She held up a tin of chicken noodle soup, and Martin said, 'Yes, please.' His stomach growled. He said, 'Your sister likes to write?'

Julia hesitated. Elspeth had told them not to tell anyone, and they hadn't. She had been tempted to tell Martin, but something always held her back; she was afraid he would think her a liar. 'Yeah,' she replied. 'Just, you know, email, not real writing.' She gave Martin a mug of tea and opened the tin of soup. Martin put the frozen peas on the table and wrapped his hands around the mug, waiting for the tea to cool. The novocaine was wearing off. He hated the rubber-lips sensation it gave, but the in-between pain/not pain was worrying too.

Julia heated the soup, microwaved a potato, set the table,

moving quietly around Martin's kitchen, thinking now about Robert and Valentina downstairs with Elspeth; now remembering Sebastian's slim gloved hands gripping the forceps to pull the tooth; and now the panicked expression on Martin's face as he opened his mouth at Sebastian's request, and the way the panic had subsided as Martin kept his eyes on her lips as she counted for him. *Numbers . . . Why numbers? What's comforting about counting?* She turned to look at Martin. He was sitting slumped with his head tilted, staring off into nothing. *He looks sad. Or maybe that's just how he looks when he isn't doing something else with his face.*

Julia served Martin and herself. There was no point in worrying over whether Valentina expected to eat dinner with her; Robert was there. Martin ate carefully, trying not to bite himself. After the meal Julia counted out his pills and he swallowed them and smiled his half-smile at her. 'Thank you, Nurse.'

'You're welcome,' she said, and began to clear the table. When she glanced at him a moment later he had lapsed back into his sad expression. 'What's wrong, Martin?'

'Oh – I know it's silly, but I'm worrying because I can't smoke. I know I ought to quit, but this doesn't seem to be the right moment – that is, I'm always quitting, but I wasn't planning to quit today.'

Julia smiled. 'When our dad had his wisdom teeth out he couldn't smoke so Mom smoked for him.'

'I fail to see how—'

Julia snapped her fingers. 'Where are your cigarettes?'

'In the bedroom.'

She came back with the blue packet and the lighter, pulled her chair very close to Martin's and lit a cigarette. 'Okay, now, like this . . .' Julia took a drag, taking care not to inhale. Martin opened his mouth and she blew the smoke into it. 'Yeah?' she said. Martin nodded and smoke came out of his nose. 'Yeah.'

Julia put her hand on Martin's shoulder. They leaned into each other. She turned her head and put her lips to the cigarette; the tip glowed. Martin's eyes were half-closed, his mouth half-open. Julia tilted her face, and when she was inches away she blew the smoke very slowly; the sound Martin made as he inhaled reminded her of Valentina's long asthmatic gasps. He exhaled, then chuckled.

'What?' she said.

'I'm awfully useless, aren't I? Can't even smoke for myself.'

'Don't be silly,' Julia said. She touched his jaw. 'Chipmunk cheek.' Martin raised his eyebrows. She took another drag on the cigarette. He leaned towards her eagerly.

When Robert went downstairs he found the door to the twins' flat ajar. He knocked and went in. There was a window open somewhere in the flat and a cool damp breeze had found its way into the hall. Valentina was sitting on the sofa in the front room, surrounded by pieces of paper. The Ouija board and the plastic planchette were on the coffee table. The evening light made everything golden: all the faded rose-and-pink velvet brightened; Valentina's pale green dress spread around her like a lily pad and her hair, electrified, encircled her face; everything merged in the golden light so that it seemed to Robert like a painting, one continuous surface. Valentina was sitting at the far end of the sofa with one foot tucked under her. She was facing the other end of the sofa as though someone were sitting there with her. Robert stood in the doorway and tried, wished and hoped to see this other. But he could not.

Valentina turned to him. He hadn't noticed before how tired she looked; her eyes were bloodshot and had dark smudges underneath. 'Can you see her?' she asked.

'No,' he said. 'Tell me . . . how does she look?'

Valentina smiled. 'She changed when you came in . . .' Valentina shook her head slightly. 'Why shouldn't I say that? Anyway, she's wearing a blue silk dress. It's tight at the waist and has an A-line skirt; her hair is short – there's just a little curl to it – it makes her eyes look huge; she's incredibly pale, except her hands and the edges of her ears . . . She's wearing dark lipstick . . . What else should I tell him?'

'Can you *hear* her?'

'No, she's pointing to things . . .'

Robert sank down until he was sitting on the floor at the edge of the scattered papers. He leaned his elbows on the coffee table. From this vantage point he thought he saw a disturbance in the air where Elspeth should be: perhaps it was like looking through perfectly clear glass; perhaps it was like trying to see music. He shook his head. 'I want to, but I can't.'

The planchette began to move. Valentina wrote down the message. MAYBE SOON.

'Yes,' said Robert. He was relieved to be back in Elspeth's good graces. He glanced at the papers on the floor. 'What have you been talking about?'

'Family stuff,' said Valentina. 'Elspeth was telling me about when she and Mom were little, growing up in the house on Pilgrim's Lane.'

'Didn't your mother tell you all that?'

'Not much. Mom told us a lot of stories about Cheltenham. You know, like, all the weird social hierarchies and boring school uniforms. Julia always says they should have gone to Hogwarts instead.'

WE LIKED IT BETTER THAN HOME.

'Why, Elspeth?' said Valentina. But Elspeth didn't elaborate. Valentina watched her watching Robert. Elspeth had leaned back slightly so that she and Robert seemed to be gazing into each other's eyes. Then Robert turned to Valentina and said, 'Your grandparents were awfully strict. Apparently boarding school was a relief; Elspeth used to talk about the school plays, and they liked to play pranks on the other pupils – you know, twin sorts of pranks.'

Valentina asked Elspeth, 'Did you and Mom dress the same?'

AT SCHOOL EVERYONE DRESSED THE SAME. OTHERWISE NO ONLY WHEN WE WERE TINY. Valentina found it disconcerting that Elspeth was so wholly focused on Robert; since he had come into the room Elspeth had hardly taken her eyes off him. *She's so used to being invisible, she forgets I can see her.*

All afternoon, and for several days running now, whenever Julia was elsewhere Valentina and Elspeth had been sitting together, conversing in halting questions and answers. It amazed Valentina how different Elspeth's stories were from what their mom had told them. In Elspeth's childhood, events tended to take dark turnings: a picnic by a lake ended with the drowning of a schoolmate; she and Edie tried to befriend a boy from next door who was later sent to an insane asylum. In every story Elspeth and Edie were a team; there was no hint of discord, no foreshadowing of any rift; they were together always, cleverer and faster than their many adversaries. The stories made Valentina long for Julia – not the Julia of now, bossy and stifling, but the Julia of childhood, Valentina's protector and second self. The suspense of each story was heightened by the laborious movements of the planchette. Out of necessity Elspeth's stories were marvels of compression. They reminded Valentina of the blue-and-white plaques in Postman's Park.

Robert picked up a few sheets of paper. 'May I?' Valentina looked at Elspeth, who shrugged. YOU'VE HEARD IT BEFORE, the planchette spelled.

Valentina had added some punctuation. WE WERE NINE. ONE DAY WALKING HOME WE SAW A SIGN THAT SAID 'PUPPIES FOR SALE' IN FRONT OF A SHOP. VERY EXCITED, WE WENT IN AND SPOKE TO THE OLD MAN AT THE COUNTER. HE WAS A TOBACCONIST. HE BROUGHT US THROUGH THE SHOP TO A SHED IN THE YARD. THERE WERE BEAGLE PUPPIES. WE PLAYED WITH THE PUPPIES FOR A LONG TIME. THEN WE WANTED TO LEAVE AND WE FOUND HE HAD LOCKED US IN THE SHED. The page ended there. Robert remembered Elspeth telling him, years ago; they had been walking in Pond Street, where the tobacconist's shop had been. Valentina found the next page and handed it to him. WE SHOUTED BUT NO ONE CAME. THE MOTHER DOG WAS BARKING WITH US. IT GOT DARK. THE MAN UNLOCKED THE DOOR. WE RUSHED AT HIM KNOCKED HIM OFF HIS FEET AND RAN HOME.

Valentina thought, *It's like a fairy tale. How much is true?* She had been enjoying herself, but now she felt apprehensive.

Elspeth remembered the cold, ugly shed, the anxiety of the puppies when she and Edie had yelled; she looked at Valentina and thought, *Why am I telling her this? She's tired and I've confused her.* Elspeth spelled TELL US A STORY V and smiled as kindly as she could.

'Me?' Valentina's mind went blank. *I'm so tired.* She wanted Robert to go away so she and Elspeth could resume their confidences. Or, she wanted to go downstairs with Robert, be kissed and hide from Elspeth. *Or I could just run away and leave them to each other.*

'What's Julia doing?' she asked Robert.

'Nursing Martin, I imagine,' he said, and told them about Martin's toothache and Sebastian's valiant dentistry. Valentina felt a twinge of jealousy; Julia was fussing over someone else. Then she thought, *No, I don't mind. Really.* She leaned sideways, her shoulder against the sofa back and her head drooping. Robert said, 'Have you eaten anything?'

'No.' She remembered having breakfast, but that seemed long ago. 'We haven't been shopping.' She looked up at him. Her eyes seemed enormous, her face pinched.

Robert said, 'You look a bit peckish.' *Starved, more like. How long have you been sitting here?* He stood up. 'Elspeth, I think Valentina needs some dinner.' He held out his hands. Valentina took them and he pulled her up. She felt dizzy.

Elspeth watched them go. At the door Valentina turned and said, 'I'll be right back, Elspeth. I just have to eat something.' The door shut behind them.

Elspeth left the sofa and went to the open window. She waited. In a little while Robert and Valentina walked up the path, disappeared through the gate. *I ought to know better,* Elspeth told herself. *She's so accustomed to being looked after.* The light was going. *I ought to be happy for them.* Elspeth watched the sky deepen. The street lights went on. *It was a lovely day, though. Almost like old times.*

It was quite dark when Julia came in. She went through the flat flipping light switches, calling 'Mouse?' When she got to the front room she turned on the floor lamp by the piano and closed the window. She gathered up the papers and riffled through them, stopping to read. Elspeth watched her, feeling pensive. *Funny having one's conversation all written out this way. It's as though anyone can overhear, like having my phone tapped. But why not? Why tell Valentina and not Julia? Mustn't play favourites.*

Julia looked up as though she had sensed Elspeth's scrutiny. 'Elspeth? Where's Valentina?'

Elspeth leaned over the Ouija board. DINNER WITH R, she spelled.

'Oh.' Julia sat down on the sofa, forlorn.

HOWS MARTINS TOOTH

Julia brightened. 'He's much better. He wanted to go to bed, so I came downstairs.'

YOU TAKE GOOD CARE OF EVERYONE

'I try.' Julia shook her head. 'I think Valentina hates me for it.'

GRATITUDE IS TEDIOUS

'I don't think there's any danger of her being grateful. It's just how it is; she gets sick, I take care of her.'

IF YOU LET HER GO SHE WILL LOVE YOU BETTER

'I know. I can't.'

Elspeth was startled to see tears brimming in Julia's eyes. They sat together in motionless silence. After a few minutes Julia left the room. Elspeth could hear her blowing her nose. When Julia came back she said, 'Why does it say "head trauma" on this page?' She turned over the papers so Elspeth could see them.

SHE ASKED HOW OUR FATHER DIED

'Oh. We never met him, did we?'

NO ONLY YOUR GRANDMOTHER

'But we don't remember her.'

SHE DIED WHEN YOU WERE SMALL

'What were they like? Mom never talks about them.'

HE WAS DIFFICULT SHE WAS MEEK

Julia hesitated. She drew a few spirals on the paper while she considered her next question. Elspeth watched her and thought, *That's amazing; is there a gene for spiral doodling?*

'Elspeth? What happened to you and Mom?'

SECRET

'Oh, come on, Elspeth—'

SORRY CANT GOODNIGHT

'Elspeth?'

But Elspeth had gone. Julia shrugged and went to bed, feeling frustrated but excited. By the time Valentina came home Julia was asleep, dreaming about numbers and teeth.

Martin lay in bed with the phone pressed against his non-swollen cheek, listening to the ring tone in the dark. Marijke picked up on the seventh ring and he felt gratified.

'Martin?'

'Hello, my love. Shall I tell you my toothy tale?'

'I've been so worried. You sound as though you've got a mouthful of chewing gum.'

'No, but I think my cheek has octupled in size. You'll never guess who Robert brought to extract my tooth . . .'

Marijke leaned back in her own bed and listened. *He must have been so frightened; I should have been there. Fancy Robert knowing an undertaker dentist* . . . Each of them warmed to the sound of the other's voice. They lay in the dark together, in distant cities, each of them thinking, *We were lucky this time.* And they pressed their phones closer to their ears, and both of them wondered how much longer this separation could go on.

There are several ways to react to being lost. One is to panic: this was usually Valentina's first impulse. Another is to abandon yourself to lostness, to allow the fact that you've misplaced yourself to change the way you experience the world. Julia loved this feeling, and she began to court it. London was the perfect place to get lost. The curving streets changed their names every few blocks, converged and diverged, dead-ended into mews and suddenly opened into squares. Julia began to play a game that entailed travelling on the tube and randomly popping out at stations with interesting names: Tooting Broadway, Ruislip Gardens, Pudding Mill Lane. Usually the above-ground reality disappointed her. The names on the tube map evoked a Mother Goose cityscape, cosy and diminutive. The actual places tended to be grim: takeaway fried-chicken shops, off-licences and Ladbrokes crowded out whimsy.

Julia's mental map of London began to fill up with oddities: the cattle and elephants of the Albert Memorial; the shop in Bloomsbury that sold only swords and canes; the restaurant in the crypt of St Mary-le-Bow Church. She went to the Hunterian Museum and spent an afternoon looking at clouded jars full of organs, a display on antiseptics and the skeleton of a dodo.

She came home each day filled with London sights, scraps of conversation, ideas for the next day's adventures. When she let herself into the flat she invariably found Valentina sitting on the sofa amidst drifts of paper, intently watching the planchette moving across the Ouija board. Julia would tell Valentina and Elspeth about her day. Valentina would share some of Elspeth's stories. They were each pleasantly surprised to find that spending the day apart gave them things to talk about over dinner, though Robert often appeared and whisked Valentina off just when Julia hoped for a whole evening of her company.

Every morning Julia pleaded with Valentina to come out with her. Valentina would almost let herself be persuaded, but then find an excuse to stay in. 'You go ahead,' Valentina would say. 'I'm not really sick. I'm just tired.' And she did look tired. Each day a little vitality seemed to leave her. 'You need some sunlight, Mouse,' Julia told her more than once. 'Tomorrow,' Valentina always replied.

Martin stood at his front door. He reached out and put his gloved hand on the doorknob. His heart was pounding and he stood immobile, trying to calm himself. *You've been in the hall countless times. It's safe there. Nothing painful has ever happened in the hallway. No one is there, nothing at all except some old newspapers.* He breathed deeply, exhaled slowly and pulled the door open.

It was late afternoon and sunlight filled the stairway. Radiant dust motes floated in the still air. Martin squinted. *See, it's quite benign.* He considered the door sill, the newspapers, the floor. He imagined himself stepping forward, planting his feet on the carpet, standing outside his flat for the first time in more than a year.

Go ahead. It's only a landing. Robert and Julia stand here all the time. Marijke was here. Marijke wants you to leave the flat. You're a rational being; you know it's safe. If you can leave the flat you can see Marijke. Martin thought of himself as a boy, standing for the first time on the high diving board, terrified. The other boys in the class had jeered when he turned and climbed down the ladder. *No one is here. No one will know if you can't do it. But if you do it you can tell Julia.* He tried to picture Julia's face, but instead remembered her lips, counting as his tooth was extracted.

He was sweating, and he took out his handkerchief and blotted his forehead. *Just step over the sill.* It was becoming difficult to breathe. Martin closed his eyes. *This is simply idiotic.* He began to tremble. He stepped backwards and closed the door, gasping.

Tomorrow. I'll try again tomorrow.

Valentina and Elspeth were playing a game with the Little Kitten of Death. It went like this: Valentina sat on the floor in the hall, near the front door of the flat. She had a bucket full of ping-pong balls she'd found in the pantry. ('Why, Elspeth?' she'd asked. Elspeth just shrugged.) Elspeth stood at the other end of the hall. The Kitten, as usual, had no clue that Elspeth was there, so when Valentina rolled a ping-pong ball across the floor the Kitten ran confidently after it, only to have Elspeth divert it at the last moment in an unexpected direction. Soon the Kitten was overexcited, pouncing madly at the little white balls that seemed to have their own ideas about where they might go, balls that might suddenly fly straight up in the air or simply reverse direction. Elspeth let the Kitten run right through her, enjoying the sensation of fur whisking through her phantom skin and bone. She lay down on the floor and let the balls roll through her, with the Kitten veering after them. Valentina saw her reach out with both hands as the Kitten approached, as though to grab her. Elspeth forgot that she was insubstantial. The Kitten ran through her hands; she felt something smooth and slippery hook around her little finger; she felt her hands fill up with something solid and she struggled with it as though she had caught a fish. The thing wriggled and tried to bite. Elspeth was holding the Kitten.

But at the same instant Valentina saw the Kitten drop to the floor and lie still. She came running. The Kitten was dead.

'Elspeth!' Valentina flung herself to the floor, seized the Kitten's body. 'What did you do? Put her back!'

Elspeth was still clutching the Kitten, who threw herself back and forth and clawed at Elspeth. Valentina couldn't see the Kitten's ghost, but she could see Elspeth grappling with something.

'Put her back! Now!'

Elspeth took the struggling Kitten and shoved her back into her limp body as best she could. It was like trying to put a live trout into a silk stocking: the Kitten Elspeth was holding was thrashing and terrified, and the Kitten Valentina was holding was inert and delicate. Elspeth was afraid she would injure the Kitten by trying to insert her back into her body. Then she realised that the Kitten was dead, and would continue to be dead if she was not firm about this. She decided to work on the head and let the rest follow. She felt as though she were using an old camera with a rangefinder, trying to align two images to make them one.

Elspeth motioned to Valentina to put the Kitten's body on the floor. Elspeth found that the Kitten's ghost was *real* in her hands; whatever the Kitten was made of, it was like Elspeth's own ghostly self, it made sense to her in a physical way. The Kitten was the first thing Elspeth had touched since she'd died that seemed to exist with her, not in another realm. *I'm so lonely*, she thought as she tried to push the Kitten into her lifeless body. *I wish I could keep her.*

The Kitten stopped fighting and seemed to comprehend

what Elspeth was trying to do. Elspeth made small pleating motions with her fingers, trying to seal the Kitten in; it reminded her of the way her mother pinched a pie crust all around the edges. Suddenly the Kitten's ghost vanished. It absorbed itself into the body. The little white cat-body convulsed – the Kitten sat up, lurched sideways and then recovered herself. She looked around, like a child caught stealing a boiled sweet, and then began to lick herself all over.

Elspeth and Valentina sat on the floor, staring at the Kitten, and then at each other. Valentina left the room. She returned with the Ouija board and the planchette.

'What happened?' she asked Elspeth.

IT CAUGHT SHE CAME OUT

'What caught?'

HER SOUL

'Caught on what?'

Elspeth crooked her little finger like a lady drinking tea. Valentina sat thinking. 'Could you do it again?'

I WOULD RATHER NOT

'Yes, but if you wanted to, do you think you could do it on purpose?'

I HOPE NOT

'Yes, but Elspeth—'

Elspeth got up – or rather, she was suddenly walking out of the room without any intermediate motions of getting up. When Valentina followed her into the kitchen she vanished. The Kitten mewed loudly and bumped against Valentina's leg.

'You don't seem any the worse for wear. Do you want your dinner?' Valentina set out the dish, opened the can, plopped the food onto the dish and placed it in the usual spot on the floor. The Kitten waited for it as though she were a member of a cargo cult and began gobbling down the food with her usual enthusiasm. Valentina sat on the floor and watched her eat.

Elspeth stood in the middle of the kitchen, invisible, watching Valentina watch the Kitten. *What are you thinking about, Valentina?*

Valentina was thinking about miracles. The Kitten looked absolutely ordinary, eating her dinner: that was the miracle. *You'd never know that ten minutes ago you were dead. You don't seem like you even noticed. Did it hurt, Kitten? Was it hard to get back in your body? Were you scared?*

She heard the front door open; Julia was home. 'Mouse? Where are you?' *Don't tell Julia*, thought Elspeth. She was ashamed of having killed the Kitten, even though it had been only temporary.

'Kitchen,' Valentina called out.

Julia came in bearing Sainsbury's bags, which she slung onto the counter and began to unpack. 'Wassup?' she asked.

'Not much. You?'

Julia launched into a long boring story about a woman in the check-out queue at the supermarket, a tiny old person who apparently subsisted entirely on fairy cakes and Lipton tea.

'Gross,' said Valentina, trying to remember what fairy cakes were.

'Cupcakes,' said Julia.

'Oh. Well, that's not too terrible.' She got up off the floor and began to help put away the shopping. The twins worked in semi-amiable silence. The Kitten finished her dinner and wandered off. Elspeth stood in a corner, out of the twins' way, with her arms folded across her chest, thinking. *That was extraordinary. That was . . . a clue . . . to something . . . but what?* She would have to think about it. Elspeth left the twins in the kitchen and found the Kitten settling down to nap in a pool of sunlight on the sofa. Elspeth curled up next to her and watched her eyelids droop, her breathing slow. It was a charming, ordinary sight, quite incongruous with Elspeth's turbulent mood. Valentina came into the room and whispered, 'Elspeth?' – but Elspeth did not reply or make herself known. Valentina wandered off to peer into all the rooms as though they were playing hide-and-seek. Elspeth followed behind her, an invisible shadow.

Robert sat at his desk on a lovely May afternoon, trying to make himself write. He was working on the section of his thesis devoted to Mrs Henry (Ellen) Wood, lady novelist. He found Mrs Wood incredibly dull. He had ploughed his way through *East Lynne*, pored over the details of her life, and simply found himself unable to care about her at all.

When he was giving a tour, he always skipped Mrs Wood. She would have fallen between George Wombwell and Adam Worth, not only alphabetically but geographically, and to Robert she seemed unworthy of their peculiar, almost dashing company. He sat gnawing his pen, trying to decide if he could omit her from the thesis. Perhaps not. He could try to make the most of her death, but that was also dull: she'd died of bronchitis. *Damn the woman.*

He was relieved when Valentina arrived to interrupt him. 'Come outside,' she said. 'It's spring.'

Once they were outdoors their steps turned inevitably towards the cemetery. As they walked down Swains Lane they heard a lone tuba player practising scales in Waterlow Park. The notes had an elegiac quality. Swains Lane, being overshadowed by high walls on both sides, existed in a permanent dusk even as the sky above them was blue and cloudless. Valentina thought, *We're like a little two-person funeral procession.* She was glad when they arrived at the cemetery's gates and stood in the sunshine, waiting to be admitted.

Nigel opened the gate. 'We weren't expecting you today.'

Robert said, 'No, but it's such glorious weather, we thought we might go looking for wild flowers.'

Jessica came out of the office and said, 'If you're going out, take some rakes. And no lollygagging, please.'

'Certainly *not*.' Robert equipped himself and Valentina with a walkie-talkie and two rakes as well as a large bag for litter, and they crossed the courtyard and went up into the cemetery. 'Well,' said Robert, as they turned onto the Dickens Path, 'I'm sorry. I didn't mean to put you to work.'

'That's okay,' said Valentina. 'I'm pretty useless most of the time. I don't mind raking. Where do all these empty water bottles come from?'

'I think people must throw them over the wall,' said Robert.

They raked in companionable silence for some time, clearing the path and collecting an impressive bag of fast-food wrappers and coffee cups. Valentina liked raking. She had never done it before. She wondered what other kinds of work she might enjoy. *Bagging groceries? Telemarketing? Who knows? Maybe I could try lots of different jobs for a week at a time.* She was imagining herself checking coats at the British Museum when Robert beckoned her over to him.

'Look,' he whispered. She looked and saw two small foxes sleeping nose-to-tail on a pile of old leaves. Robert stood behind her and put his arm around her. Valentina tensed. He released her. They walked down the path to let the foxes sleep and went back to raking.

After some time Valentina said, 'What's lollygagging?'

'I think that's an American word. Jessica and James picked up a certain amount of American slang during the war.'

'But what does it mean?'

'Oh. Well, it can mean being lazy, just fooling around. Or it can mean fooling around, in the other sense.'

Valentina blushed. 'Did Jessica think . . . ?'

'Ah – I'm sure we didn't exactly look like two people who intended to spend the afternoon collecting garbage.' He peered into the bag. 'I think we can stop now. Let's have a walk – just leave the rakes here, we'll come back for them.' He took her hand and led her towards the Meadow, an open, sun-dappled section full of well-tended graves.

Valentina said, 'It's nice to be out in the sun. I think it's been grey every day since we arrived.'

'Surely not.'

'No – I guess it just feels that way. It's like the greyness soaks into the buildings, or something.'

'Mmm.' Robert felt a bit depressed. *You can't make her love London. Or yourself, when it comes to that.* They kept walking. A number of graves had flowers newly planted on them, each one a small dense garden.

'Valentina?' Robert said. 'Tell me. Why is it, whenever I lay a hand on you, you seem to shrink away?'

'What do you mean?' she replied. 'I don't.'

'Not always. But you did, just then, when we saw the foxes.'

'I guess.' They left the Meadow and came back to the path. Valentina said, 'It just seemed . . . weird. Disrespectful.'

'Because we're in the cemetery?' asked Robert. 'I don't

know . . . when I'm dead I want people to make love on my grave on a regular basis. It will remind me of happier times.'

'But would you do it on someone else's grave? Elspeth's?'

'No – not unless I was with Elspeth. However that would work. Maybe if we were both dead,' he said.

'I wonder if dead people have sex.'

'Perhaps that would depend on whether you ended up in heaven or hell.'

Valentina laughed. 'That still doesn't answer my question.'

Robert pinched her bum and she shrieked. 'All the boring *Joy of Sex*-type sex in hell and all the good naughty sex in heaven,' he offered.

'That seems upside down, somehow.'

'There's your American Puritanism showing; why shouldn't heaven consist of all the great pleasures? Eating, drinking, making love: if it's all so wrong, why do we have to do it to stay alive and propagate the species? No, I think heaven will consist of non-stop bacchanalia. Down in hell they'll be worrying about STDs and premature ejaculation. Anyway,' Robert continued with a sly sidewise look at Valentina's cool profile, 'if you don't watch out you'll have to go to a special, fenced-off area where they keep all the virgins.'

'In heaven or hell?'

He shook his head. 'I'm really not sure. You ought not to chance it.'

'I'd better get busy.'

'I wish you would.' He halted in the path. They were near the little turning that led to the Rossettis. Valentina stopped a few feet away when she realised that Robert wasn't walking with her. She held his gaze for a moment and then looked down in confusion.

'You don't mean . . . here?' Valentina's voice was hardly audible.

'No,' Robert said. 'As you said earlier, that would be disrespectful. And I imagine Jessica would have me arrested if she ever found out. Lord, she doesn't even like it when the visitors wear shorts.'

'I think she'd just fire you.'

'That would be worse. What on earth would I do with myself? I'd have to get a proper job.' He began to walk again, and she fell in beside him. 'Valentina, do you like it when I talk to you that way?'

She said nothing.

'You invite it, and then you seem upset. I'm not . . . no one has dealt with me this way . . . at least not since I was in the sixth form. I guess the problem is the age difference.' He sighed. 'Although most of the girls I knew then couldn't wait to get shagged. It was a glorious era.'

Valentina shook her head. 'It's not about shagging.' She hesitated, both at the unfamiliar slang and at what she was trying to say. 'It's about Julia.'

Robert gave her a look of pure surprise. 'What could this possibly have to do with Julia?'

Valentina said, 'We've always done everything together, everything important . . .'

'But you're constantly telling me how much you want to do things on your own.'

'I'm sorry,' she said. 'I'm just afraid.'

'Okay. That's understandable.'

'No, it's stupid,' said Valentina. 'I wish I could leave her.'

'You're not *married* to her. You can do what you like.'

'You don't understand.'

'No, I don't.' They walked on in silence and then Robert said, 'Wait — I have to collect the rakes.' He ran back up the path, leaving Valentina standing in a patch of sun. *It's nice here*, she thought. *If I were Elspeth I'd rather be here than stuck in the flat.* Robert reappeared, rakes and bag in hand. She watched him trotting towards her. *Do I love him? I think so. Then why not . . . ?* But it was impossible. She sighed. *I have to get away from Julia.* Robert slowed as he came up to her. 'Shall we have tea in the office?'

'Sure,' she said, and they walked back to the chapels together in mutual perplexity.

Julia wanted to frolic in the beautiful weather, but she didn't feel like going out alone and Valentina had run off somewhere with Robert. So she took herself upstairs, determined to inflict her mood on Martin.

'Hello, my dear,' he said, when she appeared in his stuffy, darkened office. 'Just give me a minute or two, I'm almost finished with this. Will you make us some tea?'

Julia marched into the kitchen and began making tea. Usually she enjoyed laying out the cups and saucers, boiling the water, all the soothing habitual motions that added up to tea, but today she had no patience. She piled everything onto the tray willy-nilly and brought it back to Martin's office.

'Thank you, Julia. Let's put it here on the desk, and pull up a chair for you. There, that's cosy.'

She plopped onto the chair. 'Don't you ever get tired of sitting in the dark?'

'No,' he said pleasantly.

'Why do you have newspaper taped over the windows?'

'Our decorator recommended it.' Martin smiled.

'Yeah, right.'

Martin poured the tea. 'You seem a bit put out, Miss Poole.'

'Oh – Valentina's out somewhere with Robert.'

He handed her the teacup. 'And why is that a problem?'

'Well, she's dating him.'

Martin raised his eyebrows. 'Is she? That's interesting. He seems old for someone her age.'

Julia said, 'If you weren't married would you date me?'

Martin was so startled by the question that he didn't answer.

Julia said, 'I guess that's a no, huh?'

'Julia—'

She put her teacup down, leaned over and kissed him. After she did this Martin sat quite still, deeply confused. 'You shouldn't do that,' he finally said. 'I'm a married man.'

Julia got up and walked around one of Martin's smaller piles of boxes. 'Marijke's in Amsterdam.'

'Nonetheless, I'm married to her.' He wiped his mouth with his handkerchief.

Julia circled the boxes again. 'But she left you.'

Martin indicated the towers of boxes, the windows. 'She didn't like to live this way. And I don't blame her.'

Julia nodded. She felt it wouldn't be polite to agree too emphatically.

The words flew out of Martin's mouth despite himself: 'You're very attractive, Julia.' She stood still and looked at him, dubious. 'But I love Marijke, and no one else will do.'

Julia resumed circling. 'What exactly . . . How does that feel?' Martin didn't answer and she tried to clarify. 'I've never been in love. With a boy.'

Martin stood up and ran his hands over his face. His eyes were tired and he had an urge to shave. It wasn't a compulsion, just a feeling of untidiness and five o'clock shadow. He glanced at the computer; it was almost four. It was time — would have been time — for him to shower if Marijke were coming home after work. He could wait a little while. Julia thought, *He isn't going to answer* and felt relieved. Martin said, 'It feels as though part of my self has detached and gone to Amsterdam, where it — she — is waiting for me. Do you know about phantom-limb syndrome?' Julia nodded. 'There's pain where she ought to be. It's feeding the other pain, the thing that makes me wash and count and all that. So her absence is stopping me from going to find her. Do you see?'

'But wouldn't you feel much better if you went and found her?'

'I'm sure I would. Yes. Of course, I would be very happy.' He looked anxious, as though Julia were about to propel him outdoors.

'So?'

'Julia, you don't understand.'

'You didn't answer my question. I asked you about being in love. You said what it was like when your wife went away.'

Martin sat down again. *How young she is. When we were*

338 · AUDREY NIFFENEGGER

that young we invented the world, no one could tell us a thing. Julia
stood with her hands clenched, as though she wanted to
pound an answer out of him. 'Being in love is . . . anxious,'
he said. 'Wanting to please, worrying that she will see me
as I really am. But wanting to be known. That is . . . you're
naked, moaning in the dark, no dignity at all . . . I wanted
her to see me and to love me even though she knew
everything I am, and I knew her. Now she's gone, and my
knowledge is incomplete. So all day I imagine what she is
doing, what she says and who she talks to, how she looks.
I try to supply the missing hours, and it gets harder as they
pile up, all the time she's been gone. I have to imagine. I
don't know, really. I don't know any more.' He sat with his
head lowered into his chest, and his words became almost
inaudible. Julia thought, *He feels for his wife what I feel about
Valentina.* This frightened her. What she felt about Valentina
was insane, broken, involuntary. Julia suddenly hated
Marijke. *Why did she leave him here, sitting in his chair with his
shoulders shaking?* She thought of her dad. *Does he feel this way
about Mom?* She could not imagine her dad on his own. She
walked over to where Martin sat, his eyes closed, head down.
She stood behind him, leaned over him and put her arms
around his shoulders, rested her cheek against the back of
his head. Martin stiffened, then slowly crossed his arms and
laid his hands over Julia's. He thought of Theo, tried to
remember the last time Theo had embraced him.

'Sorry,' Julia whispered.

'No, no,' Martin replied. Julia released him. Martin stood
up, walked out of the office. Julia heard him blowing his nose

several rooms away. He came back and did his odd sideways movement through the door, sat down in his chair again.

Julia smiled. 'You left the room without doing that.'

'Did I? Oh dear.' Martin felt momentarily consternated, but the feeling faded. *I should remedy that*, he thought, but the underlying urge was not there.

Julia did a little shimmy, looked at him. 'You seem better these days. Not as freaked out as usual.'

'Do I?'

'You do. I wouldn't go so far as to say you seem *normal*, but you aren't jumping up every ten seconds to wash something.'

'It must be the vitamins,' he said.

'You never know,' Julia replied. There was something in Martin's voice that made her wonder.

'I've been working on standing on the landing,' he told her.

'Martin, that's great! Will you show me?'

'Erm, I haven't actually managed it yet. But I've been practising.'

'We'll have to give you extra vitamins.'

'Yes, I think that might be a good idea.'

Julia sat down again. 'So if you can go outside, will you go to Amsterdam?'

'Yes.'

'And then I won't see you any more?'

'Then you can come to Amsterdam and visit us.' He began to tell her about Amsterdam. Julia listened and thought, *It could happen.* She was simultaneously excited and worried: if Martin got better, would he become boring?

She interrupted him. 'Will you let me take the newspaper off your windows?'

Martin considered. No inner voice rose to forbid it, but he hesitated. 'Perhaps just a few windows? Just . . . to try it.'

Julia jumped up and darted around the boxes that obstructed her access to the office windows. She began to rip down the newspaper and tape. Light flooded the room. Martin stood blinking, looking out at trees and sky. *My goodness, it's spring again.* Julia coughed in the dust she had stirred up. When the coughing subsided she said, 'Well?'

Martin nodded. 'Very nice.'

'Can I do more?'

'More windows?' He wasn't sure. 'Let me adjust to – sunlight – first. Perhaps in a few days you can do some more.' Martin walked to within a few feet of the windows. 'What glorious weather,' he said. His heart was pounding. The world seemed to press itself upon him. Julia said something but he did not hear.

'Martin?' *Ohmigod.* Julia grabbed him by the shoulders and propelled him towards his chair. He was covered in sweat; his breath was laboured. 'Martin?' He held up one hand to forestall questions and sat down abruptly. A few minutes later he said, 'It's only a panic attack.' He continued to sit with his eyes closed and an inward expression on his face.

Julia said, 'What can I do?'

'Nothing,' he said. 'Sit with me.'

She sat and waited with him. Soon Martin sighed and said, 'Well, that was exciting, wasn't it?' He patted his face with a handkerchief.

'I'm sorry.' Nothing she did today was right.

'Please don't be. Here, let's move our chairs and sit in the sun.'

'But—?'

'It will be fine. We'll stay away from the windows.' They moved their chairs.

Julia said, 'I keep thinking I understand, but I don't.'

'I don't understand it myself, why should you?' Martin said. 'That's what madness is, isn't it? All the wheels fly off the bus and things don't make sense any more. Or rather, they do, but it's not a kind of sense anyone else can understand.'

'But you were getting better,' she said, near tears.

'Oh, I'm much better. Trust me.' Martin stretched out his legs and let the sun cover him. *Soon it will be summer.* He thought of Amsterdam in summer, the narrow canal houses basking in their allotment of northern sun, Marijke tanned and agile, laughing at his Dutch accent; it was a long time ago, but summer was coming again. He reached out and offered Julia his hand. She took it, and they sat side by side in the light, looking out at the spring day from a safe distance.

Valentina had brought her sewing machine to London, but she hadn't laid a finger on it since that first day when they'd arranged all their belongings in the flat. It sat in the guest room and reproached her whenever she happened to notice it. The sewing machine had started to feature in her dreams, needy and neglected, like a pet she'd forgotten to feed.

She stood in the guest bedroom, staring at the machine. *If this is what I want to do, I ought to do it.* She had researched fashion-design courses on the Internet; you needed a portfolio to be admitted. She had not spoken to Julia about college in weeks. *I'll apply, and if I get in, I'll just go. Dad would pay for school. Julia can't do a thing about it.* Valentina took the cover off the machine. She brought in a chair from the dining room; she found her suitcase full of fabric and emptied it onto the bed. As she picked up each piece of fabric, unfolded and smoothed and refolded it, she thought of Edie. Julia had no patience for sewing and had never learned. Valentina untangled ribbon and sorted spools of thread. She found her box of bobbins and her good scissors. Now everything was neatly laid out on the bed and she stood wondering what to make with it.

There was a pair of half-finished blouses she'd begun before they left Chicago. She could work on those. *No*, she thought. *I want to make something new. And not a pair; I'm going to make just one.*

At home she had a dressmaker's dummy, but it was too cumbersome to bring to London. She got out her measuring tape and took her own measurements. *How weird. I've lost weight.* She sorted the fabric into piles: yes, no, maybe. In the maybe pile was a swathe of black velvet. She had bought it in eighth grade, during a brief flirtation with Goth fashion; Julia hated to wear black, so the velvet had stayed unused in Valentina's collection of yardage. She unfurled it. *Four yards? That's enough for a dress.*

She was sketching the dress when Elspeth appeared. 'Oh, hi,' Valentina said. *You'd think she'd notice the door was closed and I want to be alone.*

Elspeth mimed writing and Valentina opened the sketch-book to a fresh page. ARE YOU GOING TO MAKE SOMETHING?

'Yeah.' Valentina showed her the sketch. 'It's a minidress with a built-in shroud.'

YOU'RE SPENDING TOO MUCH TIME WITH ROBERT.

Valentina shrugged.

MAY I WATCH?

'Whatever.' Valentina rubbed her hands to warm them and went back to her drawing. Elspeth curled up on the bed and vanished.

Hours went by. Valentina was trying to make a pattern and feeling frustrated. Pattern-making was one of the things she wanted to learn in college. She sat on the floor with the paper in front of her, knowing it was wrong but unable to correct it. *I'm so stupid. Maybe I should take one of Elspeth's dresses apart, to see what I'm missing.* She heard Julia's footsteps in the hall. 'Mouse?' Valentina sat barely breathing. 'Mouse?' The door opened.

'Oh, there you are. Oh, cool. What are you making?' Julia had been outside all day, roaming Hackney. She was drenched. Valentina became aware that it had been raining; she hadn't noticed.

'Why didn't you take an umbrella?' Valentina asked.

'I did. It's really coming down out there, I got wet anyway.' Julia disappeared and came back wearing pyjamas with a towel around her head. 'What are you gonna make?'

'This.' Valentina handed over the sketch reluctantly.

Julia looked at it carefully. 'Out of that black stuff?'

'Yeah.'

'Well, that's – different.'

Valentina didn't reply. She held out her hand and Julia gave her back the sketchbook.

Julia said, 'Where are we even going to wear that? It looks like a Halloween costume for Lolita.'

Valentina said, 'It's an experiment.'

'You don't have enough fabric, anyway. Maybe we could find a fabric store. You could do it in pink. That would be cool.'

'I have enough fabric to make one dress. And it wouldn't look right in pink.' Valentina pretended to correct the pattern. She wouldn't look at Julia.

'What's the point of making one dress?'

'It's for my portfolio,' Valentina said quietly.

'What portfolio?'

'For school. Design school.'

'But you're not *going* to school. We agreed, you're *not*.' Julia circled around the pattern and crouched down, trying to see Valentina's face. 'I mean, what's the point? We have money.'

Valentina said, '*We* haven't agreed on anything. *You* just keep trying to, you know, ram stuff down my throat.' She began to roll up the pattern, to put away her pencils and sketchbook.

'But you keep doing things without me. I hardly ever see you any more. You won't go anywhere with me and you're out every night with Robert. You spend all day talking to Elspeth. It's like you hate me.'

Valentina finally looked at Julia. 'I do. I do hate you.'

'No,' said Julia. 'You can't.'

'You're, like, my jailer.' Valentina stood up. Julia remained kneeling on the floor. 'Just let go of me, Julia. At the end of the year, we'll ask Mr Roche to split the estate. You can keep living here if you want to. I'll just take some money, I won't even take very much, just enough to live . . . You can do whatever you want. I'll go to school, I'll work, or whatever, I don't even care. I just want to do *something*, have a *life*, grow *up*.'

'But you can't,' Julia said. She stood up, the towel awkwardly unwrapping itself from her head as she did so. She tossed it onto the floor. She looked pathetically young, with her hair matted to her head, her baby-blue pyjamas. 'Valentina, you can't even take care of yourself! I mean, the first time you get really sick and I'm not there to take care of you, you'll just die.'

'Fine,' Valentina said. 'I'd rather be dead than spend my life with you.'

'*Fine*,' replied Julia. She walked to the door and paused,

trying to think of something else to say. Nothing came to her. 'Whatever.' Julia went through the door and slammed it behind her.

Valentina stood staring at the door. *What now?* She suddenly realised that Elspeth had reappeared and was still sitting on the bed, regarding her with a shocked expression. 'Go away,' Valentina said to her. 'Please just leave me alone.' Elspeth got up obediently and floated through the closed door. Valentina continued to stand there, her mind racing. Finally she pulled the black velvet off the bed. She climbed into the midst of the pile of fabric and pulled the velvet over herself. *I'll disappear*, she thought. She could hear the rain falling in torrents. Valentina cried for a long while. It was warm and safe under the velvet; as she began to fall asleep she thought, *I know. I know what to do* . . . and her plan was formed completely in that space between consciousness and dreaming.

⤞⚏ A PROPOSITION ⚏⤝

The next morning Valentina watched Elspeth reading. Valentina had laid half a dozen old paperbacks creased open on the carpet in the front room. Elspeth read each page spread, then moved to the next and the next. She was mixing old favourites (*Middlemarch, Emma, A Prayer for Owen Meany*) with some ghost stories (*The Turn of the Screw*, plus bits of M.R. James and Poe) in hope of finding a few tips on haunting. The effect was slightly disconcerting. When she had read all the open pages she would go back to the first book and laboriously turn the page. Then she would proceed to the others, going along the rows until all the pages were turned. Valentina could only see some of Elspeth; her head, shoulders and arms were visible, but the jumper she was wearing vanished somewhere around the bottom of her ribcage. She was floating inverted above the books; if her whole body had been there she would have appeared to be dangling from the ceiling. If she had had any blood it would all have gone to her head. As it was, she looked perfectly comfortable.

'Do you want me to turn pages for you?'

Elspeth looked up, shook her head. She made a muscleman gesture, cocking one arm: *I need the exercise.*

Valentina was lying on the pink sofa with a tattered Penguin edition of *The Woman in White*. She found it difficult to concentrate on Count Fosco and Marian with

Elspeth fluttering pages only a few feet away. She put the book down and sat up. 'Where's Julia?'

Elspeth pointed at the ceiling. Valentina said, 'Ah,' got up and left the room. She returned with the Ouija board and planchette. Valentina put her finger to her lips. Elspeth looked at her quizzically. *You needn't tell me to be quiet.* She moved to Valentina's side.

Valentina said, 'You know what happened with the Kitten?'

Elspeth turned away. *I don't want to talk about that.* To Valentina she said nothing. Valentina persisted. 'Could you do that with me? Take out my – soul – and put it back?'

NO, Elspeth spelled.

'Couldn't, or won't?'

NO NO NO. She sat shaking her head. *What a bloody daft idea* was what she wanted to say. Instead she wrote, WHY.

'Because. Why do you have to know why?'

Elspeth wondered if this was what it would have been like to have a teenaged daughter: unreasonable demands, tendered with unthinking entitlement. She wrote, WHAT IF I CANT PUT YOU BACK.

'You could practise with the Kitten.'

RATHER HARD ON KITTEN

Valentina blushed. 'But the Kitten was fine. And there's no reason it wouldn't work with me, so you wouldn't have to do the Kitten again anyway.'

CELL DEATH BRAIN DAMAGE HOW DO WE KNOW KITTEN IS FINE

'Come on, Elspeth. At least think about it.'

Elspeth stared at Valentina. Then she wrote, FORGET IT,

and vanished. Valentina sat thinking. A breeze ruffled the pages of the books lying open on the carpet. Valentina wondered if it was Elspeth or just wind. To annoy Elspeth she flipped all the books face down. She had not expected Elspeth to agree. But she had introduced the idea, and she knew she would figure out how to get her way.

Julia was restless. She sat on the landing with her back against Martin's front door, one leg thrust straight ahead of her and the other angled down the stairs. It was another rainy morning, and the light seemed to coat everything on the landing with extra dust. Julia could hear Martin grumbling to himself inside his flat. She wanted to go in and bother him, but she would wait a while yet. She changed her position so that both of her feet pressed against the piles of newspapers Martin kept on the landing. The piles were a bit unstable. Julia imagined them toppling over and burying her. She'd be smothered. Martin would never find her – he wouldn't be able to open his front door. *No, that's not right. The door opens inward.* Valentina would think she had run away; she would be sorry. *I'll be a ghost, then she'll love me again. She'll sit here all day with the Ouija board and we'll have a great time.* Robert would come up to look for them and be caught in an avalanche of newspaper; he would crack his head and die. Julia gave one of the piles a shove. It collapsed sideways, onto another pile of newspapers. This was not very satisfying.

I'm bored, Julia decided. It was no fun to be bored alone. Julia looked around, but found nothing worth looking at or thinking about. There was no point in going downstairs; Valentina wouldn't talk to her.

Martin began to sing. Julia could tell that he enjoyed singing. It was not a song she knew. She thought it might be an advertising jingle. She kicked at the papers again but they did not fall over. *Maybe I should get a job*, she thought. *I would still be bored, but at least I'd have a reason to leave the house.* She smelled toast, and felt suddenly, inordinately sad. She gave a sharp kick and this time the newspapers obliged her by falling into a heap, covering her legs and stomach. It was somewhat like being at the beach, buried in sand, but the papers were less soft; they poked her with their corners. She sat there for a few minutes, trying to enjoy the experience. *Nope*, she thought. *Pointless.* Julia climbed out of the pile of news, stepped over it and opened the door. She followed Martin's voice to the kitchen, where he sat preparing to eat – yes – toast.

The following morning Valentina and Elspeth sat at the Ouija board together. Elspeth had been doing some thinking.

I DONT UNDERSTAND, Elspeth spelled.

'I want to leave Julia,' Valentina said. Her idea had been growing on her until she thought of little else.

SO LEAVE HER

'She won't let me.'

NONSENSE

'When you and Mom split up—'

WE HAD NO CHOICE

'Why not?'

Elspeth twirled the planchette aimlessly, then stopped.

'If Julia thinks I'm dead, she'll let me go.'

JULIA WOULD BE CRUSHED IF YOU DIED EDIE AND JACK TOO

Valentina had not thought of her parents. She frowned, but said, 'Look, Elspeth, it'll be perfect. I'll die, Julia will be forced to go on without me, she'll get over it. And you'll put me back in my body and I'll live happily ever after, or, you know, I'll at least be able to live my own life. I'll be free.'

Elspeth sat with her fingers on the planchette, looking at Valentina. To Valentina her expression seemed irritated, then thoughtful. LETS CONSIDER THIS LOGISTICALLY, Elspeth spelled. YOU WILL BE OUT OF BODY FOR DAYS — THERE WILL BE A FUNERAL — BODY WILL BEGIN TO ROT — THEN BODY IS IN CEMETERY — WE ARE HERE — MAYBE — WHAT IF YOUR GHOST ENDS UP ELSEWHERE — HOW WOULD BODY AND SOUL GET BACK TOGETHER — BODY WILL BE HORRIBLE — IN SHORT YOU ARE INSANE

'We'll get Robert to help us.'

HE WONT DO IT

'He will if you ask him to.'

Elspeth felt deeply agitated. *Disaster, that's what this is. The snake, the apple, the woman: it's pure bloody temptation. It can only end badly. Tell her no. She can't do it without you. If you refuse she'll find a more sensible way to cope with Julia. No, no, no.* Elspeth became aware that Valentina was sitting very patiently, like a good schoolgirl, waiting for her answer. *Tell her absolutely not.*

Elspeth put her fingers on the planchette. LET ME THINK ABOUT IT, she spelled.

Valentina sat in the back garden drinking tea. It was a damp grey May morning, even earlier than she was wont to rise. The stone bench Valentina sat on was covered in lichen and the damp was getting through her dressing gown, an old quilted thing of Elspeth's. She slid her feet out of their slippers and tucked her legs up so that her chin rested on her knees.

Elspeth sat in the window seat, watching her.

Valentina could hear magpies calling in the cemetery. Two of them settled on top of the wall and looked at her. They shifted from foot to foot. Valentina looked back at them, trying to remember the rhyme Edie had taught them:

> *One for sadness,*
> *Two for joy,*
> *Three for a wedding,*
> *Four for a child,*
> *Five for sickness,*
> *Six for death.*

Two for joy, she thought. *That's good.* But even as she smiled to herself, three more magpies plopped down beside the first two, and a moment later they were joined by an especially large, shrieking magpie that landed in their midst and sent the others walking back and forth on the wall uneasily.

Valentina looked away, then up at their window. *Is that Julia?* A dark form stood framed in the window against the darkness of the room, like a hole in reality. Valentina stood up and shielded her eyes with her hand, trying to see. *Elspeth? No, there's nothing there.* It had been a disquieting thought, the dark thing in the dark . . . *No, it's nothing. Elspeth wouldn't be so . . . strange.*

Valentina drank the last swallow of tea, gathered up her cup and saucer and spoon, and went back into the house.

The Little Kitten of Death was sleeping on Valentina's pillow. It was afternoon, and sunlight slanted through the bedroom window, across the rug, up the side of the bed, not quite reaching the Kitten. She was almost white enough to blend into the pillowcase, *like a drawing of a polar bear in a snowstorm*, Elspeth thought. Elspeth stood in the sun, letting it pour through her, watching the Kitten sleep. *I want you.* Elspeth felt depressed. She had never thought of herself as someone who would kill a beautiful white kitten while it napped. But apparently she was that sort of person. *Don't you worry, Kitten. I'll put you right back.* Elspeth extended one hand tentatively towards the Kitten; she did not stir. She poked her fingers through the soft fur of the Kitten's belly. *How did I do it, before?* She slid her fingers inside the Kitten, who made a mew of protest and turned but did not wake. Elspeth trawled unimpeded through hot blood, organs, bones, muscles. She was groping for that snick of immateriality; her fingers would recognise the Kitten's soul because it was made of the same stuff as Elspeth herself. *Does it have a permanent location in the body? Or does it migrate? Last time it felt as though I'd hooked it with my finger. It was slippery like an avocado stone popping out.* The Kitten moaned and curled up tighter. *Sorry, Kitten. Sorry.* Elspeth moved her hand higher, into the lungs, and the Kitten woke up.

Elspeth snatched her hand back. *She can't see you.* But the

Kitten was uneasy; she arched her back, looked around warily. She padded to the edge of the bed and listened. The flat was quiet; Julia and Valentina were out. Elspeth could hear Robert hoovering his kitchen. The Kitten circled and settled at the foot of the bed, front paws crossed, chin resting on them, eyes slitted. Elspeth sat beside her and waited.

A few minutes later the Kitten closed her eyes. Elspeth watched her sides rise and fall. The tip of her tail twitched. *Gently.* Elspeth stroked her head; she liked that when Valentina did it. Now it only made her flick her ears in annoyance.

The Kitten went back to sleep. Elspeth raked her fingers through the little white body in a quick swiping motion, the way the Kitten might bat at a toy. Something caught — the Kitten's body slumped into itself like a cake collapsing — and Elspeth was holding a furious clawing, biting Kitten.

If she scratches me, can I heal? Elspeth imagined her ghost skin in tatters, and threw the Kitten onto the bed. They stared at each other. The Kitten hissed loudly. Elspeth was startled. *If I can hear her . . . ?* She said, 'It's okay, Kitten,' and held out her hand. The Kitten backed away, hissing. She turned, jumped off the side of the bed and disappeared. Elspeth flew over the bed just in time to see a white haze dissipating by the bedside table.

What now? How can I put her back now? Elspeth thought of Valentina and despaired. She curled up next to the Kitten's limp body. *Come back, Kitten. I was only practising . . . Oh dear.* The Kitten looked quite dead. Her eyes were half-open and the third eyelids had slid across. She looked like a feline alien. Her small pink tongue protruded; her head hung over her paws at an uncomfortable angle. *I'm sorry, Kitten. I'm so, so sorry.*

Where could she be? Was she even in the flat? Perhaps the Kitten had gone to prowl the back garden, or to be a little white cloud stalking the cemetery for the ghosts of sparrows and tiny frogs. Perhaps she would become a ghost kitten that haunted the dustbins of South Grove. Elspeth stroked the Kitten. Even her fur seemed to have lost its liveliness. She pushed her fingers into the Kitten's side and was startled at the change: there was life in there, but it was the life of the things that break down the body. The micro-organisms that consume every dead thing had already been unleashed inside the Kitten.

Elspeth pulled her hand out and sat up. *This isn't going to work, Valentina. Not the way you think it should. By the time the body got through a funeral, the rot would be well under way. You'd die of putrefaction. You'd die of your own deadness.*

Elspeth let herself thin and spread out into the air. She was ashamed that she'd killed the Kitten for the sake of a stupid idea. *I should have known better. Poor Kitten.* Elspeth went and curled up in her drawer. She stayed there feeling awful and monstrous, berating herself and wondering what everyone would think of her cruelty. The answer was nothing at all, because no one except Valentina had any clue what Elspeth had done.

⟁ THE FUNERAL OF THE LITTLE KITTEN OF DEATH ⟁

It was Julia who found the Kitten. It was her first death; her only thought was for Valentina; she wished that this might not be, that somehow the Kitten might wake up, that Valentina would never find out. But Valentina was only subdued. 'Oh,' was all she said when Julia told her.

Julia found a hinged wooden box in the servant's room. It had once held silverware but now had only empty spaces for utensils lined with pale green velvet. The silver had been a wedding present for Elspeth and Edie's parents. It had vanished in a burglary in 1996. Julia wondered briefly why anyone would keep an empty box which had so completely lost its purpose. She carried it into the bedroom and placed it next to the Kitten's body.

Valentina opened the box. 'I don't think she'll fit,' she said.

'Maybe if she was more fork-shaped. Wait, I think this lifts out,' Julia said. The old glue gave way as Julia ripped the insert away from the box. This released a fierce mouldy smell. Valentina made a face and pulled her shirt over her nose.

'We'll put catnip in with her. And wrap her in something pretty.' Julia went into the dressing room and came out holding a blue silk scarf that had been Elspeth's. Valentina nodded. Julia spread it out on the bed. Valentina gathered up the Kitten and placed her on the scarf. She kissed the top of the Kitten's head. The Kitten's body felt a little stiff. Valentina wrapped the scarf over her and put her in the box. The Kitten seemed more dead in the box than she had lying on the bed; the lump under the silk was utterly still and pathetic. Valentina closed the lid.

The twins went downstairs and stood in front of Robert's door, not speaking. Valentina held the box. When Robert opened the door, he said, 'I've been thinking and I think we should bury her in the back garden.'

'Why?' said Julia. 'There's a whole cemetery on the other side of the wall. It's silly to have a family crypt and not be able to put her in it.' The twins walked into Robert's flat but then stood in his front hall as though about to leave again. He shut the door.

'There are some quite good reasons why that won't be happening. First, you don't have a proper coffin for above-ground interment, so that would get ugly. Next, animals aren't permitted to be buried in Highgate Cemetery, it's a conse-crated Christian burial ground.'

'Not even Christian animals?' asked Julia.

'What if we got the right kind of coffin?' asked Valentina.

Robert said, 'We'll bury her next to the garden wall and have George carve her a little gravestone. She'll be two feet away from the cemetery and you can visit her any time you want to.'

'Okay,' said Valentina. She felt numb. She needed to talk to Elspeth, but Elspeth was nowhere to be found.

The three of them went out into the back garden. Robert fetched a spade and some gloves. After consulting with Valentina he began to dig a hole. Though the box was not large, he dug down three feet. When the hole was finally big enough, he had a new appreciation for the burial team at the cemetery; *Thomas and Matthew could have dug that grave in ten minutes, and here I am getting blisters and covered with sweat.* He laid the box carefully at the bottom of the hole.

Julia said, 'Shouldn't we . . . say something?'

'A prayer, do you mean?' asked Robert. He glanced from Julia to Valentina.

Valentina said, 'Goodbye . . . Kitten . . .' *I love you. I'm sorry* . . . She began to cry. Robert and Julia looked at each other, uncertain, each trying to allow the other to comfort her. Julia made a gesture with her hands: *Go for it.* Robert stepped towards Valentina, gathered her to him; she was sobbing now. Julia turned away. She walked to the house and up the fire escape. As she opened the door she looked down and saw Valentina clinging to Robert. Robert was watching Julia. *He looks uncomfortable. Like somebody gave him a present he didn't want but has to pretend he likes.* Julia went into the flat and left them to it.

For two days everyone avoided one another. Elspeth stayed in her drawer reproaching herself; Robert put in some time at the cemetery with the burial records; Julia rose early and went out without saying where she was going; Valentina hung around the flat and tried to work on her shroud dress. She found it difficult to concentrate, and the logic of the pattern continued to elude her. Robert had helped the twins order a new television, which arrived the day after the Kitten's funeral. Valentina abandoned the dress for *Antiques Roadshow* and a documentary about Islam. Martin had no clue that anything was amiss, and happily worked on his crosswords and practised standing on the landing. He could stand there for ten minutes now without incident; he was considering actually walking down the stairs.

Valentina was eating her dinner and watching *EastEnders* when Elspeth finally emerged. She sat a few feet away from the television, invisible to Valentina, trying to think what to say. The programme ended. Valentina turned the TV off and began to clear away her dishes. Elspeth followed her to the kitchen and then to the bedroom, agonising.

Valentina said, 'Elspeth? I know you're there.'

Elspeth touched her fingers to the back of Valentina's hand. Valentina went into the front room and sat down at the Ouija board. 'What happened, Elspeth?'

HORRIBLE MISTAKE I AM VERY SORRY

'I didn't want you to really kill her, you know?'

I KNOW I TRIED TO PUT HER BACK SHE WOULDNT SHE RAN AWAY

'Is she here now?'

I CANT SEE HER

'If you see her, will you please let me know?'

IT MAY TAKE TIME FIRST SHE WILL BE LIKE A CLOUD

'Okay.'

I AM SORRY

'Me too. It's my fault, Elspeth, I shouldn't have suggested it.'

BEST LAID PLANS OF MICE AND MEN

'Yeah, I guess.' Valentina stood up. 'Elspeth, I'm tired. I have to go to bed now.'

GOODNIGHT

'Goodnight.' Valentina left the room. Then Elspeth heard her brushing her teeth. *So much for that*, Elspeth thought. *Perhaps it's just as well.*

The following morning Julia found Valentina in the back garden. She was sitting on the bench in the sun, staring at the little mound of earth over the Kitten's grave.

'Um, hi,' said Julia.

'Hi.'

'I was thinking of going to Liberty. Do you want to come with?'

Valentina was about to say no when she remembered that *Julia doesn't really like Liberty's; she must be going to please me.* Valentina thought of the fabric-remnant bins on Liberty's third floor; she could spend a couple of hours mindlessly looking at fabric. It would make a change from TV. 'Okay,' she said. 'Sure.'

They didn't speak much on the way there. Valentina was dressed entirely in black; the clothes were Elspeth's. Julia, unable to match her, had settled for a pale pink hoodie and a short skirt with tights. *Pink and black look good together*, she thought. *We'll match without matching.* They sat side by side as the Northern line growled along, each acutely aware of the other but unable to begin a conversation. When they arrived at Liberty, Valentina went upstairs and plunged into the fabric department. Julia followed and hung back, turning over in her mind what she might say to Valentina when Valentina was willing to talk.

At lunchtime they left the store and went to a Pret; they

split a bacon, lettuce and tomato sandwich and a bag of potato chips. Julia drank a Coke and Valentina had tea. As lunch stretched on in silence, Julia grew more anxious. Finally she said, 'What would you like to do next?'

Valentina shrugged. 'I don't know. Go home, I guess.'

'Oh, come on,' Julia wheedled. 'It's such a nice day. Don't go home yet.'

'Okay.' Valentina's tone made it clear that she didn't much care what she did.

'Let's go for a walk.'

'Okay.'

Back on the street, Julia headed south. She could navigate without consulting the *A–Z* now, Valentina noticed. Soon they were strolling in St James's Park. 'Let's watch the ducks,' Valentina said, so they sat on a bench and stared at the ducks for a while.

Julia said, 'Why are you so mad at me?'

'You know.'

'No . . . I don't get it. We've always been together, and we were happy. I mean, we didn't even think about it, you know? That was just how it was. We wanted the same thing, and we were never going to be apart . . . remember?'

Valentina shook her head. 'That was *your* thing. *Your* idea about how we were. We always did what *you* wanted. You never even noticed, but you got your way *all the time*. The things I wanted to do, somehow we never got around to doing. Like school. We could have stayed at Cornell, or U of I. We could be done with school now. We could have actual jobs. But you didn't like it when I tried to do stuff without you, so you left and you dragged me along. You don't want to do anything with your life, as far as I can tell, so I'm not allowed to have a life either. So what's the point, Julia? You can't hang on to me forever.'

'But we're *supposed* to be together. I mean, look at Mom and Elspeth. They didn't want to be apart. Something really huge happened and they had to separate, but they wouldn't have unless they had to, and they were unhappy about it.'

Valentina said, 'They could have gotten back together, but they didn't. Robert and Elspeth came to America on vacation and they never even went to Chicago because Elspeth didn't want to. Robert thinks Mom told Elspeth not to be in touch with us.'

'But the point is, they didn't want to be apart.'

'Who cares about them?' said Valentina. '*I* want to go to school. *I* want to have a boyfriend, *I* want to get married and have kids. I want to be a designer, I want to live in my own flat by myself, I want to eat a whole sandwich *by myself*. Not necessarily in that order,' she added.

'You can have all the sandwiches you want,' Julia replied. She meant it as a joke, but Valentina stood up and walked off abruptly. Julia called after her. When Valentina kept walking Julia followed her. *Where is she going?* Julia worried. *She doesn't have a map, she'll be totally lost in ten seconds.* Valentina left the park, hesitated, turned right and began walking along the Mall. Julia ran to catch up. She saw Valentina glance backwards, then hurry on. When Valentina came to Trafalgar Square she stopped to talk with a *Big Issue* vendor, who pointed and gestured and seemed to be writing something down for her.

She's trying to find the tube, Julia thought. She waited for Valentina to figure it out. *I'll catch up with her on the train. She won't be able to get away then.* Valentina looked around, did not see Julia, and walked off in the wrong direction. *Why aren't you going to Charing Cross?* Julia trailed her along Cockspur Street and up Haymarket. *She's kind of invisible, wearing black.* Julia closed some of the distance between them and luckily happened to see Valentina disappear into the Piccadilly Circus tube station. Julia ran after her. She saw Valentina slap her Oyster card on the barrier, pass through and run for the stairs. Julia followed; she took the escalator and got to the bottom before Valentina did. Valentina walked by Julia without a word. Julia walked a few steps behind her, distraught.

Valentina ducked into the platform for the westbound Piccadilly line. *Where the hell is she going?* Julia stood a couple of feet away and said, 'Valentina. This is the wrong train. It's going to Heathrow Airport.' Valentina ignored her. *Is she going to the airport? She doesn't have her passport. She doesn't even have much money on her.* A train came. Valentina got on. Julia got on after her.

Just as the doors were closing Valentina squeezed through them and jumped off the train. Julia saw her standing on the platform, watching the train slide away with an expression of satisfaction.

Robert came home from the cemetery shortly after six. He made himself a drink and went out into the back garden, intending to sit just inside the cemetery wall and relax. He found Julia sitting on the bench. She had been crying.

'What's wrong?' he said, against his better judgement.

'Valentina's lost,' Julia replied. She told him some of the events of the day.

'I don't know,' he said. 'Just because she gave you the slip doesn't mean she's lost.'

Julia looked away. 'Then where is she?'

'I don't know, but surely she'll come home tonight.'

Julia looked doubtful, but she said, 'Yeah. I guess.'

Robert offered her his glass. 'Would you like some?'

'No, thanks.'

'Can I do anything, then?'

'No. But thanks.' Julia went up to her flat, leaving Robert worrying in the garden.

At eleven o'clock Julia came downstairs and knocked on Robert's door. 'Any word?' he said.

'No.' Julia continued to stand in the hall. 'What should we do? Should we call the police?'

'I don't know,' he replied. 'I'm not sure—'

The phone rang. Robert hurried to it. 'Hello? . . . Thank God, we've been worried . . . Where are you? . . . West Dulwich? How did you get there? . . . Never mind, let me get a map . . . I'll come in a minicab, just wait for me at the entrance, okay? . . . No, it's fine, just stay there. Yes, no worries. See you soon.' He hung up and turned to Julia. 'She's at a railway station in south London.'

'Can I come?'

Robert said, 'It might be better if you didn't.' He found his wallet and his keys; he stepped into the hall. 'I'm sorry, Julia. She sounded . . . overwrought.'

Julia said, 'That's okay.' She turned and went upstairs. Robert set out for the minicab office.

The journey from Highgate to West Dulwich was a long one, and Robert had time to reflect. *Perhaps I should call their parents. I'm not equipped to deal with their issues – Elspeth is no help. I could call Edie and Jack, ask them to come over . . . and do what, exactly? Take them in hand . . . I'm not their guardian . . . What they need is a referee . . .*

When the cab eventually pulled up to the station, Robert got out and stood on the pavement. Valentina seemed to materialise from the shadows; Robert saw her disembodied head floating towards him, then he realised she was wearing black clothing. Neither of them spoke. She got into the cab and he slid in beside her.

There was very little traffic. The driver was talking in Hindi to someone on his mobile. They rode for several miles in awkward silence. As the cab crossed the Thames Robert said, 'Are you all right?'

'I've made a decision,' Valentina said calmly. 'But I'm going to need your help.'

Robert experienced a qualm. Later, he thought that he should have stopped the cab, sent her home without him; he should have abandoned her then, and run through the streets of south London until his heart failed. Instead he said, 'Oh?'

Very quietly, so the driver would not hear, Valentina began to tell him about Elspeth's resurrection of the Kitten. Robert listened with increasing impatience. 'I don't understand,' he said. 'The Kitten is dead.'

'That was another day – Elspeth was practising. The Kitten didn't like it and ran away, and Elspeth couldn't put her back in her body.'

'Why on earth was Elspeth practising? Practising for what?'

'That's what I wanted to tell you. We had a plan . . .' As she explained the plan, in her soft American voice, almost whispering in the back of the minicab, Robert had a sensation of horror. He drew away from Valentina. 'You're mad,' he said.

She laid her small hand on his knee. 'That's what Elspeth said, at first. But then she thought about it, and she worked out how we could do it. You should talk to Elspeth.'

'Yes, I certainly am going to have a chat with her.' He removed her hand from his leg, then relented and held it. 'Erm, Valentina. You shouldn't . . . It might not be good to let Elspeth call the shots.'

'Why not?'

'She's – clever. Her ideas have other ideas hiding inside them.'

'She's been really nice to me.'

Robert shook his head. 'Elspeth isn't nice. Even when she was alive she wasn't very . . . She was witty and beautiful and fantastically original in . . . certain ways, but now that she's dead she seems to have lost some essential quality – compassion, or empathy, some human thing . . . I don't think you should trust her, Valentina.'

'But you trust her.'

'Only because I'm a fool.'

They rode the rest of the way home in silence.

* * *

Robert offered Valentina his own bed to sleep in, because she wouldn't go upstairs. He waited for her to fall asleep, then went up and knocked on the twins' door. Julia opened it immediately.

'Come in,' she said. He stood in the front hall; he didn't want to sit down and risk a long conversation.

'She's in my flat, sleeping,' he said.

'Okay.'

'Julia,' he said, 'has Valentina ever seemed . . . suicidal . . . to you?'

Julia said quickly, 'She doesn't mean it.'

Robert turned to go. 'I think she might. Just . . . be careful.' He went downstairs. As he reached his own door he heard Julia closing hers.

He let himself in and went to the phone. It would be almost seven o'clock in Lake Forest. He imagined the Pooles eating dinner together, pleasantly unaware that their daughter was plotting her own death and resurrection. He had picked up the receiver and was about to dial when he realised he didn't have the phone number. Could he ask Julia? Better not; he would get the number from Roche in the morning.

Robert sat up most of the night, watching football highlights and a programme on American folk music with the sound turned off. At some point he fell asleep in his chair. When he woke Valentina was gone. He went upstairs and found the twins eating breakfast together, seemingly at peace. Valentina made him a cup of coffee.

'What are you doing today?' he asked them.

'Not much,' said Valentina.

'Perhaps you could go to the supermarket.'

'We've got plenty of food,' said Julia.

'Or sightseeing.'

'You want to talk to Elspeth?' Valentina said.

'How did you guess?' he said sweetly.

Valentina looked abashed but said nothing. After breakfast Julia went upstairs to see Martin, and Valentina took her tea to the back garden. Robert stood in the dining room and said, 'Elspeth. Come here.'

He felt her cold touch against his cheek. He sat at the table with the pencil poised over the paper and said, 'Elspeth, what are you up to?'

ME?

'You and Valentina. She was telling me about this plan of yours.'

IT'S ACTUALLY HER PLAN.

'Valentina couldn't plan her way out of a wet paper bag. Elspeth, you know quite well that it won't work. For one thing, dead bodies are full of chemicals.'

ASK SEBASTIAN NOT TO EMBALM HER.

'No, I mean natural chemicals. There's all sorts of nasty stuff released by various glands to break down the body. There's gases, and bacteria—'

KEEP THE BODY COLD. ALMOST FREEZING.

'Elspeth, all of that is *beside the point*. There's no need for any of this. In six months Valentina can take her half of the estate and walk away. If she doesn't want to see Julia, she won't have to.'

WHAT IF SHE KILLS HERSELF BEFORE THEN?

'She's not going to kill herself.' He said this with more conviction than he felt.

HAVE YOU REALLY LOOKED AT HER LATELY? SHE'S FANATICAL.

'I'm going to call her parents. They can take her home.'

I SUGGESTED THAT TO V. SHE WON'T GO.

'Why not? Anyway, should she be making these decisions for herself? Edie and Jack can take her to hospital if need be – I don't have that authority.'

NEITHER DO THEY.

'Elspeth, I'm not going to help you do this, and you can't make it work without me.'

IF WE DO IT YOU'D HAVE TO HELP, OR SHE WOULD STAY DEAD.

Robert was struck silent by that. He put down the pencil, got up and began pacing around the dining-room table. Elspeth sat on the table and watched him orbit. *You never change*, she thought fondly. At last he sat down again. 'What's in it for you?' he asked her. 'Are you jealous of her?'

NO.

'Are you going to really kill her?'

I COULD DO THAT NOW WITHOUT ANY FUSS AND NO ONE WOULD KNOW.

'True.' Robert knew there was a question he should ask, the question that would lay bare the underlying contradiction inherent in the whole ridiculous plan, but he couldn't think of it. 'It's just . . . wrong, Elspeth.'

PERHAPS. BUT SHE IS VERY DETERMINED.

'She's not going to kill herself.'

BUT WHAT IF SHE DOES?

He shook his head. Her logic was circular. Surely he could stand outside the circle and see another solution? 'Let's not do this,' he begged Elspeth. 'Let's both agree we won't, and she'll have to think again.'

AND IF SHE KILLS HERSELF?

He said nothing.

AT LEAST LET ME EXPLAIN HOW IT MIGHT WORK.

As Robert sat filling sheet after sheet with Elspeth's careful handwriting, he was engulfed by despair. *I won't do it*, he thought. But it was beginning to look as though he would.

On Sunday afternoon, after they had closed the cemetery, Jessica and Robert sat with James on the terrace overlooking the Bateses' back garden. It had been a frantic day – the magnificent June weather had brought the tourists in droves, and most of the guides were on holiday; Robert and Phil had been obliged to eject two extremely large and hostile film-makers and their actors from the Eastern Cemetery; some grave owners had arrived from Manchester without the faintest idea of the location of their grandmother's grave. Now the Bateses and Robert sat drinking whisky and decompressing.

'Perhaps we ought to make another sign to post at the gate,' said James. 'All uncertain grave owners please present yourselves during office hours when the staff can attend to your very time-consuming requests.'

'We *want* to help them,' said Jessica. 'But they *must* call ahead. These people who pitch up on the cemetery's doorstep wanting us to do a grave search whilst they wait – it's beyond anything.'

'They think the records are digitised,' Robert said.

Jessica laughed. 'Ten years from now, perhaps. Evelyn and Paul are typing in the burial records as fast as their fingers can fly, but with one hundred and sixty-nine thousand entries . . .'

'I know.'

'Robert and Phil were quite valiant today,' Jessica told

James. 'In addition to vanquishing the unwanted movie people they each gave four tours.'

'My goodness. Where were the rest of the guides?'

'Brigitte is visiting her mother in Hamburg, Marion and Dean are on holiday in Romania, Sebastian is working overtime at the funeral parlour because of that terrible bus accident in Little Wapping, and Anika caught flu from her little girl.'

'It was just the three of us – Molly was on the Eastern Cemetery gate all day, poor girl.' Robert emptied his glass and Jessica topped it up.

'Well,' said James, 'I suppose that's the principal difficulty of running a cemetery with volunteers. You can't exactly tell people they can't go on holiday because you'll be left short of guides.'

'No,' said Jessica. 'But I do wish they would all make the cemetery a priority—'

'They do, you know,' said Robert. 'They drive in from all over, week after week.'

'Yes, I know. I'm just exhausted, that's all. It was a terribly long day.'

Robert stretched his legs. 'On the upside, if I did four tours every day I might get a little fitter.'

'You do look as though you've been left indoors a bit too long.' Jessica scrutinised him. 'You ought to get more vitamin D. You always seem tired.'

'Maybe I should buy a laptop. I could sit in the Meadow amid the graves and write in the sunshine.

"Oft have we seen him at the peep of dawn
Brushing with hasty steps the dews away
To meet the sun upon the upland lawn."'

Jessica smiled. 'How very Romantic. That would make a lovely advertisement for laptops.'

'How is the thesis coming along?' asked James.

'Reasonably well. I've been slightly distracted lately.'

'Don't you have a deadline? I thought your thesis committee was getting restive,' James said.

'The problem is the more I research, the more there is that ought to go into it. Sometimes I think my dissertation is going to be the size of Highgate Cemetery itself, grave by grave, year by year, every blade of grass, every fern—'

'But Robert, there's no need for that!' Jessica startled him, she sounded so urgent. 'We need you to write what happened, and why it is significant – you don't have to completely recreate the place on paper. You're a historian – history has to pick and choose.'

'I know. I will. But it's hard to stop gathering material.'

Jessica pressed her lips together and looked away. James said, 'Can we help in any way? How long is your manuscript?'

Robert hesitated before he replied. 'One thousand, four hundred and thirty-two pages.'

James said, 'That's marvellous, then it's merely a matter of winnowing it down.'

'No,' said Robert. 'Because I'm only up to the First World War.'

'Oh,' said James. Robert looked at Jessica. She was gazing out at her garden, trying to restrain herself.

'The cemetery has many histories,' Robert told them, 'not just one. There's the social and religious and public-health aspects. There are the biographies of the people buried there – the rise and fall of the London Cemetery Company. There's the vandalism and then the coming together of the Friends and all the work that has been done since then. All these things have to fit together. Then there are the super-natural things that people claim—'

'Surely you aren't putting all that rubbish in!' Jessica sat up and turned to him.

'Not as fact. But it is a part of the modern historical record—'

'A very distasteful part.'

'A small part. But all that craziness was the catalyst for forming the Friends. And I don't want to censor events just because we don't approve of them.'

Jessica sighed. 'But "history is written by the victors". And in the Battle for Highgate Cemetery the Friends are most certainly the victors. So we ought to have some say in our history.'

Robert had misplaced the reference; he thought that she was quoting Michel Foucault. He struggled for a moment with the cognitive dissonance of that, until James kindly said, 'Winston Churchill.'

'Oh, right,' said Robert. *But I'm a Marxist*, he thought. He didn't try to explain, as Jessica had always had a slightly rueful attitude towards Karl Marx (at least in terms of his presence in Highgate Cemetery). Robert wasn't sure he was up to defending current trends in Marxist academic thinking at the moment. Instead he hurriedly set off on a tangent. 'I was thinking about the nature of memory. Of memorials . . .'

The Bateses exchanged glances but didn't say anything. Robert realised that he wasn't sure what he wanted to say.

'The digitisation project,' he said finally. 'And cleaning the graves so the inscriptions can be read. And George in his workshop, carving the names onto new gravestones . . .'

'Yes?' said James.

'Why do we do it?' asked Robert.

'For the families,' said Jessica. 'The dead don't know the difference.'

'And for the historians,' James added with a smile.

'But what if the dead did know?' Robert asked. 'What if they're all there, or somewhere . . . ?'

'Well . . .' Jessica sat looking at him. *Something is wrong with him. He's all nervy.* 'Robert, are you all right? I don't mean to be a fusspot, but I am worried about you.'

Robert looked at his lap. James said, 'Is everything all right with the twins? Stop us if we're prying, but we did rather think you had turned the corner . . .' Robert looked up to find both Bateses peering at him with worried frowns.

'The twins are coming undone. If I understand correctly, Valentina wants to leave Julia, and Julia wants Valentina to break things off with me. But that's not actually the problem.'

He was aware of a resistance to telling them; he didn't want them to think badly of him and he knew he would not be believed. *My head is going to explode if I don't tell somebody. Maybe they'll understand, even if they don't think it's true.* The air was still, there on the terrace. He could hear one crow, far off, cawing. Then it stopped, and the three of them sat in the stillness, waiting.

'I've come to believe that there is some sort of existence after death,' Robert said. 'I think it's possible for people to hang around . . . or to get stuck, somehow . . .' He took a breath. 'I've been talking to Elspeth. She's in her flat and can't leave.'

'Oh, Robert.' Jessica sounded terribly sad. He knew it was sadness for him, sadness that he was losing his mind, not sadness at Elspeth's plight.

Robert said, 'The twins talk to her too.'

'Hmm,' said James. 'Would she talk to us, do you think? How do you communicate with her?'

'Automatic writing, and Ouija board when we get tired. She's very cold, so it's hard to do the writing for very long.'

'Can you see her?'

'Valentina can see her. Julia and I can't, I don't know why.' *I would give anything to see her.*

Jessica said, 'It doesn't seem to be having a very salutary effect on you.' She looked as if she wanted to say a great deal more.

'No. It doesn't.'

'Perhaps we should send you on holiday,' she said. 'A change of scenery might help. And some vitamins. Perhaps the cemetery isn't quite what you need just now.'

'More whisky?' asked James.

'Yes, please.' Later Robert wondered if they'd all had more whisky than they should have. He held out his glass. James added a little water and a generous pour from the bottle. 'But Elspeth isn't in the cemetery. I've never encountered anything in the cemetery except foxes and tourists and the occasional work party.'

'That's good,' said James. 'I'd hate to think of everyone stuck out there in all weathers. Though it seems to me that the afterlife might be a bit dull if it consists of lounging about the house for all eternity with nothing to do.'

'Apparently it started out that way. But lately she's been quite — active. Yesterday I watched Valentina playing backgammon with Elspeth. Elspeth won.'

Jessica shook her head. 'Granting that what you tell us is true — and understand, please, that I find it *most* unlikely — what good could come of it?'

Robert shrugged.

'It seems to put you in a difficult position,' James said. 'This situation never works out very well for the man.' Robert thought, *What precedent could you possibly be citing?* and looked at James quizzically. 'In literature. And myth. Eurydice, *Blithe Spirit*, that lovely story by Edith Wharton—'

'"Pomegranate Seed",' supplied Jessica.

'Thank you, yes. The lovers and husbands all end badly.'

'I asked her to kill me, so I could be with her. She refused.'

'I should hope so!' said Jessica, aghast.

'This won't do,' said James. 'Let us help you. We'll *take* you on holiday.'

'Who will run the cemetery?' asked Robert, smiling.

'Who *cares*?' replied Jessica. *How can he joke about this?* 'Nigel and Edward will sort it out between them. Where shall we go? Paris? Copenhagen? We've never been to Reykjavik, they say it's marvellous this time of year.'

'Let's go somewhere warm and sunny,' said James. The evening was becoming overcast. He felt tired, and the thought of travelling farther than Highgate High Street made his back ache. He held out his glass, and Jessica refilled it.

'Spain,' said Jessica. She and James smiled at each other. 'Or perhaps the Amalfi Coast?'

'That could happen,' said Robert. 'Any of it. It sounds fantastic.' *Why not?* he thought. *I could just walk away. Let the three of them sort it out. The twins would reconcile, and live happily ever after with Elspeth . . .* He sighed. He knew he wasn't going anywhere. Still, it sounded so simple. 'Let's talk about it.'

'We ought to eat something,' said Jessica. 'I feel my tummy flapping at my spine.'

'I'll order takeaway from the Lighthouse, shall I?' said Robert. 'Scampi?' He stood up, unsteadily, and went inside to call.

Jessica and James sat quietly, listening to Robert walking through their house. They heard him pick up the phone in the hall, his low voice ordering food.

James said, 'Ought we to tell anyone? We could call Anthony . . .'

Jessica put her hands over her eyes. *I am so tired.* 'I don't know. What does one do when one's dear young friend is being haunted?'

'Don't you think he told us so that we would do something?'

'Have him committed, do you mean?'

James hesitated. 'He talked of killing himself.'

'No, I think he was trying to get Elspeth to kill him.' She snorted.

'I don't like it at all.'

'No. Do you think he would come away with us?'

James sighed. 'Do you think we could manage if he had a breakdown in some foreign hotel room?'

'We ought to do *something*.'

Robert reappeared. 'I'm going to walk down the hill and pick up the food.' He sounded completely cheerful and normal. James offered him some money, and Robert said thanks, but it was on him. He walked off, almost sober-seeming. *Paris. Rome. Saskatchewan.* Robert hummed softly as he came out onto the street and began to walk over to the Archway Road. He walked faster; the evening was cooling off rapidly. *Adelaide. Cairo. Beijing. It doesn't matter where I go, she'll still be stuck in that flat, plotting a resurrection.* This made him laugh. *This is brilliant, I'm walking down the street giggling like Peter Lorre.* He had to stop and lean against the newsagent's; he was bent over laughing. *Cancún, Buenos Aires, Patagonia. I could get on the tube just across the street and be at Heathrow in an hour. No one would know.* He stood up, gasping, closed his eyes. *God, I feel ill.* He stood that way, eyes closed, arms wrapped around his middle, for a few minutes. Robert opened his eyes. The world tilted, then righted itself. He began to walk down the hill, very slowly. *This won't do. I have* to fetch the food. *James and Jessica will worry.* People stared at him as they passed by. *The problem is . . . I'm too responsible. She knows I'll do it because if I don't . . . if I don't . . .* He nearly passed by the fish restaurant, but habit saved him and he managed to go in and pay for the food. As he trudged back up the hill a thought came to Robert: *I ought to read those diaries. Elspeth gave them to me and I ought to read them.* He began to repeat over and over again, 'The diaries, the diaries.' When he got back to the Bateses' house the food was cold and Jessica and James were in the kitchen eating soup. Jessica put him to bed in their guest room.

In the morning he crawled out of bed with a hangover and a feeling of having forgotten something. Jessica made him drink a foul-tasting concoction that included bananas, tomatoes, vodka, milk and Tabasco sauce. Then she fried some eggs and sat with him while he ate. James had already gone to the cemetery.

Jessica said, 'James and I talked it over last night and we think you need looking after. Would you like to come and stay with us? We have loads of room.' She smiled.

Robert's heart leapt. Here was the escape hatch he had been searching for; the words of acceptance were nearly on his tongue when he thought, *Wait. If I'm staying here I won't be able to go to the cemetery at night.* He said, 'May I think about it?'

'Of course,' Jessica said. 'We'll be here.'

He thanked her and left the house in the mood of a shipwrecked man who has allowed the rescue ship to pass him by.

* * *

Robert finally remembered his resolution to read the diaries the following morning. With trepidation he heaved the boxes onto the bed and began to go through them.

Just pretend it's research, he told himself. *It won't bite.* The diaries began in 1971: Elspeth and Edie were twelve. He was relieved to see that they ended, abruptly, in 1983, long before he himself entered the picture; Robert had not been looking forward to reading about himself. The diaries were a hodge-podge of school gossip, comments on books she was reading, musings about boys; some of the writing seemed to be in code. The author carried out long conversations and arguments with herself; suddenly Robert realised that Elspeth and her twin had written the diaries together. The effect was strangely seamless. It made Robert uneasy. There were symbols in the margins that appeared only during holidays and seemed to mean something about Elspeth and Edie's parents; there was a plan to run away that came to nothing. But Robert knew her home life had been unhappy: there were no real surprises, only an ominous sadness that mixed with ordinary girl things, netball and the school play and such. The later volumes detailed university life, parties, the twins' first apartment. Jack appeared on the scene, at first as one of many handsome, eligible young men, then as someone around whom everything suddenly revolved. As an only child, Robert had a certain curiosity about other people's siblings. Elspeth and Edie seldom wrote in the first person singular; it was almost always 'we' who went to the movies or sat an exam. Robert ploughed on, wondering what he was searching for in Elspeth's juvenilia.

The bomb came in the last diary; Elspeth had tucked an envelope inside the cover. The envelope was labelled BIG, DARK, HORRIBLE SECRETS. It had a skull and crossbones inexpertly drawn under this inscription. The skull was smiling. *Oh, Elspeth. I don't want to know.* Robert held the envelope and considered burning it. Then he slit it open.

Dear Robert,

I hope you won't be too annoyed. You said you hoped you wouldn't find any lurid secrets among my papers – I'm afraid there are a few. 'Lurid' isn't quite the right word – 'awkward' might be better. Anyway, darling, they are old surprises – this all happened long before I met you.

My name is Edwina Noblin.

I switched identities with my twin, Elspeth, in 1983. It was mostly her doing, but I couldn't undo it without making her very unhappy. And I certainly was not blameless.

As you know, Elspeth was engaged to Jack Poole. During the time between their engagement and the wedding, Jack became more and more flirtatious towards me. Elspeth decided to put him to the test.

I've told you lots of stories about Elspeth and me impersonating each other. But you never saw us together – we were so alike, such a perfect pair. And we knew each other so intimately. When we were young we hardly differentiated between ourselves; if Elspeth got hurt, I would cry.

Elspeth began to be me when Jack was around. He couldn't tell the difference, and he fell in love with 'Edie'.

He broke off his engagement with Elspeth and asked 'Edie' to elope with him, to go back to America with him in Elspeth's place.

What could she do? She was hurt; she was furious. But the situation was of her own making. She came to me. We decided that she would be Edie and I would be Elspeth, and life would go on.

Unfortunately, it wasn't that simple. I had slept with Jack (only that once – we were drunk, at a party – it was just a stupid mistake, my love, just carelessness and alcohol) and I was pregnant. So in the end I was the one who went to America. I lived with Jack for almost a year, though it was Elspeth he had married. I had the twins, worked out like a maniac to lose the baby weight, cooked and kept house and almost went mad with boredom and rage and a sense of having been trapped in a farce. When the twins were four months old, I brought them to London 'to see their grandmother'. It was Elspeth (now Edie) who returned to Lake Forest a few months later with the twins. I haven't seen them since. I dream about them often. According to Elspeth, they are very much like us.

By the time I returned to London I disliked Jack intensely, and I was disgusted with Elspeth for insisting that we go through with the pregnancy (I wanted to have an abortion). The whole situation was mad. It was the sort of thing you get yourself into when you're young and stupid. I don't know what would have happened if Jack had ever found out about it. How he managed to overlook all the little differences between my body and Elspeth's I have never been able to fathom. Perhaps he knew and never said anything? We decided not to chance letting Jack see us together again. I still can't believe we got away with it.

Elspeth occasionally sent me letters, and photographs of the twins. I never wrote back until last year, as I told you. I think her life with Jack has been disappointing. Her letters are full of longing for London, old friends, me. Before she married I urged her to chuck him, or to tell him everything. It's been hard for her. If you meet her, perhaps you'll know what I mean.

So that's how I became Elspeth. I don't think it altered the course of my life too much. I regret that I never got to know the twins. It was very hard to let her take them. I'll never forget standing at Heathrow, watching her disappear with them through the gate. I cried for days. And I would have liked to have seen Elspeth one more time. It was just fear, and pride, that kept us apart at the end.

Robert, this was my only secret from you. I hope you won't think too badly of me. I hope when you meet the twins you'll find a bit of me in them, and that it will make you remember happy times.

Your loving Elspeth (Edie)

P.S. I really would have left you everything if you'd wanted it. But I knew you wouldn't. I love you. e

The letter had been written a week before her death. Robert sat on the bed, holding it, trying to grasp what it meant. *Everything was a lie, then?* No, surely not. But he had not even known her name. *Who was it that I loved?*

He put everything back in the boxes and brought it all to the tiny servant's bedroom at the back of the flat; then he shut the door and tried to put the letter out of his mind, but it intruded on him constantly, no matter what he was doing. Over the next few days Robert took to drinking more often, and stayed in his flat alone.

Valentina and Elspeth spent long hours conferring over the details of their plan. Everything had to be natural, casual. Elspeth worked out a way for Valentina to take some money from the account she shared with Julia; it would be enough for a year or two, if Valentina was frugal, and the money would not be missed until after the funeral. Valentina found a few anatomy books in the flat and spread them on the floor of the guest room for Elspeth. It was almost a game for them, to anticipate all the potential difficulties, to circumvent Robert's objections, to avoid alarming Julia. *What if . . . ?* one of them would begin, and they would converge on the problem like detectives until they had cracked it. They had private jokes, a secret language. It was all immensely satisfying, or would have been, if they had been planning a picnic, or a surprise party, anything other than Valentina's death. Elspeth was amazed at Valentina's relish for the details of the plan, and her ability to inflict grief thoughtlessly. *But I'm no better. I'm helping her to do it. She wouldn't do it if she knew . . . And what if it doesn't work? What if it does?* Elspeth watched Valentina and debated with herself. She thought, *We mustn't, it's terribly wrong.* But each night Robert would come and take Valentina away for dinner, for a walk. They always came back late, and whispered together in the hallway. Elspeth hardened her heart.

Robert dreamt that it was Resurrection Day at Highgate Cemetery.

He stood at the top of the steps next to the grave of James Selby, the coachman. Selby sat on his grave, oblivious to the heavy chain running through his chest from grave post to grave post. He was smoking a pipe and tapping one booted foot nervously against the ground.

Trumpets brayed in the distance. Robert turned and saw that the path into the cemetery was covered with a long canopy of red fabric, and the dirt and gravel and mud of the path itself were draped in white silk. It was winter again, and the silk was almost the same white as the snow that lay over the graves. He saw through the trees that all the paths were swathed in red and white. Robert found himself walking. He looked down anxiously, afraid that his muddy boots would stain the silk, but he wasn't leaving any tracks.

He came to Comfort's Corners and found tables set out for a banquet. There was no food, only places laid with china and cutlery, empty wine glasses and empty chairs. The trumpets stopped, and Robert heard trees rattling in the wind. There were voices, but he couldn't gauge where they were.

Sit down, someone said, but it wasn't a voice, really; it was more like a thought that came from outside his head. He sat at a place near the edge of the cluster of tables and waited.

The ghosts arrived slowly, picking their way along the silk paths with unsure steps. They crowded around the tables, translucent, dressed in their grave clothes, winding sheets, their Sunday best. The air became dense with ghosts. *More than one hundred and sixty-nine thousand people were buried in this cemetery.* Robert wondered if all of them could fit around the tables. The ghosts shivered in the morning light. *They look like jellyfish.* There was a ripple of dissatisfaction: the ghosts were hungry; there was no food. He thought he saw Elizabeth Siddal and began to stand up with a thought of going to speak to her, but a hand on his shoulder kept him in his chair.

There were immense numbers of ghosts now. The tables had multiplied as well. A voice, well known, long wished-for, spoke just behind him. 'Robert,' said Elspeth, 'what are you doing here?'

'I'm not sure. Looking for you?' He tried to turn, but again he was restrained.

'No – don't. I don't want . . . not here.' She was pressed close to him. He felt uneasy, confined. Suddenly he had the sense that something horrible, monstrous, was standing behind him, pressing its disgusting hands on him.

He shouted out her name, so loudly that he woke the twins in their bedroom; so loudly that Elspeth herself lay on the floor above his bed for hours in the slowly increasing grey light, waiting to hear him call her again.

The phone rang. Edie stretched out her hand and brought it to her ear, but did not immediately say anything. She was curled on her side, in bed; it was almost nine in the morning. Jack was at work.

'Mom?'

Edie sat up. She smoothed back her hair with her fingers as though Valentina could see her. 'Hello?' She sounded as though she had been awake for hours. 'Valentina?'

'Hi.'

'Are you all right? Where's Julia?'

'She's upstairs. Hanging out with Martin.'

Edie felt the adrenaline subside. *She's fine. They're both fine.* 'We missed talking to you on Sunday. Where were you?'

'Oh . . . I'm sorry. We just . . . lost track of the days, you know?'

'Oh,' said Edie. She felt a pang of neglect. 'So, what's up?'

'Nothing . . . I just felt like calling you.'

'Mmm, you're sweet. So what's going on?'

'Not much. It's kind of rainy and chilly here.'

'You sound a little down,' Edie said.

'Oh . . . I dunno. I'm fine.' Valentina was sitting in the back garden, shivering in the drizzle. She hadn't wanted Elspeth listening in on this conversation, but it was suddenly awfully cold for June and she had to make an effort to keep her teeth from chattering. 'What's up with you and Dad?'

'The usual. Dad just got a promotion, so we were out last night celebrating.' Edie could hear birds through the phone. 'Where are you?'

'In the backyard.'

'Oh. Have you and Julia been anywhere fun lately?'

'Julia's got almost the whole city memorised now. She can walk around without the map.'

'That's impressive . . .' Edie thought, *There's stuff she's not telling me.* But then she thought that was inevitable: *They move away and soon you have no idea. They make their own world and you don't belong any more.* Valentina was asking a question about a dress she was trying to make; Edie told her to email the sketch and then remembered that the twins had no scanner.

'Yeah, oh well. Never mind,' said Valentina. 'It doesn't matter.'

'Are you sure you're okay?' Edie said. *She just sounds strange.*

'Yeah. I've got to go now, Mom. I love you.' *If I stay on the phone I'll cry.*

'Okay, sweetie. I love you too.'

'Bye.'

'Bye.'

Valentina dialled her dad's work number and got his voice-mail. *I'll call later,* she thought, and didn't leave a message.

⤞═ CAUGHT OUT ═⤝

It was almost dawn. Jessica stood at the window in the cemetery's Archives Room, looking out over the courtyard at the Colonnade. The room was dark. She had lain awake most of the night worrying over the letter she had written to one of the cemetery's vice presidents. Finally she had left a note for James and walked down here to put it right, but even though her head was crowded with the phrases that would convince the vice president of the logic of her request, she had not been able to sort out the tangle of her argument. Jessica leaned against the window sill, her hands clasped together in front of her and her elbows jutting at right angles. The trees and graves above the Colonnade were dark and hazy in the indeterminate light. The courtyard reminded her of an empty stage. *So much work*, she thought. *No one realises how we worked. Every sett in that courtyard laid by hand—*

Suddenly the courtyard was filled with light. *Foxes*, she thought and swept her eyes left and right, to see them. *They've set off the motion detectors.* But then a man walked across the courtyard. He didn't seem fussed by the lights, didn't hurry or change his course. Jessica craned her head forward, trying to see him better. It was Robert.

Damn the boy. I've told him not to use that door! Jessica rapped on the window as hard as she could, not minding the pain of arthritic joints on cold glass – she was angry enough not to notice; later she would wonder why her hand was swollen and throbbing. Robert continued walking, unheeding. Jessica grabbed her keys and torch and got herself down the stairs and through the office, into the courtyard. She stood not quite under the chapel archway and shouted his name.

Robert stopped. *I'm for it now.* Jessica walked quickly towards him. He thought, *She'll fall, walking so fast.* She had forgotten to switch on her torch and carried it as though she had brought it along as a weapon rather than a source of light. He roused himself and walked to her to shorten the distance between them. They met by the Colonnade steps, as if choreographed. Jessica paused to catch her breath. Robert waited.

'What on *earth* do you think you are *doing*?' she finally said. 'You *know* better. We've *discussed* this, and yet *here you are* – flagrantly strutting about at the crack of dawn *in the cemetery* – where you have absolutely no right to be! I trusted you, Robert, and you have let me down.' She stood hatless and fuming, glaring up at him, her hair spiky; she was wearing her gardening clothes. Robert was startled to see the glint of a tear on her cheek. It undid him.

'We have rules! The rules are there for legal and safety reasons!' Jessica was yelling now. 'Just because you have a key does *not* entitle you to come in at night! You might be attacked by intruders, or fall into a *hole*. You might trip on a root and concuss yourself – you don't even have a radio! *Anything* could happen: a monument might fall on you, *anything* – think what the insurers would do to our rates – the publicity if you got yourself injured, or killed! You're just bloody selfish, Robert!'

They stared at each other. Robert said gently, 'Can we go into the office to talk? You're going to wake the dead.'

Jessica lost whatever control she had had over her temper. *Why can't he take it seriously? I'll make him see it's no joke!* 'No! We are not going into the office to talk! I am going to have your key, please' — she held out her hand, in which she already held her own keys — 'and you are going out the front gate.' Robert didn't move. 'Now!'

He dropped the key into her palm, turned towards the gate. She followed him as though escorting a prisoner. They reached the gate; she unlocked it; he pulled the massive thing open and slipped out, pulled it shut again. They faced each other through the bars. 'What now?' he asked.

'Go,' she said quietly.

He bowed his head, walked away and up Swains Lane. Jessica stood watching him. *What now?* Her heart beat fast. *No one saw him but me — they needn't find out.* She watched Robert until he vanished up the road. She had an urge to follow him, to say — what? *I'm sorry? No, certainly not. He put us at risk, thoughtless, careless . . .* She stood at the gate overcome with emotion, but unable to parse it — angry, hurt, anxious with affection, indignant. She could not sort herself out at all. *I've got to talk to him immediately*, she thought, and then: *But I've sent him away.* She turned the key in the lock and slowly walked back to her office. It was just after five o'clock. James might be awake. She picked up the telephone receiver, then put it down again.

Jessica sat in her chair, watching the room lighten. *I was right*, she thought. *I was quite right.* When it was day she got up and made tea. Preoccupied, tired, she spilled the milk and thought, *That's an omen. Or a metaphor.* She shook her head. *What shall we do now?*

Martin was stumped. He had been working all afternoon on a cryptic crossword in celebration of Carl Linnaeus' three hundredth birthday, but the clues wouldn't come to him and the thing felt inelegant and lumpen. Martin stood up and stretched.

Someone knocked. He said, 'Yes?' and turned towards the door. 'Oh, Julia. Come in.'

'No,' she said, stepping into the room, 'I'm Valentina. Julia's sister.'

'Oh!' Martin was delighted. 'At last! Such a pleasure to meet you. Thank you for coming – would you like some tea?'

'No, I . . . I can't stay. I just came to tell you . . . you know the vitamins Julia's been giving you?'

'Yes?'

She took a breath. 'They . . . aren't really vitamins. They're a drug called Anafranil.'

Martin said gently, 'I know, my dear. But thank you for coming to tell me.'

Valentina said, 'You knew?'

'It's printed on each capsule. And I've taken Anafranil before, so I know what it looks like.'

Valentina smiled. 'Does Julia know you know?'

Martin smiled back at her. 'I'm not entirely sure. I think perhaps we shouldn't mention this conversation to her, just in case.'

'Oh, I wasn't going to.'

'Then I won't either.'

She turned to go and Martin said, 'Are you sure you won't stay?'

'No – I can't.'

'Come back, then, any time you like.'

Valentina said, 'Okay. Thank you.' He heard her steps receding as she walked through the maze of boxes, and then she was gone.

Robert thought afterwards that it had been like watching ballet.

'Are you ready?' he asked.

Elspeth did not want Valentina to say yes. She wanted to pause in this moment before — before whatever was about to happen, before temptation, before disaster, before Elspeth had to do the thing she did not want to do.

Robert watched Valentina. She stood quite still. He wondered if he should open a window; the weather was still unseasonably cold for June, but who knew how long her body would lie there until Julia returned? The light was waning rapidly; crows were calling to each other in the cemetery. Julia was upstairs. Valentina closed her eyes. She stood at the foot of the bed, one hand curled around the bedrail. Her other hand clenched and unclenched around her inhaler. She opened her eyes. Robert stood only a few feet away. Elspeth sat in the window seat, elbows on knees, head in hands, her face tilted at an angle that denoted contemplative sadness. Valentina watched Elspeth and felt a spasm of doubt.

Robert hesitated, then stepped towards her. Valentina put her arms around his waist and pressed her cheek against his shirt. She wondered if the button of the shirt was imprinting itself on her cheek, and whether it would stay that way once she was dead. He did not kiss her. She thought it might be because Elspeth was there.

'I'm ready,' she said. She stepped back, into the middle of the bedroom rug, and took a puff from her inhaler. Elspeth thought, *How insubstantial she already looks, just a shadow in this dim light.*

Robert retreated to the doorway. He could not articulate his feelings at all: he waited for something to happen. He did not believe that it would happen; he did not want it to happen. *Don't, Elspeth . . .*

Valentina closed her eyes, then opened them and looked at Robert, who seemed far away; Valentina thought of her parents watching her and Julia move through the security line at O'Hare the day they'd left Chicago. Intense cold permeated her body. Elspeth moved through her, simply stepped into her; it reminded Valentina of looking at old stereoscope pictures, trying to bring the images together. *I will die of cold.* She felt herself seized, detached, taken. 'Oh!' An interval of nothing. Then she was hovering close over her body, which lay collapsed on the floor. *Ah—* Elspeth knelt beside the body, looking up at her. 'Come here, sweet,' Elspeth said. *She sounds kind of like Mom. That's so weird.* She tried to go to Elspeth, but found that she could not move. Elspeth understood and came up towards her, gathered her in her hands. Now Valentina was only a small thing, cupped in Elspeth's hands *like a mouse.* The last thing she thought was: *It's like falling asleep . . .*

Robert saw Valentina go slack. She fell: knees gave way, head lolled. She folded up and hit the floor with a thud and a crack. Then there was no sound in the room except his own breathing. He stood in the doorway and did not go to her because he did not know what was happening; unseen things must be happening and he did not know what to do next. The girl, crumpled on the carpet, continued to be utterly still. Finally he walked the short distance across the room and knelt beside Valentina. She was not bleeding. He couldn't tell if she was broken; she looked broken, but he could not touch her; she lay as she had fallen and he knew he must not touch her.

Elspeth looked down at him looking at Valentina. She could feel Valentina, heavy and smoke-like, caged in her hands. *Put her back, now. Put her back while there's some chance of it being all right . . .* She wanted Robert to move Valentina, to straighten her limbs and compose her hands. Valentina's head was arched back, she lay on her right side with her arms flailed out in front of her, legs tucked neatly together. Her eyes were rolled up, her mouth was open, her little teeth showed. The position of Valentina's body seemed wrong, an insult. Elspeth wanted to touch her, but her hands were full. *What now? If I let go, will she just disperse? I wish I had a little box . . .* She thought of her drawer. *Yes, I'll put her in there.* She would take Valentina with her into the drawer. They could stay there together, waiting.

Robert stood up. He left the room. He wanted to forget what he had seen, before he reached the front door. He stopped with his hand on the knob. 'Elspeth?' he said. In answer there was a momentary cold touch against his cheek. 'I won't forgive you.' Silence. He imagined her behind him, resisted the urge to turn and look. He opened the door, went downstairs, stood in his kitchen drinking whisky as the light failed, waiting for Julia to come home and find the body, listening for her cry of distress.

* * *

Julia came downstairs an hour later. All the lights were off in the flat. She walked through the rooms flipping switches, calling 'Mouse?' *She must have gone out.* 'Mouse?' *Maybe she's downstairs.* The flat was cold and seemed curiously empty, as though all the furniture had been replaced with optical illusions. As Julia wandered from room to room she trailed her fingers across the dining-room table, lightly touched the top of the sofa and the spines of the books, reassuring herself that everything was solid. 'Elspeth?' *Where is everybody?*

She came to their bedroom and snapped on the light. She saw Valentina lying contorted on the floor, as though frozen in a painful dance. Julia moved slowly; she went to Valentina and sat beside her. She touched Valentina's lips, her cheeks. She saw the inhaler clasped in Valentina's hand and pressed her own hand to her own chest, unthinkingly.

Mouse? Valentina seemed to be trying to see above her; her eyes were rolled up and her head thrown back as though some event of extreme interest was happening right over her head. 'Mouse?' Valentina did not respond.

Julia whimpered. She felt cold on her face and hit out at it wildly. 'Fuck you, Elspeth! Fuck off! Where is she? Where is she?' Then she began to wail.

Elspeth sat on the floor with Julia. She watched as Julia clutched Valentina in her arms and keened over her body. *I never wanted to do it, Julia.* She thought about her own twin, about the phone call someone would have to make to her, soon. Elspeth knew, watching Julia, that nothing would ever be right again. *It's my fault, all of it. I'm sorry. I am so, so sorry.*

* * *

Elspeth and Valentina stayed in the drawer together while Valentina's body was confirmed dead by paramedics, then certified dead of natural causes by the doctor she had seen at the hospital, and removed from the flat by Sebastian, while Julia cried and Robert phoned Edie and Jack. There were hours of stillness, light, dark.

Robert had a long talk with Sebastian that resulted in mutual tension. 'I can understand that you don't want her embalmed,' Sebastian said. 'I can understand why you don't want me to set her features – that's fine. But why on earth do you want me to shoot her up with heparin?'

'It's an anticoagulant.'

'I *know* that. But you aren't having her cryogenically preserved.'

'Not exactly. But we'd like the coffin packed with ice, please.'

'Robert!'

'Humour me, Sebastian. And please keep her in cold-storage as much as possible.'

'Why? Robert, I don't like this.'

'It's nothing like that . . .'

Sebastian regarded him sceptically. 'I'm sorry, Robert. But either tell me exactly what you've got in mind, or find someone else to do it.'

Robert said, 'You won't believe me – it sounds crazy. It is crazy.' Sebastian said nothing. Robert took a deep breath and tried to organise his thoughts. 'Do you believe in ghosts?'

'As it happens,' Sebastian said softly, 'I do. I've had some . . . interesting experiences. But I seem to recall that you don't – believe in ghosts.'

'I've been forced to reconsider.' Robert told Sebastian about Elspeth. He omitted any mention of a plan; he told Sebastian that Elspeth had caught Valentina's spirit when she died, and now she was going to put it back into Valentina and bring her back to life.

Sebastian had a number of objections. ('Why didn't Elspeth just revive her right away?' was the most formidable, and Robert could only say that he didn't know.) In the end Sebastian agreed to do his best to keep Valentina cold; he also agreed to say nothing to the family, in case the attempt did not succeed. But even so, Robert went away wondering if Sebastian might be calling Jessica, or the police, the moment he was out of sight.

The next morning Edie and Jack arrived.

Standing at his window, Robert watched them walking up the front path. They disappeared into the building and he heard them treading the stairs. Elspeth's ban on Jack and Edie entering her flat was inappropriate now. Robert wondered what Elspeth was doing; he wanted to drink himself to distraction, to die; anything would be preferable to meeting Valentina's parents. He had agreed to go with them to the funeral parlour.

In the cab they hardly spoke. Robert could not look at Edie. She was unbearably like Elspeth; the only significant difference was her Americanised speech. Julia was dazed. She sat next to her father, leaning her head on his shoulder. Edie began to cry quietly. Jack put his arm around Edie and looked at Robert, stricken. Robert was sitting in the fold-down seat opposite the three of them. He kept his eyes on Jack's shoes for the rest of the ride.

When they arrived at the funeral parlour Sebastian was

waiting for them. He took Edie and Jack to view Valentina's body. Robert and Julia sat in Sebastian's office.

'How are you?' Robert asked her.

'Peachy,' Julia said, not looking at him.

Sebastian returned with Edie and Jack. He began to carefully lay out the procedures and options, the prices for interment and cremation, the various certificates and signatures that would be needed. Robert listened with what he hoped was an impassive expression. He had forgotten that Valentina's parents might have their own ideas about her remains, and that Sebastian was required by law to explain all their choices. Robert's heart was racing. *What if they decide to cremate her?*

Edie said, 'We want to take her home – Jack's family has a plot in the Lake Forest Cemetery. It's right on Lake Michigan. We were thinking we'd like to bury her there.'

Sebastian nodded and began to explain how to go about shipping a body by air. Robert thought, *Well, that's it, then. I tried and I failed.* It was out of his hands now.

Curiously, it was Julia who saved the situation. 'No!' she said. Everyone looked at her. 'I want her here.'

'But Julia—' said Edie.

'But it's not your decision—' Jack said at the same time.

Julia shook her head. 'She wanted to be buried in Highgate Cemetery.' Julia looked at Robert. 'She said so.'

Robert said, 'That's true.'

'Please,' Julia said. And in the end it was decided that Valentina would be interred in the Noblin family mausoleum, just as she had requested.

* * *

In the drawer Elspeth encircled Valentina, pressed her into a soft shapelessness, kept her from diffusing, kept her close. *Here we are, Valentina, like marsupials in a pouch, waiting for developments.* She wondered what Valentina knew, what she would remember. It was like being with a baby, not knowing what this tiny being was thinking, whether it could think at all. Elspeth did not remember the first days of her afterlife. Things had come on gradually; there was no moment of awakening, of sudden consciousness. She held Valentina close, sang her little songs, chattered to her about nothing. Valentina was like a hum, a buzz of being, but no words or thoughts escaped from her to Elspeth. Elspeth thought about the twins as infants. They had never slept or fed at the same time; they had drained her of energy and milk; they had seemed even then inseparable but individual. *Well, you've managed to separate yourself rather thoroughly now, Valentina.* In the drawer nothing much happened. The days went by. Soon – though time meant little to the ghosts – soon it was the day of Valentina's funeral. It was time for something to happen.

At eight o'clock on the morning of the funeral Robert stood at Martin's door, engulfed by the spill of newspapers. He tried to straighten them into piles but gave up when Martin appeared.

'Come in.' They moved through the flat to the kitchen. Robert sat at the table and Martin put the electric kettle on. Robert thought he seemed refreshingly normal and domestic compared to what was going on downstairs. *You know you're in trouble when Martin is the most functional person in the place.*

'The funeral is at one, today.'

'I know.'

'Would you like to come? It's all right if you can't, you know, but I think Julia would appreciate it.'

'I'm not sure. I'll call down if I can do it.'

'So I'll put you down as a "No"?'

Martin shrugged. He held up two boxes of tea. Robert pointed to the Earl Grey. Martin put a tea bag in each cup. 'How is Julia?'

'Her parents have arrived. Listening to Elspeth, I'd imagined they'd have three heads apiece and shoot fire from their eyes, but they've taken Julia in hand and they're all, I don't know, subdued together. None of us really believe it – they keep walking around the flat like they're going to run into Valentina in the hall. Julia's practically catatonic.'

'Ah.' Martin poured out. Robert stared at the stream. 'They are staying in the flat?'

'No, at a hotel.'

'So Julia's by herself in the flat?'

'Yes. Her parents tried to get her to come to the hotel with them, but she wanted to stay in her flat. I don't know why.'

'She shouldn't be alone.'

'Well, that's what I came up to talk to you about. I want you to ask Julia up here tonight, and keep her here until I tell you it's okay to let her go.'

Martin regarded Robert sceptically. 'Why?'

Robert maintained what he hoped was an innocent air. 'Julia shouldn't be alone.'

'No, she shouldn't be. But surely she'd rather be with her parents?'

'If necessary you can ask them up too.'

'You're joking. You expect me to have Edie and Jack here? Have you looked at this place properly?'

'Yeah, but I didn't realise you had.' Robert switched tactics. 'Look, Martin, it's life and death: you've got to help me keep Julia out of her own flat for a few hours. I can't depend on Edie and Jack.'

'What are you up to?'

'You wouldn't believe me if I told you.'

'Try me.'

'It's . . . a seance, of sorts.'

'You're trying to contact Valentina? Or Elspeth?'

'More or less.'

Martin shook his head, exasperated. 'Surely this is *not* the moment? If you're going to play about with that, can't it wait?'

'It absolutely can't wait.'

'Why can't Julia be there?'

'I can't explain. And you can't tell her.'

'No. I won't do it.'

'Why not?' Martin got up and paced around the kitchen. Robert instantly wished he had done this first, but they couldn't both pace at the same time. That would be peculiar.

Robert said, 'It won't hurt Julia not to know. Here: I'll make a bargain with you. If you'll keep Julia here tonight, I'll give you something you desperately want.'

Martin sat down again. 'What's that?' he said suspiciously.

'Marijke's address in Amsterdam.'

Martin raised his eyebrows. He got up again and left the kitchen. Robert heard him walking across the hall into his office. He was gone for a while. When he reappeared he had a lit cigarette in one hand and a map of Amsterdam in the other.

'I thought you'd given up?' Robert said.

'I'll quit again in half an hour.' Martin smoothed out the map on the table. Robert saw that it was covered with marks, notes, erasures. Martin pointed to a tiny red circle in the Jordaan. 'There.'

Robert squinted, brought the minuscule words into focus. 'Close, but no cigar.' They stared at each other. Robert smiled. 'How did you happen to pick that spot?'

'I know her. She's careful not to say much, but I remember things. We lived nearby, on the Tweede Leliedwarsstraat.'

'I'll throw in her email address.'

'Marijke doesn't do email.'

'She does. She's had it for more than a year.'

'A year?'

'I'll give you her address, email and a photograph of her apartment.'

'She sent you a picture of her place?'

'Several. Did she mention she's got a cat now?'

Martin looked wistful. 'Does she?'

'It's a little grey cat named Yvette. It sleeps on Marijke's pillow.'

Martin sat quietly, smoking and staring at the map. 'All right, you're on. What do I have to do?'

Robert laid it out for him. It was simple, really; it was the only simple thing about that entire day.

When Jack woke up, Edie was standing in her nightgown at the French windows in the small hotel room, staring at the blue sky over the slate roofs of Covent Garden. He lay there watching her, reluctant to break into her thoughts. Finally he got up and went to the bathroom. *Amazing how life goes on. Here I am pissing and showering and shaving like it's any day, like we're on vacation. Why didn't we come and see them before?* He wiped the last traces of lather from his neck and went back into the other room. Edie was still standing at the windows. Now her head was bowed. Jack walked to her and stood behind her, put his hands on her bare shoulders. She turned slightly.

'What time is it?' she asked.

'Eight fifteen.'

'We can call Julia.'

'I'm sure she's been awake for hours.'

'Yes.'

They continued to stand that way, Jack's hands weighing on her shoulders. Edie said, 'I'll call her.' Her cell phone didn't work here, so she fumbled with the hotel phone, misdialled and redialled.

'Julia?' *I just wanted to hear your voice.*

'Hi, Mom.' *Oh God. I don't know what to do, Mom.*

'We thought we might come earlier.' *I can't stand to be in this room.*

'Can you come soon?' *I'm alone and I don't know what to do.*

'Yes, yes, we'll just get dressed and take a cab. We'll be there as soon as we can.' Edie felt a surge of incongruous happiness. *She needs me.* Edie was smiling as she hung up the phone. She walked briskly to her suitcase and began to dress for the funeral. Jack went to the wardrobe, stood looking at his dark suit hanging by itself. He forgot, for a minute; he was lost in the dark wool hanging in the shadows of the wardrobe. Then he remembered and reached for the suit. *I feel old.* The suit was heavy, as though it were lined with some soft metal. He watched Edie bustling around, brushing her hair, putting on earrings. *I don't want to go outside.* He sat on the bed holding a pair of socks. Edie saw him sitting motionless and said, 'Come on, she's waiting for us,' and it was that singular pronoun, pronounced impatiently, that finally bore down on him the fact of Valentina's death.

Julia was waiting for them downstairs in the main hallway. She watched her parents through the narrow leaded window as they let themselves in the gate and walked along the path through the front garden. It was a bright June day; the sunlight made them seem extra-dimensional and distinct. They reminded Julia of a picture in one of the twins' childhood books. *A little girl leading a bear.* Julia opened the door and wind rushed in, blowing Robert's mail to the floor. She left it there.

Edie embraced Julia and said, 'You aren't dressed yet?'

Julia looked down at her sweats. 'I didn't want to wait for you upstairs. The flat is kind of creeping me out right now.'

'Stay with us at the hotel, then,' Edie said.

Julia shook her head. 'I have to stay here.' *Valentina's here. She's got to be.*

Jack bent down to Julia and she clasped her arms around his neck. 'Come on,' she said. They went upstairs, Julia leading the way.

Once inside the flat they hesitated. 'Have you eaten?' Jack asked. He was ravenous, but felt guilty for thinking about breakfast.

'No,' said Julia, vaguely. 'There's probably some food. Have whatever you want. I'll get dressed.'

Edie followed Julia. Yesterday, when they had arrived, Edie had been grief-numbed and jet-lagged. Julia had completely occupied her mind. This morning Edie began to notice the apartment itself. Elspeth suddenly seemed present to her in the furnishings, objects, in the paint on the walls and the angle of the light coming in the windows, in the very air. It was as though their childhood had been preserved in a museum. Edie shuddered. She stood in the doorway of the bedroom as Julia began stripping off her sweats. Julia had laid out her violet dress, white stockings and black patent-leather shoes. It was the same outfit she had chosen to bury Valentina in.

'Don't,' said Edie.

'What?'

'Don't wear what she's wearing. I can't . . . I want you to wear something else, please.'

'But—'

'Please, Julia. It's too much.'

Julia looked at Edie and relented. She walked into the dressing room in her underwear and began taking things off their hangers, tossing them at the bed.

Elspeth heard Edie and Julia talking. She came out of her drawer and slowly made her way to the bedroom. She kept Valentina cupped in her hands. Yesterday Elspeth had stayed away from everyone. All night she had bargained with herself, confused and defensive. *I'll never see her again. She'll be unhinged. I don't want to see her. It's my fault. She's here and I should see her. If she knew she would never forgive me. Coward, coward. Murderer.* Valentina had seemed to catch her mood and became subdued, a little sad apprehensive cloud wrapped in Elspeth's dark musings. Now Elspeth crept towards the bedroom in a chastened state of mind.

Edie and Julia stood on opposite sides of the bed, flipping through a pile of clothing. *Oh . . . there you are.* Elspeth stood in the doorway, staring. Valentina became brighter, seemed to beat like a heart. *Oh, you. What happened? How could this have happened to you?* The last time she had seen her twin, it was 1984 and they were sobbing in each other's arms at Heathrow, the babies in a double pram beside them. *Twenty-one years later and here we are . . . You're so different. Older, but there's something else; harder. What is it?*

What happened? Elspeth stared and thought, *He didn't take care of you; you had to take care of yourself. No one loved you the way I did. If we'd been together . . . Oh, Elspeth.*

She slunk around the edge of the room. Julia looked right at her and became still, watching. *Can you see me, Julia? Or is it Valentina?* Elspeth sat down on the window seat and tried to efface herself. Valentina twisted and throbbed in her hands. Julia walked over to where Elspeth sat and put a hand out, towards Valentina. Valentina stilled as Julia touched her. Julia closed her eyes. 'Mouse?'

'What are you doing?' asked Edie. Julia stood at the window with one hand extended. 'Julia?'

'She's here!' Julia said, and burst into tears.

'What? No, Julia . . . here, come here.' Edie went to Julia and held her. Jack appeared in the doorway and Elspeth was shocked; he was so much older, softer; domesticated. Edie looked at Jack over Julia's shoulder and shook her head slightly. He withdrew. Elspeth heard him walking through the flat and down the stairs. *He's gone to have a smoke*, she thought. She watched Julia and Edie. Julia had stopped crying. They embraced, swaying back and forth slightly. Elspeth was envious. Then she was ashamed. *She's their mother. It doesn't matter. It's too late to fix anything.* Things that had once seemed important now revealed themselves as idiotic. *We thought we were so clever. We were stupid. We bollixed it all up.* Elspeth wondered if she could put things right again. If Valentina came back; if the twins went home? She would make Valentina go with Julia. She would sacrifice everything. *All this sadness for nothing.* She got up and left the room. She felt a kind of yearning, then realised that it was

Valentina's; Valentina wanted to stay, wanted to be with Julia and Edie. *Sorry. I can't bear to watch them any more. You have to come with me.* Elspeth went to the office windows and looked out without seeing, clasping her writhing daughter to her chest.

Robert answered the knock at his door, expecting to see Julia. Instead it was Jack.

'I hope you don't mind. I've been shooed out and thought maybe . . .'

He doesn't want to be alone, Robert realised. 'Right, of course. Come in.' Robert had been sitting at his desk, staring at his enormous manuscript. Anything was better than being alone. He led Jack to the kitchen. 'Can I get you anything? Tea? Coffee? Jameson's?'

'Yeah. The last.'

Robert put out two glasses, and the bottle. 'Water? Ice?'

'Yes, and no, thanks.' Robert ran some water into a carafe and put it in front of Jack. They sat across from each other. The kitchen seemed strangely cheerful, sun-bleached and empty. Jack wondered if anyone in this building had any food. Robert saw him looking at the bare cupboards. 'I haven't felt much like eating. I could make toast, though, if you'd care for any?'

'Sure. There's no food upstairs. Julia looks gaunt.'

Robert didn't reply but got up and began to make the toast. He opened the fridge and set out a jar of marmalade and a jar of Marmite. Then he sat at the table. Jack leaned back in his chair. The chairs were of the small fifties metal and vinyl variety. Robert wondered if the chair would fold up under Jack's bulk. He got up again and fetched cutlery.

Jack said, 'I wonder if I could ask you a kind of personal question?'

Robert made a non-committal sound and sat down.

'You were Elspeth's . . . ?' *Boyfriend? Significant other? What do they call an unmarried lover here?*

'Yes.' *I was Elspeth's. Creature is the word you're groping for.* The toast popped up violently and startled them both. Robert put three pieces on Jack's plate and one on his own. He handed the plate to Jack. There was a pause while they each spread marmalade on toast. Neither of them spoke until Jack had finished his toast. Robert handed him the fourth, untouched piece. Jack thought, *He seems very detached.* Robert thought, *I'm going to be sick.*

Jack poured himself a few fingers of whisky and added water. He began again. 'Did Elspeth ever tell you what happened between her and Edie?'

Robert shook his head. *That's not what I expected, mate.* 'Not while she was alive. She left me all her personal papers, and in the papers were her diaries. And a letter to me, explaining some things.'

'Ah. I don't suppose you'd let me look at any of it? The letter, maybe?'

'Erm, you've seen Elspeth's will. She most particularly did not want you or her sister to have access to any of her papers.'

'Uh-huh.' Jack ate the last piece of toast. Robert watched him. Jack said, 'I really just need the answer to one question. I know everything else.'

'What's that, then?'

'*Why* did they do it?'

Robert said nothing.

Jack said, 'I would like to know the point of this whole . . . stupid *game* we've been playing all these years. Because, as far as I can tell, nobody was fooled, but for some reason we all have to go on pretending we don't know.'

'Don't know what?'

'Don't you know about the switch?'

'I do, but according to Elspeth you don't.'

'But she knew I knew. I mean, pregnancy really changed her body – apparently *Edie* was the only one who didn't realise . . . Maybe this was all some weird thing Elspeth was doing to Edie? Look, I know you can't tell me anything,' Jack said. 'But what if I tell you the situation as I understand it? And you can just, you know, elevate your eyebrow a little when you hear something that makes sense. Could we do that?'

'All right.'

'Okay.' Jack sipped the whisky. 'I don't drink at this hour. Usually.'

'No. I don't either.' *Until recently.* Robert poured some whisky for himself. He thought the smell might turn his stomach, but it didn't. He drank, cautiously. *I love the smell of napalm in the morning.*

'So,' said Jack, 'it's 1983. Edie and Elspeth Noblin live together in a little flat in Hammersmith, in bohemian squalor and at great expense to their mother. The twins are recently down from Oxford, and I am working at the London branch of the bank I still work for. I am engaged to the woman we both know as Edie, but who back then was known as Elspeth. I'll stick to calling them by their current names, to avoid confusion.'

'Okay.'

'Elspeth – your Elspeth – was not fond of me at all. She wasn't actively hostile – she just did that British thing, you know, where somebody doesn't want to know you so they freeze you out. I don't think it was personal, but she knew where things were leading: I was going to take her twin to America. I don't know how much the twins issue affected your relationship with Elspeth—'

'Not much. Edie was gone. Elspeth very rarely mentioned her. But Julia and Valentina have been educational.' Robert wondered what Julia had told her parents about his dealings with Valentina.

'Well, the thing about twins: no one can ever replace the missing twin. I mean, Edie and I, we love Valentina – but Julia . . . I don't know how she'll . . .' Jack looked at his hands. Robert found it hard to breathe. 'Anyway. The twins – Edie and Elspeth – started acting weird. You never saw them together. They were a lot alike, but not as much as they thought they were. When they were impersonating each other there was always this extra thing, the *acting*, going on. I mean, you don't have to work at being yourself, but when one of the Noblin sisters was being the other, there was a noticeable smell of effort.

'So Edie started to impersonate Elspeth – that is, my fiancée started pretending to be her sister – and she started coming on to me, which is something your Elspeth would never have done in a thousand years, because she genuinely disliked me, in that impersonal way she had.'

'Why did she do that?'

Jack shook his head. 'My wife has always been pretty insecure about herself. She was the weaker of the two, but over

HER FEARFUL SYMMETRY · 417

the years she's taken on some of her sister's personality. I think she was testing me, to see what I would do.'

'So what did you do?'

'I got mad. Then I made a big mistake. I played along with it.'

'Ah.'

'Indeed. So, yadda, yadda . . . things got complicated. I'm ninety-nine per cent sure the woman standing next to me at the wedding was Edie. My Edie, you know what I mean. The switch happened when we got on the plane to Chicago.'

Robert imagined Elspeth sitting next to Jack on a plane. 'Elspeth was terribly afraid of flying.'

'They both were. That's why Edie and I didn't come over to visit the girls, though it seems crazy, now. That isn't what tipped me off.' Robert waited for him to elaborate. Instead Jack said, 'Please – the answer must be in Elspeth's papers. Why else would she be so hell-bent on keeping them away from us?'

Robert said, 'But I don't understand – what is it you're hoping to find out? Elspeth was pregnant, you were the father – it seemed obvious to them, in their self-absorbed way, that they should just trade identities and everything would be fine.'

Jack said, 'I never slept with Elspeth.'

Robert thought, *My brain is going to explode.* 'Stay there,' he said. He got up and went to the servant's room, found the last box of diaries with Elspeth's letter and carried it all to the kitchen. He extracted a diary and paged through it until he located the entry. 'April Fool's Day, 1983,' he said, and handed the diary to Jack. 'At a party, in Knightsbridge. You were drunk. I think the joke was supposed to be on Edie, somehow.'

Jack held the diary at arm's length, reading. 'She doesn't mention my name.'

Robert replied, 'They wrote the diaries together.' He leaned over Jack and pointed to the entry just below the first one. 'That's Edie's reply.'

Damn you. Can't I have anything of my own? Jack read. He looked up, confused.

Robert said, 'They tried to make it right, but they didn't understand what would be involved. I can't imagine they wanted to hurt you.'

'No,' said Jack. 'I just happened to be there.' He put the diary on the table and closed his eyes, pressed his lips together. Robert thought, *He didn't know he really was their dad. Oh God.* He thought of Valentina, and felt helpless, furious. Robert was unable to speak. Finally he gestured at the other diaries and said, 'You're welcome to look through all that.'

Jack replied, 'No, thank you. I found out what I needed to know.' Jack stood up, disorientated and a little buzzed. They looked at each other and then away, mutually unsure suddenly on how to proceed.

Robert said, 'I'll see you at Lauderdale House.'

'Yeah. Um . . . thanks.' Jack lumbered off. Robert heard him treading slowly up the stairs. A door opened and closed. Robert got his wallet and keys and went out to buy flowers.

Valentina's funeral was held at Lauderdale House, a sixteenth-century manor where Nell Gwyn had once lived, which now functioned as an art gallery/wedding hall/café. Her funeral was in the big upstairs room where the figure drawing and yoga classes usually met. The room was half-timbered and half-unfinished, as though the carpenters' elevenses had lasted several decades. The coffin stood at the front of the room on trestles, covered in white roses. Folding chairs filled the rest of the space. Julia sat between her parents in the front row, staring out of the window. She remembered a story someone had told them about Nell Gwyn dangling her baby from one of the windows at Lauderdale House. Julia couldn't remember why this had happened, or which window.

The coffin was white, with simple steel fittings. Sebastian moved around the room, placing a water pitcher and empty glasses at the podium, depositing a newly arrived wreath at the front of the coffin. Julia thought he was like a butler in his super-efficiency and preternatural tranquillity. *I've never met a butler.* Sebastian glanced at Julia as though he knew she was thinking about him and gave her a calm smile. *I'm going to cry, and if I start I'm not going to stop.* She wanted to disappear. Sebastian put a box of tissues next to the podium. *He does this all the time, as a job.* Julia had never thought of death as something that would happen to her, or to people she knew. All those people in the cemetery were just stones, names, dates. LOVING MOTHER. DEVOTED HUSBAND. Elspeth was a parlour trick; she had never been really real to Julia. *Valentina is in that box.* It couldn't be true.

I want to be haunted, thought Julia. *Haunt me, Mouse. Come and put your arms around me. We'll sit together and write our secrets with the planchette. Or, if you can't do that, just look at me. That's all I need. Where are you? Not here. But I can't feel you gone either. You're my phantom limb, Mouse. I keep looking for you. I forget. I feel stupid,*

Mouse. Haunt me, find me, come back from wherever you are. Be with me. I'm afraid.

Julia looked at her mother. Edie sat stiffly, white-knuckled hands gripping her small handbag. *She's afraid too.* Her father sat overspilling his chair, smelling sweetly of unsmoked tobacco and alcohol. Julia leaned against him. Jack reached over and took her hand.

People filed in and took their places on the folding chairs. Julia turned to see, but most of them were strangers. There were people from the cemetery. Jessica and James sat behind the Pooles. Jessica patted Julia's shoulder. 'Hello, dear.' She wore a little black cloche with a veil that was like stars caught in a net. *The Mouse would have been wild for that hat.*

'Hello.' Julia didn't know what else to say, so she smiled and turned to face the coffin. *I would get through this better if I could sit at the back.*

The officiant stood at the front of the room holding a clipboard and watching as people took their seats. She wore something red draped over her shoulders. Julia wondered what was about to happen. They had asked for a non-religious ceremony. Robert had arranged everything through the Humanist Society. He had asked Julia if she wanted to speak. Now she had a much-folded and crossed-out speech tucked into her bag. The speech was all wrong; it was inadequate and somehow untrue. Martin had read it for her and helped with the phrasing, but still the speech did not say what Julia wanted to express. *It doesn't matter*, Julia told herself. *Valentina won't hear it anyway.*

The red-shawled officiant spoke. She welcomed them and said some non-religious things that were meant to be comforting. She invited people who had known Valentina to speak about her.

Robert stood at the podium. He peered out at the room, which was half-filled. The Poole family sat a few feet away from him, regarding him stoically. *Valentina, forgive me.* He cleared his throat, adjusted his glasses. His voice, when he found it, was first too soft, then too loud. Robert wished to be anywhere else, doing anything else. 'This is a poem by Arthur William Edgar O'Shaughnessy,' he said. His hands held the paper steady.

'I made another garden, yea,
    For my new Love:
I left the dead rose where it lay
    And set the new above.
Why did my Summer not begin?
    Why did my heart not haste?
My old Love came and walk'd therein,
    And laid the garden waste.

'She enter'd with her weary smile,
    Just as of old;
She look'd around a little while
    And shiver'd with the cold:
Her passing touch was death to all,
    Her passing look a blight;
She made the white rose-petals fall,
    And turn'd the red rose white.'

There was more to the poem but Robert did not read it. He looked at the people sitting in the folding chairs and was about to continue, but then changed his mind and sat down abruptly. People were confused by what he had read and there was some buzz of conversation in the room. Jessica thought, *That's quite inappropriate. He's blaming Elspeth for something. He should have spoken about Valentina.* Edie and Jack stared ahead at the white coffin. Jack wondered what on earth Robert meant.

Julia was angry, but she tried to quell it; she walked to the podium. Her limbs seemed to be remote-controlled. She unfolded her speech, then began to speak without looking at it. 'We're far from home . . . Thank you for coming even though you haven't known us very long.' *What else was I going to say?* 'Valentina was my twin. It never occurred to either of us that we might get separated. We didn't have a plan for that. We were going to be together always.

'When we were little Mom and Dad took us to the Lincoln Park Zoo, which if you don't know is a big zoo in the middle of Chicago. You can see the skyscrapers while you are looking at the emus and giraffes and stuff. And we were looking at this tiger. It was by itself in this fake landscape – I think they wanted it to think it was in China or wherever it was from. Valentina fell in love with this tiger. She stood there, like, forever, just looking at it, and it came over and looked at her. They stood there staring at each other till finally it kind of nodded its head and walked away. And Valentina said to me, "When I die I'm going to be that tiger." So I guess possibly she is a tiger now, but hopefully not in a zoo, because she actually hated zoos.' Julia took a deep breath. *I will not cry now.*

'On the other hand, that was when we were eight years old, and lately we've been thinking differently about life after death.' Robert thought, *Oh, no.* Julia continued, 'I don't know what Valentina exactly thought about death. Since we moved here she seemed kind of excited about it, in a way, but that was probably because we live next to the cemetery and we're twenty-one and it didn't seem like it had any direct application to us.' Julia had been addressing her remarks to a flower arrangement at the back of the room but now she looked at her mother. 'Anyway, I don't think she would mind too much. I mean, not that she would have wanted to die, but she was into this aesthetic thing about the cemetery, and if this had to happen I think she would be happy to be there.' *What else? I love you, I don't know how to go on without you, you were part of me, you're gone, I want to die too. Don't I?*

'Anyway, thanks. Thanks for coming.' Julia sat down amid murmurs from the guests. Sebastian caught Robert's eye. Robert could tell that Sebastian thought the speeches were a little irregular. The officiant said a few things, told everyone to walk across Waterlow Park to the cemetery, thanked them again for being there. The pall-bearers lifted the coffin and bore it out of the room. People waited for the Poole family to follow it; when they did not there was muted discussion, and everyone rose and filed out in twos and threes. The Pooles sat until the room was empty. Robert stood on the landing, waiting for them. Finally Sebastian offered Edie his arm. He wondered if she was going to make it through the interment. 'Would you like some water?'

'No. No.' Jack and Julia got to their feet. Edie looked up

at the three of them. *I can't move.* Julia leaned over and whispered to her, 'You can stay here. I'll stay with you.'

Edie shook her head. She wanted to shut off everything, stop time. She was still thinking about the poem, about the garden laid waste; she imagined herself alone in such a garden, the flowers all dead and night coming; Valentina and Elspeth were buried there, and Edie thought that if she sat very still, if everyone would let her be, she would hear them speak to her. The vision possessed her and she could not shake it away. Jack reached down and lifted Edie off her chair; he enfolded her into himself. She began weeping. Sebastian took himself off to stand with Robert on the landing. They listened to Edie's sobs. Julia walked out of the room and past them, and went downstairs without acknowledging either of them.

What on earth have we done? Edie's tears were a solvent that removed Robert's detachment, his resolve to just get through the day, his sense of himself as a decent person. He was a monster. Now he knew it. All he could do was carry out the plan, but the plan was ill-conceived and monstrous in its self-ishness. 'No,' he said.

'Sorry?' said Sebastian.

'Nothing,' said Robert.

Jessica had a powerful feeling of déjà vu. Once again they all stood around the Noblin mausoleum. It was summer instead of winter; there was Nigel by the hearse, the burial team standing by, Robert looking dazed next to Phil and Sebastian. There was no minister; the woman from the Humanist Society said a few words. Valentina's coffin was placed on the floor of the mausoleum, ready to be put into its niche beneath Elspeth. The Poole family huddled together, Julia and the father practically holding up the mother. Sebastian adroitly produced a few chairs. The family sank into them, not taking their eyes off the door of the mausoleum. *Poor dears. She was so young.* Jessica turned her gaze to Robert, to whom she had not spoken since the morning she'd caught him in the cemetery. She whispered to James, 'I think he's going to faint.' Robert was quite pale and sweating profusely. James nodded. He took Jessica's arm, as though she were the one who needed support.

The service was over. Nigel closed the door of the mausoleum. People began to drift down the path. There was coffee, food and drink back at Lauderdale House. Jack Poole talked with Nigel; Julia and Edie waited quietly. Robert began to walk away by himself down the path. Jessica called to him.

He turned and hesitated. Then he walked back to her.

'We're so sorry, Robert,' said Jessica.

He shook his head. 'It's my fault,' he told them.

'No,' James said. 'Not at all. These things happen. It's terribly unfortunate.'

'It is my fault,' said Robert.

'Don't blame yourself, my dear,' Jessica said. She began to feel disturbed. There was something about the way Robert looked at them. *I used to think he was coming unhinged, but now I think perhaps he actually has done. That poem. Oh dear.* 'We ought to go down,' she said. They walked slowly together past the Egyptian Avenue towards the Colonnade.

* * *

At Lauderdale House most of the conversation was provided by people who had known Valentina only slightly. Edie and Jack had gone back to Vautravers so Edie could lie down. Julia sat bewildered and silent in a small circle of young Friends of Highgate Cemetery; Phil brought her tea and sandwiches and hovered nearby, waiting to be asked for something. Finally Robert came over.

'Can I walk you back to the house?' he asked. 'Or Sebastian can give you a ride, if you'd rather.'

'Okay,' she said. Robert looked at her and decided it would be best to put her in the car. Julia had switched off; her eyes were blank and she did not seem to have understood the question. He helped her extricate herself from the Friends. They walked in silence to the street and waited together while Sebastian brought the car.

'How long did it take Elspeth before she was a ghost?' Julia asked quietly, not looking at him.

'I think she must have been a ghost right away. She says she was a sort of mist for a while.'

'I thought Valentina was there, this morning. In the bedroom.' Julia shook her head. 'It just felt like her.'

'Was Elspeth with her?' Robert asked.

'I don't know. I can't see Elspeth.'

'No, I can't either.' The car arrived. They rode up the hill in silence.

That afternoon seemed to go on and on. Robert sat at his desk, not thinking or moving. He wanted to drink, but he was afraid he'd get drunk and things would go wrong, so he sat there silently, doing nothing. Edie was asleep in the twins' bed. Jack sat in the window seat with the curtains almost closed, listening to his wife's soft snores and reading an American first of *The Old Man and the Sea*. Julia found that she could not stand to be indoors. She went and sat in the back garden, knees tucked under her chin, arms wrapped around her. Martin was practising standing near the windows. He saw Julia; he hesitated, then rapped on the window and beckoned to her. She jumped up and ran to the fire escape. He heard her thumping footsteps and unlocked the back door just as she reached it. Julia came in wordlessly and sat in one of the kitchen chairs.

'Have you eaten?' he asked her. She shook her head. He began to make a cheese sandwich. He poured her a glass of milk, set it in front of her. He turned on the stove and put the cheese sandwich in to melt.

'You're using the stove,' Julia said.

'I decided it was okay. I had the gas company reconnect it.'

'That's great.' She smiled. 'You're getting a lot better.'

'It's the vitamins.' Martin searched his pockets for his lighter and cigarettes, extracted one and lit it. He sat in the other chair. 'How are you? I'm sorry I didn't come to your sister's funeral.'

'I didn't expect you to come.'

'Robert asked me – I went and stood on the landing, but I couldn't go any farther.'

'Um, that's okay.' Julia imagined Martin standing there, surrounded by newspapers, trying to walk downstairs by himself, failing.

Martin had been thinking all day of how he might persuade Julia to stay with him that night. He had plotted out various conversations, but now he blurted, 'What are you doing tonight?'

Julia shrugged. 'Having dinner with Mom and Dad, probably at Café Rouge. Then, I don't know. I guess they'll go back to their hotel.'

'Shouldn't you go with them?'

Julia shook her head stubbornly. *I'm not a child.*

Martin said, 'Will you come up and stay with me? I don't think you ought to be alone.'

Julia thought of Elspeth lurking around the flat and said, 'Yeah, I'd like that.' She sipped her milk. Neither of them said anything until the timer rang and Martin carefully extricated the toasted cheese sandwich from the oven, put it on a plate and set it in front of Julia. She looked at the sandwich and the milk and thought how odd it was for someone to be taking care of her for a change. Martin stubbed out his cigarette so she could eat. When she was done he cleared the dishes and said, 'Would you like to play Scrabble?'

'With you? No, too humiliating.'

'Cards, then?'

Julia hesitated. 'It seems weird to play anything when she's . . . you know. I feel like I shouldn't.'

Martin offered her a cigarette. She took one and he lit it for her. He said, 'I think play must have been invented so we wouldn't go mad thinking about certain things – but I have another idea: let's have a memorial service of our own, since I missed the other one. Won't you tell me about Valentina?'

At first he thought she wouldn't reply. She stared at the tip of her cigarette, frowning. But then Julia began to tell Martin about Valentina, in halting words; he coaxed each story from her until the words began to create the Valentina who would now live in Julia's mind. Julia spoke of Valentina for hours; the afternoon slipped into evening, and Martin mourned for the girl he had met only fleetingly, a few afternoons ago.

Jessica had his key, so Robert had taken Elspeth's. The key to the door in the back-garden wall had hung, unused, in her pantry for as long as he had known her. He had taken the key to the Noblin mausoleum from Elspeth's desk a week ago. The two keys rested with the key to the twins' flat inside his overcoat pocket. Robert stood at his window looking out over the front garden, waiting for dark.

Julia and her parents walked up the path and through the gate, on their way to dinner. Robert thought, *Now. If I don't do it now, I won't be able to do it at all.*

He went out his back door, leaving it unlocked. Though Martin's windows were papered over, Robert still looked up at them as he crossed the back garden. *That's odd. He's taken down some of the newspaper.* There was light in Martin's office; all the other rooms were dark. Robert slipped through the green door, left it ajar.

The most direct way to the Noblin grave was to cut through the Circle of Lebanon and the Egyptian Avenue. He used his torch in order to go more quickly. There was a half-moon, but the trees over the Avenue made it ink black.

He switched off his torch and listened. He was not afraid then. He was aware of being pleased to be in the cemetery. The only noises were the usual night noises: light traffic up and down the hill, a few insect sounds, muted in the chill of the night. Robert walked out of the Avenue and uphill to the Noblin mausoleum.

The key did not work easily. *I ought to have oiled the lock.* He got it to turn and swung the door open. He stepped inside the little room, put on a pair of latex surgical gloves and pulled the door almost shut behind him in case anyone came by. *Though they might be more afraid of me than I of them.* He knelt by Valentina's coffin. He felt enormous and intrusive in the tiny space, like Alice grown huge with her arm up the chimney of the White Rabbit's house. The coffin had been pushed back into its niche, so he tugged and pulled until it was out where he could work on it. *There is no respectful way to do this*, he thought as he took a screwdriver out of his pocket and began to unscrew the lid. It seemed to take forever. He was sweating by the time he managed to pry up the lid. It gasped as it came undone, as though he had opened an enormous jar of pickled gherkins.

Valentina's body lay ensconced in white silk. *She looks comfortable.* Robert reached into the coffin with both arms and scooped Valentina up; she weighed nearly nothing. She was slightly damp from the plastic-wrapped ice Sebastian had concealed underneath her. She was pliable, though very cold. Sebastian had kept his promise: Valentina gave off no whiff of decay. Robert was not sure where to put her. He stood awkwardly, turned and put her down on the floor. He took the ice out of the coffin and threw it into the bushes, then put the screws inside the coffin and lowered the lid. He pushed the empty coffin back into its niche. Robert gathered his screwdriver, torch, looked around for any other signs of his visit, found none. He took off his overcoat and laid it on the floor. He placed Valentina's body on the coat and wrapped her up in it. Now she was hidden.

He realised that the keys were in his coat pocket, so he fished them out and put them in his shirt pocket. Then Robert picked up Valentina. He carried her pressed against his body, her head on his shoulder. He held her with one arm embracing her torso while he opened the door with his other hand and passed through the doorway carefully, anxious not to jostle his burden. He relocked the door, flicked off the torch and began walking back down the path in darkness.

That was strangely easy. I always imagined bodysnatching to be a more strenuous occupation. Of course, it would be if there was digging involved. And they used to carry dark lanterns and shovels and so forth. Robert wanted to giggle. Or whistle. *I'm not quite right. I'll have a drink when I get home.* He turned into the Egyptian Avenue. In the blackness he could feel Valentina jouncing with each step he took. He slowed down and held her more tightly.

He reached the Circle and walked up the stairs. At the top he thought he heard someone breathing. He stood still, held his own breath, heard nothing.

Finally he was at the Catacombs. He came to the green door and pushed it gently. The garden was empty. The same light was on in Martin's office, *as though no time had passed, nothing has happened.* There was light in the twins' bedroom; the curtains were drawn. Robert went into the garden, locked the door and ran across the moss. Then he was inside his flat. Sweat was pouring off him.

What on earth am I doing? He laid Valentina on the kitchen table, went to the freezer and took out a bottle of vodka. He was about to drink from the bottle, but hesitated, then took a glass from the cupboard, poured some vodka and drank it down, staring at his own reflection in the kitchen window. He could see Valentina's muffled form reflected behind him, lying mummy-like, as though on display in a museum. He poured another drink, drank half of it. He locked the back door.

Come now, my darling.

Robert laid Valentina down carefully on his bed. At first he put her down crossways, so that she was parallel to the head-board and her feet stuck out over the side. He unwrapped her and threw his coat over the bedroom chair. Her little black shoes seemed to be levitating above the floor, as though Valentina's legs had nothing to do with holding them up. Robert frowned. *That's no good.* He gently gathered her into his arms and reapplied her to the bed, this time in the conventional position for sleeping. He smoothed out her dress, placed her arms comfortably beside her body, massaged her fingers. Valentina's head lolled on his pillow as though her neck no longer had bones. Robert took her face in his hands and turned it until she looked content, not broken. He stroked her eyebrows.

The room was cold – every night that June had been cold. That morning he had filled the bedroom with flowers. He had hesitated in the shop: lilies or roses? He had decided on pink roses, because the smell of lilies always made him queasy, and because Valentina had once said something mildly approving about pink roses. Now the roses sat in vases, in old tins, in pots borrowed long ago from Elspeth. There were roses on both sides of the bed, on the window sills and radiator covers. The roses were the pink of ballet shoes, the pink of old ladies' dressing gowns. In the chill of the bedroom they seemed to shiver, and remained furled, scentless. Robert had bought a shopping bag full of candles from a street vendor in Hackney. Each one had a picture of a saint on it. She had explained to him that the candles had to burn until they expired, and then the thing you had prayed for would be granted to you. Robert hoped it was true. The candles stood next to the roses, burning away.

Robert sat next to Valentina on the bed, watching her. He found it astonishing how perfect she was. He tried to remember what Valentina had said about the Kitten's revival. There were dark circles under Valentina's eyes, and though she was rather bluish in some places and too red in others, she was not like the medical-school and police-morgue corpses, which puffed up and oozed and discoloured and stank. The morgue corpses led active existences; they were trying to transform themselves as quickly as possible into unrecognisable beings, not to be mistaken for people any more. Valentina was still essentially Valentina, and he was thankful that this should be so.

He wondered if he should talk to her. It seemed unnatural to be in the room with her and not to say anything. Her hair was tangled. To distract himself, Robert began combing her hair. Very delicately, so as not to tug at her scalp, he began to work the tangles out. Her hair was like dental floss, slippery handfuls of white. The comb burrowed in, separating, smoothing. At first his hands shook, but then he became absorbed in the repetition and in the beauty of Valentina's shining hair. *This is almost all I want. To sit here forever and comb her hair.* The slight resistance of the hair against the comb was like breath, and without knowing it Robert combed Valentina's hair at the rate of his own breathing, as though this could communicate breath from his lungs to her hair, as though her hair were now going to take over the task of breathing for her.

He made himself stop, finally. Her hair was perfect and to do more would disturb it. Robert sat still and listened. Outside the wind was coming up. A dog barked nearby. But Valentina was silent. Robert looked at his watch. It was only 11.22.

The phone rang, once.

Julia was tired. Over dinner Edie and Jack talked about the funeral; about London as they had known it twenty-two years before; they offered to stay in London with Julia, to take her home to Lake Forest; they recognised that she was too overwhelmed to decide right now, then stared at her eagerly as though they might whisk her off before she had finished eating her *steak frites*. They spoke of Valentina carefully; it was difficult for each of them to refer to Valentina in the past tense, so they talked around and around her. By the time Julia had seen them into a cab and walked back to Vautravers she wanted to crawl up the stairs on all fours. *But Martin asked me to come stay with him.*

When she came into his office Martin was sitting at the computer, but the screen was dark; he sat with his hands folded and his head bowed, as though saying grace.

'Martin?'

He roused himself. 'There you are. I was getting sleepy.'

'Me too. I just wanted to say goodnight. I'm going to bed.'

'Oh, don't yet.' Martin held out his hand. She relented

and went to him. He said, 'I was thinking . . . I might leave tomorrow.'

'Leave?' She couldn't take it in. 'How can you leave? I wish . . . Couldn't you wait?'

Martin sighed. 'I don't know. If I wait, will I be able to do it at all? But perhaps tomorrow is too soon. I don't want to upset you.'

Julia bent and clasped her arms around his neck. She did it impulsively and Martin reacted as he often had when Theo was small: he pulled Julia onto his lap. She rested her head on his shoulder. They sat this way for a long time. Martin thought she might have fallen asleep when she said, 'I'll miss you.'

'I'll miss you too,' he said. He stroked her hair. 'But don't be so tragic; I'm sure I won't be gone long. Or, you can come and visit.'

'It will be different. Everything will be different now,' she said.

'What are you going to do?'

'I don't know. What do people do by themselves?'

'Come with me,' he said.

Julia smiled to herself. 'That's silly. You're going to Marijke. You don't need me.'

'Don't I?'

She raised her face and he kissed her. The kiss progressed; he broke off, panting, and took her hand away from his belt buckle. 'That's no good,' he said.

'Sorry.'

'No – that is, I would if I could . . . Julia, the Anafranil – one of the side effects is—'

'Ohh . . .'

'That's why I never liked to take it.'

'It's like a chastity belt.' She began to giggle.

'Minx.'

'I guess Marijke doesn't have to worry about me.'

Martin said quite seriously, 'In the larger sense, no, she doesn't. But Julia, you aren't meant for an old man like me. Your lover should be what I was thirty years ago.'

'But, Martin . . .'

'You'll see,' he said. He moved to stand up and she slid off his lap. 'In the meantime, come along and let me sing you a lullaby.' He took her hand and led her to his bedroom. 'Ah, wait; let me just check something.' He took out his mobile, pressed 2 on his speed dial, let it ring once and hung up. It was 11.22.

She watched him curiously. 'What are you doing?'

'For luck,' he said. 'Come along.'

Robert checked to make sure that the keys were still in his pocket. He laid two of them on his dresser and kept the key to the twins' flat. He gathered up Valentina and lifted her off the bed. He caught sight of the two of them in the mirror, an image out of a horror film: the candlelight flickering from below, dark shadow cast across his face, Valentina's head thrown back, her neck offered up, her arms and legs dangling. *I am the monster.* He felt the absurdity of the situation, and then deep, unspeakable shame.

He walked through the flat as quietly as possible. Valentina's foot banged against a wall; Robert flinched, then wondered if she would feel it when she was back in her body. He opened his front door an inch and listened. He heard traffic, wind rattling the windows. He eased Valentina through the doorway and carried her upstairs. At the twins' door he had to shift her; he stood with Valentina draped over his shoulder like a suit collected from the dry-cleaner's while he fumbled with the key. He realised after messing about unsuccessfully that it hadn't been locked in the first place.

He carried Valentina into the dark front room. His eyes adjusted, and he laid the body carefully on the sofa.

Softly: 'Elspeth? Valentina?'

No response. He sat peering at Valentina's body by the glow of his wristwatch and the moonlight, waiting.

Elspeth was there. She felt Valentina frantically squirming in her hands. *Is she trying to escape?* She was afraid to open her hands, afraid that Valentina would disperse, that she would fight or thrash around. *Be still, darling. Let me think.* She could not put off the decision any longer.

Robert watched Valentina's chest. He waited for her to breathe.

Elspeth knelt by the body. It was cool, profoundly still, alluring. She felt Valentina go quiet. She felt Robert sitting close to her, eager, unhappy, frightened. She looked at the body, lax and waiting. Elspeth made her decision and opened her hands.

A white mist gathered over Valentina's body. Elspeth watched it hover, waited to see what it would do. Robert saw nothing, but the air became suddenly cold. He knew the ghosts were there. *Breathe, Valentina.*

Nothing happened.

After a while he was aware of a change in the body. Something was present. There were faint sounds, gurgling, liquid; he had a sense of something far away coming closer.

The body opened its mouth and took a jagged, asthmatic breath, seemed to hold it for a long time, let it out and began sucking at the air again with horrible rasps. It lurched sideways and Robert caught it; it was convulsing and the breaths stopped. Then suddenly there was another agonised gasp. Robert held Valentina's hands pinned on either side of her torso. He knelt next to her, braced her with his body. The sofa was slippery and he tried to keep her from falling onto the floor. Something like electricity wracked her body; her limbs contracted; her head swerved violently back and forth, once.

She cried out: 'Uh-uh-uh!' and he said, 'Hush, *ssh*,' as though she were an infant, but now she thrashed and her eyes opened. Robert recoiled at the blankness of her eyes. It was not even animal; it was the gaze of brain damage; it looked past him into nothing. Her eyes closed again. Her breath quietened. He put his hand on her chest. Her heart was beating.

He was afraid.

'Elspeth?' Robert whispered, to the room. There was no response. 'Can I take her away now?' Nothing.

A harsh voice said his name in the dark.

'I'm here, Valentina.' She said nothing. He smoothed her hair. 'I'm going to take you downstairs now.' She kept her eyes closed, nodded awkwardly like a child too drowsy to speak. He lifted her off the sofa; she tried to put her arms around his neck, but couldn't. He carried her to the landing. She was live weight now, dense and mobile.

In his own flat he laid her back on the bed. She sighed and opened her eyes, looked at him. Robert stood over her. She seemed almost normal: exhausted, limp. Something about her expression was different, though. He couldn't think what it was. She held out her hand, palm up, quivering with the strain of holding up her arm. He took it in his; her hand was quite cold. She pulled his hand slightly: *Lie next to me.*

'Wait a minute, Valentina.'

He took out his mobile, speed-dialled Martin's number. He let the phone ring once and hung up. Then Robert placed the phone and his glasses on the bedside table. He took off his shoes, walked around the bed, sat down beside Valentina. She looked up at him and smiled, shyly, lopsidedly, a smile that happened at different rates of speed in various parts of her face. How ordinary she appeared: the violet dress, the white stockings. There were places where blood had pooled and made her skin deep red; these were becoming pink; bluish-white skin was beginning to flush. He touched his fingers to her cheek. It was pliable, soft.

'What was it like?'

Lonely. Cold. Insanely frustrating. 'I . . . missed you.' Her voice cracked; she sounded like a ventriloquist's dummy, off kilter, high, raspy and stressed wrong.

'I missed you too.'

She held out her hand again. He lay down beside her and she turned her face towards him. Robert wrapped his arms around her. She was trembling. He realised then that she was crying. It was such a normal sound, the sobbing girl in his arms was so tangible, it was easy to forget the reason for the tears, it was natural to comfort her. He stopped thinking and let himself kiss Valentina's ear. She cried for what seemed a long time. She hiccuped; he handed her a Kleenex. She fumbled at her nose, dabbed at her eyes. She tossed the tissue over the side of the bed.

'Okay, then?'

'Mmm-hmm.'

She tried to unbutton his shirt, but her fingers weren't working properly. He closed his hand over hers. 'You sure?'

She nodded.

'We should wait . . .'

'Please . . .'

'Valentina . . . ?'

She made a little noise, a mewing sound.

He undid the buttons himself. Then he undressed her. She tried to help, but seemed too weak; she let him undo zips and strip the violet dress from her, let him peel off her knickers and carefully remove her white lace bra. Her body was marked by the lace and elastic and the folds of her clothing. She lay with eyes half-closed, waiting while he removed his clothes. One of the candles guttered.

'Are you cold?'

'Uh-huh.' He carefully peeled the blankets and sheets from under her, got into bed and pulled the bedding over the two of them. 'Mmm,' she said, 'warm.' He was startled at how cold she was. He ran his hands over her thighs; they were like meat from the refrigerated case at Sainsbury's.

Robert wasn't quite sure if he could bring himself to kiss her mouth. Her breath smelled wrong, like spoiled food, like the hedgehog he'd found dead in the heating system at the cemetery's office. Instead he kissed her breasts. Some parts of her body seemed more alive than others, as though her soul had not quite spread all the way through her body yet. Valentina's breasts seemed to Robert more present, less isolated from her self, than her hands; Valentina's hands were like badly wired robots. He chafed them between his, hoping to warm them back to life, but it didn't seem to help.

Something is wrong, he thought. He drew her close to him. She was so small and slight that Robert thought of Elspeth in the last days of her illness; she seemed barely there, as though she might slip back to wherever she'd been.

'How do you feel?' he tried again.

'So cold,' she said. 'Tired.'

'Do you want to sleep for a while?'

'No . . .'

'I'll sit and watch you, make sure you're okay.' He stroked her neck, her face. Her eyes rested on his, questioning. *Something is different. Her voice. Her eyes.* She gave in, nodded. Robert got out of bed, blew out all the candles. *So much for wishes.* He turned on the light in the hall, left the door ajar so he could see her. Then he climbed into bed again. She was shivering. He lay pressed against her, watching the smoke of the extinguished candles disperse in the narrow band of light from the hall.

'I love you, Robert,' she whispered. In the corridors of his memory doors were flung open and he almost knew . . .

He said, 'I love you too . . .'

She brought her clumsy hand to his face, watching him;

stretched out her index finger, and with great concentration and gentleness touched the tip of her finger to the indentation above his nose, stroked it down and over his lips, over his chin.

'. . . Elspeth.'

She smiled, closed her eyes, relaxed.

Robert lay with her in the dark, in his bed, as the knowledge and horror of what they had done spread before him.

Martin sat propped against the pillows, smoking. Julia lay pressed against him. 'Sing,' she commanded. Martin stubbed out his cigarette in the ashtray on the bedside table. He sang, '*Slaap kindje, slaap; Daar buiten loopt een schaap; Een schaap met witte voetjes; Die drinkt zijn melk zo zoetjes; Slaap kindje slaap.*'

'What does it mean?' she asked.

'Mmm . . . "Sleep, baby, sleep; there's a little white sheep walking outside; it has little white feet and drinks sweet milk."'

'Nice,' she said, and then she fell asleep.

Julia woke before dawn. Martin was sleeping curled away from her. She got up quietly, went to the bathroom, dressed. She slipped out of the flat and went downstairs, shed her clothes and put on a nightgown. She got into her own bed and stared at the ceiling. After some time, she got up and took a shower.

In the morning Elspeth woke up in Robert's bed. She put her hand out, but he wasn't there. Instead there was a note: *I've gone to get breakfast. Back soon. R*

Elspeth lay in bed exulting in the smooth feel of the sheets, the smell of Robert on her pillow mingled with the scents of candles and roses, the twittering of little birds and the sheer corporality of herself.

Everything hurt but she did not mind. Her joints ached; her blood was sluggish. Breathing was an effort, as though her lungs were full of half-set blancmange. *So what? I'm alive!* She struggled to sit up, became tangled in the bedding. She had an idea of what her limbs ought to do but they did not respond as she expected. Elspeth started laughing. The sound was harsh and had an underwater quality and she stopped. She managed to stand and walk a few steps, clinging to the side of the bed. When she got to the footboard she stood swaying, regarded herself in the mirror. *Oh. Oh . . .* There was Valentina. *What did you expect?* She imagined Valentina upstairs, alone and cold. *I'm sorry. I'm sorry . . .* She was not sure what she felt. An indecipherable mixture of triumph and remorse. She stared at her reflection that was not herself; this was a consummately impressive costume which she would now wear as her body. This body was young, but the posture and movements were like an old woman's: hunched, lurching, cautious. *Can I live like this?* She put her hand over her heart, where her heart should be, then remembered and moved her hand to the right, found its slow beat. *Oh, Valentina.*

Elspeth let go of the bed. She staggered to the bathroom, meaning to take a bath. When she got there she lowered herself slowly to the floor, reached for the taps and turned them on with effort. *It's like the first days of being a ghost. I will get stronger. I just have to practise.* Water gushed into the bathtub. She was unable to reach the plug, so it swirled down the drain. Finally she turned off the taps and sat on the cold tile floor, waiting for Robert to return.

After breakfast, Martin packed his suitcase. He didn't put very much in it; he reckoned that either Marijke would spurn him and he would be back quite soon, or he wouldn't manage to get there at all, so why should he burden himself with extra clothing? Perhaps Marijke would let him stay and neither of them would ever come back. Maybe Marijke had found someone else, and in that case Martin knew that he would prefer throwing himself into the Prinsengracht over returning home, alone. He packed lightly.

He moved through the flat, turning out lights, turning off the computer. The flat was strange to him; Martin felt as though he had not seen it for years, as though he was dreaming this unknown flat, this lost twin which somehow housed clones of all his stuff. There were the patches of sunlight coming through the windows where Julia had ripped off the newspaper. Martin held his hands out and the sunlight filled his palms.

When it was time to leave he stood at the door, one hand on the doorknob, the other clutching the handle of the suitcase. *It's perfectly fine. It's only the stairwell. You've been there before. Nothing hideous has ever happened there. It is not necessary to count.* Martin thought it might be good to bring some gloves, though. He went back, found a wad of surgical gloves, put them in his jacket pocket. Then he opened the door and stepped out onto the landing.

There. I'm out of the flat. Martin took stock of himself. A bit tight in the chest, but okay. He locked the door. *Still all right.* He began to lumber down the stairs with the suitcase. When he arrived at the first-floor landing he stopped, kissed his fingers and touched the door just above Elspeth's name card. Then he continued on.

On the ground floor he knocked on Robert's door. He heard Robert walk to the door and stand there, breathing. 'It's me,' Martin said softly. The door opened about an inch, and Martin could see Robert's eye regarding him. It made him more nervous. The door opened and Robert silently gestured at him to come in. He did, pulling the suitcase along. Robert shut the door.

Martin was startled by Robert's appearance. The change was indefinable, but extreme, as though Robert had been ill for months: his eyes were undershadowed by dark circles; he stood hunched as though in pain. 'Are you all right?' Martin asked.

'I'm fine,' Robert said. He smiled. The effect was grotesque. Robert cleared his throat. 'I've seen a few miracles in the last day or two, but this is perhaps the most gobsmacking of them all. Where are you going?'

'Amsterdam,' said Martin. 'Are you sure you're okay?'

Robert said, 'Everything's under control. Does Marijke know you're coming?'

'No,' said Martin. 'But if you think back, she did actually invite me.'

'I'd love to see her face when she realises you've braved cabs, trains and buses for her. She'll just swoon.' He smiled again. Martin suddenly, urgently wanted to get away. But he needed to ask a question first. He said, 'Robert, do you know of any reason why I shouldn't go? . . . Has she . . . ? Is she . . . ?'

'No,' said Robert firmly, 'I don't believe she has. Or is.'

'Well, then . . .' There was a pause.

'Deep subject.'

Martin held out his hand. Robert shook it, then recognised his mistake when he felt Martin recoil. 'Her address?' Martin requested.

'Sorry. Here it is.' Robert gave Martin a large envelope.

Martin opened it, read the address. 'I *was* close, wasn't I?'

'Only two streets off. Amazing.'

Martin had the feeling that Robert was waiting for him to leave. 'I'd better go. But . . . thanks.'

'Erm . . . not at all.'

Martin turned and then said, 'Did it work out all right?'

'What's that?'

'The seance. The matter of life or death.' Martin stood not quite touching the doorknob, thinking about Julia.

'Things derailed a bit, but the end result was . . . interesting,' Robert said. 'By the way, how *did* you manage to keep Julia upstairs?'

'Duct tape and charisma.' Martin opened the door, stepped into the hallway.

Robert said, 'Ring us up sometime. Tell us how it goes.' He smiled more naturally as he shut the door.

Martin glanced at his watch, saw that he should hurry. This propelled him across the hall and out the front door without too much hesitation. Halfway up the garden path he turned and looked back. Julia was watching him from her parlour window. He waved; she waved back. He glanced down at the ground-floor parlour and saw someone – *Julia?* – sitting in the dim room. *Well, it can't be Julia. How odd.* He shook his head, looked up at Julia and smiled. She stood and watched as Martin turned away and walked through the gate, carrying his suitcase lightly. *What did he see?* Julia wondered.

Elspeth watched Martin disappear through the gate. *Goodbye, my friend.* She heard Robert come into the room. He stood behind her. 'There he goes,' he said quietly.

'It's quite inspiring, really. He must be terrified.'

'He seemed calm enough. Julia's been slipping him pills.'

'Ah. I hope they linger in his system long enough to get him to Marijke's doorstep.'

Robert said, 'Martin came to your funeral.'

'Did he? How sweet. And brave.'

'Very brave.'

'Robert. Why only "interesting"?' she asked.

'Sorry?'

'You told Martin the end result was "interesting". Would you rather it was Valentina and not me?'

'I can't seem to justify sacrificing Valentina to have you.'

With some effort Elspeth turned to face him. 'What exactly do you think happened last night?' He was standing near her, but not touching. Robert looked down at her, hesitated before he answered. 'I couldn't see anything until you came into . . . Valentina's body. All I know is that you're here, and she isn't. What am I supposed to think?'

'She couldn't do it. She wasn't strong enough. I could have put her back a few minutes after she died – or she would have had to be a very strong ghost like me, and it took me months to get to the point where I could move a toothbrush, let alone a body.' She put the palm of her hand on her chest. 'At first you have to make everything go by pushing and willing it. You have to breathe with lungs that don't know how to breathe. You have to make the blood move. You have to seal yourself in and become the body. Valentina was just a sort of mist. She hovered over the body and then . . . dispersed. And I thought, *Right, I'll take it then.*'

'But do you think she knew? Do you think she decided not to come back?'

'I don't know. I don't remember that phase very well.'

'But the whole thing was a deception, then. It would never

have worked. She couldn't have come back – why didn't you tell her?'

'How was I supposed to know? It's not as though we were scientists; we made it up as we went along. She would have killed herself anyway.'

'No . . . she might have run away. She just wanted to leave Julia – she didn't want to die.'

'She was in love with you,' Elspeth said. 'She was trying to be your ideal girl, and you were in love with a ghost. Now your ghost is alive and Valentina is a ghost.' She paused. 'So what are you going to do?'

'I don't know. I can't . . . Elspeth, right now I just despise myself for having any part in this.'

'Are you going to leave me for your new ghost?'

He turned away from her. They had been speaking very quietly, for fear of Julia overhearing them, and somehow this increased the horror he had of her; this whispered argument in the dim parlour suddenly became painfully absurd to him.

'You said you wished I could come back . . . You wanted me to come back . . .'

He could not answer.

Julia stood at Robert's door. *I know you're in there.* It was quiet behind the door. She didn't knock. She stared at the little card that said FANSHAW. *What was Martin looking at?* She tried to come up with a plausible reason to be standing at Robert's door. She couldn't think of a thing. She knocked anyway.

In the parlour Elspeth and Robert were silent, listening. Finally Elspeth looked up at him. He bent to her and she spoke into his ear. 'I'll go out the back door. See what she wants.' Robert helped her to take off her shoes, helped her walk to the back door. She sat down on the fire escape, breathing strenuously with her shoes in her hands.

Robert walked very slowly. He stood at the door for a moment, then unlocked and opened it. Julia stood there. She looked tired and distraught, her dress hanging askew, mis-buttoned, her hands clasped in front of her like a penitent.

'Hello, Julia.' *I'm sorry, Julia. I've killed your sister.*

'Hey.' *You look really freaked out, Robert.*

'Are you okay?' *I didn't mean to kill her. She insisted.*

'Can I come in?' *What are you hiding?*

'Erm, yeah, sure.' *It didn't work out quite the way she thought it would.*

Julia walked into Robert's hallway. She took a few steps and turned back. 'Can I look around?'

'Why?'

She didn't reply, but ran into the front room, stood looking for a moment, raced into the parlour, through the dining room, across the hall and into his bedroom. She stood panting, taking in the candles and roses, spent matches, dishevelled bedclothes. She went into the bathroom and came out holding a comb. Silvery hairs wafted around it like the iridescent tendrils of a deep-sea creature.

'This is Valentina's.'

'Yes.'

'Where is she?'

'Julia . . .'

'I know, but . . . something is wrong.' Julia was turning,

trying to see, looking for the thing that would explain what was wrong. 'I don't feel like she's dead.'

Robert nodded. 'I know.'

'She's here.'

'No,' he said. 'Julia . . . I know it's impossible to believe, but she's gone.'

'No,' she said. Julia began moving through the flat again. Robert followed her.

'Do you want some breakfast?' he asked. 'I have eggs, and orange juice.' She ignored him, kept orbiting through the rooms as though velocity would answer her question. In the dining room she turned on him.

'It's your fault. You killed her.' This was so much his own feeling that he could not answer. He stood with his hands at his side, ready to accept her verdict. 'You . . . if you hadn't . . . You killed Elspeth, and then you killed Valentina.' He saw that she was only trying to hurt him.

'Elspeth died of leukaemia. Valentina had asthma.' *How delicately language skirts the issue. How meaningless it is.*

'But . . . I don't know. Why did she die?'

'I don't know, Julia.' She stared at him, seemed to be waiting for him to say something more. Suddenly she ran out of the room. Robert heard her slam his front door and run up the stairs.

This is unbearable. He wanted to go to the cemetery, to walk off this sense of things being too real, too wrong. But Elspeth was sitting on the fire escape. He went to collect her. When he opened the door she was huddled on the bottom step looking miserable and boneless. He scooped her up and brought her in without a word. When he had settled her on his bed he sat next to her, facing away. 'We have to leave here,' he said.

'Of course,' said Elspeth, relieved. 'We'll go anywhere you like.'

He left the room. She heard him dialling. *Where are we going?*

'James? May I come over? I'm bringing someone . . . I'll explain when I get there . . . No, the situation is a bit unusual . . . Yes. Thanks, we'll be there directly.'

Martin had imagined this journey countless times. In his head parts of it were quite tangible and specific and other things were left vague. There was no question of flying. He knew he could not bear to sit strapped in 30,000 feet up in the air; his heart would burst. He had decided to take the train.

First he had to convince himself to get into the minicab. The driver had waited patiently, had finally opened the door for him and let him insert and extract himself several times before he sat down and allowed the driver to shut the door. Martin sat with his eyes closed for a while, but eventually felt secure enough to look out the window. *There's the world. Look at all the new buildings, and the cars – there are so many strange cars.* He had seen pictures of the cars in adverts: here they were. A black Prius cut off the minicab and there was a mutual exchange of hostility at the next light. Martin closed his eyes again.

Standing in Waterloo station he was immediately over-whelmed. It had been completely refurbished since he'd been there last. He was an hour early. He made his way very slowly across the open space of the station, looking straight ahead, counting his steps. People flowed around him. In the midst of his anxiety Martin was able to discern a kernel of excitement, pleasure in his re-entry into the world. He thought of Marijke, of what she would say when she saw him, how proud she would be of him. *Look, darling. I've come to you.* Martin shivered in the cool dead air of the station. Unconsciously he closed his eyes and arced his head forward, as though expecting a kiss. A few people looked at him curiously. He stood still before the board that announced the trains, imagining Marijke's embrace.

He had bought a first-class ticket on the Eurostar, one-way for luck. He waited in the lounge, standing apart from the other travellers. Finally he was able to step onto the train and walk to his seat at the end of the compartment. The train was quieter and cleaner than the trains he remembered. Martin bowed his head, clasped his hands and began counting silently. It was a five-hour journey. He was grateful not to have to take the ferry. The train would move straight ahead, on rails. It would not fly through the air; it would not sail the seas. He had only to sit still, change trains in Brussels, and take one more cab. It was doable.

Jessica opened her front door. Robert stood on the doorstep clutching what seemed to Jessica at first to be a wounded child; he held it under its arms as if it were about to slide to the ground. Though the day was temperate, the figure was shrouded in a scarf. Robert's head was bowed over the small figure and he slowly raised his face and looked at Jessica with an expression of profound sorrow.

'Robert? What's happened? Who is that?'

'I'm sorry, Jessica. I couldn't think where else to go. I thought you might help us.'

The figure turned its head; Jessica saw its face. *Julia? No.* 'Edie?'

'Jessica,' it said, and tried to straighten, tried to stand on its own. There was something about it that made Jessica think of a newborn foal, unsteady but ready to flee.

'It's Elspeth, Jessica,' Robert said.

Jessica put out her hand and braced herself against the door jamb. She experienced one of those rare moments when understanding of the world alters and a previously impossible thing is admitted, if not understood. 'Robert,' she cried out, 'what have you done?' From inside the house James called, 'Jessica, are you all right?' She paused, then called back, 'Yes, James.' She stared at them, uncertain and fearful.

'We'd better go,' said Robert. 'I'm sorry. I shouldn't have—'

'But how is it possible?'

'I don't know,' Robert said. He realised the enormity of his mistake. 'Jessica, I'm sorry. I'll come back and see you when I've thought it all through more carefully. Just . . . please don't mention this to Julia or her parents. I think they would rather not know.' He picked up Elspeth and turned to leave.

Jessica said, 'Wait, Robert . . .' But he was already walking away. Elspeth wrapped her arms around his neck. James came to the door as they reached the pavement and were hidden from view by the hedge. 'What happened?' he said. 'Come inside,' said Jessica. 'I have to tell you something.'

* * *

Martin sat on the train and the world flowed. *Everything is still out there: the rooftops and chimneys, the graffiti, the office towers and the cyclists; soon there will be sheep and that immense sky they keep out in the countryside . . . Once I thought there were two realities, inner and outer, but perhaps that's a bit meagre; I'm not quite the same person I was last night, and when I get to Marijke's I won't be the same man she married or even the one she walked out on . . . How will we recognise each other, after all that's happened? How will we manage to realign our realities, which are moving away from us even as we travel towards them?* Martin wrapped his fingers around the vitamin bottle, which Julia had slipped into his pocket. *Everything is so fragile, and so glorious.* He closed his eyes. *Here it comes . . . here's the future . . . and here it is again . . .*

At the railway station in Brussels he bought a ham sandwich and a pair of sunglasses; he was nervous and the extra protection soothed him. He peered at himself in the shop's mirror. *Bond . . . James Bond.* The Thalys train was more crowded than the Eurostar had been, but no one sat next to him. *Three more hours.* He began to eat his sandwich.

The cab disgorged Martin at Marijke's front door. He stood in the crooked narrow street and tried to remember if he had ever been there before. He decided he hadn't. He stepped up to the door and rang Marijke's bell. She wasn't home.

Martin panicked. He had not considered what would happen if she didn't answer. He had imagined the scene exactly as it must happen; he had not allowed for having to stay outdoors for any length of time. He tried the doorknob.

He felt his heart racing. *No. Don't be silly . . . just breathe . . .* He sat on his suitcase and breathed.

Marijke wheeled her bike into the street; preoccupied, fishing in her bag for her keys, at first she didn't notice the man gasping on her doorstep. As she came closer he stood up and said, 'Marijke.'

'Martin – *oh goh – je bent hier!*' She was immobilised by the bike, then hurriedly propped it against the building and turned to him. 'You've come to me,' she said.

'Yes,' he said, and held out his arms to her. 'Yes.'

They kissed. There in the sun, under the kindly gaze of anyone who happened to walk along that street, Martin embraced Marijke, and the years fell away. He had found her again.

'Come inside,' she said.

'Of course,' said Martin. 'But we'll go out again later?'

'Yes,' Marijke said, smiling. 'Of course.'

THE END OF THE DIARIES

Edie and Jack stayed in London for two weeks. Every day they showed up at Vautravers before breakfast, collected Julia and whisked her off to visit their old friends, to see London through the prism of Edie's childhood, Jack's first days of working at the bank, their courtship. Julia was grateful to be busy, though the pace seemed forced and there were moments when she caught her dad looking confusedly at her mom, as though the stories weren't quite the same ones he remembered.

One day, when Edie and Jack arrived, Robert went out and intercepted them in the front garden. 'Edie,' he said, 'I need to talk to you. Just for a sec.'

'I'll go upstairs,' Jack said.

Edie followed Robert into his flat. The flat had an abandoned feeling; there was little furniture and though it was tidy enough Edie sensed that things had been subtracted from it.

'Are you moving out?' she asked.

'Yes, slowly,' said Robert. 'I can't bear to be here alone, somehow.'

He led her through the flat to the servant's room. It was almost bare except for a number of boxes filled with ledgers, photographs and other papers.

'Elspeth left me these,' he said. 'Do you want them?'

Edie didn't move. She stood with her arms crossed protectively, looking at the boxes. 'Did you read them?' she asked.

'Some of them,' he said. 'I thought they might mean more to you.'

'I don't want them,' Edie said. She looked at him. 'Will you burn them for me?'

'Burn them?'

'If it were up to me I'd have a big bonfire and burn the lot. All the furniture too. Elspeth even kept our bed, from when we were kids; I couldn't believe it when I walked into her bedroom and saw it.'

Robert said, 'It's a pretty bed. I always liked it.'

Edie said, 'Will you burn these for me?'

'Yes.'

'Thank you.' She smiled. Robert had not seen her smile before; the effect was painfully Elspeth-like. She turned and he followed her back through the flat. At his door he said, 'Is Julia going to stay here?'

'Yes,' said Edie. 'We thought she might want to come home, but she won't. She seems to feel that she's somehow abandoning Valentina if she leaves the flat.' Edie frowned. 'She's become very superstitious.'

Robert said, 'That's understandable.'

Edie paused. 'Thanks again; you've been very kind. I can see why Elspeth and Valentina both cared for you.'

Robert shook his head. 'I'm sorry—'

'It's all right,' Edie said. 'It's going to be all right.'

Later, after the Poole family had gone out, Robert lugged the boxes into the back garden and burned everything in them, piece by piece. Edie saw the scorched area on the moss the next morning and was glad.

On an overcast day in mid-July, Jack and Edie sat together on the plane to Chicago, waiting for take-off. She'd had two drinks before they boarded, but that hadn't helped much. Sweat streamed down her back, armpits, forehead. Jack offered his hand and she gripped it. 'Steady,' he said.

'I'm so daft.' She shook her head.

Jack took a calculated risk. 'Not you, Elspeth love.'

The plane began to move. She was so surprised to hear her own name that she could only gape at him. She almost forgot to be afraid as they were lifted into the sky and London receded under them. 'How long have you known?' she asked him once the plane had levelled itself.

'Years,' he said.

She said, 'I thought you'd leave me . . .'

'Never,' he said.

'I'm sorry,' she said. 'I am so, so sorry.' She began to cry, the kind of messy, hiccuping, uncontrollable weeping that she had always refused to allow herself – a lifetime's worth of crying. Jack watched her and wondered what would come of it. The flight attendant hurried over with a small packet of tissues. 'Oh God, I'm making a spectacle of myself,' Edie said at last.

'That's okay,' Jack said. 'This is a plane full of Americans. No one will mind. They're all watching the movie.' He raised the armrest between them and she leaned into him, feeling empty and strangely content.

⟞⟝ REDUX ⟞⟝

Julia woke up late and confused after a night of bad dreams. Edie and Jack had reluctantly gone back to Lake Forest two days earlier. Julia had been relieved to see them go, but now the flat was too quiet; she seemed to be the only person left in Vautravers. Since it was Sunday, she pulled on yesterday's clothes (which were also the clothes of the day before and the day before that) and walked to the corner shop near the bus stop to buy the *Observer*. When she came back there was a large motorcycle blocking the path to Vautravers. Julia edged around it with annoyance. She walked back to the gate and into the house without realising that she was being watched.

She made tea and opened a packet of chocolate digestives. She poured milk into the tea and arranged everything on a tray along with her cigarettes and carried it into the dining room. The ghost of the Kitten was curled up on top of the newspaper, one eye open and the other closed. Julia set the tray down on the table and reached right through the Kitten, plucked the paper off the table and began to separate the sections. The Kitten looked reproachful and began to lick her nether parts with one leg stuck up in the air. She vaguely resembled a cello player, but Julia couldn't see the Kitten, so she didn't make her usual joke about it.

Julia spread out the newspaper and ate a biscuit. She idly wondered where Elspeth was and what she was doing; Julia hadn't noticed any sign of her in weeks, beyond the occasional cold patch of air and quivering light bulbs. As Julia read each section she did not bother to refold it: the Mouse was not here; the Mouse was not going to read the paper or be aggravated by Julia's selfishness. Julia lit a cigarette. The Kitten made a face and jumped off the table.

Somewhat later Julia had finished the *Observer* and was smoking her fourth cigarette when she heard sounds. The sounds were so much like footsteps that she tilted her head back and stared at the ceiling, which was where the sounds came from. Martin? Was Martin back? Julia ground out her cigarette in the dregs of her tea and ran from the dining room onto the landing and up the stairs without thinking.

The door to Martin's flat stood ajar. Julia's heart accelerated. She walked into the flat.

She stood still, listening. The flat was silent. Julia heard birds singing outside. The boxes and plastic containers were still dusty in the dimness. Julia wondered if she should call out; then she thought that it might not be Martin after all. She stood undecided, remembering that first night, when Martin had woken them up with his deluge and she had found him scrubbing the bedroom floor. It was so long ago; it had been winter then. Now it was summer. Julia slowly, silently walked through Martin's rooms. All was stillness. Most of the windows were still blacked out with newspaper. Some windows were clear and daylight streamed through them; the newspapers lay where she had thrown them. Julia crept through the parlour and the dining room. In the kitchen someone had left a beer cap and an opener on the counter. Julia couldn't remember Martin drinking in the morning, but then she wondered if it was still morning; she'd gotten up so late.

She crossed the hall and looked into Martin's office. There was a tall, angular young man standing at Martin's desk, reading a piece of paper which he held to the light. The tableau reminded Julia of a Vermeer painting. The young man had his back to Julia. He was wearing jeans, a black T-shirt and motorcycle boots. His hair was longish and darkish. As he read he sighed and raked his fingers through his hair. If Julia had ever met Marijke, that sigh, that gesture, would have told her who she was looking at. As it was, she had no clue until he turned and she saw his face.

'Oh!' Julia said. The young man started. They stared at each other for a moment, then Julia said, 'I'm sorry,' and the young man said, 'Who are you?' at the same time.

'I'm Julia Poole. I live downstairs. I heard footsteps . . .' He was looking at her curiously. Julia realised what he must see: an unwashed, too-thin, stringy-haired girl in ratty clothes. 'Who are you?'

'I'm Theo Wells. Martin and Marijke's son. I haven't heard from Dad in over two weeks. Or Mum. They're usually so . . . communicative. They haven't been answering their phones. And now I come here and he's gone. Do you understand how peculiar that is, that he should be gone? I can't . . . I don't understand it.'

Julia smiled. 'He went to Amsterdam to find your mom.'

Theo shook his head. 'He walked out of the flat voluntarily? He got on a bus or a train? No. The last time I saw him I had trouble coaxing him out of the bathroom.'

'He got better. He took medicine and he gradually got better. He went to find Marijke.'

Theo sat down at Martin's desk. Julia could not get over how much he resembled Martin: younger, less hunched, larger in his movements, but still so like Martin in his face and hands. *Genes are strange.* She had always thought so. She wondered if he was like Martin in other, less conventional ways.

Theo said, 'He hated taking antidepressants. He was afraid of the side effects. We tried to talk him into it. He always refused.' Theo passed his hands over his face and Julia wondered if she and Valentina had affected people like this, if they were unable to see one without thinking of the other. *This is what the Mouse hated so much. The layering, the intertwining. When someone looked at her and saw me.* Julia looked at Theo and saw Martin. This excited her.

'He didn't know. I tricked him.' She couldn't tell if Theo approved of this or not. He seemed lost in thought. 'Is that your motorcycle?' she asked.

'Hmm? Yes.'

'Can I have a ride?'

Theo smiled. 'How old are you?'

'Old enough.' Julia blushed. *He thinks I'm, like, twelve.* 'I'm your age.'

He raised both eyebrows. 'I *am*,' she said.

'Prove it, then.'

'Stay here,' Julia ordered. 'Do not leave without me.'

'No worries, I have to pick up a few things. If I can find them,' Theo said, glancing at the boxes.

Julia raced downstairs. She stripped off her clothes and showered, then stood in Elspeth's closet, confused. *What would Valentina wear? No, forget that. What would I wear?* She emerged clad in jeans, Elspeth's chocolate suede high-heeled boots and a pink T-shirt. She put on lipstick, blow-dried her hair and went back upstairs.

Theo was kneeling beside a pile of boxes. 'This is pointless,' he said.

'Probably,' said Julia.

Theo turned to look at her. 'Well,' he said. 'Would you like a motorcycle ride? I have an extra helmet.'

'Why yes,' said Julia. 'I would.'

⇥⇒ VISIT ⇐⇤

At first Valentina was almost nothing and she knew almost nothing. She was cold. She moved aimlessly through the flat, waiting with a sense of anticipation.

Time passed very slowly in the flat. Valentina paid no attention at first, but as the months went by and she began to understand that she was dead, that Elspeth had somehow gone away, that now she was stuck with Julia forever; when she started to grasp what might have happened to her, time slowed until Valentina felt as though the air in the flat had turned to glass.

The Kitten was her constant companion now. They spent days following pools of sunlight, lolling together on the carpets; they watched television with Julia in the evenings and sat in the window seat at night while Julia slept, staring out over the moonlit cemetery. *It's like an endless dream, where nothing ever happens and you can fly.* Julia seemed to be watching for her, waiting; sometimes Julia would say her name uncertainly, or look in Valentina's direction, and at those times Valentina would remove herself to another room: she did not want Julia to know she was there. Valentina was ashamed.

Summer ended and autumn arrived. On a cold rainy evening Valentina saw Robert come up the front walk. In the garden was a For Sale sign; Martin and Marijke had put their apartment on the market. Julia was upstairs helping Theo unpack and repack boxes for the move.

Robert let himself into the flat. The small typed card with Elspeth's name on it was still tacked to the door, causing him a spasm of sadness. He had taken off his muddy shoes downstairs, and walked noiselessly through the hall into the front room. He turned on the light by the piano and looked around. 'Valentina?'

She stood by the window. She waited to see what he would do.

'Valentina . . . I'm sorry. I didn't know.'

She had been longing to see him for months. Now he was here, and she was disappointed.

Robert stood in the middle of the room, his head tilted as though listening, his hands hanging empty at his sides. Nothing moved. There was no cold presence, only vacancy.

'Valentina?'

She wondered if he had loved her.

He waited. Finally, receiving no encouragement, he turned and padded out of the flat. She watched until she saw him walking up the path and through the gate, dark against the darkness. *Where are you going, Robert? Who will be waiting for you when you get there?*

Julia walked down Long Acre, window-shopping. It was a sunny day in January, a Saturday, and she'd woken up that morning with an urge to go somewhere there would be people; she had gravitated to the shops thinking she might buy a present for Theo, or something cute to wear when she went to visit him at the weekend. Julia was dressed carelessly in yesterday's jeans and a sweatshirt under one of Elspeth's coats. She felt extra thin, as though she were barely occupying her clothes. She walked like an astronaut, swaggering in furry moon boots. She wandered into a tiny shop in Neal's Yard that was full of pink things: hi-top sneakers, feather boas, vinyl miniskirts. *Mouse would have been in love with all this*, she thought. Julia imagined herself and Valentina in fluffy angora sweaters and Day-Glo green fishnet stockings. She held the sweater to her chest in front of the mirror, and was repelled by her own reflection; the girl that peered out of the mirror looked like Valentina with the flu. Julia turned away and returned the sweater to the rack without trying it on.

Back on the pavement she stood for a moment, thinking about a Pret she had passed a few streets back and trying to remember which direction she had come from. A girl brushed past her. There was something, perhaps, about the smell of the girl, which was compounded of lavender soap, sweat and baby powder, that made Julia notice her. The girl was walking fast, dodging tourists. She moved without hesitating, circumventing *Big Issue* vendors and buskers instinctively. The girl had dark chestnut hair that bounced in ringlets as she walked. She wore a bright red dress and a little fur capelet. Julia began to follow her.

As she followed the girl she became more and more agitated. *Sherlock Holmes says you can't disguise a back. Or maybe it's Peter Wimsey. Anyway, from the back that girl sure looks just like the Mouse. She doesn't walk like her, though.* Valentina would never have moved with such forthright strides through a crowd. The girl ducked into Stanfords, the map shop, and Julia did too.

'Please, I'm looking for a map of East Sussex?' The girl's voice was a rich alto, unmistakably Oxbridge.

'D'you want the road map or Ordnance Survey?' asked the shop assistant.

'Ordnance Survey, I think.'

Julia loitered at a table full of books about Australia while the girl followed the assistant downstairs. A few minutes later, the girl came up the stairs holding a shopping bag and Julia got a good look at her face.

She was like Valentina, and she wasn't. There was an extraordinary resemblance, and none at all: the girl had Valentina's features, and none of her expression. The girl was heavily made up, with dark lipstick and eyeliner. Her eyes were brown, and her face had an assurance that Valentina could never have matched. She radiated confidence.

The girl had her hand on the door; she was about to slip away, and Julia couldn't bear to let her go.

'Excuse me,' said Julia. The girl stopped and turned, saw

that it was herself that Julia meant to address. Julia saw that the girl was pregnant. Their eyes met: was the girl surprised? Afraid? Or just startled to find a stranger's hand clutching her arm?

'Sorry?' the girl said. Julia stared so hard she felt as though she were eating the girl's face. She wanted to scrub off the make-up, to undress the girl to see if all the familiar moles and vaccination scars would be there.

'You're *hurting* me,' said the girl loudly. It wasn't Valentina's voice. Around them the shop went still. Julia heard heavy footsteps behind her. She let go of the girl's arm. The girl flung open the door, stepped onto the street and hurried away. Julia followed her out and then stood watching as she disappeared into the crowd.

Elspeth forced herself not to run. She was panting, and she tried to slow down. She didn't look back. Here was a Starbucks; she went inside and sat down at a table. When her heart stopped racing she went to the loo and splashed water on her face, fixed her make-up. She scrutinised her reflection. It had not passed the test. She was changed, but apparently not changed enough; Julia had seen her twin underneath the difference. Did Julia know? If she knew, why hadn't she chased after her; why did she look so uncertain? Elspeth visualised Julia's face: so thin, so tired. She leaned over the sink, braced her arms against it and hung her head. Her chin rested on her chest, and her belly swelled like a red balloon between her arms. Elspeth began to weep, and once she had begun she could not stop. The little fur capelet was wet with her tears.

When she finally emerged from the loo, three women were

standing in the queue and they each gave her a dirty look as she passed. Elspeth decided to skip her remaining errands. She ducked into the tube and exited twenty minutes later at King's Cross St Pancras. She was standing on the doorstep of the tiny flat fumbling for her key when Robert opened the door.

'Where have you been?' he said. 'I was almost worried.'

'We have to leave London, Robert. I saw Julia.'

'Did she see you?'

Elspeth told him. 'I don't think she was sure. But she was confused, and she frightened me. We have to leave.'

They were sitting in their squalid kitchen. Elspeth sat at the table with her elbows on it and her head propped in her hands, and Robert paced. The kitchen was so small that he could only move a few steps in each direction. It made her nervous. It reminded her of Julia. 'Please don't do that.'

Robert sat down. 'Where can we go?'

'America. Australia. Paris.'

'You don't even have a valid passport, Elspeth. We can't get on an international flight.'

'East Sussex.'

Robert said, 'Why Sussex?'

'It's pretty. We could live in Lewes and walk on the Downs every Sunday afternoon. Why not?'

'We don't know anyone there.'

'Precisely.'

Robert got up and began pacing again, forgetting that Elspeth had just asked him not to do this. 'Maybe we should confess. Then we could live in my flat, and eventually things would be normal again.'

Elspeth just looked at him. *You are barking mad.* After a moment Robert said, 'I suppose not.'

'We could get a little cottage. You could finish your thesis.'

'How the *hell* am I supposed to finish my thesis when I can't go to the *cemetery*?' he yelled.

'Why can't you go to the cemetery?' Elspeth asked quietly. She felt the baby kick.

'Jessica saw you,' he said. 'What am I supposed to tell her?'

Elspeth frowned. 'Tell her as much of the truth as you can. And let her sort it out. There's no reason to lie, just omit a few things.'

Robert stood looking down at her upturned face, her borrowed face. *That's how you do it*, he thought. *I never realised it before.* 'How long have you been plotting to move to Sussex?' he asked her.

She said, 'Oh, since we were tiny. Our parents used to take us to Glyndebourne, and we'd get off the train at Lewes with all the other people in fancy dress. I always wanted to live out in the countryside, there. Actually, I wanted to live in the opera house, but I don't imagine that's practicable.'

'Oh, I don't know,' said Robert, irritably. 'It seems to me if you can come back from the dead you could probably live anywhere you like.'

'Well, we can't live in your flat,' said Elspeth.

'No.'

'Right, then,' said Elspeth. 'Can we at least go and look at East Sussex? With an estate agent?'

'Fine,' said Robert. He scooped his keys off the table and grabbed his jacket.

'Where are you going?'

'Out.' He turned to look at her as he put his jacket on; she had a chastened expression he could not remember ever seeing before. 'To the library,' he said, softening. 'I ordered some books.'

'See you later?' she said, as though she wasn't quite sure.

'Yeah.'

As Robert walked along Euston Road in the sunshine he thought, *I have to talk to Jessica.* As he entered the library he thought, *I can't imagine leaving London.* He put his things in a locker and went upstairs. *What am I going to do?* He was sitting and waiting for his desk light to activate when the answer came to him, and he laughed out loud at the obviousness of it.

Robert and Jessica sat in her office with the door closed. It was after hours; all the cemetery staff had gone home. He had told her everything, as best he could. He had tried to place all the evidence before her; he had not spared himself. Jessica listened impassively. She sat in the waning light with her fingers steepled, leaning forward, regarding him with serious eyes. Finally he was silent. Jessica reached out and pulled the little chain of her desk lamp, creating a small pool of yellow light that did not reach either of them. He waited for her to speak.

'Poor Robert,' she said. 'It's all very unfortunate. But I suppose you could say that you got what you wished for.'

'That's the worst punishment,' Robert said. 'I would undo everything, if I could.'

'Yes,' she said. 'But you can't.'

'No, I can't.' He sighed. 'I'd better go. We're leaving tomorrow. There's still packing to do.'

They stood up. She said, 'Will you come back?'

'I hope so.' He turned on the overhead light and followed her slowly down the stairs. When they were standing at the cemetery gates she said, 'Goodbye, Robert.' He kissed her on both cheeks, slipped through the gates and walked away. *There he goes,* she thought. Jessica watched until Robert disappeared from her sight. Then she locked the gate and stood in the dark courtyard, listening to the wind and marvelling at human folly.

THE END

It was the first day of spring. Valentina sat in the window seat, looking out over Highgate Cemetery. Morning sun slanted in, pouring through her onto the worn blue rug without pause. Birds wheeled over the trees, which were bursting with new leaves; Valentina could hear a car crunching the gravel in St Michael's car park. The outside world was shiny and clean and loud today. Valentina let the sun warm her. The Kitten jumped up onto her lap, and she stroked its white head as she watched pigeons building a nest in the top of Julius Beer's mausoleum.

Julia was asleep. She slept sprawled out now, as though trying to cover as much of the bed as possible. Her mouth was open. Valentina got up, still holding the Kitten, and walked over to the bed. She stood watching Julia. Then she put her finger in Julia's mouth. Julia didn't wake. Valentina went back to the window seat and sat down again.

An hour later Julia woke up. Valentina was gone; Julia showered and dressed and drank her coffee alone. She found the silence of the building disturbing. Robert had moved away; the upstairs flat hadn't sold yet (perhaps because it was still half full of boxes). *Maybe I should get a dog. How do you get a dog in London?* English people were so fanatical about animals; maybe you couldn't just go to the pound and pick one out. Maybe they had to approve of you. She imagined what the dog-adoption people would think when they saw her living like an orphan in huge silent Vautravers. *Maybe I should be one of those women who have one hundred cats. They could swarm all over. I could let them into Martin's flat and it would be a cat Disney World. They would go bonkers.*

Julia sat with her mug of coffee at the dining-room table. It was littered with sheets of paper and pens; the paper was covered with Valentina's writing. The dog-adoption people would see that she was insane. She began to gather up the papers. She strode into the kitchen and threw them in the bin. When Julia returned to the dining room, Valentina was standing by the French windows with the Kitten draped over her shoulder. Julia sighed.

'I can't leave that stuff sitting around,' she said. 'It looks weird.'

Valentina ignored this and made the gesture they'd always used to get waiters to bring the bill: she pretended to write on her upturned palm.

'Fine,' said Julia. 'Okay.' She took a sip of her now-cold coffee, just to show the Mouse that she didn't have to jump when told. Valentina stood patiently by her chair, and Julia sat down and drew a piece of paper to her, picked up a pen and poised it over the paper. 'Go ahead,' she said.

Valentina leaned over and the Kitten jumped onto the table and stood on the paper. Valentina brushed her aside and put her hand into Julia's.

I FIGURED IT OUT.

'Figured what out?'

HOW TO LEAVE.

'Oh.' Julia looked up at Valentina, resignedly. 'Well. Okay. How?'

IT TAKES A BODY. OPEN YOUR MOUTH, GO OUTSIDE.

'Go outside and open my mouth?'

Valentina shook her head.

OPEN MOUTH, CLOSE MOUTH, THEN GO OUTSIDE.

Julia opened her mouth as though for the dentist, shut it and pressed her lips together, then pointed to the window. 'Right?' Valentina nodded. 'Now?' Valentina nodded again. 'Let me get my shoes.'

Valentina gathered up the Little Kitten of Death and waited for Julia in their front hall. She thought she saw a hint of her reflection in the mirrors, but she wasn't quite sure.

Julia reappeared wearing one of Elspeth's favourite cardigans, baby-blue cashmere with mother-of-pearl buttons. Valentina stood looking at her for a long moment, and then leaned to Julia and kissed her on the lips. To Julia it felt like the ghost of all the kisses the Mouse had ever given her. She smiled; her eyes welled.

'Now?' Julia repeated, and Valentina nodded.

Julia opened her mouth wide and closed her eyes. She felt her mouth fill with something like dense smoke; she opened her eyes and tried not to gag. *How will I breathe?* The thing in her mouth was becoming more solid. Julia felt it in her throat, and she coughed and gasped. It was like a mouthful of fur, a big hairball. She closed her mouth. Julia struggled to draw breath, and then felt the thing become smaller and heavier, leaving space around itself, fitting itself between her tongue and the roof of her mouth. It tasted metallic and moved slightly but constantly, like an excited child trying to hold still. Julia looked around the hall. Valentina and the Kitten had disappeared.

Come on, you two, let's go. Julia stepped across the threshold onto the landing. Valentina and the Kitten were still in her mouth. Julia raced down the stairs and out the front door of Vautravers; the strange bulk still quivered on her tongue. She ran along the side of the building into the back garden, to the door in the wall, and fumbled with the key. She got the door open, stepped into the cemetery and opened her mouth.

Valentina flew out into the air. She hung suspended for a moment, spread out in the morning breeze like a rainbow created by a garden hose. The Little Kitten of Death was intermingled with her, and as Julia stood watching they seemed to separate and resolve.

Valentina felt the breeze carry her, extend her, divide her from the Kitten. At first she could not see or hear, and then she could. Julia stood with her arms clutched against her chest and a desolate little smile on her face, looking up at Valentina.

'Goodbye, Valentina,' Julia said. Tears ran down her face. 'Goodbye, Kitten.'

Goodbye, goodbye, Julia. The Kitten squirmed out of Valentina's arms, jumped off the roof of the Catacombs and went racing into the cemetery. Valentina turned and followed.

Her senses were flung open like doors and windows. Everything was speaking, singing to her, the grass, trees, stones, insects, rabbits, foxes: all stopped what they were doing to watch the ghost fly past; all cried out to her, as though she had been long away from home and they were the spectators at her victory parade. She flew through gravestones and bushes, revelling in their density and coolness.

The Kitten was waiting for her under the Cedar of Lebanon, and Valentina caught up with her. Together they flew above the Egyptian Avenue and streamed down the main path. If there were other ghosts, Valentina did not see them; it was nature that greeted her; the angels on the tombs were simply stones. Valentina could see through things and into things. She saw the deep grave shafts with the coffins stacked in them; she saw the bodies in the coffins, with their postures of yearning and gestures of supplication, bodies long turned to bone and dust. Valentina felt a hunger, a desire to find her own body that was visceral, almost ecstatic. They were flying faster now; things streamed by in a blur of stone and green, and now, at last, here: the little stone shelter that said NOBLIN, the little iron door that was no obstacle to Valentina, the quiet space inside, Elspeth's coffin, Elspeth's body, Elspeth's parents' and grandparents' coffins and bodies. She saw her own coffin, and knew before she touched it that it was empty. *So it's true, then.* She saw the Little Kitten of Death rub her face eagerly against the white box. Valentina laid her hands on the varnished wood of Elspeth's coffin, just as Robert had once done. *What now?* She picked up the Kitten and went outside. She stood on the path, uncertain.

A little girl came walking up the path. She hummed to herself and swung her bonnet by its strings in time to her own footsteps. She wore a lavender dress in a style from the late nineteenth century.

'Hello,' she said to Valentina, politely. 'Are you coming?'

'Coming where?' said Valentina.

'They're mustering the crows,' said the girl. 'We're going flying.'

'Why do you need crows?' Valentina asked. 'Can't you fly on your own?'

'It's different. Haven't you done it before?'

'I'm new,' said Valentina.

'Oh.' The girl began walking and Valentina walked with her. 'I say – are you an American? Where did you get your cat? No one has a cat here – when I was alive I had a cat named Maisie, but she's not here . . .' Valentina followed her to the Dissenters' section of the cemetery, where many ghosts stood around chatting in small groups. The trees in this section had recently been cut down; it was open to the sky, with stumps jutting between the graves. Ghosts glanced at Valentina, then looked away. She wondered if she should try to introduce herself. The little girl had wandered off. Now she returned, dragging an extraordinarily fat man who was dressed as though he were about to go fox-hunting.

'This is my papa,' said the girl.

'Quite welcome, I'm sure,' said the man to Valentina. 'Would you care to join us?'

Valentina hesitated; heights made her nervous. *But why not?* she thought. *I'm dead. Nothing can hurt me now. I can do whatever I want.* 'Yes,' she said. 'I'd like that.'

'Splendid,' said the man. He raised his arm and an enormous crow flew down and plopped in front of them, cawing and strutting. Valentina thought, *It's just like hailing a taxi.* Soon there were hundreds of crows milling about. Each ghost seemed to shrink until it was a suitable size, then hopped aboard a crow. Valentina imitated them. She clasped one ethereal arm around her crow's neck and held onto the Kitten with the other, hugging the crow's body with her knees.

Now the vast throng of crows rose out of Highgate Cemetery in unison, and the ghosts with them, their dark dresses and winding sheets flapping wing-like in the sky. They flew over Waterlow Park, circled around to fly across the Heath, and on and on, until they came to the Thames and began to follow the river eastwards, past the Houses of Parliament and Westminster Bridge, past the Embankment, London Bridge, the Tower, and on, and on. Valentina held tightly to her crow. The Kitten purred in her ear. *I'm so happy*, she thought with surprise. The sun passed through the ghosts undimmed, and the shadows of the crows darkened the river.

After Valentina had vanished from her sight, Julia stood in the open doorway for a little while, listening to the birds. Then she shut the green door. She went back to her flat and made herself another cup of coffee. She sat in the window seat and watched trees swaying in the cemetery, with flashes of white gravestones peeking through the leaves. She listened to the quiet of the house, the hum of the refrigerator, the flick of the numbers on the old clock radio turning over. *I am definitely going to get a dog*, Julia thought. She spent the afternoon dusting and talked to Theo on the phone after dinner. Julia went to bed contented and alone, and slept without dreaming.

It had been one of those vivid days: the fields around the cottage were radiantly green, and the Sussex sky was so blue it hurt her eyes. Elspeth had gone for a walk with the baby in the early evening. He was a colicky baby, and the walking sometimes soothed him when nothing else could. Now he was breathing quietly, asleep in his little pouch pressed against her breast. Elspeth came to the long drive that led to their tiny home. It was dark now, but the moon was nearly full and she could see her shadow moving before her up the drive. The summer insect songs pressed at her from all sides, a shimmering choir that lay like a blanket of sound over the fields.

For weeks she had been watching Robert carefully. There had been a long bad patch after they'd moved here. Robert could not adjust to the spaciousness, the quiet; he missed the cemetery and would take the train into London on the least pretext to visit it. He seldom spoke to Elspeth; it was as though he had withdrawn into his own invisible London and was living in it without her. His manuscript sat vast and untouched on his desk. Then the baby was born, and Elspeth had found herself in a purely physical world: sleep was an elusive prize, breastfeeding more complicated than she remembered. The baby cried; she cried, but at last Robert seemed to wake up and notice her. He seemed almost surprised by the baby, as though he'd thought she was joking about being pregnant. And to Elspeth's surprise, the arrival of the baby did what she could not: it brought Robert back to writing his thesis.

For months now he'd worked with perfect concentration in the midst of baby-wrought chaos. She tiptoed around him, afraid to break the charm, but he told her there was no need. He said he found the din oddly helpful. 'It's as though it wants to be finished,' he said, and the printer whirred each night, emitting increasingly pristine pages.

Tonight she felt a pause, suspense: the world was adjusting itself into a new pattern. Something was going to happen; the manuscript was almost finished. Elspeth walked with the baby in the dark between sweet-smelling fields and rejoiced. *I'm here. I'm alive.* She placed her hands on the baby, felt his soft head against her cool palms. The ever-present regret lapped at her, and she thought of Valentina broken on the bedroom floor. Elspeth had no answer and no defence against this image. It flared in her mind vividly, then faded. She kept walking.

The cottage reminded her of a jack-o'-lantern, its windows blazing orange. All the lights were on. Elspeth walked through the garden and came in the back door, into the kitchen. The insect sounds diminished. The house was very still.

'Robert?' she called, careful to keep her voice low. She went into the front room. No one there. On Robert's desk was a neat pile of paper. *A History of Highgate Cemetery.* All the files and notes had been cleared away. There was a look of finality about the scene. Elspeth smiled. 'Robert?'

He was not in the house. He did not come back that night. Days went by, and at last she understood that he would not return at all.

⤞⤜ ACKNOWLEDGEMENTS ⤚⤟

I could not have written *Her Fearful Symmetry* without the extra-ordinary generosity of Jean Pateman, Chairman of the Friends of Highgate Cemetery. In addition to teaching me about the Cemetery and allowing me to become a guide there, she has been a great friend and an inspiration.

I am very grateful to the staff of Highgate Cemetery: Hilary Deeble-Rogers, Richard Quirk, Simon Moore-Martin, Pawel Ksyta, Aneta Gomulnicka, Victor Herman and Neil Luxton, for help with funeral customs and practices and for answering my many questions with great humour and patience.

I am especially indebted to Dr Tony Jelliffe and to John Pateman, whose research and scholarship have been particularly relevant to this project.

Many thanks to Christina Nolan, Susan Norton, Alan Peters, Eddie Daley, Tracy Chevalier, Stewart Thorburn, Ian Kelly, Mary Openshaw, Justin Bickersteth, Greg and Becky Howard, Jean Ettinger, Judy Roberts, Rowan Davies, Ken Carter, Bob Trimmer, Christian Gilson, Steve Hanafin, Matthew Pridham, Samantha Perrin, Alex Mahler, Judith Yuille and all the Guides and Friends of Highgate Cemetery, past and present, who kindly let me tag along on their tours and badger them while they did the accounts. It has been a privilege to work with them.

Love and thanks to Joseph Regal, for his derring-do,

fortitude and unconventional thinking, as well as his immensely helpful editing. Thanks to Lauren Schott Pearson, Markus Hoffmann and Howard Sanders for their excellent advice and guidance in literature and life. Thank you to Barbara Marshall and Michael Strong. And thanks, Caspian Dennis of Abner Stein, for friendship and excellent agenting.

Thank you to Dan Franklin for wise editing and sideways thinking, and for correcting my Americanisms (French windows; who knew?). Love and thanks to Rachel Cugnoni, Suzanne Dean, Chloë Johnson-Hill, Alex Bowler, Liz Foley, Roger Bratchell and Jason Arthur of Random House UK; thank you to Marion Garner and Louise Dennys of Random House Canada. And *Dank und Liebe* to Hans Jürgen Balmes, Isabel Kupski and Brigitte Jakobeit of S. Fischer Verlag.

Thank you to Nan Graham, for her incisive editing and lightness of touch; I look forward with pleasure to our future collaborations. Thank you, Susan Moldow, Paul Whitlatch, Rex Bonomelli and Katie Monaghan of Scribner.

I am grateful to the Ragdale Foundation and the Corporation of Yaddo for residencies that gave me time and space to work, and to the British Library for research assistance. Thanks also to the Highgate Scientific and Literary Institution for a productive afternoon in their library.

Thanks and love to Lisa Ann Gurr, Ethan Lavan, and the little Gurr Lavans Jonathan and Natalia for their delightful hospitality. Special thanks to Lisa Ann Gurr for permission to use her story of the ghosts of the trees, and also for letting me borrow the Little Kitten of Death. (Sorry I had to kill her.)

Much love and thanks to Hayley Campbell, Neil Gaiman,

Antonia Rose Logue, and to David Drew for all the wonderful afternoons at the ballet.

Many thanks to Noah D. Frederick for his Latin translation and his help in translation-related matters. Thanks also to Ana Rita Pires for her Portuguese translation of Martin and Marijke's fantasy taxi ride. Thank you to Daniel Mellis for his help in arranging that.

Love and special thanks to Bert Menco for his help with the Dutch language and all things *Nederlandish*.

Thanks to John Padour for his indispensable drawing of the layout of the flats in my imaginary Vautravers, which saved me from many gaffes. Thanks to Janet Lefley for the long days of writing and chatting at Kopi's; thanks to Jesse Thomas, Mary Drabik, Catalina Simon, Jesus Mendes and Jesus Reyes for all that Russian tea and sympathy.

Thank you for inspiration, advice, research assistance and/or reading the manuscript: Lyn Rosen, William Frederick, Jonelle Niffenegger, Riva Lehrer, Bert Menco, Danea Rush, Benjamin Chandler, Robert Vladova, and Christopher Schneberger. Thanks to Patricia Niffenegger for help with sewing enquiries, and to Beth Niffenegger and Lawrence Niffenegger for their support.

Thank you to Sharon Britten-Dittmer for her friendship and for keeping chaos at bay.

And thank you to April Sheridan for her quiet strength and good sense, for her astonishing writing and art, and for helping me to make my art.

⊰⊱ THE LITTLE GREEN BOX ⊰⊱

At the end of every tour at Highgate Cemetery, someone stands at the elaborate gate with a green plastic donations box, and visitors often put in their spare change as they leave. The money supports the upkeep and preservation of the Cemetery, which in 2009 cost approximately £1000 per day. Sumptuous old cemeteries are expensive to maintain, alas.

If you would like to help the Friends of Highgate Cemetery to carry on with their work, please consider making a donation. You can do this no matter where you live by logging on to PayPal.com. Click on Send Money, and enter the Cemetery's PayPal address, donations@highgate-cemetery.org.

Thank you,
Audrey Niffenegger